THE LOST LIBRARIAN'S GRAVE

edited by

ANN WYCOFF

"Three Bad Things" by Kathy Kingston was originally published in Dark Moon Digest. Copyright © 2011 Perpetual Motion Machine Publishing.

Editor: Ann Wycoff
Assistant Editor: Donald Wycoff
Proofreader: O.V. Anderssen
Interior Artwork: Stefan Ljumov, Shibu Prabhakar, Ann Wycoff

www.redwood-press.com

Redwood Press
6101 Gushee Street
P.O. Box 111
Felton, CA. 59018

Warning: This anthology primarily features horror fiction. As such, this book contains scenes, themes, and representations that some readers might find disturbing.

Welcome, mortal. You have finally discovered that place they told you about where hope crawls off to die.

Where sorcery, vile experiments, and the supernatural are as real as killers from around the corner and those things you cannot see that buzz and wriggle and chew narrow, twisting tunnels under your skin and inside your skull.

Surrender to the unclean darkness living in this malevolent tome. Treat yourself to a bevy of tales where revenge, greed, and malice are the orders of the day and watchwords of pitiless night.

Travel through blood-stained vistas set in forgotten pasts, along rolling centuries of iron and pain, into the strange apocalypses of our present day and several possible near futures. Enjoy this diverse collection of horror, occasionally mixed with other ingredients of speculative fiction and leavened with an osseous dusting of bizarre adventures, verse, and weird fiction, written by a loose cabal of thirty-nine authors from around the world.

Unearth... The Lost Librarian's Grave!

TABLE OF CONTENTS

THE SAVAGE NIGHT

Pedro Iniguez

Just before the sun set over the horizon, Kushim, the medicine man, heard their dying wails bellow out from beyond the ridge of the ravine. He squeezed the spear in his hand, his feet rolling over a swath of sharp twigs and pebbles as he sprinted toward the terrible cries of his kin.

Kushim winced. He had seen too many winters. His muscles strained, and his lungs burned as he sprinted across the valley. He was fortunate to have loyal Akito. His dog ran alongside him, matching his every step.

Suddenly, the screams of men died, and the howls of wolves filled their place. Those fools. He could have helped them fend off those fanged terrors.

For countless seasons he had been their healer, sewing and mending their wounds, sacrificing woodland beasts to appease the gods for successful hunts. And despite this, he had been made to keep his distance from the rest of the tribe, being left to tail them like a bastard child or wounded pack animal.

He scowled as he dwelled on the thought. Not even the warmth of their fires was offered to him any longer.

Jarag, the tribal elder, had accused him of unnatural practices. Rituals that disrupted the harmony between the natural and spirit worlds. His own family had accused him of bringing about bad omens—they feared what they did not understand. But to be an outcast among his own people was akin to torture. Regardless, they were all he had in this world.

1

By the time he and Akito arrived, the sky had turned violet, and the first stars began to shimmer.

And the entire tribe was there waiting for him. Men, women, children, even the dogs and their pups. Two dozen bodies lay mangled around the fire, their limbs gnawed and torn from their sockets. Some bellies had been ripped open while their blood and masticated innards spilled out, left to irrigate the ground.

He inspected the wounds. The deep punctures of canid teeth marked their flesh. Only a large, hungry pack could do this.

Kushim raised his head and lifted his spear to the sky. In wild, twisted tongues he screamed and muttered curses at the gods for their betrayal. They were cries of sadness and anger all at once. He knew not what he said, only that in his heart, he wished his family back.

And so, he pounded his feet in the dirt, dancing the dance of life, hoping that in turn, his spectacle would please the gods and restore existence to the departed.

When his voice became hoarse and he could no longer scream, he ceased the dance. Kushim then set to burying the bodies in a mass grave on the fringes of the camp. He laid each member to rest, touching his head to theirs before rolling them into the pit. He capped the site with a mound of stones: one for each person.

As the moon rose, he feasted on the tribe's rations of rabbit giblets, now nearly burned to a crisp as they roasted beside the fire.

He felt a weight press against his chest, and he knew it was loneliness. How would he go it wholly alone now? He turned to Akito and threw him a piece of meat.

Wolves had been stalking the tribe. How could Jarag have been so blind?

As he nestled closer to the fire's warmth, he heard the startling sound of a moan followed by the rustling of dirt.

Akito barked. Kushim spun around, his spear cocked. The sound of shifting soil came again, only louder this time. The noise arose from the direction of the grave.

It couldn't be.

Kushim stepped forward, his eyes narrowing as he focused on the darkness ahead. Another moan. Akito's lips curled as he snarled in response.

"Aughh. Aughhhh," a familiar voice groaned.

A bloodied arm sprang from the earth, its hand clawing at the air. Kushim dropped the spear and clutched the arm. He heaved with all his strength until, like a root, he plucked a man out from the grave.

Dragul writhed and convulsed in agony atop the bloodied soil, his trunk missing both right arm and leg, while a deep gash ran like a fissure atop his head. As Dragul opened his mouth to groan, Kushim peered inside. His tongue had been ripped apart as blood seeped from his maw like crushed berries.

Kushim nuzzled his head to Dragul's and carried him toward the fire's warmth. There in the light, he gauged his injuries.

The man's body was severely maimed. The work of wolves. He was certain now, as their saliva still bubbled on the man's punctured flesh.

Dragul reached his hand out to Kushim, pleading for an end to it all. Kushim clenched his teeth in response. How could Kushim end this man's life? He'd be left to face the horrors of the world, alone, without a companion.

Akito approached Dragul and licked the blood from the open wound where his shoulder bone lay exposed. Kushim flailed his arms and shooed the dog away.

Kushim pulled madly on his hair, groaning as he struggled to think of a solution. Then, he smiled. If he hurried, there was a chance it could work. He sprinted for the burial mound and retrieved the body of another man. This man was Kalkama, whose throat had been pierced and crushed by the same canid teeth. Kushim examined his body. Besides a few scrapes, his limbs were intact. He dragged Kalkama and set his corpse beside Dragul, whose skin had turned pale from the loss of blood.

Kushim retrieved his stone knife and thrust it into Kalkama's right shoulder. He made an incision into the meat and cut until the arm was severed.

He did the same with his right leg, grumbling as he sawed deep into the bone.

Kushim uttered a prayer under his breath and proceeded to peg Kalkama's arm and leg into the missing gaps in Dragul's body. He entwined the sinew and ligaments to the bone and muscle until they were a part of Dragul. He then sealed Dragul's wounds by thrusting his knife into the fire, removing it, and pressing the heated stone blade to his skin.

Dragul screamed until he nearly passed into darkness.

Kushim retrieved a deer stomach pouch and tilted it to Dragul's lips, wherein he gently poured a sliver of water inside his mouth.

After a while, Dragul fell into sleep.

Kushim mumbled soft, rapid words directed at the gods. His prayer was the only magic he could invoke. It would have to do.

Kushim would fight for Dragul's life lest he displease the gods and the spirits of the tribe. Lest he be alone in this world. Amidst the distant howls of wolves, Kushim cradled Dragul's cold body until the sun rose.

Ten moons and ten suns had passed. For all of Kushim's mending chants and remedies, Dragul remained dumb and his right limbs partially paralyzed. All the hair had fallen from his scalp, and his skin remained pale like death. To Kushim's dismay, his companion could not throw a spear as before.

Dragul afforded Kushim little choice; hunting had become difficult for them during the day as the animals became frightened of his uncontrollable shrieks. Along with his frail body and the knowledge that most predators hunted during the day, the men adopted the nighttime as their domain.

On this night, while they approached their next meal, Kushim placed a hand on Dragul's chest and motioned for him to remain silent. Akito stalked noiselessly through the weeds, moving alongside his master. Kushim stepped forward, both hands clutching his spear should anything spring forth from the darkness. Nothing stirred except the soft buzzing of the mosquitoes as they wisped past his head.

There, splayed out on the grass, lay their dinner. It had almost been picked apart completely, but Kushim whispered a prayer to the spirit of the animal nevertheless. The corpse was a gift that would not go to waste.

Tonight, they would feast on the carrion remains of a mountain goat. Kushim knelt beside its open ribcage, scraping apart the hanging shreds of meat from its fur with his knife. He tossed a handful of raw flesh to Dragul, who immediately set about to devouring his meal. He bit into the meat like a crazed beast, pulling on the flesh until it snapped apart, strand by strand. The blood that coated his face lay in stark contrast to the pale moonlight that now tinted his body. Dragul had become bestial. Half alive, half dead, like a reflection in a pond; it was similar to a man but not real.

Lowering a ribbon of meat into his own mouth, Kushim noticed the two large, deep puncture marks embedded in the neck of the goat. A long-fanged cat must have roamed these lands in the daytime. It would be best to head back to the cave before it returned.

Kushim looked to the sky. The sun would rise soon, and the terrors of the world would come to claim the land once more.

After their meal, the three of them departed for the cavern alongside the coast, where the waves crashed against the rocks like thunder.

They entered the cave, greeted by the throng of bats hanging on the roof of the cavern. They screeched and fluttered like restless birds. Dragul took curiosity in their fervor, mimicking their cries, before losing interest and curling into his own body as sleep took him.

The sun rose on the horizon, and Kushim felt the weight surface in his chest once more. The pain traveled with him despite Dragul's company. He embraced Akito and wondered why the gods had not gifted him with another family and instead cursed him with a ravenous shell of a man who could not think, speak, or hunt.

Then as the tears rolled down his face, sleep took him, too.

Dragul groaned as the last of the water trickled down his cracked lips. The pouch had nothing else to offer, and there had been no source of water as far as Kushim could see. The back of his throat felt dry and coarse now, burning with every breath.

They sat quietly on a small hill overlooking the plain. No animals stirred or cried out. Not even the smell of rotting flesh permeated the air around them. The wolves were silent, and the tracks of the long-fanged cats were nowhere to be found.

Beyond the plains, the woods rolled as far as Kushim could see, but that trek would take them another night's travel.

Kushim grunted and cursed the gods for abandoning them and leaving them to starve and thirst.

As the moonlight glimmered on his body, Dragul rolled in the dirt, flailing his arms like a child. Kushim knelt beside him, placing a hand on his mouth to silence his cries, but the man bit into his palm. Kushim yelled and jerked his hand free. A small piece of flesh had torn loose; blood flowed down his wrist. Dragul licked his lips and reached his hands out to Kushim.

Kushim lightly jabbed his spear in Dragul's direction. Dragul's legs buckled, sending him stumbling to the ground.

Kushim dwelled on his hand before returning his gaze at the man on the ground. Dragul brought both hands to his mouth and motioned to his lips, screeching like a cave bat.

Kushim retrieved his knife and cut deep into his palm until the blood flowed freely. He raised his arm and let the blood trickle into Dragul's mouth.

Dragul knelt underneath the stream with his mouth agape. The blood poured into his maw, and the pale man drank until the flow stopped. He then crawled toward a bloody puddle that had collected on the floor and lapped it up like a dog.

The night began to give way to the morning, and Dragul turned to Kushim, baring his teeth, his gums stained red. He was smiling.

Kushim turned away and tried to push the image from his mind for fear that his dreams would match the horrors of reality.

The burning pain boring deep into his neck woke him. Then came the warmth of liquid flowing down his skin. He opened his eyes in the dark of the cave, Dragul's red face greeting him, his teeth latched firmly onto his throat. Over their heads, the bats thrashed their wings and shrieked wildly.

Kushim thrust his right hand into his pouch, retrieved his knife, and plunged it into Dragul's left shoulder. Dragul's grip on his throat loosened while he howled in pain. Kushim shoved Dragul from his body and turned to reach for his spear but found it already embedded in Akito's carcass. The dog's body had been split down the middle, half of his innards missing.

Before he could turn back to Dragul, the man-beast leaped onto Kushim, knocking him to the floor. Dragul then wrapped two icy hands around Kushim's neck. He opened his mouth, bearing forth his rotting teeth. His breath carried the rancid promise of death and decay. Kushim lifted a knee and bucked him over his head.

Dragul landed on his skull, and the sound of shattering bones echoed through the cave. Kushim pushed himself off the floor and hobbled toward the cavern entrance. Dragul's wounded howls echoed shrilly across the mouth of the cave.

Kushim thought of turning to face Dragul one last time but decided against it and limped away instead.

Kushim heard Dragul's wails fade over time as he trekked toward the rolling plains.

He placed a hand over his throat, meandering through the wild, tripping over fallen branches. The night was cold and unforgiving, the breeze nipping at his muscles as he struggled to move his legs.

Until by chance, under the light of the moon, he stumbled into another tribe's camp. Startled and woken by his grunts, the strange people looked upon him in confusion while he fell to his knees. He extended two pleading hands while the blood poured from the wounds on his neck.

He tried to speak, but the words would not form. Only the wet, guttural sounds of a dying man escaped his lips. He knew then that he would not be able to warn them of the abomination who had been resurrected from death only to be sewn anew from the body of another; who traveled by night and shrieked like a bat; who drank the blood of men and beasts alike.

And before the world faded to darkness, he mustered the last words he would speak and prayed the warning would suffice.

"Dragul," he said as his last breath left his body.

Then under the gaze of strangers, the night took him for all time.

INSIDE A REFRIGERATOR

Adrian Ludens

I am ashamed of what I have done. I am remorseful for the actions I have taken. It is important to convey that upfront. Sitting here now and reflecting, I wish I could hit a cosmic reset. That kid, Darren, did not deserve what happened—what I did. He was innocent. But then again, that was why I chose him.

I'm not a horrible person. I work hard. I do my best. I live paycheck to paycheck, and I guess what happened pushed me into doing something I would have never considered under normal circumstances.

Darren's dad and I were colleagues, even friends. Or so I thought. We said we'd stand together in solidarity against the out-of-state company who'd bought our newspaper. Jeff and I raised our glasses and toasted the merits of independent reporting and journalistic integrity. In less than a month, Jeff had a new office and a promotion. My friend became my editor and supervisor. A paltry two weeks later, he fired me. Jeff offered a strained smile and a few empty platitudes, but I knew he'd barely hesitated before sacrificing me to the corporate gods of downsizing.

I packed the personal items scattered around my cubicle into a cardboard box and relocated the carton to the back seat of my salt-rusted sedan. I drove out of the Employees Only parking lot with bitter bile roiling like magma in my throat. I stifled the eruption and aimed my vehicle toward the suburb where Jeff and his family lived.

I'd been there before in happier, more optimistic times. We'd hung out, cracked open a few beers, played an amateurish game of pool, and commiserated. Funny how the events of four months ago now seem like ancient history.

When I slid my car up to the curb, fortune smiled upon me. I found both of Jeff's kids bundled up and playing in the snow-covered front yard. Looked like a scene from one of those feel-good holiday movies you find on cable. I vowed to scar this family, make Christmas a time of mourning.

Darren's sister, a pale, elfin girl named Lily, recognized me first. "Uncle Brian!"

I let myself in the front gate and grinned at each of the kids in turn. "Hi, guys! Your dad wanted me to tell you to get ready to go out for pizza as soon as he gets home from work." The kids' faces lit with excitement. "Lily, run inside and tell your mom, okay?" Lily didn't think twice. She raced into the house.

A voice in my brain screamed at me to get in my car and drive away. I ignored it. Instead, I scooped up Darren and loaded him into the back seat.

We chased the headlights out of the city while the lies tumbled from my mouth.

We arrived at the abandoned structure just after dusk. It hid from view behind a stand of overgrown trees just off the highway, fifteen miles north of the suburb we'd left behind us. I'd been here before and explored the building several times, in fact. What had once been a roadside tourist attraction had also served as a residence for the onsite caretaker. When the business failed, he'd moved on to parts unknown, abandoning what possessions he couldn't load. Pickers had taken the best items, and vandals had destroyed the rest, but something I remembered seeing in the cellar during my last visit drew me onward.

Snow had begun to fall, and a breeze swirled the moonlit flakes around the towering evergreens like fairy dust. I parked and pawed through the personal items in the box in the back seat until I found an item I could use to my advantage.

"Darren, remember when I first picked you up, I said I was taking you to meet Santa?"

The boy nodded, but I could see in his eyes that the unexpected drive had rattled him. He still had not decided between fear or trust.

"It was a long car ride, wasn't it? But we're here. We are at Santa's Workshop at the North Pole."

Darren knelt on the seat and gazed at the shambling, darkened structure before us. "It doesn't look like Santa's Workshop."

"Of course not! It's disguised by magic, so people won't know." I twitched a photograph I'd removed from the box between two fingers, attracting the boy's notice. "Aren't you curious why you get to meet Santa early?"

He nodded, still wavering between curiosity and mistrust.

"It's because me and your dad both work for Santa." I flipped over the photograph, and Darren's mouth fell open in guileless amazement. I knew I had him. The snapshot, taken at last year's staff Christmas party, showed Jeff and I decked out in ridiculous red and green elf hats, complete with plastic pointed ears glued to the sides. To a four-year-old kid, it was indisputable proof. His father and I both grinned for the camera, our drinks just out of frame.

"Lily didn't get to come because she hasn't been as good as you have," I confided. "That's why it had to be a secret surprise."

Darren nodded. He'd composed his features to match the solemn honor of the occasion, but his eyes danced with excitement.

"Santa has lots of secrets. The elves are making all kinds of new toys for good boys and girls, but you don't get to see any of those, okay? You only get to meet Santa and tell him what you'd like for Christmas."

I got out from behind the wheel, walked around the rear of my car, and unlocked the trunk. I rummaged around until I found a cheap plastic flashlight that was part of my half-assed survival kit. I pressed the thumb switch and found the beam of light serviceable. I slammed the trunk and approached Darren's passenger-side door. I paused, contemplating the desolate road over the roof of my car. I could still walk away. I could return the boy to his home, use the journey back to fabricate an excuse for taking him.

The bitter wind hissed its derision at my indecisiveness, and the snow-laden branches of the trees shook with laughter at my weakness. I pressed my lips together and threw open the car door. "Since there are certain things inside Santa's Workshop that you aren't allowed to see, we're going to do something silly, okay buddy?"

Darren's lips upturned in a shy smile.

"We're going to take your coat off super quick and put it right back on again backwards!"

"Why?"

"Because your coat has a hood. We'll put your hood up as a blindfold so I can carry you in past all the elves until we get to Santa's special meeting room."

Darren let me unzip his puffy parka, and I had it reversed and his face covered in all of fifteen seconds. I lifted him into my arms, and we crunched through the freshly fallen snow toward the back of the old house, where I knew a busted door would allow us entrance.

I don't understand Jeff's betrayal. It felt so spiteful and unnecessary. Sitting here now, stiff and uncomfortable, I keep pondering his actions, turning them over in my mind. I keep examining the situation from all angles, trying to find the reason. Professional jealousy? Did he fear accusations of nepotism? Am I a slipshod journalist?

Jeff wasn't content with the promotion and the raise. He'd climbed a rung or two up the ladder and still felt the need to stomp on my fingers, to kick me off the ladder entirely. It was so damned sudden, so malicious.

Two could play that game. I would show him "sudden." I would show him "malicious." That's what I thought at the beginning of all this.

Now, I'm not sure what I did or didn't do.

Carrying Darren in my arms, we made our way through the accumulating snow toward the back of the ramshackle structure. Each footstep caused a muffled crunch as I eased around the edge of the house. I could hear the wind blowing through the trees; unknown animal tracks zigzagged across the snow. I stumbled in a deep drift left over from a previous storm.

At last, we reached the rear entrance. My breath came in ragged gasps. The rotting wooden door hung from one hinge. Ice melt and drifted snow turned the three descending steps into an invitation to break a leg. I lowered Darren down, took his hand, and led the way. "Watch your step, buddy," I cautioned. I turned on the flashlight app on my phone. I had other plans for the flashlight.

I ignored the stairs that led to the main level and guided the boy left, past a rusting washing machine, dryer, and two deep basin sinks. I pushed open the creaking door below the stairwell into what had once been a workshop and storage area. I shone the light along the floor, now covered in a thick carpet of scattered pinecone scales—the nest of something I hoped was deep in slumber. I noticed an old-fashioned grade school desk. Rusty tools used by the long-departed caretaker hung like bloody crucifixes on the concrete walls of the foundation. Wooden shelves leaned beneath the weight of gift shop fossils, petrified wood, minerals, and faux gemstones. A machine used for sharpening blades sat on an oblong countertop; the rusted blades hung like macabre trophies above it on the wall.

Among the jumbled detritus, I saw several straight-backed wooden chairs encased in cobwebs, leaning stacks of dust-covered boxes, bundles of moldering newspapers, and a high wooden cabinet. Coffee cans and glass jars filled with nails, screws, washers, and other workshop miscellanea filled the shelves.

Beside me, Darren's breathing came fast. Whether from walking or excitement, I couldn't say. Maybe it was just hard to breathe through the backward-facing hood.

We took another left, ducking through a door beside the wooden cabinet, and moved deeper beneath the building into a sunken, T-shaped root cellar. We passed burlap bags of rotten potatoes and onions. Jars of seeds and of homemade canned vegetables lined dust-caked shelves. I saw beets, asparagus, and other produce I could not identify floating in cloudy yellow fluid.

The path was so narrow I had to steer the boy ahead of me. We passed canned goods, a dark brown pelt that may have come from a bear, and a cardboard box, white and rotten with mold. I shined my phone's light and relayed verbal warnings. We stepped over broken jars of stewed tomatoes—now black and desiccated—dried hawthorn and a spilled profusion of empty prescription pill bottles.

Someone had stacked chopped wood on a second set of stairs at the end of the walkway, completely blocking that egress. Rather than proceed farther, we turned right, into the heart of the cellar's maze. Here I would wall in my Fortunato-by-proxy. No catacombs or stones this time. The boy and I stood before a 1960s vintage Tru-Cold refrigerator.

"Step back, okay?" I steered Darren a few feet out of my way. "Santa has a special area where he will meet you, kind of like in the mall, but the one in the mall is just pretend." I raised my voice while I worked. I had opened the door and removed the wire shelving, placing it on the scat-covered concrete floor.

"Remember, don't make a peep." I guided Darren toward the refrigerator. "Climb up one step." He did so, hands outstretched, feeling the sides of the interior.

"Okay, buddy, now sit down." The boy sat with his legs crossed.

"When do I get to meet Santa?" He hadn't spoken for so long his muffled words startled me.

"Soon," I said. "Here, hang onto this." I placed the bulky flashlight from my trunk into the boy's hand. The air felt dank and oppressive. Using the light from my phone, I tore the Christmas party photo in half and pressed the piece containing his father's image into Darren's other hand. I noticed my own face in the other half of the photograph. My image seemed to be imploring me to stop this madness. But, I realized, that was the old me, a previous, inferior incarnation—his knowledge of the situation was incomplete by default.

I knelt beside the shivering child. "This is a magic portal. I need to close the door, but don't be scared. When the door opens, you'll be able to meet Santa, okay?"

"Okay." The hand holding the picture of Jeff shook. I rose and closed the refrigerator door. The old-fashioned handle latched.

Darren lasted ten seconds—the time it took for him to put his hood down and turn on the flashlight—before he started yelling.

The boy pounded on the inside of the fridge. "Let me *out!*" he screamed.

"Darren!" I shouted. "*Darren!*"

The noise stopped for the moment.

"If you feel scared, just look at the photo of your dad. Okay, buddy? If you be good, he'll be there to open the door for you."

I felt a cruel thrill at providing him with false hope. I wondered how soon before his hope crumbled, how soon until he panicked, and claustrophobia had him screaming again. I speculated over how long he could last in there without air circulation. Perhaps I could adjust the fridge just enough to crack the door and allow a little airflow; then I could string him along and torment him into tears. I'd build him up again with reassurances, rekindle his hope, and douse it. Maybe he'd wet his pants when he couldn't hold his bladder any longer, and I would scold him for it. My mind raced with the possibilities.

I could just leave him, alone and afraid, until he suffocated. If I gave him some air, perhaps he'd die of dehydration. Undoubtedly, the ordeal would drive the boy insane first. Part of me relished the idea, wanted to be there for every moment of the boy's suffering. Another part of me wanted nothing more of this, wanted to flee as if waking from a nightmare.

Perhaps some fresh air and a chance to collect my thoughts would help me decide my course of action. I rose and crunched through broken glass and discarded pill bottles. Inside the refrigerator, Darren started to sob, then to scream.

I moved along the passage and turned left. Jars of peaches and beets lined one shelf. A dark brown pelt sat on another. This seemed like familiar territory, but at the end of the passage, shelves barred my path. Before me, jars of seeds, dried hawthorn, and pickled asparagus lined the shelves. I looked over my shoulder. At the far end of the walkway, split logs were piled up on the steps. This had to be the right way.

I reached out, shoved the jars aside. A bottle of stewed tomatoes fell to the concrete and exploded like a shot. I jumped back a step. The light from my phone caught the mess of shattered glass and blackened vegetables while behind me, Darren had started pounding on the confines of his makeshift tomb. I looked again at the shelves in front of me and at the wall behind them. I reached out, rapped on the surface. I expected wood, a closed door, perhaps, but the wall behind the shelves was solid concrete. I'd turned myself around. I just needed to go back to the refrigerator and get my bearings.

I spun around and followed the light from my phone's flashlight to the piles of stacked firewood. In an attempt to expose the second door, I grabbed three chunks of wood and tossed them over my shoulder one by one. My phone's light diminished markedly. I paused to check the battery and saw I'd hit fifteen percent. A quick glance showed me I was not in cell tower range. I shoved the phone into a gap in the firewood and squinted. I was confronted by another concrete foundation wall.

I muttered a few curses, turned and retraced my steps, then my breath hitched in my throat: two pieces of firewood lay ahead of me. *Two*, I realized, not three. I did my best

16

to ignore Darren's terrified cries as I passed the refrigerator and tried to rationalize the missing piece of wood. I used my flashlight to examine my surroundings. More jars of canned vegetables sat on the shelves to my left, definitely no longer safe to eat. As I watched, something in one of the jars shifted. I flinched before realizing it had to be dust motes floating in the air in front of the jar, causing the illusion.

The flashlight app on my phone shut down. I slid my thumb on the screen, and it illuminated, albeit dimly. My battery sat at eight percent.

I turned again, glancing at a cardboard box covered in frostlike white mold that should have been around the corner, ten feet away. My phone's screen faded, leaving me in darkness. I stood still, trying to get my bearings. That's when I noticed the silence.

"Darren?" My blood seemed to pound against my eardrums with each heartbeat. I strained my eyes to no avail; no light penetrated the bowels of the basement. I needed the flashlight.

"Hey, buddy? Knock on the side so I can hear you."

A tapping came in response, ahead and to my left. My feet crunched broken glass as I shuffled forward. The sound stopped. "Keep knocking. I'll open the door and let you out of there."

The tapping resumed. I realize I'd overshot my mark. The tapping now came from behind me—and to the right. I started to turn but stopped. I forced myself to remain calm and use logic to solve my predicament. "Darren, I need you to holler, okay? If you keep calling my name and knocking on the wall of your special room, I'll come let you out, okay?"

"I'm here, Uncle Brian!"

The voice and the tapping overlapped and echoed from every direction in the concrete maze. I reached out with both hands and felt my way along the passage, doing my best to ignore how my skin crawled every time my fingers encountered something unsavory or unexpected. After what seemed like much longer than it should have taken, I relocated the refrigerator. At my touch, the cries and tapping fell silent.

I'd decided if the boy had fainted, I would take the flashlight, close the door, and be on my way. I had no desire to remain any longer.

I opened the door, and something rolled out and fell onto my foot. I fought the impulse to kick it. If it was the flashlight, I didn't like my chances of finding the damned thing in the dark. I crouched and felt the hard plastic casing. With a relieved sigh, I stood and clicked the flashlight's switch. A bright beam of light stabbed the darkness, and I recoiled, blinded for a moment. I pointed the beam at the floor and let my eyes adjust. The shadowy interior of the refrigerator arrested my attention. I lifted the beam.

Darren wasn't inside.

For half a minute, I just stood there staring into the boy's would-be tomb, now miraculously vacant.

I took a deep breath and held it. Nothing changed. I kept silent, hoping he would make a sound, betray his location. I stepped around the appliance and shined my light down all three walkways. No sign of the boy. I returned to the refrigerator, knelt, and felt the interior with my fingers, tapping and shining the flashlight's beam. Could there have been a false back, some Houdini-like explanation for the boy's seeming disappearance? I found none. Rising, I aimed my light down all four passageways.

My hand shook. There should have been three corridors. I looked again down four passageways, at four dead ends. Now, even the woodpile was gone. My mind was playing tricks. I decided my own guilty conscience had caused my confusion. The way out had to be right in front of me.

I explored this idea further, following the thread of logic to see where it led. Darren was not here. Maybe he never had been. What did I have as evidence to prove his physical presence? Perhaps I'd left him in the car, or maybe I hadn't abducted him at all. Possibly I'd just imagined it, had a psychotic break that allowed me to release my pent-up rage. With this realization came a liberating sense of relief.

If my theory was true, it seemed only rational that I should also now be able to find the door and make my escape. As

I turned, the flickering beam of my flashlight fell on the torn photograph taken at the Christmas party. It had dropped out of the fridge and lay face down under the toe of my shoe. I crouched, picked it up, and turned it over.

The fading light revealed Jeff's grinning face. He seemed to be laughing at me. My flashlight's beam faded to nothing.

The blackness disoriented me. I couldn't even detect the motion of my own hand in front of my face. Something touched my back, and I instinctively recoiled, arching forward and away. My fingertips found the bottom of the now-empty refrigerator. I felt reapplied pressure on my back; a small pair of hands shoved me forward. As I floundered against the force of this push into the unyielding confines of the antique appliance, something hard struck the back of my head. False bursts of light illuminated my vision, and throbbing pain followed. My arms and legs felt numb and heavy. Hands shoved me forward into the painted steel interior of the antique appliance.

Before I could protest or react, the hands fell away, and I heard the door of the Tru-Cold's old-fashioned handle latch close with a subdued, yet horrible, click.

Now I am inside what I had intended to be Darren's tomb. My knees are shoved up under my chin, and my tailbone aches, but I refuse to give up hope.

I do not pretend to understand what happened. How much of this have I imagined? Is Darren in the basement, waiting for me to beg for my release? Did I leave him upstairs in the car, freezing but unharmed? Is he still safe at home?

Or did Jeff follow my car to his house and then pursue me to the abandoned basement?

Tiny bursts of light sparkle across my field of vision. My pulse is racing, and it's hard to breathe. I feel dizzy. I want to take it back, to behave differently. I am not a killer, nor do I deserve to die. If Darren got out of here, maybe I can too.

But what if I can't?

I am inside a refrigerator in the cellar of an abandoned building fifteen miles from town. My flashlight battery is dead, and it is so very dark. I will not give up hope. Someone will find me.

Eventually.

MEDUSA'S MIRROR

Paul L. Bates

What I am about to relate is a fiction, a blatant lie. Not because I wish to deceive or impress you—far from it—but because, as Enoch was wont to remind me, *it is in our unwavering nature to lie whether we wish it or not. A man must perforce relate everything through the prism of his own distorted vision, for at best he sees only components of the greater truth—a pale reflection of reality; and at worst he denies the simple truths that cloy at him from every shadowed corner of his feeble mind, even to himself.* So, I will lie and lie again, despite my every effort to tell you the unvarnished truth.

Have you ever felt as if your skin were about to erupt into an independent crawling horde? That your body was inhabited by—or composed of—countless squirming maggots or mites scrambling about on tiny legs, living just below the surface, busily transmogrifying all that was not them into more of them? Such was the sensation I experienced every time Enoch insisted I accompany him on one of his *outings*, as he called them—*excursions into the darkness within and without.* And while I never shared his somber vision, I was forced more and more to accept his perception was, at the very least, a significant portion of the greater whole. I still feel that crawling sensation when I think about him. Thankfully, now as then, it lingers briefly and passes.

I had met Enoch my first year at college, long before he became, in his own words, a *purveyor of arcane oddities, catering to a diverse and deranged clientele with equal contempt.* Even then, he had a reputation for acquiring nearly anything our classmates might desire, for a price. In those bygone rosy days of youth, he specialized in intense aphrodisiacs, rare hallucinogenics, and outré pornographic materials. Later, our mutual friend Greta insisted, he became a pimp.

Enoch was a gaunt figure, tall, stoop-shouldered with deep-set eyes and grayish skin, leaving one the impression he had bypassed childhood altogether—that he had been born middle-aged. His movements, always languid, were theatrical; his speech, never hurried, was painfully meticulous and often biting. Willis, a mutual acquaintance, once swore to me Enoch never slept. He shunned close personal contact, disdained studying, yet he was popular and graduated with honors. Women, especially, were attracted to him, but he seemed to barely notice them. Those who persisted were inevitably left the worse for their loyalty. I am uncertain why, but he always treated me with a calculated respect, which left me both flattered as well as wary, lest he want something I was not prepared to give.

After graduation, I lost track of Enoch for over twenty-five years although I would occasionally hear tales of his misadventures from mutual acquaintances. These stories were always highly implausible and usually conflicting. For no reason I ever understood, I inevitably broke off contact with those who felt compelled to relate these dubious episodes to me. In one, Enoch was languishing in jail for desecrating a little-known historical monument—a tree—in Texas; in another he had become a CIA consultant specializing in the overthrow of small South and Central American democracies; in another he had recently emerged from a decade long opium haze to form his own ruthless drug cartel and was actively eliminating the competition. On and on these wild adventures went, until, finally, I had severed contact with nearly everyone we knew in common.

So, it came as a complete surprise when Enoch approached me one afternoon where I sat in an uptown café contentedly nursing a cappuccino while engrossed in perusing a battered volume of epic verse. He looked exactly the same as the last time I saw him, wearing a new black silk scarf and an impeccable camel hair coat. He left me with the distinct impression that for him time was just an illusion, that he had simply stepped out of the past.

"Are you up for an adventure?" he asked quietly, without greeting.

"Not really," I replied, doing my utmost to remain unruffled. My skin began tingling madly, the first time I experienced that annoying sensation he could evoke by his mere presence.

"Come along anyway," he said with a practiced smile. "I promise no harm will befall you. I have a client whose penchant for self-destruction might amuse you—an old friend, if memory serves. Surely you would wish to witness what has become of him. It will prove to be an enlightening outing for both of us, I assure you."

His strange declaration had an odd effect on me. Logically, Enoch could in no way guarantee my safety; nor did I have an interest in witnessing any manner of masochistic behavior, especially that of an old friend. Yet, in spite of the absurdity of his statements, I gave in without argument. I shut my book, drained the dregs of the cold coffee, left a tip beneath the saucer and joined him. A monstrous, uniformed chauffeur held the door to a sleek silver limousine for us, and Enoch waived me on.

"Do you remember Willis?" he asked after we rode several blocks in relative silence.

Willis had told me years before about Enoch's supposed desecration of an ancient tree with historical significance in some Texas backwater. I hadn't seen or wanted to see Willis again since—he had somehow become *contaminated* in my estimation. A judgment I did not quite understand at the time but maintained steadfastly nonetheless. Now, with Enoch grinning next to me, I felt as if something were attempting to burrow through the skin of my arms and back on tiny, filament-like feet. "Yes, of course," I replied. I wanted to scratch my arms, my chest and back furiously—but I, in an endeavor to maintain my composure, resisted the maddening urge.

"He's long begged me to find something very special for him—a little-known artifact last described in an obscure treatise dating from the early days of the Ottoman Empire."

I politely expressed some mild interest prompting Enoch to tell me at length about his singular profession and his diverse and deranged clientele. Thankfully the itching sensation passed. I nodded whenever he stopped to stare at me, not wishing to interrupt his narrative, and he obliged by continuing with his rambling tale. After some little while, I suddenly noticed the wide boulevards lined with trendy galleries, smart bistros, fashionable boutiques, and newly gentrified apartment towers, which marked the start of our journey, had long since given way to filthy narrow streets, lined with deplorable graffiti-covered ruins, many of them with doors and windows boarded. Shabby derelicts slouched in languid cabals upon the stoops of three- and four-story buildings ritualistically passing paper bags back and forth to one another and taking swigs from the small liquor bottles they surely contained. The whole place looked as if it was about to collapse beneath its own depressing weight and crumble into an abyss of infinite despair.

"It will soon collapse beneath its own weight, crumbling into an abyss of infinite despair," Enoch said, watching me peer through the tinted glass surrounding us as if he had read my thoughts, or perhaps I his.

"Yes, truly," I said, suddenly realizing he had finished his long-winded narrative. "What has this miserable place to do with Willis?"

"Everything."

"How so?"

"Wait and see."

The chauffeur, that silent, obedient colossus, eased the limousine into a constricting service alley layered in crushed glass, mounds of trash, and the odd, fluttering newspaper page. He stopped the limousine, shut off the engine. We were parked before a rusted steel door crudely marked with a singular black pictograph that left me feeling more ill at ease than I could possibly explain. Whereas the crumbling stone walls on either side of the door were covered in seemingly endless depressing layers of garish images, barely intelligible slogans, and run together initials, the door had but one. As I was registering this oddity, a trio of shadows came to life further down the alley, approaching us guardedly with no good intent until Enoch's chauffeur emerged from the limousine, at which time, they turned tail and galloped off howling in abject terror.

The rusted door with the odd sigil was not locked. Enoch opened it with a flourish, led the way within. The chauffeur remained behind with the car. We were greeted by the foulest odor I had ever smelled, as if the shadows contained decomposing cadavers scattered amid mountains of fresh excrement. I covered my face with my handkerchief at once. Enoch watched me amusedly.

"It's all illusion," he affirmed, "an approximation of an underlying reality. Decay engenders life, my friend. Remain mindful of that fact and all will be well."

Just beyond the marked door, we came upon an unlit rickety wooden staircase. Enoch clomped up into the heart of the grime-covered slum, and I followed him reluctantly to the next floor. He removed a pair of small flashlights from his overcoat pocket and handed one to me. By their pristine white light, I watched a portly rat the size of a raccoon waddle into the gloom, mildly put out by our presence. The upstairs hall was filled with dark plastic bags overflowing with reeking refuse and wriggling vermin. We negotiated the obstacles, passed yawning openings, some with crumbling wooden doors teetering on disintegrating hinges, until Enoch shined his light on another steel door marked with the same black pictograph.

He knocked once.

"Is that you?" a broken voice demanded.

"It's me, Willis," Enoch intoned. "I've brought your instrument as well as a mutual friend to hear you play it."

Enoch opened the door without waiting for an invitation, ushered me into the cramped apartment, shut the door behind us. The stench was even worse than that permeating the corridor.

I shined my flashlight at piles of litter, stopping at an emaciated figure squatting on a filthy, bare mattress in the far corner. All that remained of his once thick black hair were a few scraggly grey wisps insufficient to conceal the riot of pink and brown splotches covering his scalp. I had to study the stained, sagging features carefully to even recognize Willis within this utter wreck of a human body wrapped in layers of mismatched rags. In the years since I last saw him, Willis had aged a lifetime. He squinted into the beam, his wild eyes watering.

"You have the harp?" he croaked at us.

"I have it," Enoch averred. He reached into an inside pocket of his impeccable camel hair overcoat, removed a slender package wrapped in brown leather, perhaps a foot long, shaped like a kite. "Orpheus' Lyre," he announced, "able to mesmerize the gods, rend the illusion in all its deceptions, cut to the ultimate reality. Nothing can resist its clarion voice."

"Give it to me," Willis growled. "I've paid for it. I've done everything you demanded, damn you. Give me the harp."

"As you wish."

Enoch extended the leather package toward the discolored mattress whereupon Willis snatched it from his gloved hand. The pathetic wretch clutched his prize against his torso with a hideous laugh, rocking back and forth for several minutes before unwrapping it lovingly. Inside was a graceful silver dagger. The sharp outer edges curved free from a slender central shaft but were connected to it at the haft and tip, creating two narrow crescent-shaped openings. Willis was clearly elated.

"You do know how to play it?" Enoch asked.

"Of course," Willis snapped back.

Gripping it with two hands, Willis plunged the thing into his own abdomen, swiftly cutting a large round circle, grinning like a fool all the while. I watched in horror, my skin crawling once again, awaiting the inevitable gush of blood and entrails across the litter-strewn floor. But to my surprise no such thing occurred. Instead, a great segmented worm several feet long the diameter of his arm forced the skin away, emerging from an eight-inch hole. Its blind antenna twitching in the cold air, its tiny arms groping. A second worm forced its head beside the first, and then another. I backed toward the door as Willis dropped the *harp* onto the mattress. With some effort, he wrenched one then another of the things free, devouring them greedily until there were no more. He turned his grimy face toward us, and by the glow of the flashlights I watched his black-stained lips and broken teeth twist into a leering grin. Ignoring us completely, Willis began rocking back and forth anew, clutching his knees and moaning ecstatically.

Enoch snatched up the harp and its covering. He carefully wiped the blade clean on a rag he tossed into the shadows. He rewrapped the thing, tucked it back into his inner coat pocket, then told me to open the door.

"I know he paid for it but I can't, in good conscience," Enoch said as the chauffeur eased the car through the alley, "leave the harp lying about, although no one in this neighborhood is likely to pry behind any door marked with my sigil." He allowed himself a brief laugh. "Perhaps I'll have another call for it someday."

We said nothing more as we rode back to the uptown café where he found me. As soon as we stopped, I scrambled out of the limousine before the chauffeur could open the door. I was amazed I had been able to contain the contents of my stomach. Still, the horror of what I had just witnessed was in some way mitigated by the dark truth, however obscure, that lay at its core.

Enoch popped his head into the opening behind me. "Until next time," he said jovially, then shut the door.

The limousine slid from the curb and was soon lost in traffic while I stood frozen to the spot, watching it disappear.

I hailed a cab, rode home—my skin itching mercilessly—and remained beneath a scalding shower for twenty minutes which by degrees relieved me of that soon to be familiar sensation that had nearly overwhelmed me at the end of our first *outing*.

Thankfully, I did not see Enoch again for almost a year.

He found me one evening at a lecture I was giving at a small upstate college. My subject was the title of my most recent book, *Human Cosmologies Across the Ages*. Standing at the lectern in the auditorium, I felt my skin crawling for a moment, paused in my delivery, scanned the sparse audience until I saw a smiling Enoch sitting in the back row. He was clearly much amused by my proffered views but did not dispute or debate them. "We all need to earn a living," he said with a shrug by way of critique. Enoch waited while I sold and autographed copies of my book.

"Have you spoken with Greta lately?" he asked as we walked the otherwise deserted stone halls afterward.

"No, not for several years," I admitted. "We lost track of one another."

"Really? I thought you were sweet on her."

"I was once, but to tell you the truth, I came to accept the fact she only tolerated my company."

His eyes twinkled mischievously, and he laughed aloud. "Then you won't mind joining me on another excursion tonight, as I've got something she's craved for a while now. You might find her paradoxical transformations informative."

Once again, his odd choice of words utterly seized my attention. A look of revulsion must have distorted my features for he was quick to insist it was nothing remotely similar to his previous commission for Willis. "I promise you will witness no harm to her," he added to assure me. "In fact, I guarantee our visit will markedly improve her demeanor and she'll reevaluate her relationship with you accordingly."

He let me mull his odd assurances for a moment before continuing. Once again, I wanted more than anything to scratch my arms, back and chest, but I would not give Enoch the satisfaction of witnessing the strange effect he had upon me. Thankfully the sensation passed.

"Was she still peddling real estate the last time you saw her?" he asked as we stepped into the chilly night air.

"Yes."

"Well, you should know she's moved into another, although not altogether dissimilar, profession."

I sighed, resigning myself to whatever unexpected mystery Enoch was about to reveal as he steered me through the cheery campus to where the gargantuan chauffeur again awaited us beside the silver limousine glistening in the moonlight. We drove in silence as I mused my long-standing unrequited affection for Greta and how the last time I had seen her, she had told me that Enoch had become a pimp.

The nearest town to the campus was small, seemingly existing solely to service the college and itself. There were no more than two dozen streets about five miles beyond the isolated campus, speckled with declining one- and two-story wood frame houses that looked as if they would buckle beneath the next strong wind. They were clustered around a drab main street lined with dreary storefront businesses including a post office, barbershop, beauty parlor, hardware store, grocery, repair shop, and diner. About five miles past this miserable village we came upon another part of town, perhaps ten ramshackle one- and two-story buildings including motels, liquor stores and bars, some boasting exotic dancers. Ornate bright red and green neon signs flashed, advertising these businesses and their dubious pleasures. A continuous parking lot that faced them was filled to capacity with battered cars and rusted pickup trucks. The chauffeur slowed the limousine, circling the last business on this strip of ill repute, revealing a second parking lot behind them. He stopped at the back of the largest of the nightclubs. I felt my heart pounding with dark anticipation. I wanted to be anywhere but here.

"Think of what you are about to witness as a chance to rid yourself of a burden—nothing else," Enoch advised as we climbed the ancient wooden steps leading to the upper story. He patted me on the back then knocked once on the rear door, which also bore his sigil.

A few moments later, a full-figured woman reeking of tobacco smoke with pocked pale skin and brittle bright red hair, wearing a revealing smock, opened the door. She smiled eagerly at Enoch, eyed me suspiciously. She looked to be in her late thirties, wore way too much makeup.

"He's OK," Enoch vouched for me. "Is Greta free?"

"Yeah, she's just finished. You know where to find her."

The woman stood aside to let us pass, closed the door after briefly scanning the rear parking lot. The air was thick with smoke and contending aromas, from cheap perfumes to tobacco, marijuana, sweat and sex. Moans and creaking springs assailed us from every direction. Enoch led me down a corridor whose dingy walls had lost their color, stopped at a door with that same large pictograph painted crudely in black over its flaking surface. He rapped again. A wretched creature, overweight with stringy brown hair and a small tumor on her neck pulled open the door. She wore a torn negligee, although to my eyes there was nothing remotely alluring about her bloated body or her ravaged face. She glared at Enoch. Once again, I had to stare long and hard to see the person I had once known within this dismal, defiant caricature. And once again this total wreck of a human being took no notice of me whatsoever. I was uncertain if I was sad or glad to be ignored, under the circumstances.

"You've brought it this time?" Greta demanded, a feral glare in her eyes.

"I have."

"Come in, then."

We were ushered into a foul-smelling compartment, with the same filthy colorless walls, furnished with dilapidated junk store furniture—a sagging bed with dirty sheets, battered night table, mirror, lamp, armoire—and an adjoining cramped bathroom without a door from which the low steady whine of faulty plumbing could be heard. As usual, I felt my skin crawling.

Enoch reached into his jacket pocket, and as before, removed a brown leather parcel, much smaller than the one he gave Willis. "The Yucatan Fountain," he said, handing it to her with a grin.

I watched Greta deftly unwrap the package. She removed a gold necklace with an oval medallion resembling a miniature convex mirror surrounded by a ring of small black pearls. Greta put the thing around her neck, quickly fastening the clasp beneath her greasy, broken hair. I watched in amazement as she changed into the girl we knew at school, the medallion somehow transforming her before my eyes. But there was something definitely wrong with my vision, as the image appeared skewed—disjointed and strangely illuminated, as if covered with some fine iridescent mold and seen through a wavering dark corridor.

Greta looked in the mirror, then smiled playfully and reached in my direction, but I jumped away, avoiding her touch. Enoch laughed, pushed me into the hall and we left. Begrudgingly, I had to admit he was right about everything— he had freed me from the burden of my desire for this sad broken creature and the memory of the girl she had been, and the evil charm did all he claimed it would after a fashion. I remained lost in thought for much of the ride back to the campus.

"What else does it do?" I demanded as the comforting glow of the college appeared before us in the distance.

Enoch turned to me and smiled. "She'll appear forever young so long as she wears the amulet and plies her trade in that room accordingly."

I cringed. Enoch laughed at my discomfort. The chauffeur, as always, took no notice. Enoch assured me it was Greta who insisted he find the bauble for her and not he who foisted the corrupt thing upon her.

"You know me," he added. "I'm strictly a purveyor. Like you, I have no agenda whatsoever." He smiled confidently, leaned forward and stared at me, defying me to refute his statement.

I said nothing.

After that, Enoch appeared upon my doorstep every few months on a more or less regular basis for several years, each time to gather me up to witness his delivering some new, malignant artifact to another hapless customer, the customers inevitably being mutual acquaintances who had once told me twisted tales concerning Enoch's many misadventures after graduation. Each time he appeared I protested, not wishing to witness any more of his dark business, always afflicted with that same itching sensation spreading across my skin for several minutes. But Enoch always made some cryptic remark that convinced me to join him, which inevitably caused the itching to abate. These comments inexorably proved true, in a most perverse sort of way, and always at enormous personal cost to his clients.

Never once did I break their confidences to him concerning the unlikely stories they had told me; never once did Enoch make mention of the fact either. And, as before, I barely recognized these prematurely aged friends within their shattered bodies and broken minds, who craved and paid for his panorama of sinister curiosities.

At last, however, I made mention of these grotesque mutations to him, asking him not to show me anymore. At first Enoch dismissed my concern altogether. He claimed my powers of observation remained horribly flawed; that I had steadfastly refused to grasp the essential unifying truth which linked the smaller truths I had come to belatedly accept; that I had taught myself to hide within my comforting academic fallacies. As my friend, Enoch insisted, he had chosen to help me rise above this personality flaw. He went on to say I had *barely scratched the surface of the great mire which surrounds us—the mire which had so totally embraced the meager essence of these incredibly inconsequential souls.* He, on the other hand, had chosen to earn a thriving living by catering to that mire which those, like me, who preferred to *scratch out a subsistence by weaving glowing fantasies for the gullible,* made it a point to ignore.

"It's all around us, you know," he confided with a shrug and a wave following our penultimate outing. "One can even witness it in all its disgusting glory with the proper tools. In fact, the only proof of our sentience is our ability to witness it—witness it and accordingly change ourselves for the better by manipulating it; change ourselves to become immune to its many afflictions by willfully merging our will with its irresistible intent."

"Witness what, exactly?" I asked.

He turned to me and flashed that icy smile, the one he reserved for those rare moments I lit upon the intellectual junctures where our divergent world views intersected.

"Why, the living mire through which we slog," he said and laughed, "the one whose presence I embrace while you do your utmost to deny—even in the face of everything I have demonstrated to you."

"What tools?" I asked without enthusiasm.

"There are any number of devices fashioned specifically for that exact purpose, all manufactured at various notable declines in mankind's ever absurd efforts at civilization. The one I'd recommend, however, is Medusa's Mirror."

"Medusa's Mirror," I scoffed, "now that's a warning to keep one's distance if ever I've heard it. Have you located this abomination yet?"

"No, not yet—but I'm certain I could. I have the gift, you know. The cost of such an object, however, would be quite dear."

"Don't look to me to finance this thing you are proposing," I objected. "The entire idea is yours and yours alone. I'm inclined to heed the warning inherent in the name. Better you stick to catering to the wants of your disturbed clientele and leave me to weaving my glowing fantasies for the gullible. I'm content and don't wish to be counted among your deranged."

Enoch was clearly disappointed. He smiled understandingly and wished me goodnight. We had arrived at my home after witnessing a poor, misguided fool swallow a moldy, desiccated root upon which he swiftly disintegrated into a bubbling puddle on a basement floor. The hideous thing he became frothed and tittered until it shrunk, leaving only a sickening sulfurous odor and an oily black stain on the fractured concrete. I could still hear the ghastly sound as we drove off into the night as if its disembodied author had become entangled in Enoch's monstrous will and followed us from the crumbling tenement with that now all too familiar black sigil crudely spray painted across the door.

I watched the limousine disappear into the starless night, the pathetic tittering seemingly still clinging to it. I had hoped that was the end of my association with Enoch, for although these demonstrations of his dark gifts had inevitably been of some small interest to me, I had tired of them. More importantly, I had no wish to become the object of one of these demonstrations myself. But this was not to be.

At our last meeting some months later, I found Enoch waiting for me outside my loft one summer evening. I had stepped out for a brief walk in the stagnant air and constant roar to find his chauffeur looming beside the silver limousine. Both were bathed in the icy glow of a humming streetlamp, which cast their wavering shadow across the sidewalk, like some spectral barricade. I had felt the familiar itching as soon as I reached the street, made for the limousine like a moth to a candle flame. The silent chauffeur opened the back door as I approached.

"I have it," Enoch called to me. "I have the mirror."

I stopped and asked him what he intended to do with it.

"You and I will gaze upon the dark heart of the mire together, sharing its organic embrace. And you shall see firsthand, my friend, the colossal secret of my success."

"The mechanics of the abyss?" I asked.

"Oh yes. Will you join me?"

"Only if you will allow there might be something I can show you, as well."

"Done," Enoch said and laughed as if the notion were all but absurd.

"Tell me," I asked as we pulled away from the curb, "why have you cultivated my friendship given the obvious incompatibility of our perceptions and the conclusions we draw from them?"

"Because you, like me, are clearly unaffected—save for that singular discomfort you always exhibit and clumsily attempt to hide—by the allure of the mire. All those I've shown you have foolishly demanded something from it—something illusory, something addictive, something which I procured and you witnessed."

"Something which inevitably destroyed them."

"But of course."

"Which makes you an apex predator, them easy prey, and me—what?"

"Exactly."

"I see. So now you have procured something you think I might secretly want and wish to see the effect this object has on me."

"You've grown too cynical, my friend. I'm offering to share the experience with you. I don't imagine either of us will emerge any the worse for wear. Neither of us have the personality defects that proved fatal to the others. Think of what I am doing as another attempt at removing your blinders, a widening of your perception."

The dingy twilight lingered at the avenue's end, squashed between the crooked towers, drab with smog against the city's demanding electric glow. We headed uptown, eventually disappearing into an underground garage below a sleek, black monolith whose top three floors, Enoch claimed, *were his lair*. He assured me the spacious elevator in which we rode was his alone—that he, in fact, owned the entire building, one of many. I said something about the profitability of arcane oddities and he laughed, saying only that he had other interests. As the rigid formality of our relationship appeared to be dissolving, I mentioned the CIA and the drug cartel. Enoch laughed again, obviously delighted, but he neither affirmed nor denied anything.

The imposing copper-clad entry doors beyond the elevator each bore a raised black likeness of that spray-painted sigil I had often seen, only there was nothing crude about them. We passed into a dark corridor whose length was marked by widely spaced cones of muted light poring through tiny openings in the ceiling. At its end we passed through another pair of identical doors into a modest windowless room at the very heart of his citadel, dimly lit by similar lighting.

Floor, walls and ceiling were a porous black, like moist charcoal, with a faintly glowing surface. It creaked softly with hidden life beneath our feet and smelled strongly of decomposing vegetation, like a dense forest after a long, soaking rain. Against the far wall stood a simple dais about four feet high made of the same black stuff, an altar of sorts, upon which leaned a matching oval frame with an opening perhaps two feet high by a foot and a half wide.

"So, you've actually owned the mirror all along," I observed.

"Yes," Enoch confessed. "I'm sorry I wasn't completely forthright with you about that. The other way would have been so much more dramatic. Drama is good for magic, you know. The mirror was the first object in my collection—it facilitated the others."

"I guessed as much," I said. "In fact, were I a betting man, I'd bet even money almost every one of your clients developed their unhealthy fixations in this room."

"That's a bit harsh, and you'd lose your wager in any event. Each and every one of them began their quest here, I'll grant you. Their fixations, however, were always a part of them, albeit often latent. The mirror merely offered clarification as to their specific needs."

"No matter—I've not been altogether forthright with you, either," I replied.

"I, too, suspected as much."

"Shall we see what your oddity has to show us?"

"Please note that the only thing required on my part is that I allow the mirror to act upon my true nature, that I give myself over to that nature completely, and that my nature and the nature of the greater whole function as one without reservation."

And with these simple instructions, Enoch picked up the empty frame with both hands, held it before his face and smiled. I watched his features gradually darken, take on the color and texture of the room itself, his visage reduced to subtle shadows, barely suggested by the pale lights struggling to penetrate the living darkness within that unholy place. I watched every part of him contained within the oval frame of Medusa's Mirror disintegrate into a maze of undulating black tendrils, wet and dripping as if coated in a thick black sap.

They quivered through the mirror's invisible surface, crossing the space between us. I felt their clammy touch, atop the almost unbearable itching beneath my skin as they wrapped about my arms, legs and throat, completely engulfing me in their viscous embrace. I stood my ground, indifferent, until I felt them release their hold, slither back through the frame where I watched Enoch gradually emerge from the writhing field of black vegetation.

"I'm impressed by your reserve," he said, "truly I am."

"My turn," I said, extending a hand toward him.

Reluctantly Enoch placed the frame into my open hand without releasing his grip upon it. The thing was cold, as if it had been stored inside a freezer, and much heavier than it looked. I understood why he had abruptly stopped his demonstration—just touching the mirror was monumentally taxing. I put my other hand upon it.

"At least tell me what you plan to show me," he insisted before he would part with it.

"Of course. You displayed your understanding of the mechanics of the abyss—that vast, all-engulfing shadow, rent here and there by those annoying pinpricks of light, much like this very room. A shadow, I surmise, you expect will eventually seal itself against such paltry intrusions forever; a shadow in which you find an absolute kinship—an affirmation of yourself. I no longer dispute the validity of your shadow and its workings—its colossal intolerance—and your willing compliance. You have taught me that much. But my researches, such as they are, spurred on by our outings, have led me to those pinpricks, where, oddly enough, those same stark and predatory principles you've so long espoused find a somewhat different expression."

Resignedly Enoch released his grip upon Medusa's Mirror, allowing me to accept its full weight. He stared at me with no small amusement, confident in his absolute grasp upon the situation as well as his total mastery over the dark nature of reality, as I hefted it before my face as he had done, albeit with much difficulty.

"Please don't drop the mirror," he cautioned.

It came as no surprise, to me at least, as I had felt them stirring beneath my skin so many times before. But for Enoch, I suspect, it came as a thunderbolt. Small and white, they emerged en masse as I gave myself over completely to their demands for the first time. Their numbers legion, their nature electric, the tiny voracious spiders scrambled upon their long delicate legs, celebrating their freedom with complete abandon. Famished after a lifetime of fasting, they surged through my skin, my clothes, and the mirror's leaden frame as a throbbing white tide, descended like miniature glowing acrobats on glistening electric threads, swarmed across the black floor all over a flailing Enoch, until even the echo of his screams was no more.

THE MAZE OF MOONLIGHT AND MIRRORS

Gerri Leen

I remember our final fight, magic streaming
Amid the stench of sulfur and burnt feathers

You think you won, locking me here
In this maze of moonbeams and reflections

A maze with no exit, where time hasn't
Fully stopped but only pops in

Occasionally like a neglectful friend
A quick hug, a look around the place

Then gone, leaving me alone
In my prison, with only

My reflections for company
Reflections that have changed little

In the time that's passed
Did you think I would go mad in here?

I'm well acquainted with being alone
And skilled in using moonlight

I've created a forest, a castle, architecture
So strange you might not recognize it as such

Building my illusions out of the subtle light
You left here in misguided kindness

Growing stronger as I embrace
Rather than reject the solitude

My final work spins on the floor
A vortex that in time will become a portal

And I have all the time in
This world to perfect it, to use

My off-kilter doppelgangers
As foci, as anchors that will disappear

As soon as I do, when I force the exchange
Use the portal to both escape and ensnare you

Let's see how you do in a maze
That never goes dark but is never day

And you a sorcerer who requires sunlight
And other people to siphon energy from

A pity you spent so little time on inner work, forsook
The solitary path in favor of a livelier existence

I think you truly will go mad in here
Hoist on your silently luminous petard

OCULAR

Nidheesh Samant

I got down from the carriage and contemplated the old boarding house standing in front of me. The sign read, "Kamath Lodge." The architecture was typical of the villages in the region. The lodge reminded me of my ancestral home, which was constructed in much the same way. I was born and brought up in the city, so I only had vague memories of my family's home in our village. I remember a childhood of long evenings roaming the fields with my grandparents, and the charm of the countryside with the fond memories it held for me.

As I opened the gate and entered the verandah, my sense of nostalgia faded. The carvings on the walls were unlike any art I had ever seen: they all looked like irregularly shaped eyes. Inside what I assumed to be the irises were spiral designs. The longer I stared at them, the more I felt they were drawing me inside like a doomed ship being pulled to the bottom of the sea by a hungry whirlpool. My stomach churned as the scene spun in a dizzy cavalcade of monstrous eyeballs. I closed my eyes for a moment and became very still. From there on, I consciously avoided looking at the etchings as I walked into the hall, which served as a lobby. The man at the front desk greeted me with a curt *namaste*.

"Greetings, sir! I am Ramnath, the owner of this lodge. A room for one, I assume. Yes?" he asked while studying me from head to toe.

"Yes, please. I am Suraj Thakur. You do have a room free?"

"Of course, Mr. Thakur. All our rooms are free, but I will put you up in our best room. Let me take your trunk."

I smiled at the man, although something about him felt off to me. There was nothing strange in the way he looked or spoke, yet there was something different. Suddenly it hit me. The man just did not blink! His gaze lingered on me as he motioned that I should follow him. As we walked up the staircase, I noticed more of the ocular symbols and could not contain my curiosity or, rather, my uneasiness any longer.

"What exactly are these markings on the walls? I saw them outside as well."

The proprietor waved his hand dismissively.

"It is just some tribal art, sir. The villagers are very fond of it."

"Do you like it?"

"It is not a question of liking."

"What does—"

Ramnath cut me off.

"Your room, sir."

He gestured behind me. I turned and looked at the door, which stood slightly ajar, and then back toward the lodgekeeper.

"Thanks!" I said, but he wasn't there anymore. He had vanished in a moment, leaving my portmanteau behind. I shrugged, bending down to pick up my luggage. Maybe all the traveling had tired me out.

It was a long trek from the city and a journey I would have never taken had it not been absolutely necessary. Mr. Humes had made the same trip a fortnight ago and never returned. Not surprisingly, Mrs. Humes had grown worried and contacted me, his long-time friend. I could not refuse. So, here I was in the middle of nowhere. I entered the room, which was both small and very tidy, set down my trunk, and latched the door behind me.

The windows opened to a view of the dense forest that bordered the lodge. I stood at the window and stared at the dark skies, contemplating the summer rains that would soon be upon this community. I walked back to my trunk and opened it, retrieving my clothes from within. I hoped this would be a short trip. As I turned the mystery of Mr. Humes's disappearance over in my mind, the prospect seemed less and less likely. This was the only lodge in the village, or rather in this entire district, and Mr. Humes was not a liar—he would not deceive his wife about the location of his trip. There were questions that still required answers, and I intended to find them. I changed into a fresh pair of clothes and neatly tucked the rest into the armoire, which was large enough for me to comfortably fit inside, and yet have space to store all my clothes. I shut the wardrobe and lay down on the soft mattress. I was glad that this room contained none of the vertiginous ocular carvings found on the walls.

I shifted to my side, trying to get comfortable, when my gaze fell upon a wooden figurine lying on the table beside me. The figurine, or idol perhaps, was of a faceless man, covered in miniature detailing of the same ocular carvings. I turned over, unable to face those symbols. An odd sensation, something between fear and anger welled up inside me.

I twisted and turned in my mind and must have fallen asleep even though I didn't remember doing so, but I did recall the odd sensation of awakening into a threshold somewhere between dreams and reality. I was being watched! Those eyes peering at me. I could feel them drawing me within them, inside their spirals.... I could not move. I woke with a throttled scream at the abrupt shock of sinking into nothingness or some terrible, black void. I was drenched in sweat. Finally, I pushed myself off the bed. Muddy, black storm clouds had let loose with a torrent of rain that battered the land. I seized the hateful idol and tossed it outside the window in a sudden fit of revulsion, then slammed the window behind me. I grabbed my coat and charged out of the room. I couldn't wait any longer to have my questions answered.

The lodgekeeper was wiping the tables in the dining room when I entered. Two strangers were seated inside, drinking tea. I guessed the men were villagers from around these parts, though their faces were covered by *gamchas*. I ignored the pair and walked straight up to Ramnath. He looked up and greeted me with an awkward smile.

"Good evening, Mr. Thakur. You are right in time for supper. Should I set up a table for you?"

I dismissed the question with the wave of my hand.

"I need to ask you something."

"Yes, sir. What do you wish to know?"

I looked over my shoulder and noticed that the strangers had stopped sipping their tea. Their heads were tilted in my direction. I turned back to Ramnath.

"Not here. Come with me to the reception."

The lodgekeeper nodded. I followed him outside the dining room and into the reception area. He leaned on the desk.

"You can ask me now, sir. Is there any trouble?"

I scoffed.

"I won't waste any time here, Ramnath. I am looking for my friend, Mr. Alan Humes. Do you know where he is?"

He stared at me blankly.

"How would I know that, sir?"

"I am sure he boarded here in your lodge. He was an Englishman, as tall as I, with a bushy mustache. You must recall him."

The lodgekeeper continued staring at me as he shook his head.

"I'm sorry, but that does not ring any bells."

I slammed my palms on the desk.

"Don't lie to me. There is no other lodge in this area, and I know he couldn't board anywhere else. Check your register!"

Ramnath scratched his bald head in what seemed like a play for time. He retrieved a shabby book from a shelf behind him and placed it on the desk. He opened it to reveal pages inked in a crabbed hand I did not recognize. The script looked like some sort of tribal dialect.

"I will check the register, but it will take some time as my daughter handles these things. I can't read or write; she makes all the entries. She will be here in a while. Why don't you please wait in your room till then?"

I sighed.

"Very well. I will stay in my room until she arrives. Bring supper up as well—I'm famished. I don't think I can eat here with these eyes hovering over me anyway. It's good that the room doesn't have any of those atrocities."

Ramnath nodded.

"Other than the figurine you mean."

I put up my arms, feigning ignorance.

"What do you mean?"

The lodgekeeper's eyes widened, but he did not retort.

"I will bring your supper up, sir."

I turned around and headed toward the staircase. On my way, I glanced into the dining room, only to find it empty. The two strangers were gone.

As I walked up the stairs, I thought back to what had happened so far. Had Humes experienced the same? Were the two strangers involved in his disappearance? And what on earth were those bizarre ocular designs about? Even thinking about them made me shudder. I opened the door to my room only for a cold, moist draught to hit me in the face. The window stood open. I was certain that I had previously closed it, and sprinted toward the window to shut it. Halfway there, I was suddenly grappled by a pair of strong hands. Before I could make a sound, another man clamped his hands over my mouth. They dragged me into the wardrobe.

"Stay quiet!"

I turned to face my captors. As my eyes adjusted to the darkness, I realized they were the same strangers I had noticed in the dining room.

"Be still and we will not harm you. Understand?"

I nodded. Their accent was thick, but I could apprehend what they were saying. The one man lifted his hands from my mouth.

"Who are you?"

One of the strangers placed a finger on his lips. The other pointed a knife at my face.

"Shhh! Keep your voice down."

"Who *are* you?" I asked again, this time in a whisper.

"We are not fools like you. Why did you have to throw away the idol from this room?"

"The figurine? What has that grotesque piece got do with anything?"

"You are just as clueless as that stupid Englishman who was living here before."

"It was you! What have you done with Humes?"

"We have done nothing to him."

"Liars! You, Ramnath, all of you."

"Shut up!"

They both pressed knives against my neck and one man said, "Look outside!" I peered between the slats in the door of the armoire. I had a clear view of the window and the storm raging outside. Everything seemed normal, so I tried to look back at my captors, only to have both of them bear down with their knives on my neck.

"Alright!" I hissed.

I peered at the window again, trying to spot something new.

A bolt of pink lightning momentarily lit up the sky as a hairy, taloned hand clutched at the windowsill. I gasped at the cadaverous horror that pulled itself, or herself rather, into the room. Another stroke of lightning revealed the intruder's gaunt, leering face. The hag was searching for something, growling as she darted her bloodshot eyes from side to side. Terror and loathing welled up inside me as I realized this astonishing harridan was searching for me. She lurched forward on crooked, seemingly broken legs. Her feet pointed backward as if they had been hacked off and reattached by some hideous Frankenstein.

From the stories I had heard, this grotesque entity perfectly fit the description of a *Daayan*—an unholy product of malice and dark magic.

The witch made her way to the bedside, hunching over the bed. She unhinged her jaws, revealing a mouthful of crooked shark teeth. Suddenly, the creature vomited out a blood-curdling shriek. She ripped through the bed sheets and mattress with her hideously long, bony fingers. More like elongated, flexible needles than digits. Then the *Daayan* froze. The smell of rot and piss almost unmanned me as I struggled to remain silent. Her ravenous gaze lingered over the wardrobe. Cold sweat trickled down my back. I waited for what felt like an eternity. I stood transfixed, staring at the witch and trying not to scream. Finally, she glared about the room, and with a loud, liquid hiss bounded out the window back into the raging storm. I stood rooted to my spot; I don't know for how long. The two men stepped out of the wardrobe, one after the other. I turned to them.

"Was that a *Da... Daayan?*" I realized I was still shivering.

One of the strangers looked toward the window with his teeth bared. The other favored me with a hard smile. They moved toward the door. I noticed neither man had sheathed his knife. I called out after them again. One turned and looked me dead in the eye.

"Your *moorakh* friend had tossed away the idol as well. We only told you the truth. We did nothing to him."

The men left long before I could bring myself to move again. After what I had just witnessed, I had no reason to find any doubt in their words. How by all that is holy was I going to explain all of this to poor Mrs. Humes?

VOYAGE OF THE PFV-4

David Rose

A spy shouldn't be soaking wet, Jimmy told himself as he watched the sweet, pink liquid drip off of him and run down the drains. Having been dumped onto the ship's floor, he untwisted the lingerie he was in—that someone had *stuffed* him in. He was alone, fine. But missing all his gear? Not good. Especially not good if on one of Monagle's Pathfinder spacecraft, ran by a crew rumored to be equally as ruthless.

Jimmy knew from deep-space voyages that his fire-watch partner, that ogre of a man of an assistant team leader, should've been reanimating right alongside him.

The first watch, the other two men in this four-man outfit, they should've been just outside of arm's reach, ready to walk nude into their own tubes to "freeze up" for a year. But he looked about as he rose, confirming what he already knew: he was alone. And more, suspended animation would only make sense if they'd left the hangar. They hadn't, or, racking his brain as he stumbled out of Tube Bay 2, he hadn't remembered.

A rail prevented him from falling. Through eyes still gunked, above the haze of lights and the flickers of control panels, he could see the black square of the bridge's front viewing port.

Black, yes, Mammon's Egg was a hangar darker in places than moonless midnight. But still, there'd be the glow of at least a service lamp. Wouldn't one be bolted somewhere against a concrete wall? There were none. Straining, continuing forward, he began to see out the viewing port what appeared to be a dull and rusty sphere. It was growing, as if drawing near.

A noise he suddenly realized he'd been hearing just as suddenly ended: thuds following, like, like boots? Jimmy turned to see Denis Punchie.

"Ready for fire watch, Acko?" the ogre growled.

Acko—that was it, that's what he was supposed to be. Shorthand for Atmosphere Control Operator: the Pathfinder team's communications bubba, tasked with clogging up the airwaves when all the other ships arrived. New planets didn't just need their resources sucked dry; they needed organization. The radioman designated airspace and guided down the drillers.

Punchie broke from the tower routine to duck through a hatch and point a finger at the Acko locker.

"Thought we were second watch?" Jimmy said, fiddling with his bra.

Men who look like steroided corpses can still smile, though the result is as unsettling as if they'd howled at the moon. The assistant team leader's mirth was short-lived.

"That freeze fucked you up somethin' good. You know your name right now? Yeah, newbies never fair well, do they? Especially radio-humpers like you."

Freeze? Yeah right, and what for? They were still on Earth, and Jimmy nothing more than the victim of some gag. And damn right he knew his name. He was Jimmy Fureen, the high-level operative who killed the real Acko days before altering his creds and assuming his role on this dismal spacecraft. He was their sworn enemy. He opened the Acko locker. Flinging aside the garments and getting dressed in that dead man's flight suit, Jimmy didn't need to rely on any training to remain timid while in the crosshairs of a man like Denis Punchie. He knew this Monagle scum's kind. Still, he couldn't entirely resist.

"Affirmative. Radio humpers, like me."

"Yeah, you're still good an' dumbed up," Punchie sigh-smiled. "Look, we tranquilized you, a little zap in the neck before we set sail. Then tossed you in your tube. That and the women's underwear, just a bit of tradition." His voice turned grim. "I don't spend a year on watch with some fuck I don't know. So I had Cy—he's your team leader, case you forgot—I had Cy delay your unfreezin' until we were a day or so out. Figure you'll need time to tweak your comms and whatnot. That's less woke time for you. You're welcome." Punchie sat at a table and whipped out a deck of cards. "You know how to play six-card cribbage?"

"A few days out?" Jimmy said. He only planned on boarding the Pathfinder Vessel 4 to blast everyone inside, then spend the next few hours poring over logs, snapping photos, and dropping thermites before hauling ass.

"Yep," the assistant team leader said. "Some things changed while the two of us were froze up, though. We got tasked a different planet." The gunk was out of Jimmy's eyes in more ways than one. Jimmy could see clearly now. He could see the nomenclature below controls he'd been tasked with learning, the sloppy "Wicked Tenants" sign pasted over the ship's placard. And he now knew what that dull, rusty sphere had been, what it was. Why it had appeared to be getting closer.

Punchie nodded to a point beyond Jimmy, toward the main windshield in the bridge: "just look at that ugly fucker."

He wasn't on Earth. He was on a flying spacecraft and would soon be doing a full year on this planet, looming at him through the front viewing port like a bloodshot eye.

"The comm gear is... where?" Jimmy shut his eyes.

"In the comm locker, dipshit. All these questions you make a man think you're no Acko at all." Punchie leaned over the table and leered. "Damn that freeze fucked you up."

"It did." Jimmy felt his patent slyness, his presence of mind. They were returning. "Getting tranquilized probably didn't help none, Punchie. Let me get outfit first, then maybe some cribbage."

"Your pistol's in the armory. Not that it'll do you any damn good. Only Glock-53s have the spring cups that adjust to planets." Punchie shuffled his deck, refusing to look up.

"*Tisk tisk*, bringin' contraband on board, and tucked under your shirt? With no holster even? Cy wasn't too happy."

Jimmy got out of there before his brutish co-habitant could pry any deeper. Picking a hall appearing best fit to house a comm locker, he soon came to a new room.

A placard read above the open hatch: *Here Ye We Do To Trouble*. Inside the small menagerie of horror, he saw an array of suspended animation tubes.

Most housed men, or parts of them. Jimmy knew Clinton Yates, that operative who liked to go by "O." They both worked for Dobshire Drilling, Jimmy and O, Monagle Mining Corp's most aggressive competitor. Opposite as two could be, Yates worshipped good ol' Beelzebub, Jimmy had been raised Methodist. One a knife-wielding badass, the other more a bookworm. They were both good, real good. But the bookworm was alive, and the other's head now floated jawless in a queer-lit jar.

Jimmy had long recognized the fierce reputation of Monagle's moon-skinned PFVers, but it didn't paint any glitter on these barbarians.

"We're a member light," Punchie said from behind him.

Punchie pointed.

Jimmy froze as if the reaper had touted, "you're next." Floating in a tube, little different than a dark towel stuffed into an aquarium, a muscular body was shot full of holes. The ship's terrestrial equipment operator, the engineer they called: "Quadz?"

"No panties for that newbie on the way back," Punchie growled. "Apparently the sonofabitch tried to turn the ship around when we were given our new rock. Cy wasn't about to lose that money. I would've fed 'em to the dogs over it." A mammoth hand landed on Jimmy's shoulder. "Ever done that, Acko? Fed a sonofabitch to a pack a dogs? You hear the screams, not just all the hungry, hungry snarls."

Jimmy ran from the room and that foul laughter. Back in the tube bay, he gasped and leaned against the tube glass that had held his fetal position for—god almighty, for an entire year.

The reflection looking back at him cooled his nerves. His greasy brown hair hadn't aged a day, still hanging down to a sharp jaw on an angular face that held eyes that had seen worse.

He wasn't back to a hundred percent yet, but he would be. There was a job to do. Jimmy went back to the Acko locker and pulled out his personal bag that these assholes had graciously remembered to put away.

Passing that wretched trouble room, Jimmy soft-stepped the lit gangway until he came at last to the door of the armory. Of course it would be locked, leaving him to admire through impenetrable glass a rack of M7A2 rifles and those highfalutin Glock-53s. He didn't have access, and even if he did, chances were poor he'd come out on top if he roped off with the guy two rooms over, solemnly admiring torture.

In this year of our Lord, 2225, cigar-puffing moguls didn't mind outfitting their monkeys with the latest weaponry, as much as they didn't mind sending them onto high arid steppes or down into boiling marshes that crawled with hostile life. He'd done his research. Pathfinder scum were no rookies to combat. They had lathered the hulls of the PFV-4 with extraterrestrial blood, gunked the tread of their boots with amputated pods and still-twitching organs from Betelgeuse all the way out to the Kocher Belt.

When he walked by the trouble room again, he glanced inside. Punchie must've returned to the bridge. These metal caverns held his comm locker, somewhere. At least there he could hide and drum up a semblance of a plan. Moving, Jimmy knew his bag was just a few pounds of useless leather. He opened it anyway. He couldn't put his pistol inside, nor anything else that had stared at him from the other side of armory glass. Though, his hand confirmed as he dug around, he may actually have *one* weapon.

He laughed. He couldn't help it. "Weapon, my ass," he said.

The egg—the size of a damn emu's—and the big blue veins that still pulsed against its shell had lasted the year, though the thought of *using* it may mean he'd become as mad as the questionable priest he'd stolen it from. Jimmy grabbed some wall. There hadn't been a meteor to avoid; the ship hadn't jerked. Still, he'd nearly fallen. Had that spiritual leader back on Earth placed a curse on this devilish egg, that its thief was to experience heart-stopping vertigo whenever he ogled at its ugliness?

Little different than the sign housing Yate's head's grave, *Do Unto Others* had been embossed on the plaque adorning the egg's former home. In that museum of religious oddities, a weapon of sorts seemed likely, to say nothing of fitting. Now Jimmy held it in his hand.

"Do unto others." That was bible talk for sanctioned death.

Nonsense. Black magic was as fictitious as five loaves and two fish feeding a bunch of greasy ancients. More pressing, as he entered a garage full of land vehicles to weave past their tracks and wheel wells, was a headache and wooziness that had beset him. What a joke. If there was a maligned force that could actually be unleashed from a damn egg, he'd gladly dress himself again in that soggy lingerie and ignite a one-man parade.

"I'd love to hear *you* scream while being eaten," he said to himself, thinking of Punchie. Seized by a sudden throbbing behind the eyes, he dropped the egg. From between his fingers, he soon looked down. The egg, it lay in pieces. Though it had felt heavy, almost uranium-like, now broken, not a curse or a slime or a fetid batwing wafted up his way. Just as he'd figured, only dry air and a foul stench, the latter helping none for his pounding head.

Tranquilized, yes, suspended animation, that too, but something beyond these pestered him. Coming to an intersection, the gangway lit red one way, green the other. Could it have been that shot of liquor right before Punchie or Cy had crept up from behind to needle-gun his artery? Green seemed less ominous, pushing him past more confidential information and a medical locker.

The comm locker was at the end of the green tunnel, though when he got there, he was uninterested. It was as if— the med locker! Jimmy ran back and flung open its doors.

Scanning the vials and bottles, "No, no, no," he said. Here it was, proof the cosmos had it out for him once and for all. Punchie's voice crackled over an intercom, though about what Jimmy wouldn't know. He hated his own brashness, always volunteering for certain death to taunt those exact things—certainty and death. Because they'd found him at last. A day full of wonderful discoveries and an even more wonderful reminder. All he could do was blow out a hopeless laugh. Jimmy suffered an affliction, one that would claim his life out in the swirling nothingness of space. The headache made too much sense.

Tucked within the belly of some beast, or so it seemed, orange lights overhead began to flash. Was this a joke too? Who had stolen what, and from whom? If Monagle Mining Corp was the same as Dobshire, these intervals meant they were nearing that horrid rock's atmosphere.

When the orchestra ended, Jimmy was almost done checking off his symptoms. When had his last dose been, excluding that infernal, non-counting year in a tube? Dizziness was something he'd experience whenever blood would start shunting from the brain. This was the earliest sign. That the ship's walls now appeared soft, however, fleshy even, that was harder to explain.

He recoiled his hand when it corroborated his tested vision. The bulwark didn't feel like cool, clean metal, but a porous, slimy sheet. Punchie was barking on the intercom again, providing an ironic assistance that pulled him back to reality. Waiting for Punchie to fall asleep then beating him to death with a wrench was viable. After, he could easily waltz into the other tube bay, kill Cy, their frozen team leader, then set a new course. He didn't know the ship well, though he willed himself to believe he could learn, given enough time puttering around in the void. But this grand scheme relied on the one thing he didn't have: medicine to counter Noaraexis, to slow his ailments and to give him a fighting chance.

Noaraexis. A condition that had developed in modern times, due to, as one story goes, all the outer-space clutter now mixed with human food. Another yarn had to do with the latest apparel and the Martian poly-fibers stitched in their seams. But Jimmy and the rest of the Dobshire boys knew the truth. Still battling it out with their union, Noaraexis was a rare illness, suffered only by Dobshire Drilling operatives who caught something nasty on a planet orbiting Proxima Centauri. They usually fought it off well. But eventually, without meds, shunting would progress, headaches would worsen, the afflicted would go unconscious, then die from cerebral hypoxia.

But he would not end up with his head in a jar. He braced himself against the frame of the locker, repelling self-pity. He'd boarded this ship to merely execute Monagle scum and gather intelligence, but he stood inside a Pathfinder that could be his coffin. The only mission now was to survive.

Yet, how could he? He couldn't just strut into the bridge and ask a maniacal space sailor to refreeze him, head back to Earth, and all because of an ailment that *only* the maniacal space sailor's enemies suffer.

Mixing the meds onboard! He'd seen it done before.

Pilfering through the shelves, Jimmy loaded his bag. Labels on serum-laden vials played no trick on his eyes, showing soon and clearly that the cocktail to delay his death was short one component. When he had the last useful item, he looked up. The walls had changed again, or, he felt his mind calibrate, change *further*. Pillars had partially detached themselves. Their right angles now round. Had the broken egg done this? These... these tubes, not of glass and freeze fluid but stinking bile, they were a corpus that actually moved!

Moved nothing! Being tranquilized and frozen for a year plus being without meds was screwing with his head.

He reverted back to the V in the gangway to follow the red lights this time. He soon wished he hadn't. Gut instinct had served him, bringing him to the ship's galley. The first compartment he released revealed chunks of raw meat floating in vats of blood. The second, the third, all the same. It was a cannibal's kitchen from hell until at last flinging open the cabinet that contained a strikingly normal masonry of bagged goods.

The cabinet, unfortunately, didn't have anything that contained Allicin.

A former colleague had been notorious for his savant-like polarity. Though a renowned chemist, usually beset to poison other spies, the dunce would come to work wearing mismatching shoes or his shirt inside out. Such feats reached their zenith when it got out he'd been stranded on a margarita cruise-liner, forcing him to discover a second solution to his own Noaraexis dilemma.

Jimmy flung the bags behind him, making cursing despairs as his desperation exceeded amazement. If ingested with insulin and coagulants, Allicin would slow Noaraexis significantly. The savant chemist had proved such. That would buy enough time to grab that wrench, enough hours to wait for bed. Not a mixed spice medley or a string of garlic; the last ingredient was not onboard.

He had to have missed one. There would at least be one! Jimmy picked through the bags on the floor, scrutinizing their labels before hurling them again. His eyes had been correct, though his attention was pulled suddenly to another of his lamentable senses. Boots pounded, marching toward the galley from out in the red hall. Tissue crawled up the walls with the gleaming texture Jimmy had seen once in an exposed stomach. Coming with this nightmare was a stench like what had come from that egg. Above the meal-prep table swung kitchen hooks, all losing their spoons that now clanked on the floor. Knives and pots were being sucked into the vileness of the wall. Jimmy grabbed the meat cleaver.

"Get your ass to Tube Bay One," Punchie said, shouldering into the galley. "Now! Start unfreezing Cy. Somethin', somethings gone wrong. I gotta push the landing." His grisly face degraded to an obvious question: "What the fucks goin' on?"

Jimmy watched him scan the bulges and the drips. "Then you see it too."

"...Yeah—you're goddamn right I do!"

Then it wasn't a hallucination. No freak symptom. That goddamned egg, Jimmy knew, sudden, certain.

"Okay," Jimmy said. He'd believed for a moment Punchie would storm in and brain him for initiating a haunting. But Punchie hadn't a clue. "Okay, let's move." Jimmy waited for Punchie to turn, leading them out of the galley. The nerve-frayed Monagle scum was unable to see Jimmy slip the meat cleaver from behind his back and into his bag. Jimmy wiped the sweat from his brow. The air had become hot and moist.

Jimmy had hoped he would give him an easy target, but Punchie kept turning, looking and twisting as if to make sure his Acko was still behind him. The red lights still hummed, casting the almost palpable humidity into a fog of pinkish heat. The gangway gave irksomely below their boots, all the while the air grew warmer.

Oddly, at least to Jimmy, when they spilled out into the garage, the place was entirely normal. Though unaware of the horror that had originated here by way of a dropped evil egg, Punchie joined Jimmy, searching below ATVs and land-movers for lurking flesh or an exploding boil. Jimmy thought of the wrench, saw a locker labeled *Demo*, rejoiced in the miraculous familiarity of a dull wall and a clean floor. He might have thought more on these things if it weren't for Punchie opening the next hatch.

The return to sanity was short-lived. If it wasn't for the fact that Tube Bay 1 was only accessible from Tube Bay 2, there was little doubt in him that Punchie would've crawled through the air vents rather than enter. The tube bay they'd both been housed in was now engulfed. Unknown fluids dripping from the ceiling, a giant artery blocking a door, rubbery sacks pulsating against the ladder well. The once calmness of recirculating air had been replaced by rhythmic swooshes, as if in a giant lung.

Moving together, Punchie opened the hatch to Tube Bay 1. *Tube room, ha!* Jimmy giggled. The diaphragm of a leviathan had risen between the two bays. He continued to laugh like a lunatic. He couldn't help it, even when Punchie roared in his ear. He may have told the Monagle scum their blessed head honcho was blocked in *the other lung*, but of such discourse he was deprived. Thankfully the floor was a soggy mat. It didn't even feel hard.

"Get up," Punchie demanded.

"I can't," Jimmy said, rolling onto his back. "I can't. I have Noaraexis."

"No Aces?"

"Noaraexis," he giggled, "and we're both gonna die."

It took a moment for the Monagle scum to put it together, but he did. And when he did, Jimmy was grinning deliriously amongst ground-floor slime, reaching into his bag. "You did this," Punchie then said, "Didn't you?"

"Fuck you, Punchie."

All that remained of their light was a lone overhead, blinking and fizzling with whatever ungodliness was burrowing into its wires. Punchie took a hard step forward. "You double-crossin'," Jimmy was back on his feet, putting Punchie's volume up to a scream; "double-dealin' Dobshire fuck!"

Jimmy pulled out the meat cleaver and lunged forward. Punchie disarmed him as coolly as he would have taking a purse from an old lady. Jimmy's world became pain and white light. After a time, he realized he was once again on his ass.

Punchie raised the cleaver. Then he flung it. "No... you ain't goin' out this clean."

"Feed me to the dogs?" Jimmy said, holding where Punchie had blasted him with a fist.

"Nope." Punchie freed his belt and wrapped it around that same fist. "Just gonna smash, smash you up."

He had come to believe in the forces of darkness, but Jimmy felt for the first time in a long time that traditional divine intervention may be afoot. Because right then the ship made a terrible noise, a growl so strong every flap of flesh quivered and every bolt left thrummed. The stalled assistant team leader on this doomed voyage took his attention off of Jimmy to gaze at the sudden expansion of the room.

61

A protrusion from the lung-wall shot out and wrapped around Punchie's leg. Jimmy rallied as Punchie cursed, wildly, beating the smooth sinew with his belted fist. Jimmy thought he heard the thing shriek when it finally let go. Two of these same attackers came up from the floor, on either side of Jimmy, pinning him flat.

"So much for divine intervention," he sighed.

"So much for a lot of things," Punchie said. "Your ass breathin' for much longer bein' one." Punchie also watched as these fleshes grew over Jimmy, apparently realizing an instant quicker what was dawning on Jimmy now—a most awful suffocation.

Punchie smirked, refitted his belt, then ran frantically back toward the garage.

He had no tools, no blade. Straining his neck, Jimmy attempted to bite his way free. Despite his position, it struck him as strange he'd inadvertently pay such close attention to the clatter of Punchie's flight. Once gone, once the garage hatch had slammed shut, it seemed the sheet-like protrusions began to take cue. They wiggled, caressing, sensing him and the other protrusions like mindful tongues. They rolled back, releasing him.

Shambling to the bridge, he felt an undeniable delight when he was able to recover the cleaver from a sodden patch of shadow. Delight, whatever had just happened, whatever understanding the ship had of him, it was the first good news in a year; that *do unto others* must've meant others than he.

His eye hurt. His head swam. He stared out a porthole and tried to breathe. And he tried to think:

Light had once been thought the galactic speed limit. As is often the mother of invention, some nerd hoping to get laid more had discovered ways to combine jet propulsion, magnetism, and a good old rip in the space-time continuum, thus hailed a hero and stuffing an old theory forever in its grave. Stars, systems, the outer reaches of the Milky Way herself, all good window-viewing if just willing to freeze a few years away.

Not long after this revolutionary discovery, space exploration had destroyed people's belief in the Book of Revelations. More planets equaled no seal-opened apocalypse to pen the human race its doom. Christianity crumbled to a mere fragment of its former glory, as its monotheistic cousins had before it. Turns out, getting your ass smacked with fiery paddles was the only thing keeping most asses warming church pews. But old ideas, the ones about man's quest for knowledge, brought Satanism back with a fury. Most classic Satanists, as the old books read, had merely been proud individualists adorned in black. All the hellish planets humanity had discovered, however, supported the sprawling growth of a revised maltheism.

Jimmy had come from the fragment still opposing it. Though he had rid himself of his upbringing, attached like hooks under the skin were the remnants of a mother hell-bent on going to Heaven. This ship was both mechanical and alive, sparing this porthole just before the bridge. When Jimmy was a kid, he'd wondered if heaven was in the sky, and that, if so, would angels and demons be able to breathe in their final war if it took them swirling up into outer space. Now, flaps of wings blotting out the stars, expansions so great they bowed and rattled what few planks remained. These wings gave him an answer. A thing, a dragon? Something propelled itself in the void. And he was inside it.

When Jimmy entered the bridge, the hatch's frame was made of nothing but bone. As half-expected, the ceiling and floor shined and glimmered with the same alabastrine. He slipped his way to the front viewing port, its massive clear block now separated twenty feet or more by hard skull. These two new windshields were rounded, like ovals laid sideways, contracting and easing at their edges.

He was looking through the dragon's eyes. Stretched out before him was an impossibly long snout, thicketed with horns, crowned at the end by one large enough to skewer a whale. A collision with the inner-skull he was spared, for when the monster swung its stare to gaze upon the ridge of its own scaled back, Jimmy felt nothing.

David Rose

The ride, nevertheless, forced him to vomit. It was like being stuck inside a car as it flipped down a hill. Stars one moment, the admiration of claws that could raze a building the next, the beast seemed proud to be alive, taking inventory on all that it was.

The planet they'd been heading toward reappeared with stomach-churning suddenness. Regaining his footing, it occurred to him the planet's surface should've been getting closer, not farther away. The great wings flapped. This summoned dragon was resisting the planet's gravitational pull. The idea of being in this thing. *Ugh,* he thought. He'd rather his bones turn to dust than be subsumed by this ship. Stuck out in space, perhaps forever.

The line of sight shifted again. What the dragon saw— what they both saw: Punchie swam clumsily outside, trying to activate his spacesuit to jettison him down to the red rocky desert of an alien world.

How Jimmy wished it was his doing—tampering with the suits—then he could die knowing that at least one of his plans had worked without error. The dragon was tracking Punchie, little different than a dog following an insect with its snout. Jimmy saw the spray begin to flicker behind Punchie's jetpack.

Punchie didn't get far. Changes from outside suggested the dragon had reached forward at the neck. Just before the Monagle scum went under the rise of the great horn, into the dragon's mouth, Punchie screamed silently into the glass of his helmet, looking toward Jimmy, though Jimmy doubted his face was the face that Punchie saw.

He listened. Unbelievable, dull screams and thuds passed below, down into whatever the throat was in this devil-haunted ship.

The skull wasn't done growing, nor was the new brain— rising from the floor, sealing off the only exit, sticking to Jimmy's boots. He would be closed in, crushed somewhere against the ceiling. He tightened his squeeze on the cleaver. In thoughtless desperation he hacked at the tissue between his feet.

"Yeah, that's it!" He screamed like a blind man seeing light for but a second. The floor underneath not only retrograded to bone, but back to plain ordinary metal.

A spree commenced, flinging his sweat and chunks of the beast all over the bridge. Part of a piloting control emerged, as did lights that shined as if being freed. But, sending him spiraling; when he would abandon one area to work on another, the aliveness undoubtedly returned. It was no use.

The garage!

Dying in a brief fiery crash beat suffocating inside ghastly innards. Parsing the files in preparation for his mission, he read that explosives may be onboard for the purpose of creating landing zones. The demolition equipment, the "Demo," it had to be in that pray-to-god still unaffected garage. Jimmy fought off waves of collapse, traversing first the nightmarish length that had become the dragon's neck.

About time you were right, he jabbed, stuffing into his flight suit an ANFO sack, detonator, and all sorts of doomsday paraphernalia.

Commonsense would normally dictate that he blow in place, but the garage's continued normalcy somehow chilled him more than if it had become an organ. He squeezed through what was left of the hatch and crawled back into Tube Bay 2.

He had stood and tried to calm himself. If this same fiend was the one witnessed by John of Patmos, surely Jimmy wagered his own soul was destined for Hell, having buddied up in some odd way with the great dragon of Revelations. He tried and failed to think of some soothing biblical verse.

So be it. Akin to a shotgun blast to the lung, the soon-to-be explosion brought to mind: "And the great dragon was thrown down, that ancient serpent...."

He set the explosives against a vein. Tree-like and throbbing, it probably led right to the polluted heart. He jammed in a blasting cap and unspooled the det cord, tracing his way back until his heels met the perilously long hall. He initiated the fuse. Of course the detonation cord would be of the slow-burning type. Though a dead man, instinct demanded he scramble on all fours, up through a tightening tunnel toward a brain plotting some unknowable corruption.

The tunnel, black and stinking, narrowed until, at last, he was unable to move. His tomb rubbed against his face and hair, not to pop him like a parasite, but to caress, to trap and keep him a while. Jimmy felt a strange remorse. He never got to see the dragon's face.

The explosion shook every bone, filling him with a painful surge that became euphoria. The air was demanded out of his lungs then the tissue released, limp and convulsing, allowing him a final, futile sucking in of pointless air. He cocked his head. A porthole slowly returned amidst the cataclysmic roar of space sucking out parts of the ship. Soon, such would give way to atmosphere.

Beyond the porthole's seal rolled the crimson plains that would be his grave. It was no church cemetery, but he'd made peace with all that. The planet would receive Monagle scum and their godforsaken ship. But perhaps Good existed after all, and more—perhaps he'd briefly been its agent, for at least none would be alive.

THE INFINITY OF WORSE

Ken Hueler

"Too old," Lowell grumbled and limped on.

Paul scampered behind the lowborn thug, who was lurching grave to grave in the twilight, too terrified and desperate to flee. Again, he glanced to a stand of alders, where Lowell's horse and drag were dissolving into the darkness and sour mist. To him, this chilly fog felt like England's breathy, disappointed sigh as it watched him dishonor his bloodline.

Lowell crouched to grip the low iron bars of a mortsafe and peered inside. "Heh! Couldn't ask for fresher. Bring us the rod and find the edge." He dropped his buttocks onto the cage and pulled out a flask. A thought changed his features, and he sneered. "If it pleases the gentleman."

Paul lowered the sack gently, to lessen the noise, and slid out a long metal spike. Partway to the grave, a hiss stopped him.

"Tssch! The other end, ninny—where the head will be." Lowell waved his unoccupied hand and snorted. "Why did I pick you? As thick as pig shit and half as useful!"

Paul stabbed the rod several feet from where the bars entered the ground and rocked the point. He hit the metal plate and tried again a foot further. This time, the shaft sank deeper.

Lowell lit the bullseye lantern. "Lovely. You first."

Paul fetched the spade. The wooden blade made for more work, but struck stones did not sound out so loudly. Lowell delivered a stream of complaints about Paul's strength and

67

ancestry until, exasperated, the big man took over. Three feet down, past the mortsafe's locking plate, he began tunneling under. Paul checked the position of the moon, diffusing through the fog, and calculated the time until dawn. His pocket watch, along with other sacrificed belongings he'd been carrying when the doors of his home had been closed to him, lay in a pawnbroker's case.

Finally, Lowell hit wood and cleared around it. He tossed out the spade. "Right, shirkster, empty the sack and fetch it here with the rook and the rope."

Lowell inserted the rook's chisel between the lid and the headboard. "Wrap it," he ordered. When Paul just stood, confused, Lowell loosed a riper string of abuse and wound the sacking around the end of the crowbar. "Hold that in place," he ordered. The cloth muffled the squeak of parting nails and wood as Lowell worked the crowbar under the lid, then circled the board. Tearing the panel away revealed hair so blonde it glowed in the faint light like knucklebones through skin.

"Be glad she's embalmed," Lowell chuckled as Paul turned away, coughing. Lowell shouldered past and climbed out the hole. He snatched up the rope and tossed it at Paul. "Pull her out, the way I told you."

Paul crouched and reached into the coffin, his head turned sideways, and he slid his hands along the ears and jaw. Fighting the tangling hair, he passed the rope's end under the neck and tied a clumsy knot. He clambered away, queasy.

Lowell nodded. "Done? Let's test your work, then."

The two dragged her out to the waist, and then heaved her up onto the grass by her arms. The smell, while diffusing in the open air, followed Paul, smeared into his clothes. Resentful, he glanced at the girl. She appeared sixteen or a whisper beyond and lay with head askew and limbs forgotten, the way a drunkard sleeps. Her ring, cameo choker, and blue satin dress spoke of money—Paul had met many girls attired so—and her face and skin of good diet and leisure. Pleasant company, usually, unless out to snare a careless bachelor.

Lowell pulled out his flask. "Now's when you'll want to rest, but longer we stay, the likelier us getting nicked. Gather up the kit but for the shovel and load it on the drag. Then come and help carry her like a good lad."

Walking alone unnerved Paul more than anything so far. Without Lowell, he felt exposed, and being spotted near the road felt more probable than within the cemetery. Had anyone noticed their unattended wagon? Would anyone be on the road this hour—what hour was it? How long had they been working? Additionally, without the palliatives of loud company and drink, he felt the crush of his failure all the more keenly, as if some final blow would suddenly and finally press him into the earth as it had the men and women surrounding him. He glanced warily at the procession of headstones sliding past. The farther ones crouched in the fog like shadowy animals.

He slid the sack into the wagon bed and ran back.

Lowell had stripped away the woman's clothes. Seeing the exposed body—young, pretty, odd-angled, helpless—sent Paul stupid with outrage.

"You fiend! I'll do theft to keep from starving, but I will not allow you to disgrace this innocent."

Lowell grabbed Paul's coat, swaying slightly from his bad leg but powerful in his arms and hands. "Keep your voice down or we're both done! Takin' a body's jail and a fine, but stealing the belongings gets you transported to the colonies or hung. Your great, loud gob betrays us, you want to face the law? And we're knapping a corpse, so don't expect pity if time comes for a judge to look down his nose. Got it? Well, do you? Say no, and I'll stuff you in that coffin and fill the dirt after."

Paul nodded, terrified. He'd seen Lowell round on a man who'd cheated him. The crowd's cheering had faded at the thorough brutality, and though the unfortunate had lived, he neither moved nor looked the same after.

Lowell rolled the jewelry into the dress and shoved it into the coffin. "I did most the work so far, skiver," he growled. "Fill it in."

Paul propped up the headboard and started shoveling. The looser soil made for faster work, but the moon had shifted noticeably since their arrival.

Lowell tied the rope beneath the shovel head and slung it over his shoulder. "Right, you take her legs. Mind your eyes."

The loose-limbed corpse proved difficult. He hooked his arms under her knees and, to keep them from slipping, pressed them hard into his sides. He knew the ground-in smell of death would never leave his only coat, and the bare heels and calves tap-tap-tapping the back of his legs would ruin his trousers. Angry again, he glared down at the smelly woman. Noticing the marks on her abdomen and inner thigh, where she had been drained, brought a vague remorse, but when he looked up, he spotted the alders and felt elated. He was nearly done and appeared to have escaped detection! And Lowell was with him—with all his faults, Lowell was big and knew how to fight. People drifted away when Lowell got "the look": those flushed cheeks, widened eyes, and curled lips.

They loaded her into the wagon bed and put away the spade. When they had ridden to the graveyard, they'd sat up front conversing over the clatter of the horse's hooves and the wheels' wooden rims, but now Lowell exiled Paul to the back with the corpse. Paul didn't mind the distance: Lowell was visibly cross at his apprentice's ineptitude tonight and would be tempted to "teach some smarts." Both knew the low-born thug needed a partner—had run through several, in fact—and though Lowell declared Paul's gentle face and cultured manners apt for situations requiring bluff and finesse, not testing the strength of their bond seemed wise.

And Paul needed Lowell. After being disowned and seeing his supposed friendships evaporate, Paul had thought he'd hit bottom, but, as the corpse beside him attested, worse is infinite. He needed to travel to a distant part of the country, perhaps even to the Continent, and start a new life. That required funds. He pulled the filthy stable blanket over the girl. Yes, one could always go lower, and he refused to discover what rotten, degrading misery might be waiting.

He gazed forward. The carriage lamp imparted a sad warmth to the fog. Trees were sliding by, charcoal sketches on rough paper. Paul could not see much from where he sat in the wagon bed—and likely Lowell on the bench not much farther.

"What the hell?" Lowell barked.

Paul crouched, ready to leap into the woods. Being caught with a stolen corpse—that would magnify his shame if the newspapers and penny dreadfuls eternalized his name and face far and wide. Where could he go after? Nowhere but back to his current home of drink, lodge houses, and men like Lowell. He held his eyes to where Lowell was staring: a wheel-sized section of the fog was parting into a shaft of clear air. The carriage lamp brightened as the tunnel passed the driver's bench and reached Paul. Then, as the road curved, the tunnel shifted, sliding off Lowell and toward the woods. The wagon continued, the rapt men listening for unusual sounds over the clop of hoofs and the creaking of wood. Fog once again blurred the driver, but Paul could see straight down the pivoting tunnel into the woods.

"Bloody unnatural," Lowell muttered, subdued. "What did you make of it, college boy?"

"I've never seen or heard of the like," Paul replied.

Lowell snorted. "Wasted your time on them books, then, di'n you?" He hunched his shoulders. "Damn this slow horse."

Paul glanced across the wagon bed, but the fog remained a wall; the phenomenon terminated exactly where he sat. Already chilled from the sweat damping his clothes, he trembled at a deeper internal freeze. He almost cried out to Lowell, but what could that illiterate commoner do? Again, he considered running, but to where? And if the abomination followed—if he were indeed its focus—that knowledge, that horrid confirmation would be much worse even than this current dread. He cocked his ear. "What?"

"Eh?" Lowell called back.

"Did you say something?"

"If I did, you wouldn't mistake it. Now keep it down. We're nearing town, and I, at least, don't want ta' fetch no notice."

Silence descended again. Then a soft flutter of sound:

"I am Delilah. Delilah Heatherington."

Paul searched for the source. Lowell was perched forward, trying to keep to the road in the thickening fog, and the voice had been too soft, too refined and feminine, for that lout.

The corpse's lips trembled. "Yes, I'll talk to you. What do you want to know?"

Paul trembled. He drew back the section of blanket within the clear air's circle, exposing the corpse's head. He leaned close, studying the slack features, the rope-scraped throat. A whisper wiggled out.

"Yes, I can see all of your futures... but mine is getting much more interesting. Wouldn't you rather to hear about that?" The eyelids peeled apart, loosing the small puffs of gauze under them, and wide pupils, pressed hard into emerald-green irises, rolled out of hiding. They stared over Paul's shoulder.

Paul whipped around and gripped the sideboard. The girl's line of sight flowed exactly down the eerie tunnel.

"Here, stop mucking about," Lowell growled. He snorted a foul laugh. "Hasn't she had a hard enough time?"

The wagon rounded another turn, and the tunnel swung with Delilah like a leash. Paul sank down. The girl's mouth was straining against the undertaker's jaw-set, her words slurring, as when a child imitates a ventriloquist.

"Unless these two gentlemen choose to reinter me, I am currently bound for the house of one Mr. Wheaton of Downs Road, where I am intentioned to be sold for dissection at King's College." The pupils glided to settle on Paul. "But that will not come to pass should there be police. They would take Mr. Wheaton away, what with the implicating cadaver he bought an hour past in residence. And how then might my future change?"

As Paul stared, unable to find the courage to cover up the horror lying on the wagon's bed, the clear tunnel began to deflate, but then, rapidly, it spread again.

"Lowell," he croaked.

"Shut your bone box," the man hissed. "I need to mind the road."

Paul kept his face turned from the awful girl to Lowell. The man, occupied in steering toward the occasional dim prick of gaslight and enveloped within the clatter of the wagon and horse, remained oblivious to the faint murmuring. Paul turned his attention to the side of the wagon, toward the vague, filmed pavement. A pedestrian, caught in the sudden cleared air, stopped, bewildered, met Paul's eyes, and then vanished as the event passed.

"You'll have two children, madam," Delilah answered into the tunnel, "one to bury, one to rear. That son will return from France to court a fine woman, and they will later mind you in your dotage." The corpse raised a corner of her lips. "I can't tell you that, but a war will start, and he will, at least, be on the side of right and live beyond."

Paul shoved his palms to his ears and squeezed his eyelids: He was small again, back at home, head under the covers and fearing what lurked under the bed. If he cried out, his father would appear solely to brand him a coward, and after the man had stormed back to bed, Paul could only lie there, shoving himself smaller and more invisible.

Something hard struck his forearm, sprawling him sideways.

"I said look lively. We're almost there."

Paul rubbed his arm and decided that he didn't need the back of Lowell's hand across it again. He peered around. Everything appeared the same in this leveling gray. Indistinct houses drifted by, but through the clear circle he could tell the color of the paint on each door, even read the numbers.

"Will you put me back?" Delilah rattled—to him, Paul realized.

Up ahead, they heard a pea whistle and an order for pedestrians to disperse. Lowell reined in the horses. "Sounds about where we're headed. Not sure if Charles got himself nicked, but not going over to find out. Now, before we decide where to go, we need to be clear: You try to cut a lucky on your own, I'll track you down and kit you a coffin. Got it?"

"Yes," Paul stammered.

"Any peelers come by, use those high manners and fancy talk to send them off, or why did I pull a daft bringing you for a man's work?" Lowell guided the horses down an alley across the street. "Well, now what? Now what?"

"Paul," Delilah whispered, "try to imagine me, a maid stripped of her modesty and handled by two utter strangers, and then, my shame hid only by a filthy blanket, paraded through the streets in a cart—can you? Can you? Lowell will go down for this crime. Time to part company, don't you think? I'll make you a bargain—will you listen? I want to be put back. Follow my instructions, and in exchange you can lay your hands upon the wherewithal to buy your new life—that is what you want, is it not, eh, *mandrake*?"

"I'm not a mandr—that was once! Just once."

"I told you to shut that blabber," Lowell snapped. "I need to think."

Delilah sighed. "Check your hand."

Paul felt an itch on his left palm. The crease arcing from his wrist to between his thumb and index finger was melting together at the terminus.

"Not much time," Delilah urged. "Not much time at all. Like me, scarcely sixteen and felled by Scarlet Fever. Think fast, my Paul, for I know where cash and jewels are to be found. Enough for a clever man to start over. People will be at home, but they are all occupied with visiting in the parlor. They won't catch you. Will you trust me?"

Paul listened. "Lowell, I know a place we can expect help."

"Yeah?"

Paul gave the address, and Lowell guided the wagon toward a better section of town.

"Leave Lowell outside," Delilah whispered. "Park him in back, and afterward, leave by a side window. He would take most the money for himself, and besides, you don't need a lowlife such as he dragging you down. Yours is a different destiny."

Twenty minutes later, Paul told Lowell where to stop. "Thank you," he whispered to Delilah and drew the blanket over her head. He would, as agreed, report the wagon to a bobby after he'd escaped. Delilah would be returned to the cemetery and not, knowing the jittery, callous Lowell, slipped into the Thames or dumped in an alley.

"Wait here," Paul announced as he climbed down. "Let me make sure my friend is at home. He'll be able to sort this out."

The back door was unlocked, as promised. Inside, he heard a strong female voice from the forward end of the house. He slipped up the servants' stairs to the second floor and through the third door on the left. Just enough light seeped through the window sheers to make out the bedroom dresser. In the top drawer, Paul found the small jewelry box, which he shoved into his jacket.

A commotion rose outdoors, a loud one. He crept to the window. Indistinct shadows had surrounded a large, flailing blob next to the wagon, and over the men's shouts, he identified Lowell's angry swearing. One of the bobbies went down, but their barrage of nightsticks finally collapsed the thrashing smear that was his partner.

Fear gripped Paul. What if the police, too, could hear Delilah? He had to run before she betrayed him. As he turned, the door swung away from the wall. Behind it stood a policeman, and from the closet another emerged. A servant, a stout, gray-haired man dressed as if he'd just returned from errands, appeared in the hallway. He addressed the constable.

"I thank you and your companions for listening to me." He sniffed. "You must be Paul. Gentlemen, please allow me the gratification of escorting this creature from the house."

The policemen recovered the box from Paul's pocket, grabbed his arms, and marched him down the stairs. The servant led them toward the front door. Mortified, Paul tried to walk faster, to hurry past the owners and their guests, but the policemen gripped tighter. When they neared the entry, a woman called out.

"Paul, please wait."

Six gentlemen and ladies sat at a circular table in the parlor, their hands spread and touching upon a black tablecloth. A seventh, an Asian woman in satin robes, faced the doorway. Underneath the dark skin of her face and bared arms, scattershot flashes of pink flickered, like the gasping, dark-then-light pulses of embers. Her hazel eyes locked on Paul's.

"Do you recall," the medium intoned, "how a maid, one who had lived a decent life, came to be dragged about unclothed and treated like refuse?"

One of the officers crossed himself. "Lord protect us."

"I see the face of Lowell, your companion, peering through a barred window. At what? For him, nothing outside remains—what little he owned has been confiscated for fines." The lips parted into a rictus grin. "And what of you? Your future? Transported or swung, swung or transported?" She tilted her head. "I can see that, too, but what fun is life without a little mystery, hey?"

The flickering in the medium's skin extinguished, and her eyes ripened to brown. She sagged in the chair, exhausted.

The servant opened the entry door and stood aside. "It is my dearest wish," he declared, "that resurrectionists should unearth you—and all your loathsome ilk—to be sliced into shreds upon tables and thrown onto middens like garbage."

The policemen led Paul down the steps to a waiting Black Maria. He sat on the bench, regarding himself in the dim light: graveyard dirt smeared his hands, his shabby clothes, his shoes. He reeked of death. This was how he appeared to Delilah and to the police and the servant and the occultists, and this would be how, even cleaned up, the judge would see him.

The doors shut.

"Father was right: No one was in the room with me. All along, I was what was under the bed." He kicked Lowell, sprawled on the floor. "We all are."

SNAKE AND SINEW, FLAME AND BONE

Amanda Cecelia Lang

Amid the pebble-bones of a forgotten village, beneath ancient soil consecrated by moonlight and venom, Lilias Proctor, a daughter of the nocturnal garden, awakens to the whisper of a shovel. Her grave has always been shallow, her sisters won't need to dig deep to unearth her. O, praise the Velvet Goddess who walks beyond the veil of men, their time has come! Forked voices uncoil around Lilias in the dirt, her long-serving burial companions, every manner of snake. Agitated by the prospect of her freedom, they glide like oily shadows across her bare skin, cursing and reviling her name. They strike at her as their starless sky is dug away. Firelight appears in the crumbling void above, and the exquisite, ageless hands of her sisters reach downward and deliver Lilias into a flickering summer midnight. Supple grass trembles along her mudded curves, and in the vast open air, she exhales the smoldering remains of her final, long-ago breath.

All around her, loathsome snakes spill from the open grave, eager to escape back into the world, frantic to avoid their judgment. But Lilias is swift now, too. She rakes them up, every last one, capturing fistfuls of toxic twisting muscle. Their beady hell-hot eyes burn at her with boundless contempt. They writhe between her fingers and lash fangs against her impenetrable wrists. Laughing, Lilias stretches her arms wide, rises onto sturdy feet, and basks in the miracles all around.

The yews and sweet chestnuts have grown to giants, their craggy boughs reaching infinitely higher than when she last glimpsed them. And the smoking chimneys and sloping roofs and hearth-lit watchful windows have all fallen to knees of cold rubble. O, praise the Velvet Goddess! The elemental breath of Her garden washes over Lilias, wind and dew, leaf and ember. Somewhere far, far beyond the trees, the electric pulse and shine of the new world greets Lilias's keen and curious senses. But the outside can wait.

She turns toward her sisters.

Miracle of miracles, every last breathing one.

They await her. Beyond a vast garden of unearthed, unmarked graves, countless fresh-risen souls gather in union around a savage bonfire. They stand tall and whole and skyclad, illuminated by firelight and spirited resilience. Strong coltish legs, heaving breasts, and swaying hips. O, praise Her! Lilias can't resist a glimpse of her own maiden form, unscathed skin, lithe and lovely limbs, a glorious spill of raven hair.

Her sisters welcome her forward with purest love and soaring triumph.

She steps inside their circle. They clasp hands around her and call upon the Goddess with potent rhythmic voices. Lilias draws near the bonfire, radiant and righteous. The heavy, knotted snakes thrash in her upraised fists, desperate in their primal fight as if they've scented death before—the destructive heat, the crackle of flesh, the depraved little devils.

Her sisters' voices beat higher, louder, rising around the circle, around the world. Tears and breeze, spark and seed, the fire flares and spits embers toward the crescent moon. Lilias's vision ripples and triples, and in the tremulous space between the flames the Velvet Goddess smiles out at her.

"They are Yours!" Lilias cries in a voice lush of garden and ripe of destiny. She casts the snakes into the fire and with them an epoch of atrocity. Their sleek bellies bloat with deadly sin, and the Goddess's flames erupt in vengeful ecstasy around them. One by one, they blister and char and unhinge their jaws in a spectacle of desperate human screams, voices of women and men and children, begging for mercy they do not deserve.

When the final cry sizzles to silence, the Velvet Goddess licks the ash from Her lips, tips Her tailored hat, and vanishes in a flourish of smoke and resonant laughter.

A tiny fanged adder skull appears in Lilias's mouth. Delicately, she spits it into her palm. The empty eye sockets observe her, hold her accountable for the deeds she will accomplish with this new life.

O, praise Her!

Lilias opens her arms to embrace the coming season. "Raise voice in jubilation, blessed sisters! Through flame and scale and centuries, our hard-won reign is now!"

Earlier...

Lilias waits with spirit brave in the purgatory of her grave. This season of suffering cycles toward its end. The loamy velvet arms of the Goddess cradle Lilias's slowly waking body. Her flesh tingles, her blood pulses anew.

Yet, inside her meaty cavities, the snakes still nest and burrow, still chew away at her hidden injuries. After all this time, their bellies must surely be distended and sore. She prays for the moment when they choke down their final mouthfuls. Even before they entered her corpse and began to feed, even when she walked above the ground, she carried their torments inside herself. A lifetime of unprovoked bruises, of brazen cruelty. Beaten down, laughed upon, spat upon, until she limped through her final days with eyes downcast, gripping a hemorrhaging womb of fear, of shame, of otherness—her very flesh saturated with the venoms of their intolerance and hypocrisy and loathing.

But no longer!

At last, their needle fangs withdraw from her heart and lungs, brain and womanhood. At last, they recede. Slipping through her many hollows, winding in and out of ribs and up the silent channel of her throat.

Her jaw unhinges, her lips part in a miraculous smile. A forked tongue flickers out... followed by a greasy head with slit belligerent eyes.

O, praise the Goddess for making it so!

One after another, they slide from her throat and mouth, falling out of her like the severed rope of nooses. They strike at her jugular, spiteful still, even after tasting of her pain. Yet she does not hate them. She no longer has it in her to hate, though she pities them, for they knew their deeds were hideous and they performed them anyway. But now, below, they have played an integral role in the Goddess's blessed cycle—much as maggots devour decay. Lilias is grateful for them.

In the long dark, they twitch and coil restlessly atop her bare skin, though it is not the same torment as bearing them inside. In the spaces they once filled, her heart and filigree arteries throb, empowered with the victorious rhythms of supple, radiant life.

Often, the snakes attempt to tunnel away, to escape judgment. But Her soil binds, and like Lilias they must await the night when the black sky parts and the Earth as it was falls away.

Earlier...

In the shallow dirt where they left her, she exists in searing inhuman agony. She is blackened-raw sinew on the bone. She cannot move, breathe, pulse. She screams inside herself. The pain is her only living piece. It threatens to consume her even as the burial bugs ignore her.

The ordeal is crueler and slower than she expected. Awaiting the Goddess's promise, Lilias can still hear the echoes of their hatred. Yet *they* are the ones walking the misguided path. They mistrust the Goddess and the vastness of her love. They could be living in harmony. Instead, they posture and spew and insist on the wickedness of those they refuse to understand—willfully blind to the evils they themselves inflict. They poison the air with pompous abuses of stature. They cry out as victims while they grind meek lives into the dirt.

Yet time will remember them with fiery eyes.

Already, the miracles of Her natural law condemn them.

As the seeds of hours grow to sapling years, the Goddess's loam sinks like a cool salve into Lilias's blistered, scream-gaping mouth. Gentle earth soothes her bodily misery and allows her mind to flicker past the gloom, toward her sisters and their lives ahead.

All the natural freedoms of their given world. All the laughing and shouting and celebrating, all the untamed joy and uncaged love they were once forbidden. All the possibilities of home and craft, all their untethered potential crackling inside maiden flesh and hardened bone, bud and spark, cloud and wing.

And, O, to soar on mind and voice, to rise above and have the world hear!

O, to be a newborn daughter of the Goddess's garden!

But first, to endure the final agonies of their waning season.

Lilias clings to faith with charred and shattered fingerbones.

And is rewarded.

One enchanted night, the stillness breaks to the doleful echoes of a village's lament.

Soon after, the first of her persecutors arrives. Compelled by flame, bound by soil. The ophidian fiend finds Lilias in the grave and slithers in through her eye socket. Hissing past the pulpy char of her brain, sliding along the quieted curve of her jawbone, twisting down the bent knobs of spine and into her chest cavity. He latches his fangs to her heart and the meaty, gruesome indignities that discolored her life. Force-fed by his own cursed fate, he gnashes and suckles, slowly taking his brutalities and blasphemies back into himself.

Soon dawns another night, another lament, and another companion arrives. This one enters through her navel and begins a long-choking meal of prejudice and rancor.

Like a flood unleashed, more follow. Each on the tail of woeful indignant sobs from above. The mighty falling and crawling on bellies to serve Lilias in her awakening.

One by one, they slip inside and devour her poverty, her ruin, her needless suffering and disgrace, all the ills inflicted. As their sleek bodies bloat on a lifetime of grotesque injustice, her fractured bones knit with fortitude of stone. Her scorched flesh revivifies, and her blackened organs blossom with virtue of petal and root, fine-veined, divine.

At last, the final snake appears and the scales tip, and Lilias's heart constricts with the first pulse-beat of new life.

O, praise Her!

Earlier...

They race the sunset, eager to be rid of Lilias before Her moonlight rises.

The cinders they made of her bones still glow like brimstone as they drop her into the ground. Serpent trails of black smoke rise from her gaping jawbone and into their lungs as they recite their prayers over her. Poetic words aspiring to grace even as they spill from pits of vehemence. Dirt rains down. They cover her quickly. They tell themselves they cannot abide a witch an hour more. In truth, they tremble to look upon what they have done.

They are right to be afraid.

Earlier...

Though her brick cell remains damp and sunless, the crowing of the rooster alerts Lilias to her blessed final day.

She runs her hands along the wretched floor, coming to rest on the small pile of elemental debris she collected when they weren't dousing her in river water or walking her until her naked feet bled. The skull of the night adder is a lacework of delicate, spiky bone. Her mangled fingers shudder in agony, but she manages to grasp the tiny head. Their thumbscrews and other tortures have not yet done her in, and they are fools if they think she is not exactly where she wants to be on this chilly autumn morn.

Murmuring potent verses only the Goddess can hear, Lilias packs the skull with dirt from her cell floor, blood from her feet, and breath from her rasping crone lungs. Earth, Water, Air.

The Fire they will provide.

They gather as the daylight rises outside the village keep, chanting a righteous mob-song of bloodlust. All this in the battle against a stooped and gaunt old woman.

As the Witchfinder General turns his skeleton key inside her cell door, Lilias slips the adder skull between her lips, concealing it in hollow of teeth and tongue.

Her body sags, too aged and battered to stand upright, so they hook her beneath the arms and parade her through the village as their bedraggled puppet. They do not see the strings of Her providence tied fast around their wrists, tugging them onward. Past the embroiled mob. Past their vain cottage homes, past the parallel roofs of their church and courthouse.

Past the vast garden of unmarked burial mounds where they plant all the unfortunate souls they love to despise.

Lilias prays her fallen sisters rest in the Goddess's loamy embrace. She prays their ordeal will be remedied by today's sacrifice. That they will be delivered, together, avenged and whole, into an epoch of enlightenment, free to live the lifetimes that were stolen.

The gallows tree is the largest of the juvenile yews. The rope sways from a reaching bough, caught in a breath of Her wind. The sight of it imbues Lilias with pounding exhilaration.

It takes two of them to assist her shaky climb onto the high stool they will soon kick sideways. They are absurdly courteous as they hold her balance and tighten their noose around her ancient throat.

The Witchfinder General recounts her crimes while the onlookers hiss and curse. Lilias Proctor, spinster of a despicable life, scourge of men and babies in the womb, has by his very ears confessed to walking the impious path, to partaking of impure unions, to gifting favors of beastly sacrifice and oily entrails to the Devil Herself in exchange for lurid powers and the blight of her neighbors!

And confess she did, though her hands are bloodless.

There is no need for black rites in a village so willing to enact them itself. Let these snakes offer up the atrocities that will doom them.

With no further ceremony, they demand her dying words. They expect her to flail and beg for mercy because it is what they would do.

Past a lifetime of torment, Lilias inhales her final strangled breath. Despite the adder atop her tongue, the Goddess's verse intones from her, charged and echoing:

"Snake and sinew, flame and bone, let the sacrifice be—"

They kick the stool away.

Her fragile neckbones snap.

The skull cracks like an egg between her teeth, flooding her mouth with a yolk of tiny, slithering seeds.

Silence all around. Only the yew branch moans.

Slowly, the rope spins Lilias to face her rapt audience.

With bulging, blood-laced eyes, she blinks at them, blinks again.

Her teeth part and the seeds swell from her undying lips, rising smoke, voice and verse:

"Let the sacrifice be your own... In serpents many, your souls I bind; in death I bid ye my grave to find..."

Their uproar is instantaneous. Women and children gasp and whimper and scutter back, astonished that Her power is true. The men break into a frenzy of tinder gathering. The pyre they build nearly touches Lilias's dangling toes by the time the rope twists her around for a second look at their fevered faces.

They could've lived in harmony.

Instead, they strike the flames.

The kindling erupts with the power of their wrath. Inside their gleeful inferno, Lilias's rags and grizzled hair vanish and her wizened flesh blisters on the bone. The air fills with the stench of burning fat. Her screams feed the blaze, feed their self-righteousness. The ordeal is savage and terrible and harrowing, ash and sinew, cinder and bone, but it does not extinguish her.

It ignites her.

As her eyelids crisp and her vision ripples and triples, she finds grace amid the spectacle of their vile, beady souls. This is only the beginning. The Velvet Goddess glimmers among them, unseen, watchful, fierce.

And it is not Lilias whom She narrows eyes upon.

O, praise Her!

THEY NEVER LEFT

Matthew McKiernan

"**W**ho's ready for winter in Chernobyl?"
My cousin Dmytro shouts from down the road.
It's not even afternoon, and I can tell he's already stoned.
Borysko, who is carrying most of our gear, is struggling to
keep up with us. Maybe it would be a lot easier for him if he
weren't such a fat sack of shit. I shake my head, wondering
why I am stuck with such dickweed companions. I'm Hedeon
Stanislav, and today I arrived in Chernobyl. It's my country's
greatest tragedy, but it's my ticket to passing film class.

Borysko manages to catch up with us. He is panting like
a dog and takes a gulp from his thermal mug. He offers me a
sip, but I wave my hand to decline. Whatever he's drinking,
I know it's not anything healthy. Borysko and I have been
friends since we were in strollers. He always complains about
his weight but never follows any of the dietary advice I have
given him. Every time we make plans to go to the gym or run
together, he always bails out. Still, he's a good friend. We're
attending different colleges, and he's taking time off from his
classes to go on this little adventure.

As for my cousin Dmytro, he's a lot older than me. I don't
think he ever attended school. Instead, he sold drugs until
he ended up in jail. After his release, he showed up at my
dorm since he had nowhere else to go. My roommate had just
dropped out, and Dmytro took his place. He does nothing
but sit around and get high all day. Eventually, I told him it
was time to earn his keep. He's a skinny guy with huge bags

beneath his eyes, and even though he's still a young man, his hair is starting to turn gray.

As for me, I'm not like that at all. I work out whenever I can, always eat right, and never put any poisons in my body. I was on the wrestling team in high school. My goal is to become a stuntman and hopefully do well enough to escape this hellhole of a country. Ukraine is a broken and corrupt mess; it always has been and always will be. I don't give a fuck about it, and I will do whatever it takes to get out. Initially, I was going to make a short action movie for my film class, but because of Covid there was no way I could do that. So now I'm filming a documentary in Chernobyl.

Since we probably won't encounter anyone at our destination, my friends and I have already put away our masks. We're going all the way into the Exclusion Zone. I'm holding a Geiger counter, which shows that the radiation action levels are no worse than they have been for the past few decades. I mean, I wouldn't wanna build a house here but staying a couple of days won't take any meaningful time off our lives. We brought backpacks filled with supplies, including a first aid kit. Our cellphone signals died out hours ago; nevertheless, they are good for taking pictures. Even though I have a camera, I do plan on using my cell phone for some video footage. All of us brought airhorns to scare off any wild animals that get too close, and I have a bottle of pepper spray as a last resort.

We head toward a tollbooth. All the windows are broken, and the inside is filled with dust and snow. As I whip out my camera and begin filming, a fox trots over to us. Its fur is a mixture of brown and red. The radiation here hasn't physically mutated the critter as much as people would think, but it has given them a much shorter life span, although I don't think the animals know the difference. Borysko pulls out a piece of bread, and the fox comes over and takes it from him. After eating the bread, it rolls over, showing its belly and balls.

Borysko laughs. "Oh man! This is so cool!"

He rubs the fox's belly. I can tell the fox isn't rabid, but Dmytro looks unsure, and soon we're both feeding the little guy pieces of ham. When we finished feeding him, the fox gets back up on its feet and scampers away. Borysko brushes some snow off his legs. "Boy, I can't believe that the wildlife here is so friendly."

I sigh. "That's not a wild animal. Not only did that fox come to us for food and take it right from our hands, he wanted us to pet him. That means someone raised that fox since he was a kit."

"Are you saying that there are people living here who are taking care of that fox?" Dmytro asks.

I nod. "I heard when the Soviets evacuated Chernobyl, some people refused to go, even at the point of a gun. They chose to remain here, and they never left."

Dmytro chuckles while shaking his head. "Yeah, and I am pretty sure they are all fucking dead by now."

"Or maybe they all turned into a bunch of cannibalistic mutants?" Borysko shouts.

Dmytro taps Borysko's chest. "You would make a great meal for them, tubby."

Borysko takes a step back and snaps. "Well eating you would kill them, because of all the shit in your veins. You damn junkie!"

"Fuck you, asshole!"

Dmytro and Borysko go at each other like a shark and a whale. I break up the fight before it really starts. "Guys, guys come on, let's just drop all of this and get back to filming."

Dmytro backs away from Borysko and says, "Whatever you say, cousin. Tell big fatso here that I've been off the hard stuff for years. I just smoke weed now."

"Can I have some?" Borysko asks.

"No! No one's smoking anything until it gets too dark to film," I say.

Dmytro looks at me like I just took all his birthday presents away. I film ten more seconds of the tollbooth, and then we make our way down the road. I step on something—a rag doll in a red dress. I pick it up and hold it in front of the camera. It's covered in dirt, and time has eaten its legs away. The black button eyes still remain, and I feel as though they are looking right at me. This must have belonged to some little girl who dropped it when they were evacuating. I wonder if she's still alive. I think about putting the doll in my backpack and taking it with me, but I decide to just leave it against a rock by the side of the road.

We arrive at what looks like the beginning of a small town. It's just four houses and a gas station; there is a blue pickup truck near the pumps. Dmytro hops inside and honks the horn. The noise scares some crows sitting on a telephone line. They fly away and Dmytro keeps honking until Borysko reaches into the car and grabs Dmytro's arm. "Cut that out man."

"Fine, hey your dad's a mechanic, right? Why don't we see if we can fix this car up and get it moving again? You can get your fat ass in the back. Hedeon can ride shotgun with me, then we all just cruise through Chernobyl."

I shake my head at my cousin's stupidity. "That's not a good idea. I don't think you can get any car here to work. Even if you could, the roads here are fucked up beyond belief. We walk."

"What if I find a motorcycle?" Dmytro asks.

"Those things are a death trap," Borysko responds.

The three of us walk away from the gas station and find ourselves surrounded by humongous, crumbling apartment buildings. Their paint has peeled off, along with whatever signs were on them. Oh God, I can't deal with how dead this place is. I don't think any place filled with manmade structures should be as quiet as this. Borysko taps me on the shoulder and points upward. "What's that?"

I look up and see someone standing on top of one the apartments. He is wearing green snow pants, blue gloves, a white facemask, and a red winter coat with a hood on it. I don't know how he got up there because I see that the entrance to that building has been sealed up with what seems like a thousand chains. I guess whoever owned it thought that they would be going back.

My cousin waves at him. "Hey, what's up, dude!"

The figure says nothing nor makes any kind of gesture. Instead, he just walks out of our sight.

My cousin sighs. "Man, what a dick."

Borysko taps his chin. "I wonder how he got up there?"

I feel a tingle at the back of my skull. I shouldn't be surprised that there are other people here. I mean we can't be the only ones who want to tour this place. But this guy, I know, I just know that something isn't right about him. I rush over to the apartment building. As I go around it, I see no other entrance, and the windows are too small for someone to climb through. It doesn't even have a fire escape. That means this guy either climbed to the top or jumped from another building. I don't say anything about this to my companions as we eventually make our way to a hospital.

The hospital doors are shut, and the windows are broken. I glance through them and see that there are gurneys all over the place. Also, the floor of the hospital is covered in glass and syringe needles. "Yeah, we're not going in there. Unless you want your feet to become like hamburger meat."

Dmytro shakes his head. "That's a bummer, dude. So then, what do you want to do now?"

I reply. "The sun is starting to set. Why don't we just do a little more filming and find a place to make camp for the night."

"Instead of doing that, how about we find a house or an apartment to spend the night in?" Dmytro suggests.

"That's pretty ghoulish. Let's just find a place to pitch our tent."

We wander to a small thicket of trees. We set up a tent, make a fire, and put our backpacks in a net that we fashion around a high tree branch. This ensures that no animals will be getting our food or messing up our stuff. We have ramen noodles for dinner and when we are done, Dmytro whips out a lighter and some blunts. "Who's ready to get high?"

Borysko blushes. "I have never done any drugs before. What about you, Hedeon?"

I respond. "I've taken Adderall. It's crazy how much work I was able to get done. It makes me want to clean my room nonstop, even when there's nothing left to clean. I didn't bring any with me though."

Dmytro scoots over next to me. "That stuff is going to string your brain out, cuz. You needed to chill and relax, and this blunt here is the way to do it. It's our ticket to fun town."

Dmytro hands me the blunt and the lighter. I'm about to light it up, but I pause. "This is only marijuana, right? You didn't add anything else to this Dmytro?"

He replies. "Smoke it and find out."

I shake my head and take a drag. I cough like crazy, and Dmytro pats my back to get me through it. Then I take another drag, and this time I don't cough. It feels like I have eaten dirt, and I don't feel any kind of high yet. I hand the lighter over to Borysko, and he takes his turn. Dmytro goes last. Now I'm starting to feel kind of happy, and I don't know why. I live in the most corrupt country in Europe, which is so poor that most buildings still don't even have electricity. Apart from Chernobyl, we got most of our electrical power from Russia, and when the Soviet Union ended, they stopped giving it to us.

They haven't updated our infrastructure since the 90s, long before I was born. My personal life sucks more than my country though. My father was a lecherous drunk who tried to rape a barmaid, and he got thrown in prison, where his cellmate killed him in his sleep. As for my mom, she left when I was a baby. One day in high school, one of my classmates showed me a porn video on his laptop, and I saw that the woman being fucked in it was my mother. I recognized her since I still kept her photo in my room, even though she abandoned me. I broke my classmate's laptop, and then I broke his nose.

It's a miracle I wasn't expelled—maybe because the teachers just didn't care. My parents' actions destroyed my social life. I've lost count of all the girls who rejected me every time I spoke to them and all the guys I got into fights with whenever they spoke to me wrong. None of that matters now because now I'm stoned. The three of us are laughing so loud it's echoing everywhere. I don't know what we're so happy about, but we're happy.

The sky is glowing red and blue. I'm quite sure Dmytro put more than weed in here. Dmytro lies on the ground and starts making a snow angel. Borysko and I do too, and the sky keeps flashing. Suddenly Borysko gets up, and even though it's cold, he takes his coat and all his undershirts off. He bangs his man titties like they were drums. We all take our coats and shirts off and dance around the fire while howling at the sky. The sky keeps changing color, and I find the strength in my legs fading.

Dmytro and Borysko have collapsed onto the ground, and I drag them into the tent along with our shirts and coats. I zip the tent up, and then I lie down on my sleeping bag. Everything goes black. When I wake up, I'm alone in the tent; Dmytro and Borysko are gone along with their clothing. I guess they're out taking a piss or something. I put my coat and shirt back on and step outside. The morning sun shines brightly. Someone tore our backpacks down from the tree and rummaged through them. My camera and our cellphones are scattered around the fireplace, torn to pieces. The camera was in the tent, and the cell phones were in our pockets. How did someone take them out of here without waking us up?

I check out the backpacks. Our map, all our food, and everything else is undisturbed. This wasn't done by animals. They would have wrecked everything and eaten all the food. I examine the rope and net; it doesn't look like anyone used a knife or anything to cut them. They just tore it all apart with their bare hands. I call out. "Borysko, Dmytro! Where are you guys? Someone just trashed our camp!"

I call out their names several more times, but the frigid wind is my only response. I wonder if one or both of them did all this? I mean, I don't think Borysko would do anything, but I can see Dmytro destroying my camera as a prank. However, I don't think he would wreck our cellphones unless he was too high to know what he was doing. It's snowing now, and I spot a set of footprints that I can barely make out. If there were others, the snow must have covered them up.

They look like imprints of Dmytro's boots. I can tell because his boots are way too large for his feet. I check our Geiger counter and see that the radiation is the same as yesterday. I make sure I have my pepper spray, put the map in my coat pocket, and follow the tracks. I would like to think that I'll find Dmytro and Borysko stoned somewhere, but I can't help feeling that's not going to be the case. I just can't stop thinking about that guy on top of the apartment. Was he the one who raided our camp? I have no proof it was him, but I haven't seen anyone else since I got here.

I keep following the footprints, and then suddenly they are gone. There's nothing but untouched snow before me. There is a big barn in the distance and even with the wind blowing, I hear a sound coming from it. I rush to the barn and realize it's Dmytro's screams. "Hedeon! Borysko! Anybody, please help me! It hurts! It hurts so bad! I can't take it; I can't fucking take it!"

I get to the barn and shout. "I'm here, cousin, don't worry!

The barn is made of brown wood with flecks of red paint scattered on it. The door is closed, but I see no lock. Hopefully, it's not locked from the inside; I kick the door open and step into the barn. Dmytro! He's sitting on a wooden chair with dry hay surrounding him. His hands and feet have been nailed to the chair's arms and legs. He's squirming as blood drips from his nailed-down appendages. Someone has poured gasoline all over him, and there's a white blindfold tied around his eyes. They're probably coming back to burn him later. He hears the door opening and cranks his head in my direction. "Hedeon!"

"Don't worry, Dmytro, I'm going to come over and take all those nails out. You're going to be fine, okay?"

I go to him, and my leg bumps into what I realize is a spider web-thin tripwire. When it breaks, Dmytro's lighter descends downward on a thin string into his lap and flips open. Dmytro bursts into flames. He screams and writhes in the chair. The straw by him catches fire and it's spreading everywhere.

"Snow! I'll get snow and I'll put it out. I'll put it all out!" I sprint outside and get as much snow as I can carry!

The fire is covering the entire barn already. I can't get through without burning alive myself. The heat of the flames melts the snow in my hands. I just stand there listening to Dmytro scream. He screams louder and louder, then stops. Now all I hear are the flames eating away at the barn. Dmytro is dead. I killed him. No, it wasn't me; I didn't see the wire. That's why they blindfolded him so he couldn't warn me about it.

I should have seen it! Dmytro, I am sorry. Oh God, there may not be anything left of his body when the fire's done. I can't... I can't. I can't look at this barn anymore. I turn around and walk away. I can still hear it burning behind me. I collapse to my knees and pound my hands against the snow-covered ground. Who, who could have done something like that? Borysko? No, Dmytro may have been a real asshole to him sometimes, but Borysko would never even think of doing anything like this. Besides, he couldn't do something as elaborate as that. It must have been that man on top of the apartment. I mean, it had to have been him as there's no one else around.

Oh Christ, what did he do to Borysko? Is he inside some sort of twisted trap too? If he is, I won't make the same mistake again. I won't! I decide to look at the map. There's really nothing there that tells me where I am. I put it away and just keep going. The snow has already covered my tracks, so I can't find my way back to camp. All I can do is keep going, keep calling out Borysko's name, and hope to God that I hear a response.

I find myself facing a vast green forest with snow-covered trees standing a few feet before me. Do I want to go through it? There's no telling what could be waiting for me there. Besides, I don't know if going in there will take me closer to wherever Borysko is or take me further away from him. Then I see the man in the red coat hunching on one of the trees. Without thinking, I race toward him. He leaps from tree to tree like a lemur. Going after him is not a wise idea, but I'm going to do it anyway.

I shout. "Stop running from me and get down here. I need to speak with you!"

The man ignores me as he hops from one tree branch to another, but one breaks. He falls on his feet and takes off running.

"Wait!" I yell.

There is no way I can catch him if I just run behind him. However, I zig-zag and manage to close the distance between us. I leap at the running man and try to tackle him, but he shuffles backward. I reach out with my right hand tearing his mask off and knocking his hood back. Oh Christ, this guy's a fucking monster! His face is like an ape with a person's big ears, but his skin is a dark pinkish color with patchy wisps of hair. He has large deep brown eyes, and they look angry. Is he a shaven monkey or something? No, that's not it. He's something else.

"What in God's name are you?" I ask.

"I'm a human being! I'm a human being!"

He grabs me by my coat and lifts me from the ground. He's shaking me while he keeps screaming, "I'm human! I'm human! You, you should leave! Leave now!"

He drops me and I land flat on my butt. He runs away even faster this time, and I get up and stand motionless. I weigh almost two hundred pounds, mostly muscle, and he picked me up like I weighed nothing. His voice, every word he said sounded like a growl. There must be a reasonable explanation for what just occurred. I couldn't tell how old he was. Maybe his family stayed in Chernobyl after the disaster, and the radiation mutated their DNA? Or maybe that guy's some kind of evolutionary throwback?

I know I still need to go after him, no matter how dangerous he is. I follow his footprints and soon find myself out of the forest and facing a frozen lake. It's free of snow, so there are no more footprints. It looks rock solid, but I hesitate to step on it. There's a radio tower in the distance, and I see a house beneath it. The house is a two-story log cabin with a black tiled roof and a red brick chimney. Next to the building, there is a green boat and some skates. I take a deep breath and start walking across the ice. It's slippery, and I stumble a few times but manage to keep my balance. Step by step, I inch along as slow as a snail. When I'm about halfway across, the ice beneath my feet starts to crack. Shit! Should I keep going or turn back? I have no idea how strong the ice in front of me is. I know how to swim; however, if the ice breaks and I fall in, I won't be able to climb back out.

I'll drown. I can't die like that! I can't. What do I do? What do I do?

The door to the house opens, and a middle-aged man walks out. He's wearing a gray *ushanka* hat and a brown fur coat that looks like it just came fresh off the beast it was made from. The man is huge and seems to be in great shape. He has a long scruffy red beard with streaks of gray in it. He waves to me. "Comrade, walk where I tell you, and you'll make it here!"

The man has a thick Russian accent. I obey all his instructions and make it to the other side of the lake. He pats my shoulder. "Congratulations, comrade! You would not have liked to take a dip in that lake. I'm about to have dinner. Come inside and join me."

Only now do I realize that I'm starved. Maybe it's from all the running or all the weed I smoked last night. I notice fresh footprints by the front door—whatever answers I am seeking are in that house.

"Sure, I could use a bite to eat, and I really need to get warm. My name is Hedeon; what's yours?"

The man smiles, and there is a twinkle in his eyes as he replies. "You may call me Ivan."

I follow Ivan into his home. The first thing I see is a Soviet Flag draped over an unlit fireplace. I hang my coat on a nail rack and then glance around. There are plenty of Soviet propaganda posters everywhere, but not a single photograph. In front of me, there's a staircase. To my left, there's a living room with a big 80s-looking TV and a leather couch with VHS tapes scattered everywhere. I smell boiling meat cooking in the kitchen, which is to my right. My pepper spray is in my left pants pocket. I'm going to keep it concealed from Ivan, and if he's a threat, I'll use it on him. Ivan goes to tend to the stove while I sit down at the kitchen table. It has two chairs.

"You don't live alone, do you?"

Ivan keeps cooking as he responds. "No, I live with my half-brother Arthur. He told me about your encounter in the woods. It got him really upset, so I gave him a sleeping pill and sent him to bed. He's out like a light and won't be joining us."

I fold my hands against the table and sigh. "Okay, I don't mean to sound rude, but does he have a disease or some kind of mutation or something?"

Ivan stirs one of the pots and then turns to face me. "No, he looks the way he should. I mean, he's a Humanzee after all."

"Humanzee?"

Ivan turns the stove off. "It's simple. If you crossbreed a horse and a donkey, you get a mule. If you crossbreed a lion and tiger, you get a liger. If you crossbreed a human and a chimpanzee, you get a Humanzee."

Fuck no! I shoot up to my feet and slam my hands against the table. I can't believe what I have just heard, but that makes sense. It's the only logical explanation for Arthur's strange appearance, the way he moves, and his strength.

"Please, please tell me that one of your parents didn't fuck a chimp!"

"No, Arthur was conceived through artificial insemination. Like the rest of them were. Although my father's cum was the only one that led to anything."

"What do you mean?"

"Hold on, I'm starving. Let's get dinner started, and we'll continue our discussion. Help me set the table."

I help prepare the table. I notice all the steak knives and forks are dull, while Ivan's are ultra-sharp. I'm overthinking things. He probably wants the best cutlery for himself. Ivan pours some vodka, and I don't know if I should drink any. Maybe I'll just have some small sips. We clink our glasses together, and I get started on the meat. It tastes kind of like pork, but not exactly.

"What kind of meat is this?"

Ivan replies. "It's from a fat hog I slaughtered."

I guess any animal in this place would taste odd, but this meat's great. I can't get enough of it. I clean my plate and take another piece. Ivan scratches his beard. "Tell me, Hedeon, do you believe in God?"

"Yes."

"I do not and neither did Ilia Ivanov. He was a Soviet scientist who was an expert in artificial insemination and used to create all kinds of hybrids. He wanted to prove that evolution was true and strike a death blow at religion. So, in 1926 he asked Stalin for permission to create a Humanzee. Stalin funded his research for ten years, but sadly nothing came of it. So, Stalin exiled him to Kazakhstan."

"Well, it looks like it still happened."

Ivan takes a large sip of his vodka. "Indeed. In 1971 the KGB decided to continue where Ivanov left off. They realized that a Humanzee with the strength, speed, and climbing skills of an ape, but with a man's intelligence, could be the ultimate assassin. So, they artificially inseminated a dozen female chimps with the sperm of the Russian army's best soldiers. They all miscarried, except for the one who received my papa's man milk!"

Ivan slams his glass against the table, making me flinch. "So, your brother was created to kill people. Did he ever do it?"

Ivan sighs and shakes his head. "Arthur has the mental and emotional capacity of a six-year-old, although he was smart enough to name himself after King Arthur. He can really hurt people when he's upset, but he's never been angry enough to kill. I didn't know about him until I joined the KGB. They assigned me to be his handler. They thought he would understand and conduct assassination orders if they came from a family member. I think I was making progress, but then the Soviet Union collapsed. The new government ended up putting us here, and we can't leave."

Ivan has another large shot of vodka and fingers his glass. "At least they built this cabin and send us a helicopter drop of supplies every six months. I won't deny that it gets lonely, and I wish they'd given us cable. But honestly, as long as my brother and I have each other, we don't need anyone else."

I eat a few more pieces of meat and respond. "Did Arthur tell you that my friends and I saw him on top of an apartment yesterday?"

"Yep, and I did what had to be done."

I stop eating. "What do you mean by that?"

Ivan picks up a piece of meat and twirls it in his hands. "I tell Arthur not to be seen. But if people see him, I ask him what they saw him do. You saw him stand on top of an apartment building with no feasible way to get up there. I couldn't have you boys blabbing about that. So, I decided you all had to die. I made sure to have fun killing you. I watched you through my binoculars when you tried to save your cousin. If you hadn't done that, he would have died of hypothermia. I don't know if that would have been better or worse than what ended up happening."

I grab my steak knife and stand up. "What the hell did you do to Borysko?"

Ivan remains seated and replies. "He's right here."

"Do you have him chained in the basement or something?"

Ivan waves the meat in his hands. "Nope, we just had him for dinner. Didn't he taste great?"

I wrench over as the knife slips from my grasp. I can't breathe! Borysko, I ate him! No, no, God, Borysko, I didn't know! I'm a cannibal now. I can't go back; I can't go back.

As I struggle to breathe, Ivan snatches up one of his sharp knives, gets up, and grabs me by the hair. I should let him kill me. I burned my cousin alive and ate my best friend. I don't have a right to live anymore. If I do that, nobody will make Ivan pay for what he's done. Just when the knife is almost touching my throat, I elbow his stomach and free my hair.

Ivan falls to his knees with the wind knocked out of him. I still can't breathe. I need to move. I rush away from Ivan and head for the door. He comes after me and cuts me off. He throws the knife at me. I duck down, and the blade embeds itself in the wall. Ivan roars like a bear, and before I know it, he's chasing me up the stairs. I open the first door I see, hoping it's not Arthur's room. Lucky for me, it's a bathroom. I lock the door and make myself vomit inside the toilet. I don't think I managed to throw up all of Borysko, but at least I can breathe again. An ax breaks through the door, creating a hole through which Ivan sticks his head.

"Here's Ivan!"

I whip out my bottle of pepper spray and shoot it in his eyes. Ivan screams. As he backs away, I unlock the door and go for his ax. We both have our hands wrapped around it. We struggle and end up falling down the stairs. The ax springs from our grasp and slides to the living room, bumping against the couch. Ivan and I stand up. His face is red and puffy. Tears are seeping from his eyes as he yells. "You think you can take me on? I'm KGB!"

Ivan comes at me, and I evade his right hook and land two fists on his face. He stumbles back. His hands go for my throat. I drive a knee into his groin, and we wrestle each other to the ground. He tries to get me in a headlock, and I give him an elbow to the jaw. Ivan spits out two teeth and goes for the ax. I knock him aside and yank it from the floor. His left fist speeds toward my head as I dodge and slice the upper part of Ivan's left arm off. He screams and falls to his knees as blood gushes from the stump where his elbow was.

"That was for Dmytro!"

Ivan starts crawling away while looking at the stairs. "Arthur, wake up! Wake up! This dumbass Ukrainian is going to kill me!"

I cleave off Ivan's right foot, and he screams as blood bursts from his leg like a broken pipe.

"That was for Borysko!"

Tears pour from Ivan's eyes as he writhes on the floor. "Brother, save me, save me please! I don't want to die!"

I raise the ax up and over my right shoulder.

"And this is for God!"

I bring the ax down with all my might and bury it in Ivan's head. Blood sprays everywhere as his brains literally burst from his ruined skull. His body spasms several times and then becomes motionless. Ivan's dead. I killed him. Never once in my entire life did I think I could murder someone. I had to do this to save myself and avenge my friends. But I don't know if this was right.

"Brother!"

Arthur's on top of the stairs dressed in white footie pajamas. He growls and jumps, sailing through the air. I pull the ax out of Ivan and swing it at him. Arthur knocks the ax head off. He rips what's left of the weapon from my hands and breaks it in two. He drops the pieces and strikes me in the chest. I go flying. I slam against the door, and it breaks free from the house. I'm down in the snow coughing up blood. Arthur leaps at me, and I manage to roll over. I stand up, make my left hand into a fist, and try to slam it against his head. He grabs my left arm and breaks it. I scream as bloody pieces of bone are protruding out of my broken arm. Arthur lifts me up by it and throws me across his yard. I hit the ground hard, and the snow scrapes my face.

"Brother, brother! You killed my little brother!"

Arthur walks toward me, and I can't get up. I stretch out my right arm. "Wait, Arthur, listen to me. I know how much you're suffering, but what your brother did wasn't right!"

Arthur stops in his tracks as I continue. "He tricked me into burning my cousin alive and eating my best friend! Then he tried to kill me even though we weren't a threat to either of you! You told me you were human. If that's true, then you know what he did was wrong!"

Arthur just stands still and then goes back into the cabin and comes out carrying the knife that was buried in the wall. He walks up to me and strokes it. "I destroyed your camera and phones. I told Ivan that was enough. But he didn't listen. I'm sorry for what he did to you. Still, I loved him, and you took him from me. But it's okay. I'm going to go where he is now, and we'll never be apart again. Take care of Camelot for me."

Arthur raises the knife to his throat.

"No, Arthur, don't!"

He slashes his neck open. Blood gushes from the gaping wound like a waterfall, and the knife tumbles from his grasp as he falls to the ground. I find enough strength in my legs to go to Arthur and press my right hand against his neck. There's so much blood, so much that there's nothing I can do to stop it. Arthur's he's... he's gone. I take my hand off his neck and close his eyes. I need to tend to my injuries and get out of Chernobyl. I don't want to be here a moment longer. I go into the cabin, sit on the couch, and check myself out: I have at least three broken ribs, and I really need to do something about my left arm, which is dangling at my side.

I take a slow and painful walk up the stairs, where I find a first aid kit in the bathroom. It has liquid stitches and a triangular bandage. I use them to fix my left arm up as best I can and turn the bandage into a sling. I also find some strong pain killers. I look around and find a *Spider-Man* backpack. I fill it with bottles of water and soda from the fridge. I don't bother looking for any food to take with me. I'm not hungry, and I don't know when I will be again. When I exit the cabin, I see the fox from yesterday. He's by Arthur's body, licking his face and nudging him with his paws. The fox whines, and I bend down next to him, patting his head with my good hand.

"So, I guess you're Camelot."

Then I get up and start my long walk out of Chernobyl. I just know if I keep on going south, I'll find my way out. The fox follows me until we hear the call of a vixen, and he scampers away to find her. I continue on even when night falls. Eventually, I find myself on a highway, a bus appears from the darkness, and I wave it down. I realize now that I lost my Covid mask. The doors to the bus open, and a skinny, pink facemask-wearing bus driver looks me over. He says nothing and just hands me a surgical mask. I take it, but don't put it on since I'm the only passenger on the bus.

I take a seat and remove my backpack, placing it beside me. I'm crying. I'm crying harder than I ever have in my entire life. I have no tears for Ivan. As for Arthur, while I feel extremely sorry for him, his existence was a disgrace to science and an insult to God. I'm sobbing for my best friend

Borysko and my cousin Dmytro. They were always so good to me. I should have treated them better. After all, they came with me to Chernobyl. They never left.

FACE TO FACE

Tom Leveen

The exorcist arrived in a custom 1941 Cadillac Fleetwood limousine. He carried his materials on a broad leather belt. Iron chains and hooks clanked and sparked as he walked.

The shadow cast by his broad black hat concealed his face, obscuring his race and age. He walked with a purpose like a younger man, but an older man's beard stretched out of the shadow across his visage as if seeking light. The hairs waved and squirmed in the sunlight.

He strode up the steps of the old Victorian and let himself in without knocking. He had no time for formalities.

No one waited to greet him in the parlor or escort him up the stairs to the bedroom of the possessed. But then, the Catholic priests barreling down the narrow staircase coupled with the inhuman shrieks from above them were all the indication any sensible soul would have needed to locate his destination.

There were three priests all together, each of them older and balding, but they fled with the vigor of a mother snatching a child from traffic. The first two paid him zero attention as they thundered past, stoles trailing like pennants.

The third priest looked at the exorcist, eyes wide.

"Jesus *Christ!*" he cried, though not at the appearance of the exorcist; it was plainly in reaction to whatever he'd seen upstairs.

The front door slammed behind them as they evacuated.

Humming thoughtfully, the exorcist hiked the stairs and stood at the open doorway of the bedroom of the possessed man.

David Matthew White clung upside down from the ceiling, his bare and bloody feet planted flat as if nailed in place, his hair hanging down. His arms stretched wide, completing the obscene, inverted image of Christ crucified. David White, naked now with a pile of shredded plaid pajama rags lying on the bed beneath him, laughed with such broad ferocity that his cheeks had split at the corners.

The exorcist ignored the acidic stink exuding from a brew comprised of every fluid the human body could produce. The fetid mixture coated the walls; it lay in thick puddles on the floor; it stained the white sheets. The thing inside David White had been busy.

Huddled in the far corner, a man and a woman held one another, trembling. When they faced the exorcist, the man let out a little gasp.

The exorcist strode into the room and gazed at the possessed man.

"Well, now," he said. His voice hinted at Dublin.

"*Not... this... time,*" the thing inside David White laughed. It sounded like a demented choir.

The exorcist grunted. Down to business, then.

"Were I you," he said to the couple, whom he presumed to be David's parents, who'd made the call that summoned him, "I'd head downstairs and cozy up till this is finished."

The woman licked her lips. Mothers were always stronger. "He's our son. We're staying."

"Who in God's name—" the father said.

"Suit yourself," the exorcist interrupted. "But you'll need a couple good prescriptions by the time we're done."

The exorcist hiked his robe like an old washerwoman, revealing colorless baggy leggings. With one booted foot, he pulled himself onto the bed and stood face-to-upside-down-face with David White.

The breath coming out of the young man reeked of dung excreted by cancerous cattle.

"*We will never let him go,*" the thing—the *things*—said.

"Save it for the Catholics." The exorcist turned his head over his left shoulder to get the parents in his periphery. "Whatever happens, don't come up here. Don't touch me. Don't touch your boy. Don't do a blessed goddamn thing. Understand?"

They nodded.

The exorcist turned to the possessed.

"Right," he said and opened the heavy ebony box hanging from his belt.

The box folded out to form a tray, upon which a variety of implements and bottles were strapped tight with leather and tacks. He plucked two instruments from his tray and set to work.

The exorcist slammed an iron choke pear into David White's mouth, cutting off a round of poetic, perverted profanity from the demons within. The demons glared through shocked-wide eyelids as the exorcist turned the key of the pear. The four iron leaves expanded, forcing David's mouth open to its further extent. The exorcist adjusted the key by degrees, listening closely for signs of his jaw about to give way entirely.

Satisfied he'd found the young man's physical limit—aided somewhat by the damage his possessors had already wreaked on his mouth—the exorcist chanted spells from the old times, the old ways, the era before man.

David's body convulsed. The demons within tried to curse, hiss, and spit, but the pear of anguish prevented anything more than a garbled choking.

The exorcist spoke over the noise as he gripped a pair of narrow tongs in his left hand. He struck suddenly, jamming the needle-nosed tool into an opening in the pear.

David White screamed. Flecks of larynx blood spattered across the brim of the exorcist's hat. He pulled, forcefully but with care, at the bit of stuff his pliers had gripped.

With a final pull, the thing came free.

A face.

Of what it was made, even the exorcist could not say. The face was mask-like, rubbery, and nearly human in its proportions. The face bellowed like some animal dying in a cave, its features twisting the thin skin—or whatever it might be—into unrecognizable grimaces.

The exorcist hung the writhing face on a sharp hook depending from his leather belt, and went back in with the pliers.

Face after face the exorcist pulled and yanked and tore from within the young man. Each visage was distinctly male and had its own features: one with widely-spaced frog eyes, another with a broader forehead than the last, and so on. The faces groaned and wailed in an incessant song of fury and pain. The exorcist ignored their screams, jamming the hooks through their skin-like membrane to join the others. Desiccated gray faces from previous exorcisms rattled beside them, long dead from exposure. He liked to keep them for a while after they'd served his purpose.

After a dozen such extractions, David White fell from the ceiling. The exorcist drew his cloak across the faces hanging from his belt so the darkness would quiet them like petulant birds. He knelt gracefully and expertly removed the iron pear. He replaced his tools in the box and slid off the bed.

"The boy will be well now. I will return in forty days for my payment. I recommend lots of water and rest. For all three of you."

The exorcist stepped from the room, cinching his robe tightly to muffle the last gasps of the faces. He moved quickly for the staircase, intuiting what was to come and wishing to avoid it.

He was right.

Most people took his work as a necessary evil and were simply relieved to have their loved one back in their right mind. Every so often, though, an outlier overreached. Wanted to know more than they really ought to know.

The exorcist heard the father's footsteps pounding behind him.

"What did you do?" the father said. He grabbed the exorcist's shoulder and yanked hard to spin the man around. *"What did you—!"*

The exorcist's hat fell as he turned, revealing what lay in the shadow beneath. It was apparent the father instantly and deeply regretted his impertinence.

The exorcist had no face. The white hairs most people took for a beard, at closer examination, were not hairs at all, but thin, independent nematodes writhing. Apart from this grotesque detail, the exorcist's head was a smooth, fleshy egg.

Gagging, the father raised a fist to his mouth and stumbled backward.

The exorcist calmly bent and swept his broad hat back upon his head. Once he had it comfortably in place, he spoke.

"As I said. Forty days. Till then."

He swooped soundlessly down the stairs and left the Victorian. Climbing into the Fleetwood, he spared a look at the second floor.

David White stood at his window, his face—his real face—quite pale. The young man lifted a palm in thanks, his expression betraying simultaneous gratitude and terror.

The exorcist tugged the brim of his hat in response, climbed into the limousine, and drove to his next appointment three states away.

He stopped only once, at a remote gas station that looked as though murders had been committed there, probably more than once. The exorcist did not fuel up. The limo didn't exactly run on gas; rather, it ran on something more... unconventional.

The exorcist opened his cloak and removed one of the faces from his belt hooks. It struggled against his touch, as they always did, but the face was no match for his grip. He pulled it taut against the smooth surface of his head. The face stuck instantly. The exorcist used the rearview mirror to tug and tweak at the skin until the face sat just right. A seamless mask.

He moved the new jaw around. Popped the lips. Stuck out the tongue. Flashed the teeth.

Perfect.

Smiling, he pulled back onto the freeway and went on toward the next exorcism, drawn to it by cosmic instinct. Forty days would give him enough time to drive coast-to-coast, hitting exorcisms along the way, then return to the home of David White and his parents to extract and use for his own longevity one year each from their lives. A small price to pay for David White's peace.

Laughing, the exorcist drove west.

THE PROBLEM WITH THE BOTTLING OF TROUBLESOME SPIRITS

Juleigh Howard-Hobson

Blue bottles hanging from a tree won't hold
a ghost forever. Trees will die, branches
will break, blue bottles will fall. I've been told
that after a bottle shatters, what was
inside it is unrecognizable
as a ghost anymore, having been turned
into a cold mass of hate over all
that time stuck in that blue prison, concerned
with one thing and only one: revenge on
whoever hung those bottles. Ghosts can take
as long as they need to find a person,
and they always do, living or dead, makes
no difference. A ghost, once freed from its glass
will ruthlessly avenge its bottled past.

RATHBONE

Zach Ellenberger

Twenty-eight years have passed, and there's not a single day that I soundly rest. I am forever cursed by the consequences of my failure as a soldier to uphold my rightful duty, to protect those to whom I'm sworn. Eternally tormented, history will remember me as the man who failed to save Lincoln.

I was there that night at Ford's Theater with my future wife, Clara, at the invitation of President Lincoln himself. Seated next to the president and his wife, Mary Todd Lincoln, we became first-hand witnesses to the president's assassination by John Wilkes Booth. The vile look on Booth's face perpetually haunts my dreams, thirsting for blood as he brandished the dagger that sliced open my arm after shooting the president in the head; the bloodcurdling scream coming from Mary Lincoln at the sight of her husband slumped on the floor of the theater box. The moment is forever burned into memory, painfully vivid as it repeats each and every day. How could I ever look upon myself again with pride for letting a good man die? To have been welcomed into his company as Clara and I were was such a privilege that I feel as though I've been cursed since that tragic day, to be haunted until the end of my days as a reminder of how I could not save this man's life; a man cherished by so many.

Life was much simpler back then. I was a leader of men in the fight to preserve the American Union, respected and distinguished. Clara's and my relationship was still fresh, a young couple seduced by new and vibrant love. I can only assume that is what endeared President Lincoln to me, who was a romantic at heart. The Confederates had surrendered just days before, bringing the war to an end after four years. There was an air of elation throughout the North, a cause for celebration. It was only to be a quiet evening in good company at the theater and nothing more. That evening saw Lincoln's murder at the hands of Booth in front of hundreds, who also witnessed me failing to save his life.

Now, here I stand only a shell of a man, sent abroad to do away with such undesirables as myself, who bring discomfort to everyone's presence. Since that day, I have felt the strained looks of others upon me at every moment, wielding scrutiny in their eyes like a weapon. My children look upon me with pity. Once utterly in love, Clara and I have since grown estranged from one another. My wife harbors lingering thoughts of other men, of this I'm sure. I cannot stand to let her out of my sight, for I know if given the chance she would certainly leave me. And what would I be then without her by my side? Thus, I bear this shame of a mandated isolation here in Germany serving as a representative of the U.S. Consulate, where I resolve to wither away toward an inexorable fate marked by dishonor. It was Clara's belief that with her sister Louise's help, this move to Germany would be a fresh start for us, that it would be a chance to find worth in myself once more and let go of the past. There's a particular charm to her naive positivity despite its wholesome inaccuracy.

Clara, herself, had also suffered in her own right as a result of that night at Ford's Theater. The white dress she had worn that evening was permanently stained with blood after Booth's attack on the theater box. She suffered repeated nightmares, alleging to have seen the very spirit of Lincoln. The nightmares had gotten so bad that Clara had the closet in our Albany summer home in which the dress hung walled up so as never to look upon it again, hoping its curse would eventually fade away. It was my belief that the dress would have been better suited if it were burned to ash. But, I've since learned the hard way that some things can't be so easily discarded.

A light snowfall graces the evening as the holiday approaches and yet, long are the sleepless nights that plague me. There was once a homely warmth in the thought of the Christmas holiday, long lost to the emptiness that is my becoming. Food is no longer nourishing. The stomach pains that have afflicted me for some time have rendered me inert. The only comforts to remain are the warmth of a fire and the bite of a good whiskey, for nothing else can steady these trembling hands and constant headaches. The apartment creaks and moans under the winter weather, writhing as if to come alive. The crackling fire dims, so I feed it a few more logs and a couple jabs of the poker as I lean against the mantle. On the wall to my right hangs the very portrait of Lincoln himself. In death, I can still see his face looking down on me with the utmost contempt, the same look he held upon his death. I'd imagine someone thought it awfully amusing to hang that portrait here in our apartment. No doubt a slight orchestrated by my colleagues back in D.C. Even here in Germany, I feel as though I am the butt of everyone's jokes. I stare into the flames of the fireplace, hearing softened echoes of the voices that plague my mind nightly. Within the softened echoes, there is a sinister cackle that grows ever more present. I lift my head from the fireplace to the window and am suddenly frightened by the appearance of a silhouette peering in from outside. As quickly as I react, it dashes out of sight, so I hurry to the front door.

Outside, all remains quiet in the early morning. My eyes are now open, looking desperately in every direction for the source of the sound. I can hear it, the laughing and cackling of someone within earshot. In the hue of the streetlights dances a shadow like a half-crazed demon. As it disappears behind one corner, it remerges from another. I already know it to be the ghost of old John Wilkes Booth, back to haunt me. It bounces back and forth from each side of the street, from one direction to the next, until it is nearly in front of me.

"Just leave me be, damn you!" I shout into the night. "Let me die in peace."

I am answered by nothing but the silence of the night. Until I can feel someone whisper into my ear from behind me.

"Where's the fun in that?"

I turn swiftly to see who it is standing behind me, but no one is there. Immediately, the doors slam shut. The cackling continues from inside the house.

"Where have you gone, devil?"

I take my knife and pistol out of the living room table drawer and sneak through the house in search of the intruder. Approaching the kitchen, there appears a head leaning out from behind the doorframe. Only half of it is visible. I can see Booth's apparition smiling sinisterly as its hand creeps around the corner.

"Henry, Henry. I see that the years have not been kind to you. I wonder if you see what I see."

I point my pistol at the door frame.

"Step out from behind that wall, demon, and I will tell you."

"Ah, you are still very much the soldier you used to be, Major. But, lest you forget, you could not stop me from killing Lincoln. What makes you think you can stop me from killing again?"

"Because you're nothing more than a dead man, a damn curse. There is nothing else you can take from me, ghost."

"We shall soon see."

He retreats behind the wall. I storm through the doorway, ready to fire, but he has disappeared. The room is empty. I have once again become victim to my unraveling psyche. In one hand I hold a knife and a gun in the other. I remind myself that he is nothing more than a bad dream, a waking nightmare from my past. He is dead and can do no more harm. As I lower my weapons with a sigh of relief, I hear the heavy thud of footsteps go running up the stairs behind me, accompanied by the cackles I have been hearing all evening. The ghost of Booth may be nothing more than a hallucination of my own invention, but I've no doubt the footsteps I hear are most assuredly real. I give chase to the intruder, skipping several steps at a time up the staircase. Have I become so delusional to truly believe the intruder to be Booth? I know the man to be dead, and yet, I know what I heard. There is surely someone lurking within the house! Is it someone intent on doing harm, or perhaps a secret lover of my wife arriving for a romantic rendezvous?

I see the door of my children's bedroom close as I reach the top of the staircase. The cackles echo from within the room. There is an innate sense of panic warning me that danger abounds. I throw open the door. There is nobody inside besides our three children, Henry Jr, Gerald, and Clara Pauline, fast asleep. In their slumber, there is an angelic presence to them that I notice. My heart swells with emotion as I look down at my beautiful daughter, Clara Pauline, knowing that I have failed her as a parent. I whimper with the knowledge that I could not be a better father to them, stronger, more confident, and more reliable. The truth is hard for me to accept.

"Father?"

I pivot quickly to find my son, Henry Jr., wide awake, sitting up frightened with his hands in the air. In my hysteria, I did not realize that I was pointing the gun at him. It is then that my wife, Clara, appears at the bedroom door.

"Henry? What's going on? Why do you have a gun?"

She sees me pointing the gun at our oldest son.

"Where is he?"

"Who?"

"Don't lie to me, Clara. There is an intruder in this house. I saw someone come into this room. Where is he? Who is he, one of your lovers?"

"Henry, what on earth are you talking about? Have you gone mad? You're my husband; there's not been anyone else."

"Stop that, Clara. Just stop lying to me!"

By now, all the children are awake. Clara Pauline is sobbing loudly, terrified of me.

"Henry, please. I love you. I have never in my life been unfaithful to you. You must believe me."

The children no longer look upon me in pity but in fear. Yet, they have betrayed my trust to the whims of my wife's infidelity. I can see them lying to me, hiding something. I will not let them take me for a fool.

Clara steps into the room and in my way of the children.

"Fetch the groundskeeper!" she shouts at Henry Jr. He runs out of the room as Clara Pauline and Gerald move behind their mother. Suddenly, I find myself pointing the gun at Clara and the children.

"Henry," Clara speaks softly. "Henry, please. You're scaring the children. Just lower the gun, please."

"Poor, Henry," whispers the eerie voice of Booth. *"Don't let her fear stall you from your deed. How can you truly trust her anymore? Are you going to let her weakness keep you from stopping me? You know I'm here in this house, so come find me. Until then, tell me what you see."*

The faces of my wife and children share the same sinister smile as Booth's ghost. It fades in and out on their faces as my wife pleads with me to stop this madness. But, the haunting cackle reminds me just who is responsible for all of this, for all of my pain and torment.

"Henry, please talk to me," Clara pleads.

"Why would you want to hurt your family?" the voice questions.

"I don't want to hurt my family."

"I'm glad to hear that. It's alright, Henry. I'm here for you. We won't hurt you either," Clara speaks softly as she inches closer. I begin to lower the gun, resorting to the broken man I've come to be. Tears pour from my eyes like an unfit child. In this moment, the cackling finally dissipates, and Clara's voice is the only thing to ring true.

"Come, Henry, everything is going to be alright."

Clara holds me close, as do Gerald and Clara Pauline. She leads me back to our bedroom, where she closes the door behind us. I sit on the bed with my head hung low, distraught and unstable. Clara keeps her distance from me, still fearing my unpredictability.

"Henry, please. I want to help you, but I don't know how. Tell me what I can do."

Suddenly, the cackling is louder than ever before. It seems to be coming from the closet at the corner of the room. The tears stop and the panic returns.

"Henry, what is it?"

Standing from the bed, I approach the closet and throw open the door. There before me hangs Clara's bloodied dress from that night at Ford's Theater, the same dress my wife had walled up years before.

"*Tell me what you see, Henry,*" the voice demands as I stumble backward in fear. The terror is paralyzing as the cackle grows deafening within the room.

"What do you see?" I hear Clara cry out at me. With one quick glance at the mirror, I see her reflection, but it is possessed by the insidious spirit of Booth. Her face gnarls with laughter at watching me suffer. In the blink of an eye, I fire the gun at Booth without reacting, all of three times. In my mind, I've done it. I've finally stopped him. But, once reality sets in, I see my wife's body collapsed to the floor, gushing blood from her abdomen, her upper right chest, and the right frontal lobe of her skull; her white nightgown now soaked in blood in the same way as the dress from Ford's Theater.

What in God's name have I just done?

"Dear God, what have I done?"

I kneel at her side, trying helplessly to bring her back. Her body twitches from the gunshot wounds as if trying to cling to the last moments of life. But, I can see in her empty eyes that she is already gone. My sobbing has become uncontrollable. I hear knocking at the door.

"Henry, what was that?" I hear Louise call. "What's happened?"

I'm not capable of answering her.

"Why is the dress here?" I whisper to Clara's body. "Why did you even keep it? I told you to burn it. I told you to throw it in the fire. Why did you keep it? Don't you see it's cursed us? Why would you do that? Why would you curse us? This is what you wanted, wasn't it? All you ever wanted was to destroy what we had. This is your fault!"

In a fit of rage, I slam the dagger into her chest several times. The body has finally ceased twitching after having become a fine, bloody mess. I stand and turn to face the mirror. I see my reflection covered in Clara's blood. Standing directly behind me is Booth with a wide grin from cheek to cheek.

"That, my dear Henry, is worth a standing ovation."

There lies my wife, dead on our bedroom floor. What I've done is unforgivable and irreparable. Louise continues to batter on the bedroom door. Now, the maid has arrived to help. Standing with them are my children, wondering what's going on between their mother and father. I can never look into my children's eyes again. I have destroyed their lives in a way that can never be forgiven. The damage is irreversible.

Clara is gone, taken by my hand.

I am forever nothing.

There is nothing left to do except introduce this dagger to my own heart.

I thrust the dagger forcefully against my chest cavity—again and yet again. The pain is excruciating, and with every stab it becomes harder to draw the blade from my flesh. It takes every ounce of me to continue until, at last, my blood has spilled onto the floor, and I can no longer tell the difference between mine or Clara's. Just as everything begins to go numb and my sight fades, Louise bursts through the door with the maid at her side. The last things I witness before I pass out are the hysterical cries of Louise and the maid, the children standing behind them staring in utter shock at the sight of their parents, and the ghost of John Wilkes Booth behind them, gushing with pride at the damage done.

I close my eyes and wait for death to take me.

Imagine my crushing disappointment in discovering my survival as I awake in a hospital bed days later. God's poetic justice weaves another tragic tale of misery and woe. How could I have been so inept as to botch my own suicide after murdering Clara? The doctors and nurses pass with disdainful and disgusted looks for the man who murdered his wife. They whisper among themselves, pointing their fingers in my direction. Why couldn't they have just left me to die? But, deep down I know that whatever fate comes to me, I more than deserve. I know that I am guilty of taking my children's mother from them, guilty of suffering from a broken mind that can no longer allow me to be among others and will always brand me a threat to society. I am guilty of insanity, and for that I willingly give myself to the powers that be.

Time pays no kindness to an asylum patient such as me as it chips away at whatever remains of my soul. The years I've spent pent up in this hell weigh heavily on me, with each second of the day bearing a physical burden upon my being. Before I know it, it is now 1910. I remain incarcerated in an asylum for the mentally deranged in Hildesheim, Germany. A lifetime has passed since I murdered my wife. My son, Henry Jr., now comes to visit me for the first time since his mother's death. He is a grown man, successful, and admired in his own right. As warm and elated as I feel to see him, I know this will not be a joy-filled reunion accompanied by loving embraces. As I remain shackled within a confined, solitary cage in the center of a circular room, Henry Jr. appears before me. The look on his face says it all: unwelcoming, scornful, and indifferent. I feel as though I am the child and he the parent. The orderly who escorted him into the room steps away to give us privacy.

"Henry, my dear boy, is that you?"

"It is. Hello, Father."

"Well... I just don't know what to say. I'm so overjoyed to see you now. I've prayed for this moment for many years. Look at you; you're a man now. You seem to be well kept and in good health. For that we're grateful."

"We?"

"Your mother and I, of course. Your mother's spirit keeps me company here. I hold her in my prayers, and we speak to each other every day. She's very proud to see the man you've become."

"I see," Henry Jr. answers. He looks back toward the orderly with concern.

"So, tell me about yourself. You must be quite successful."

"I practice law in Chicago."

"A lawyer, that's fantastic. And what of your brother and sister? How are they?"

"They're well. Both married with families of their own."

"Oh, that makes us very happy."

He pauses, unwilling to further engage in any subtle conversation.

"I know how this may seem. I'm not entirely foolish as to believe that your mother is actually here in this room speaking to me. I am still conscious of the horror I've committed and the pain I've brought upon our family. It just... I always loved your mother. I need you to understand that. That is no lie, our relationship had its struggles. I was not a great husband to her or a good father to you and the others. I know it means nothing and that you'll never forgive me, and I don't blame you, but I never intended to hurt you guys or your mother. I just hope that you can at least recall the good times that we had together despite all the bad."

"So, Mother speaks to you then?"

"In a way, she does."

"Does she forgive you for murdering her?"

"Henry, it's not like that."

He scoffs loudly. His composure has waned and given way to anger.

"Now, listen to me and you listen well. I did not travel halfway around the world to make small talk with you. I haven't had any correspondence from you in years, nor have we any desire to speak with you. The only reason I am here to see you is that the letter I received said the business you had with me was of the utmost importance and involved the well-being of our entire family. That and only that is the reason I'm here, to protect what honor this family has left. So, whatever you have to say, I suggest you get to the point and quickly before I decide to cut this visit short."

"You must make for a good lawyer," I remark. "Yes, right to it. Do you remember the summer home in Albany?"

"Yes, it still stands."

"On the night President Lincoln was murdered, your mother wore a beautiful white dress that was heavily stained with my blood after I, myself, was attacked. Your mother was keen to not let go of the dress, following the whole ordeal. It was a stark reminder of that awful night, one no doubt history will remember for a long time; the tragic death of a good man, one who put much stock in your mother and me. One night at the summer home, I found her awake and in a frenzy. She claimed to have been visited by Lincoln's ghost. The next morning, she had the closet in which the dress resided walled up with brick. I tried to convince her to just get rid of the thing, but she wouldn't do it."

"I'm sorry, but I don't understand. Why are you telling me all of this?"

"Because you need to go to the house, tear down the wall, and destroy the dress."

"What? Father, what are you talking about?"

"Ever since that night at Ford's Theater, our family has been cursed. Because she wouldn't rid herself of that awful dress, we've known nothing but struggle, and I fear that curse may pass to you and your brother and sister. Whatever has happened between us in the past, I just want to make sure you guys are safe and remain that way."

"So, you're telling me that this curse caused you to be such a terrible father and husband, that it's the reason you decided to kill your wife in cold blood?"

"No. Please, that's not what I'm saying."

"Why couldn't you have written this in your letter to me? Why did you make me come all the way to Germany just to tell me this?"

"I feared you would not believe me."

"And what makes you think I believe you now that I'm standing here in the flesh?"

"Because now you can at least see what I've become. There's nothing I can do or say that will excuse my actions or who I am, for that matter. I believe myself to be a God-fearing man, and I will gladly serve my penance in the pits of hell where I belong. But, with that, I also believe in the evil that seduces men like me, who are weak of mind. It has made a fine example of our family. If there is any chance that I can save you, Gerald, and Clara Pauline from the same evil that has consumed me, I'll not waste a moment in taking it. So please, burn the dress. That's all that I ask."

For the first time, he weighs my words with careful consideration. That is when he asks me.

"What about Booth? Do you still have visions of him?"

"There's no need to concern yourself with my struggles. You are the eldest; the family is your responsibility now. That should be your only concern. Now, best be on your way. You have a long journey home."

The orderly approaches to escort him out. No goodbye is necessary. There's so much more I want to say, but it's all too little and too late. He gifts me with his last words of encouragement.

"This will likely be the last time I ever see you, Father. I'm certain there will be a special place in hell reserved for you."

Henry Jr. accompanies the orderly out of the room, but not without flashing one more disappointed look.

The next day, I'm taken to a room for psychological testing. Instead of being strapped into the usual torture machines, the space is empty save for a table and two chairs. The orderly places me at one end of the table, then leaves, and a man in a white lab coat I've never met before steps in. He is a young and enthusiastic fellow.

"Mr. Rathbone, allow me to introduce myself. I am Hermann Rorschach; I am a medical student studying psychiatry at the University of Zurich."

"Hello, doctor."

"Oh, I am not yet a doctor, though hopefully soon. Please call me Hermann. Good morning to you, Major. May I call you Major?"

"I haven't been called that in many years," I answer, surprised. "But that's alright with me."

"Splendid. The reason that I am here today is because I specialize in a specific area of psychiatry we call psychoanalysis. In this field, we have been experimenting with new and innovative ways of helping to diagnose certain mental diseases in patients such as yourself. Being made aware of your condition, I believe you to qualify for these types of experiments, namely one. We call it an inkblot test. This test has taught us that different individuals, when looking at the same exact image, can have completely different perceptions or interpretations of what they are witnessing. It has proven to be a useful tool in developing new techniques and applications."

"Well, whatever you think might help me. I'm willing to give it a try."

"Beg your pardon, Major, I was not completely clear. This test will not help you. If I am being truly honest, I am afraid there is no helping you. But, administering this test can help *us* with future patients to more accurately diagnose any conditions that may infect the brain. It does allow you the opportunity to make a contribution to the scientific advancement of new psychiatric techniques. In a way, you will be saving many other people who would potentially suffer the same as you. If anything else, it could offer you a chance to find personal redemption and improve your reputation."

"I see. Well, I don't see much point in refusing."

"That's the spirit. Now, let's get started."

Hermann holds up a white canvas in front of me. On the canvas, there is a blot of black ink resembling a crooked, sinister-looking smile. As I gaze at the figure on the canvas, I begin to hear a faint cackling that sounds terrifyingly familiar.

"Tell me, Major," Hermann asks. "What do you see?

THE OCEAN'S MISFORTUNE

Alison McBain

When Father came back from the ocean that day, he said nothing as he took off his *sashiko no donza* and handed the heavy coat to Mother. He simply looked at each of us, his grown daughters, with blank eyes. There was an odor coming off him that was not the normal stink of fish from his long hours on the waves, but colder and wilder, like the sea during a thunderstorm—one part salt and one part electricity. The fetor was hard and unnatural, and it wrinkled my nose like ammonia. I could barely breathe standing right next to him.

He met my eyes, and I couldn't look away from his black gaze. The stench filled my nostrils, and I knew that if I couldn't tear myself away, his eyes would consume me in a flash, like fire on paper. I struggled against it, trying to move or speak, but it was impossible.

When he turned his back on me and took Mother into his arms, I nearly fell. My head throbbed in reaction, an agony as sharp as the moment after a blade slices flesh, when the edges of the wound are still white. Release from Father's gaze was the red welling up in the wound when pain follows the cut in a sudden slap.

Father led Mother into their bedroom and closed the door, still without a word to anyone. It was an unusual action for the middle of the day, but one didn't speak of such things—and after my earlier reaction to him, I was deeply afraid. I was too frightened to stop him, to gain his attention, to fall under that black and horrible gaze.

For the rest of the day, my sisters and I did our daily chores. The closed bedroom door was a backdrop to the tick of time. I cooked a simple supper of rice, cabbage and fish. The food grew cold as we waited for Mother and Father to emerge from the bedroom, but there was nothing, no response to my knock on their door. We ate, cleaned the house, and my sisters went to sleep.

I unrolled my sleeping mat and lay down next to them, although I couldn't close my eyes for a long time. When I did so, all I saw was my father's black, staring gaze that seemed to suck the oxygen from my blood. Eventually though, the quietness lulled me and I drifted off. I was swimming underwater through the ocean with long, clean strokes of my arms, marveling at the serene coolness. Fish tickled my feet, and I dove deep. On the ocean floor were treasures: pearls and rubies and sapphires. I scooped them into my pockets and swam upwards. There was a boat waiting for me.

But, somehow, I couldn't find the surface—everywhere I looked had turned black, with no light shining from above to guide me. I was just beginning to feel the claws of airlessness sink into my chest and the pounding of my heart turn to panic when I woke in my own bed, gasping.

The bedroom was dark, and my heartbeat slowed. Next to me were the sleeping mats of my sisters, and I could hear the deep, peaceful sound of their breathing. Their dreams were untroubled, and it somehow reassured me.

I pulled my robe around me and crept into the kitchen on bare feet, leaving my slippers behind so as not to wake my younger sisters. It was even too early for Mother to be awake yet, and the kitchen was dim. I moved up to the window and peeked through the curtain. The rain had passed sometime in the night, and I could just see the sky filling with streamers of pale light, so early in the day that the sun's advancing rays were still colorless against the fading shadows.

My eyes might have passed right by it, but I registered something wrong, and my attention turned back to the cherry tree planted by Father when he was just a boy. An unmoving shadow rested on the ground against the gnarled trunk of the tree. From this distance and in the fitful new light of morning, I couldn't make out the person's features, but the form was too familiar for me to mistake it for anyone but him. It was Father.

Outside, the grass was wet and cold against my bare feet as I ran, a remnant of yesterday's rains. The chill crept up from my feet and into my calves and spine. Like yesterday, I registered that something was wrong—completely and horribly wrong. Although Father was leaning against the cherry tree with pink blossoms drifting gently down and covering him in a blanket of petals, the petals were still once they landed. They did not flutter away from his nose or mouth.

That is when I saw his stomach—red as the cherry fruit, red like a second sunrise across his belly. In the gaping wound was the knife he used to gut fish, his hand clasped around the plastic handle.

My screams brought the household running. After that, I remember Mother lying over Father's body, her face wet and shining, her hands scarlet with his blood. My sisters formed a chorus behind her, the echoes of their crying like the shriek of seagulls on the distant beach. Through it all, I stood in the midst of the tumult. I was a stone, my nose filled with that wrong smell of salt and power that still clung to the corpse of my father. Even his blood seemed strange, the tint of it shifting toward blue as if seen underwater.

Time passed, and the neighbors came. They took my mother away and my younger sisters. When they would have moved me, I said, "Wait." I bent down to the damp grass and ran my hand across it until my palm was wet. Then I performed *matsugo-no-mizu*, water of the last moment. Father's lips against my hand were cold as the ocean in winter, and I shivered. After that, I followed the neighbors of my own will. But I saw in their eyes and faces a reflection of what was wrong. They could sense it, as I could. But none of us said anything.

We began the necessary preparations. Mother closed the house shrine and covered it in white paper to keep out the impure spirits. Father was laid out on the bed and we burned incense. My sisters and I gathered flowers.

Still, in the midst of everything to be done, my eyes were continually drawn to the windows. In the background beneath the bustle of frantic activity was a rumbling sound, uneven and threatening. If the sky hadn't been cloudless, I would have thought thunder, a storm coming. As it was, I had no explanation.

I couldn't ask Mother. She was shrunken in on herself since that morning. I noticed for the first time the lines around her eyes, her mouth, the white in her hair. In the space of a few hours, she had become an old woman.

It took several tries to find an auspicious time for Father's wake since all the signs kept on returning as bad luck. It was postponed until tomorrow, the funeral to follow the day after.

The next day, after the wake, the sky grew overcast. Mother remained to keep vigil for the night and invited me to join her. But looking into her eyes, I noticed something that stopped me. They had become blank like Father's eyes had been. When she moved, a foulness drifted in her wake, which made me gag.

On the walk back home with my family, all of us spent with sorrow, my neck began to itch. I stopped several times to look back down the path, seeing nothing. Just the village receding in the distance. I hesitated as my family trudged past me, not noticing I had stopped again. One last time, I turned around and faced the ocean.

This time, it was not nothing.

The sea had erupted with dark drops of water, rain falling upwards. Each drop bloomed into a shape, and each shape was a horror. My eyes flickered over strange creatures twisting through the air—black shadow-birds flying with five wings, fish flapping above the ocean like carrion crows.

The wind sang past me, blowing back my hair with a breath as foul as Father's stink. It carried a voice, and the voice whispered into my ear, *Bake-Kujira ni ki wo tsukero.*

At the sibilant sound, I was struck by a lance of cold through my chest so painful that my limbs dissolved. The world reduced to fragments of color and uncolor as it spun and collapsed. I heard shouting in the distance but had no power to keep my eyes open.

I woke when the sun gleamed a baleful orange through the window. My body was wet, and cold arced up my spine. As my fever spiked and the tremors worsened, Mother mopped my sweaty brow with a damp rag.

"Mother." At my croak, she moved closer. "Father's vigil is over?"

She nodded. "He has been cremated."

Haltingly, I asked her about the words carried by the wind. "What is *Bake-Kujira*? Why should I beware of it?"

Her lips tightened. "Your father must have seen *Bake-Kujira* from his fishing boat and taken his own life to prevent this disaster," Mother said. "But too late—he was marked. He should never have returned home to say goodbye to us."

To me, her tone implied. As always, Father had returned to her. And now he was dead and cremated, and behind him was the ruin caused by his decision.

"Mother," I croaked. "*What* is *Bake-Kujira*?"

She placed the cool cloth on my head, but the action seemed reflexive. Already, her eyes were drowning with blackness, and the stink of her skin filled my nostrils. I knew it would not be long. She was already corrupted.

But she gave me an answer, regardless. "The ocean's misfortune."

I was suddenly overcome by coughing and couldn't answer. After the fit passed, I noticed an absence. "Where are they?"

"Who?" Mother leaned over me, her black gaze holding me down.

I tried to say the names of my younger sisters. Mariko, to be married in three months. Sakura, bitter that Mariko was marrying Daiki but resilient enough to flirt with Hiro, our neighbor's son. But my lips were too dry, and I couldn't form the syllables with my tongue.

Overwhelmed, I closed my eyes. The blackness of Mother's gaze became the blackness of rest, of sleep. I sank into the lack of color, feeling it fold around me like a soft blanket. I was no longer afraid of death. It would be a welcome visitor, a bringer of peace from this pain.

But floating behind my lids, waiting for me, were vivid images. They sucked me down into a darkness that had grown cold and sharp. A swarm of ivory bones swam through the black waters of stormy seas and resolved into a creature made of borrowed relics—giant ribs from deep-sea animals, femurs of the unfortunate drowned, the vertebrae of a million eels and fish. The creature passed by me so closely that I spread out my fingers and reached to touch its gleaming, ivory sides in dreamlike curiosity. This couldn't be real; I couldn't be fathoms underwater, watching a bone-whale swim by me like a giant and malignant messenger of the grave.

My outstretched hand was grasped in an unbreakable grip. Opening my mouth to scream, I found that my tongue was stoppered with the ocean's filth, and I choked instead. I remembered my dream that had woken me the morning that Father died, the dream of blackness and breathlessness, the feeling of drowning. That dream had become real, and the reality was the realm of nightmare. The only thing that brought me back to the present was the pain in my arm as I was pulled sharply upwards.

The pressure eased and stopped, and I found my feet suddenly flat and stable, my arm my own again. I'd reached the top of the creature, and all around me was a crowd of people with twisted faces, hissing with avaricious glee. I shrank back from their drawn-back lips and bared teeth. Eyes gleamed from ivory sockets, and bits of nacreous flesh drifted gently from their bodies. A shudder ripped through me. They were *kyonshī*, the reanimated bodies of the dead.

The wave of lifeless flotsam from their corpses floated past me, and I could see in my mind's eye as it was carried by the ocean currents to the four corners of the earth. This blighted cargo would spawn evil wherever it washed ashore, leaving behind a growing trail of despair. It would destroy villages like my own, bringing deadly disease wherever it spread.

Click, click, I heard next to me. I turned to look before I was ready to see what waited for me.

Grinning, the skeleton king bowed low in greeting. His teeth were a percussive counterpoint to each word he spoke. *Welcome home*, he said.

I recalled the hard grip on my hand, and I glanced down at his fingers. If he had been a man with skin, he would have been tall, much taller than I was. And so his finger bones were long and thick, reflective of his size.

The king moved toward me. A black unlight winked from his eye sockets, a glowing darkness that was the birthplace of Father's dead, cold eyes. The king's bones were bleached by the ocean to a soft white. I watched him approach like a seal watches the oncoming rush of an orca.

I tried to jump away but could not lift my feet. I glanced down and saw that the bottoms had melted into *Bake-Kujira's* skin. I put my hands over my mouth but couldn't feel my fingers touching my own skin through the cold caress of ocean water. Each part of my body tingled and began to go numb, so it felt as if I had flippers instead of fingers, that my appendages belonged to someone else.

I crouched down and scrabbled at my feet, but the whale skin was impenetrable. If only I had a knife or other sharp object to tear through it. I didn't care at that point if I had to saw off my own feet at the ankles.

I stood up and searched the crowd. The farther back I looked, the more flesh had eroded from the corpses until all that was left were the stark sticks of bones jutting out from the *Bake-Kujira's* skin like people-shaped thorns.

My eyes passed over him once, then paused and went back. Was that, there ... no, it couldn't be. It looked like Father!

I started to lift my hand to do something—perhaps reach out to him, perhaps ask for something to free myself—when I remembered how he had left our family. It couldn't be him. He was dead and cremated. There would be no flesh to cover his corpse. Not unless my mother had been lying to me.

I remembered her black, black eyes, drawing me down into darkness. I remembered the smell that clung to her, and thought about how I had collapsed after Father's wake and never seen the cremation of his body.

Father faced me, and the crowd of *kyonshī* hissed and pulled back to create a path between us, their stiff arms held out like crosses. He seemed different from them, although the skin was beginning to flake from his cheeks. His eyes were lucid, although the darkest black I had ever seen.

"Help me," I pleaded.

He nodded at me. But it was not an agreement or even an acknowledgment—it was a direction. I glanced down.

The fingers of my hands were chalk-white, the skin so transparent that I could see the bones underneath. Around the nails, the skin had started to crumple and peel. As I watched, a piece twisted itself loose and was carried up, up, up by the ocean currents and out of sight.

"No..." I whispered, horrified.

Click, click, I heard beside me. The skeleton king laughed, a crazed bark of sound that echoed strangely underwater. *Welcome home*, he repeated and lifted his hands above his head, revealing the two figures behind him.

On either side of the king was a woman. And each figure was familiar to me. My two beautiful sisters. But their skin was pale and drifting, their eyes the black of the deepest sea. When I choked on a sob, they did nothing, not even blink. All they did was stare at me with their black eyes, and I knew in that moment a drip of pain so severe and profound that it was like I was stabbed from the inside out with shards of ice.

Father's jaw gaped. His face distorted as the bones of his jaw unhinged and his mouth opened wider and wider and wider. At the same time, he drifted closer to me until all I could see was the yellowed ivory of his molars and the red flesh of his uvula as tall as a mountain, as tall as the sky. Either I had shrunk or he had grown to encompass the entire world.

I flung my useless flipper hands over my head. The skeleton king's mad laughter did not drown out the sound of my screams.

THE JUMP

Pauline Yates

The dead know it as The Jump—a thirty-meter cliff in the heart of a remote forest. It's not marked on any map. No trail leads to the edge. It is found by following the scent of grief, guilt, loss, and loneliness. I follow the scent, too. Not to jump. I catch Jumpers before they leap to give them a reason to live. If they survive me, they'll never jump again.

Your name is Jenny. I caught you just before you stepped off the cliff. Most Jumpers startle when grabbed by a masked stranger in a place only ghosts frequent, but not you. You sag in my arms, making me wonder if I'm too late, and you're already dead.

You smell of loss. I've caught enough Jumpers to know. But though I taunt and tease, the cause of your suffering eludes me. The usual suspects: death of a family member, breaking up with a partner, losing a close friend, draw no reaction. You're a closed book. My toughest catch yet.

You're gagged and bound to a chair while I sift through your digital footprint. I leave the tools of my trade in full view while I work—a meat cleaver, a dental cheek retractor, and pair of orthodontic pliers. I like the dental tools because their insidious connotations are usually enough to incite the fight in a stubborn Jumper. Not you. When I laid my tools on the bench, you didn't blink, didn't cringe. Maybe I'll have to use the cheek retractor. Your gasp when the retractor forces your mouth open, your whimper when the soft skin in the corners of your lips starts to tear would be better than no sound at all.

You have as much as anyone in the way of digital records. Social media accounts, email, phone, medical records. A gym membership, a student loan, driver's license, bank accounts. You still live with your parents and have a younger sister, Poppy. She recently celebrated her twelfth birthday.

Photos show a loving family, a devoted sister, a broad circle of friends. I print out their pictures and dangle them in front of your face. I whisper how I can get to anyone, anywhere, and do worse to them than what I've planned for you. You don't flinch. You look at something beyond my sight. Wherever you are, it's not here.

Frustrated by my lack of insight into your loss, I pull medical records, wondering if you terminated a pregnancy. You wouldn't be the first. Finding nothing, I download phone messages and scour through hundreds of recent conversations. I write the names of your friends on a whiteboard and draw red lines to show how everyone connects. One name stands out. Miranda. She doesn't connect with anyone.

Miranda has no last name, no photo, just a week old *"can't wait to meet you again"* text message taken from your phone. I pick up the meat cleaver and whisper, "Miranda, Miranda," while running the blade across your knees. You tense. Your breathing grows heavier behind the gag.

Returning to my computer, I run a search for Miranda. There's nothing. She's a ghost, an enigma, a figment of your imagination. I grab your shoulders and scream Miranda's name in your ear, demand to know who she is, but you slip behind your vacant expression and hide the information I need.

I rip off your gag and jam the cheek retractors into your mouth. Pry open your jaws to force you to spill your secret. You gasp, but though your mouth stretches and your lips tear, you still refuse to speak. I grab the pliers, touch the metal tips to your teeth. Behind me, the computer beeps.

I leave you to the mercy of the retractors and hurry to the computer. Displayed on the screen are the results from a search through your parents' records. Unconscionable. You're one of a twin; Miranda, your sister, the other.

Separated at birth. No knowledge of each other's existence until a chance meeting a week ago. Further searching about Miranda reveals photos that are identical to you. Your clothes, your hairstyle, your fashion choices, all the same. But how cruel is fate?

Miranda is dead.

A hit and run while jogging in the early hours of the morning. No suspects. No witnesses. She died on the side of the road, alone.

Ignoring your ragged breathing caused by the pressure of the retractors, I flick back through your photos. Now I see your torment. Your smile masks the loss you've always suffered. A soul's sadness shows in your eyes, grief from knowing it is one half of a whole. How crushing that your soul found its other half, only to lose it again? No wonder you want to die.

I load up a picture of Miranda and turn the screen so you can see her. Then I sidle back to your side and remove the retractors. Your eyes lock onto the screen, but you stiffen when I whisper in your ear; I tell you how fast I drove on the morning Miranda died; describe the dent in my car's front fender from the impact of hitting her body; how I sped off, knowing no one saw my license plate. And how the dead can't talk, no matter how wide I pry open their mouths.

Tears pour down your cheeks. You scream obscenities. You spit, you choke on your hatred for me. You struggle against your binds, promising to kill me for what I did. I shove the gag into your mouth to shut you up and swear to reunite you with your twin. Then I throw a hood over your head, carry you to my car, and toss you into the trunk with a shovel.

I release you on the side of a road near a one-pump gas station. I leave your hood on and hands tied, but it won't take you long to break free. You're a survivor now, not a Jumper. Searching for me will keep you anchored to life, even though everything I said was a lie. You won't find me. No Jumper I've ever saved has. I'm a survivor, too.

GOOD BOY ANYWAY

Briana Una McGuckin

I did the digging for Anne's grave myself, the day after she died. I did it the right way: just her coffin, six feet deep. It was honest work and—if she could, wherever she was—I wanted her to see me do it, to look down on me and think me good. But, however well I kept my extra jobs from Anne during her illness, a man can have no secrets from a bride gone up to Heaven. The very next night, I found myself staring at an inky rectangle of sky, from the pit I'd dug twenty feet down in quite another cemetery, thinking: *now she knows what I really do.*

This cemetery was full, as many in London were. Yet people went on dying, and the church couldn't afford not to bury them. I was hired to make room.

I climbed out of a steep ditch and dug up the row of graves behind it. With my shovel, I unearthed one, two, three coffins; all of their inhabitants were so long dead that there was no one left alive to miss them.

With straps and a winch, I raised the coffins from each grave and lowered them again into the deep pit, stacking one on top of the other. I did this by myself, under cover of darkness, so no earthly soul could see me. But Anne's soul was in Heaven now. Surely, she was watching as I worked— judging me. For all the graves I emptied that night would be made ready for the newly dead, whose family would pay the church for the plots. The church, of course, paid me.

Down in my fourth hole of the night was a coffin that had been trapped under the soil for an age. I could tell by the smell, so putrid and indecent that the very wood of the pine box bulged to get away from it, that there was almost nothing left of the poor soul inside. The body had decomposed into something like the breath of Death himself. No point even in reburying this one.

I struck the coffin with my shovel. The rotten lid gave at once, and the noxious smell overtook me: Miasma. The poison rooted in the stench made a gravedigger's back ache, they said, but then so did digging graves all day. Miasma could apparently kill a man, choke him on bad air in close quarters. Some died in an instant, the stories went. But I didn't put much stock in stories. The smell was awful, true enough, but it had never done me any worse than bringing me to tears. Coughing and gagging, I wiped my eyes and struck again, again, again—until the coffin was in pieces.

I hugged the soft wood to my chest with one arm, climbed out of the hole, and set the pile aside in the grass, with the headstones from all the dug-up graves. I went back to digging, and, when there were enough coffins, I used the straps and winch again to stack one atop the other into the deep ditch I'd made. I filled the pit, then topped it with the headstone for the fellow who was near the surface.

By midnight the ground was level as if I'd never been there, but still I wasn't done. Arms aching, I loaded the rest of the headstones, then the rotten wood, into a wheelbarrow. I weaved my way to the front of the cemetery, round by the church where a light still burned in a window. On the street, the barrow rolled easier, and I moved a few buildings down, stopping outside a public house. Business had been slow when I had first started, but by now people knew what I was selling and where to find me. A man waiting in an alley approached at once.

"Any kindlin' tonigh'?" he asked me. He had a limp, and a lot of his teeth were missing. I didn't judge him. Doctors are expensive.

He paid me his penny and I gave him an armload as more folks edged out of the dark toward me. My whole stock was gone in minutes. The poor didn't mind about the smell or where the wood came from. They couldn't afford to.

But as pavers couldn't keep one warm or cook a dinner, those took longer. I waited an hour before the village builder came, easy as you please, the sky lightening with dawn.

"Can't use any what are obvious," he said, just the same as every morning.

"They're too worn to read," was my line, and it was true.

He inspected the stone at the top of the barrow a long moment, though its blankness was plain to see, and paid me.

I wheeled the empty barrow back toward the church, morning light trying feebly to shine through all the smoke of the city. The figure of the priest grew sharp as I reached the cemetery gates. He held out his hand, and I dropped the money I'd made into his palm without slowing. All I had left was to return the barrow to the shed and collect my cut. That— taking the priest's money—was the hardest work I did of a night. Afterward, my feet dragged on the steps of the boarding house where I lived, my head heavy as I bent to unlock the key to my rooms.

Anne won't be in here anymore, I thought. Then: *Anne is everywhere.*

And she knows me better now.

I grimaced and swung the door in.

At once, Toby put his front paws up and danced backward until I got down on my knees and let him embrace me. "All righ'," I said, turning my face from his tongue. "Good boy, all righ', hello."

We'd gotten Toby because of the strange hours I worked digging graves, which left Anne alone each evening. All of London seemed to mean her harm, she'd told me, stirring fretfully over a stewpot not long after we'd moved in. She said it was as if, once the lamplighters had all come and gone, all the smoke and soot of the city turned sinister, and any man around to breathe it might go mad. She'd said a dog would make her feel safer.

I hadn't known she was sick, then.

But he hadn't been a bad idea, Toby. Knowing he was at home with her eased my mind a bit. I'd come home late and find them both drifted off, his heavy head on her knee, her hands in his fur. Maybe that's why I never expected I'd bury her, even as I buried near everybody else in London. There were no madmen or murderers on Toby's watch. But a year after we got Toby, Anne died another way. One hand in mine, the other on Toby's head.

I sighed as I rose, patting Toby's head but looking around for Anne. I could feel her in the apartment still as if she might walk out from the bedroom. I minced about making myself dinner, guilty as an adulterer, but by and by I had to admit to myself that she didn't seem angry after all. The warmth of the cooking hearth was like her hand. And when I'd finished eating and seen to Toby, the corona of my candle was like her kind eye, watching me safely off to bed. On the mattress in the dark, with Toby curled up in the space behind my knees, his gentle breathing might have been hers.

But I woke the next day with the septic stench of miasma in my nose. Toby whined, and when I lifted my head to look at him, the bedroom rippled like water disturbed by a stone.

I opened my mouth to belch, thinking in my sleepy state that this would get the gas out of my nose. Too late. I felt my stomach churning, and I vomited into my lap.

Toby licked his gums.

"Not so well this morning, hey," I told him, shivering. I groped at my chest to feel my heart pounding against my ribs like a horse across cobbles. I took a deep breath to steady me and gagged at the sour reek of sick. I dragged myself to the kitchen, boiled water, and cleaned the vomit off my bedsheet. I tucked it tight around me, damp as it was, and lay down again.

Toby's whining woke me from a stale sleep. It was dark, and I thought maybe Anne had shut the curtains because sometimes the light hurt her eyes. But Anne was dead now, I remembered. The curtains were open. It was night already.

There was a heaviness to my chest that made it hard to breathe.

Toby whined again.

"Hungry, boy?" I wheezed and dragged my feet around to the edge of the bed. I couldn't lift them properly. I shuffled to the kitchen with a lit candle and found the last raw bits of beef to put in Toby's dish.

He was giving me his biggest eyes. "What?" I said, then sniffed.

He'd relieved himself inside, somewhere.

"It's all right," I said and patted him. "Good boy anyway."

He lowered his head, began to eat.

"Anne loved you more in the end." I rubbed his velvet ear between my finger and thumb. "You deserved her love more 'n me."

And as my words died, there was another sound—a ringing, getting louder. Everything in the room shuddered again, this time more violently, so it seemed to me that the pot over the hearth swung back and forth as the whole apartment tossed like a ship. The ringing wound into my ear, piercing it as real as a knife would do, and then: then there was Anne.

She was like a shadow come right off the wall, gray as smoke, stretched long by my candle so she towered over me. "How could you?" she asked me, and her voice was not in the air but in my head, part of the awful ringing. "You couldn't be my husband and do this horrible, evil thing, so who are you? What are you?"

I shut my eyes against her glare, but this made tears come. "I'm sick over it, I am." I had to shout, for the ringing grew louder.

"I'm glad," she said, the words echoing between my aching ears. "You wretched, lowly thing. I would be a fool to wait for you in Heaven when you do the devil's work."

"Please," I said, clutching my head with the hand that did not hold the candle. "It was for you. For the doctor."

"For the doctor?!" The ringing reached such a pitch I thought my skull would split. I screamed—or perhaps I only did it in my head, for all was silent.

Still.

I exhaled, opened my eyes.

Toby whined.

I licked my lips and found him standing before me.

"You need something?"

He barked, the tone of it exasperated like a person could be. Lovingly so. A little like a wife, even. I blinked down at him, at his big eyes, and felt myself tipping over. I gripped the kitchen table. I was slipping on him. He needed me; that's what he needed. "And I need a doctor," I said, frowning. "But you don't understand about money, boy. I'm down three days' pay. Doctors are expensive."

Happy to be talked to, Toby thumped his tail. It happened to tap the wall, and a black oval frame clapped facedown onto the floor. A portrait of Anne in her burial clothes, it was, taken by daguerreotype—the only photograph I had. They'd offered to draw her eyes open. Let her sleep if she's sleeping, I'd said.

I rose on unsteady feet to pick up the photo. I brushed the dust from Anne's cheeks, from the ruby necklace I'd bought her as a wedding present.

"You sap," she'd said, eyes wet. "These are real. You could've bought so many more useful things."

I'd buried her in that necklace.

I looked from the rubies to Toby. He whined.

I hunched over my shovel as if it were a cane all the way to the cemetery where Anne was buried. When I reached her grave in the dark, I set down the lantern I carried, then lay flat, running my fingers through the grass, imagining her hair.

"Hello, my love," I said. "I'm sorry."

When I was ready, I staggered to my feet and began to dig.

I was weak, but the work was not so hard because the earth had not yet settled. I dug wider than I needed to, not wanting to step on Anne's coffin. The hole grew deeper, and I felt myself sinking with it, into shame. "I won't disturb you much," I said.

The shovel scraped the top of her coffin.

"Hey there, chum."

I jumped and, landing badly, fell. Scrambling around to squint in the direction of the voice, I held up both my open hands, thinking of the police. But the man carried a lantern, and he did not wear a uniform.

"Noticed you was digging," he said, jumping down to join me in the grave. "Thought maybe we could split the spoils. That'd make us friends, and I don't tattle on friends."

"It's just one bit of jewelry I need," I said. "For a doctor."

"That's fine. I want the body bits."

"God," I said, my stomach turning as I swallowed a tide of bile. "Why—"

"For a doctor," he parroted.

I shut my eyes, cringing.

"Open it up," he said. "S'what you're here for already, ain't it? So do it."

"I can't," I said, but in my head I thought, *you're the same as him. You are, you are—he sees it,* and the earth seemed to roll under my feet. The ringing started up again.

"Look."

I opened my eyes, dizzy. The man had pulled a revolver.

I blinked at it. I didn't mind if I was shot, but I thought of Toby waiting for me. I turned to face my wife's coffin. I raised my shovel to strike.

But something was wrong.

The lid was bulging. I turned my head, willing the shape to be a trick of the light. But it was there, no matter the angle of my gaze, and it didn't make sense. It was too soon for miasma. There was no hint of smell.

The ringing was louder now.

I'm sick. That's what I'd said to Anne's angry shadow.

And she'd told me she was glad.

I wiped my eyes, the tears leaking out like pus. "All right," I said, my voice tight. "Yes. I understand."

I struck the latch of the casket. The lid popped off, and a wall of hot, rotten wind struck me down. I fell willingly, for I knew I was weak, and I knew I was wicked. I had known it for years, and now Anne knew it too. I coughed once, on impact with the earth inside the grave, but after that I made myself breathe the gas. I lay on my back beside the coffin and listened to the bodysnatcher as he wheezed and retched and kicked. I stared at the rectangle of black sky, inhaling death like anesthesia.

In my addled mind, I made a constellation in the stars that was Anne and fashioned a cloud that crept across it into a nightgown for her.

"It wasn't for me," I murmured. "It was for Toby."

"I know," she said, and this time her voice was like the wind, rustling, outside the ringing. The ringing, in fact, had stopped. As I gazed, the stars grew sharper, and the wholesome smells of dirt and grass returned to my nose.

I sat up, and the world did not tilt.

"Snatcher?" I called lowly.

No answer. The lantern was out, but the moon gave enough light to see by now. The lid of the coffin had burst open, but Anne was whole and lovely like I'd left her. I reached out and shivered, but only at the coldness of her neck. I took the rubies gently. "I'm so sorry," I whispered, and the wind whispered back; it dove down into the grave with me, pushing the jewels hard into my hands.

I spotted the snatcher as I turned away, lying against the other side of the grave. His eyes were open wide, but they didn't seem to see me. I put my hand over his mouth and nose. Nothing. He seemed dead.

I lit the lantern again, so I could see to clasp the coffin lid shut. It wasn't heavy, but I panted, and spots appeared before my eyes. I had to wait for my heart to calm afterward. I stared at the place I knew Anne to lie, behind the now swollen wood, and I wondered.

When I was ready, I climbed out. I left the snatcher where he was, for he could do Anne no harm anymore. I replaced the earth, one shovelful at a time. When I finished, the sun was rising. I hobbled back into the city. First to the jeweler, then to the doctor, and at last to the market for meat.

I went home. I fed Toby and took my medicine. He slept beside me in the place Anne should have been. And all the time, I do think she was watching.

BOTTLED RAGE

Owen Auch

Wesley glanced at the front of the bar, then back at his list. Magnolia's. The last bar in Dogpatch where someone hadn't thrown a punch at him. He'd have to make a new list for next week. The bouncer checked his ID, and he walked in. It was a standard Thursday night bar crowd—busy but not jammed wall to wall, with a crackle of energy in the air. Wesley ordered a Stella and sat down at the bar.

Wesley had been starting bar fights regularly for four years. He never threw the first punch. He didn't want to end up in prison for assault, and besides, getting someone to swing at him was easy by now. Most men were like a frozen lake. Seemingly stable under your feet, it only took a bit of direct pressure in a weak place, and the whole thing would violently crack.

He spotted his target a couple seats down the bar. Tall, white guy with a tidy brown haircut, a pastel button-down, and boat shoes. The guy was in his late twenties and was chatting with a girl in a black dress who was almost out of his league. Judging by their posture, it looked to be their second or third date.

Wesley kept his eyes on the couple, waiting. Fifteen minutes passed, then twenty. Finally, Boat Shoes walked to the bathroom. Wesley counted down a minute, then stood up and walked over to a vacant chair next to the girl.

"Hey, I saw this seat was empty. Could I buy you a drink?" Wesley said.

149

She blushed, then shifted awkwardly in her chair. "That's nice of you, but I'm actually here with someone."

"Oh, Boat Shoes? I thought he might have left to get to Easter brunch."

She blushed again, grabbing a strand of shiny black hair and twirling it nervously. He knew he was making her uncomfortable, but he just needed to stall a little longer. When she said nothing, Wesley continued.

"So, if I can't buy you a drink, can I at least get your name?"

"Kaley. And you?" He glanced over Kaley's shoulder toward the bathroom and saw Boat Shoes walk out, his eyes widening when he saw Wesley in his seat. Wesley ignored the question and addressed Boat Shoes. "It looks like our friend decided to come back after all."

Kaley whipped her head around. "Oh, hey John," Kaley said, even more flustered than she'd been before.

"That seat's actually taken." John stepped between Wesley and Kaley.

"Oh, my mistake. I thought you might have left to pick up some slacks at the dry cleaner," Wesley said.

"What's that supposed to mean?" John asked.

"Caring for your Dockers is important—you seem like you would know. I just thought Kaley here might enjoy a drink with someone more her type."

"And you think you know her type?"

"Of course. It's a pretty safe bet most girls don't want to drink with the human embodiment of corporate casual Friday."

Kaley's mouth twitched into a smile for a split second. John noticed. He took a step toward Wesley.

"You should go now," John said.

"John..." Kaley put her hand on his shoulder.

"Can't take a joke? Kaley and I were enjoying ourselves," Wesley said, leaning back in his chair. Nonchalance was lighter fluid for men's anger.

"Walk away," said John.

"Or what?"

John swung at him.

Three years ago, Wesley saw a therapist for the first time. He'd landed a job at a prestigious law firm straight out of law school, and it was crushing him. The firm knew that student loans and industry expectations meant that Wesley and the other newly minted lawyers couldn't afford to quit for at least two years, and they took advantage of it, working them at least eighty hours a week. He rarely left the office before 10 pm and never took a weekend off. Wesley had initially hoped to spend a few years at the firm to pay off his loans and then transition to a more meaningful job. Now he just hoped to survive long enough to get promoted to a new role with fewer hours. After six months, Wesley had lost ten pounds and couldn't sleep through the night, no matter how tired he was.

Wesley couldn't tell the other lawyers he worked with how much he was struggling, so he confided in his older sister, Lily. Wesley and Lily had always been close, with a similar sense of humor and spontaneity. They'd seen each other much less since Wesley moved to California, but they still talked regularly.

Lily pleaded with him to quit his job, even offering a portion of her modest teaching salary to help with his student loan payments. When he insisted that quitting wasn't possible, Lily talked him into seeing a therapist.

"Wes, if you're not going to quit, you need to see somebody. You can't keep going this way," Lily said.

"I know, but time is the one thing I don't have right now. And what if the partners find out? They'll think I can't handle it."

"They won't find out. I'll set it all up for you. It'll be quick, just thirty-minute sessions. Say you're going to the doctor or something. They can't ask why or you can sue them—they're lawyers, they gotta know that. But I hate to see you like this."

Wesley sighed. "Fine. But if it doesn't help, I'll stop going."

The following week, Wesley left work for his "doctor's appointment" and walked five blocks to the therapist's office. He and the therapist, an older man with white hair who had an exceptionally calm presence, sat in green armchairs, and talked about Wesley's job. This was a relief—Wesley had assumed he'd be looking at inkblots or reliving childhood trauma. After asking if he would consider quitting his job, which Wesley reiterated was impossible, the therapist taught Wesley a relaxation technique. For ten minutes each morning before work, he was supposed to sit on the ground with his legs crossed, breathe slowly, and meditate on a happy memory. It sounded like a waste of time, but Wesley had promised Lily he'd follow through with what the therapist told him.

For the next two days, he started his morning by meditating. Wesley thought about childhood memories. The experience was pleasant, but after the ten minutes was up, he felt the same stress weighing on him as before.

The third morning was different. Wesley meditated on something more recent—his law school graduation, just seven months before. The memory was far more vivid in his mind as he sat on the floor. He could see the enormous red and white banners billowing in the wind again. Green quad grass stretched out in front of him, covered in hundreds of identical white chairs. He walked with the procession of graduating students, his roommate Patrick practically hanging off him. They were both hungover and exhausted from a long night of drinking in the law library with their classmates, a night before graduation tradition that the school turned a blind eye to. The loudspeaker boomed with the sound of Dean Sarang's voice as she encouraged them to make the most of a future full of possibility. He drank in the sun on his face as he made his way to the stage for his name to be called.

Wesley's timer went off, snapping him out of the waking dream. After taking a moment to reorient himself, he looked down at his hands. Wesley froze. His hands were covered in hundreds of translucent blue drops of liquid. Was he still in his head, meditating? He poked at a drop on his left hand with his index finger. It was cold but otherwise felt just like water. Maybe it was just sweat? He touched his tongue to a drop to see if it tasted salty.

Every emotion from his graduation memory hit him at once. Excitement for the future, sadness at leaving his friends behind, and pride in his accomplishments welled up in him again, all compressed into a split second. The emotional weight flattened Wesley like a possum on a busy street, and he passed out on the floor.

He woke up an hour later and scrambled to work. The rest of the drops on his hands had evaporated while he was passed out. Wesley spent hours searching the internet for a medical or even paranormal story similar to his experience with the droplets. He found nothing.

Later that afternoon, Wesley slipped out of the office and called his therapist.

"Hello, Wesley," the therapist said. "How has your meditation practice been going?"

"That's what I was calling about. Something... strange happened yesterday when I was meditating. After the ten minutes were up, I opened my eyes, and my hands were covered with a weird liquid."

"Hmm... I have read cases in the literature of meditation provoking a physical response like exercise can. Do your palms normally sweat?"

"That's just it. I thought it was sweat too, but when I tasted some of the drops, it provoked this incredibly intense feeling." Wesley paused. "And then I passed out."

"Remarkable." Wesley heard the therapist rifling through the pages of a book through the phone. "Have you ever been diagnosed with narcolepsy?"

"Narcolepsy? My problem is that I can't fall asleep."

"Oh, well... right. Losing muscle control in moments of intense emotion is a symptom of narcolepsy. But that can't be it. Hmmm..." Wesley heard pages flipping again. "Can you describe these intense feelings?"

"It was the same feelings I felt while meditating: pleasant. Only more intense. Feeling all those emotions in one moment makes you realize how complex it all is."

"Yes, yes, but feeling the complexity of our emotions is the path toward health!" The therapist spoke as emphatically as he could without breaking his calm monotone. He sounded like someone who had finally found a dropped contact lens after a few minutes of blind groping around on a carpet. "And perhaps the release of all those positive emotions allowed you to unwind enough that you were finally able to get the sleep you needed. Your body might have needed rest so badly that the stress was the only thing keeping you awake."

"But it happened as soon as I tasted the liquid on my hands. It wasn't just meditation."

"Immediately after finishing a meditation session, emotions can still be fresh. I imagine it just took a moment for your mind to comprehend what you'd experienced. I assure you that the only thing on your hands was sweat."

"I suppose that's possible." Wesley was skeptical. This was something more than a strong release of emotions. But this guy was the expert, after all. For Lily's sake, he told himself he would put aside his skepticism and listen.

"You should certainly continue your daily meditation practice," the therapist said. "Give yourself extra time if you're worried about passing out again. But this is remarkable progress after only three days." Wesley said goodbye to the therapist and hung up.

The next morning, Wesley woke up early to meditate. He chose a recent but less intense memory this time. About a month ago, Wesley finished work far earlier than usual. He headed straight from the office to Delores Park. It was warm, and Wesley was in a celebratory mood, so he decided to get ice cream. Strawberry cone in hand, Wesley trekked to the park benches at the top of the hill and sat down facing the city. He looked out over the skateboarders and burnouts and couples laying on blankets to the skyline, watching it turn pink and orange as the sunset behind him, the taste of sugar and summer on his tongue.

When his timer roused him, Wesley looked down to find his hands covered in droplets again, this time a yellowish-orange. He scooped as much of the droplet liquid as he could off of his hands with a spoon, dumping it into a glass on the kitchen counter, then washed his hands. The glass had about an inch of liquid in it.

Wesley wanted to make sure it was these droplets that provoked his intense reaction. He took a shower, brushed his teeth, and put on his suit and tie for work. He felt normal the entire time. None of the intense emotions from yesterday returned. Then he came back to the kitchen, scooped up the smallest amount he could with the spoon, and tasted it.

A warm blanket of comfort enveloped him, still strong but gentler than before. The emotional strands coiled in his mind, satisfaction and melancholy and connection braiding together into one vivid feeling. Wesley exhaled and found himself back in his kitchen, spoon in hand.

Wesley canceled his therapy sessions over the next few weeks, making excuses to Lily about work being too busy for him to go. It was clear to him that the therapist didn't know what was going on, and Wesley didn't want to be treated like a crazy person. Instead, he meditated daily, experimenting with the droplets.

Different types of memories had different effects. Droplets from sad memories paralyzed him—the orange droplets from the recollection of his most recent breakup glued him to his bed for hours, and he had to call in sick to work. Lavender-colored fear droplets caused him to withdraw from others. Green droplets from memories of triumph intoxicated his ego, making him brash, while purple droplets from memories of failure or embarrassment made him passive and indecisive. Even after the initial emotional intensity of the droplets wore off, the effect on Wesley's mind would persist, altering it slowly over time the way that glasses with the wrong prescription can alter one's eyes.

Like he'd suspected, more vivid memories produced more emotionally potent droplets and drinking more of the liquid provoked a stronger reaction. But the droplets also had some strange properties. When Wesley tried to meditate on the graduation memory again, it didn't produce droplets a second time—memories could only be used once. He also discovered that if he focused closely on another person in the memory he meditated on, the droplets would contain that person's emotions rather than his own.

A few weeks later, Wesley came home from work furious at 3 am. His boss, Clint, had assigned him that afternoon the task of drafting a contract that the partners would need by tomorrow for a deal. Most likely, Clint was given this contract weeks ago and forgot about it until today, at which point he dumped it on Wesley. This last minute notice doomed Wesley to a late night and a dressing down from the partners the next day for low-quality work. He took off his suit jacket and shoes and flopped onto the bed, hoping to be able to fall asleep tonight, then paused. He hadn't meditated on an angry memory yet, and here was one, fresh as a wound in his mind. Wesley dragged himself out of bed, sat down on the floor, and meditated on the day's events.

When he finished, the droplets on his hands were a translucent red. Wesley scooped them up into a bottle like usual, then dipped his finger in and tasted it.

Rage. Fire welled up in him, melting away the exhaustion he felt before. Wesley's blood pumped in his ears, his heart beat faster and his mind raced, weaving from thought to thought like a skier through slaloms.

"Fuck Clint," Wesley said, pulling his laptop from his bag and sitting down at the table. He opened the contract that he'd spent the entire day trying to escape and went back to work.

Wesley dodged John's haymaker, dipping his head to the left. While John wound up another punch, Wesley drank in the scene. His eyes darted around the room, taking in details. Tacky faux-vintage Guinness prints on the wall. Dusty mirrors and half-full liquor bottles behind the bar. Faces of onlookers— the horror of Kaley and other bargoers, the tired resignation of the bartender. He lingered on John's face, tucking away the details in his mind. It was red and contorted, his jaw jutting forward as he ground his teeth into a snarl. His nostrils flared, drawing a complex network of paths in the wrinkles of his face.

The second punch came, this time to the stomach. Wesley let it connect, sucking in to soften the blow. Wesley was a good fighter, but he took care not to make it obvious. Ecstasy splashed across John's face as his fist connected with Wesley's gut.

"I told you to walk away, but you wanted to fuck around," John said as he swung again, this time at Wesley's head.

Wesley didn't get hit in the head anymore. He wheeled around, dodging the fist, and tripped John, using his momentum to throw him into the now-vacant chair from which Wesley had instigated the fight. John's legs tangled in the chair, and he crashed to the ground. Someone in the corner of the bar whooped.

John bounced back up, face redder than before. Kaley used the moment to stand in front of John, blocking his way to Wesley, but he brushed past her. John swung at Wesley's head again, even more recklessly than before, and Wesley dodged, this time adding a stiff right to the gut for good measure. John clawed at him, furiously trying to grab his shirt.

Wesley felt himself yanked back by the shoulders. Shit. He'd forgotten about the bouncer. The massive man pulled Wesley away from John and spun him around.

"Get the fuck out of here," the bouncer said, his face inches from Wesley's. "Go start fights somewhere else."

John was uncoiling. He looked down at his feet with embarrassment. Kaley picked up her jacket from the back of her chair and made for the door as the rest of the onlookers turned back to their conversations. The evening's entertainment was over.

The bouncer led Wesley to the door and shoved him out into the street. He walked half a block away, then pulled out his list and crossed off Magnolia's.

Wesley was a junior partner at the law firm now. He worked relentlessly—a massive increase in the quantity and quality of his work had seen him quickly promoted. Instead of working fewer hours and enjoying his higher salary, Wesley worked harder. It was just a matter of time before he would become the youngest partner in the firm's history. He had no friends at work, but all the other lawyers respected the firm's golden boy. Wesley didn't mention much about his life outside the office, and no one bothered to ask. The only unusual thing about him was the pale red liquid he sipped at all hours of the day from a bottle on his desk. It was "an energy drink he made himself," and the other lawyers joked that they should steal it to get his edge.

When he got home from Magnolia's, Wesley took off his shoes and coat, sat down on the floor with his legs crossed, and meditated on the fight. In the weeks following the night he had meditated on rage for the first time, he'd quickly exhausted all of his angry memories. He started boxing in gyms, and for a while, getting punches thrown at him was novel enough to provoke anger. But as he became a better fighter, boxing stopped eliciting an emotional reaction in him or anyone skilled enough to spar with him. Desperate for more rage droplets, he turned to bar fights. Easy to start, usually free of consequences other than being thrown out and soaked in alcohol to intensify emotions, bar fights were a consistent way to harvest memories of the rage of others.

Wesley didn't like starting fights at first. It felt manipulative and wrong, but he needed the droplets to power through hard days at work. After a couple months, Wesley started diluting the droplets in water and drinking them constantly throughout the day. As his productivity at work increased, starting fights became more natural for him. Eventually, he began to enjoy the art of choreographing other men's rage.

Wesley closed his eyes and relived the fight through John's emotions. He felt the confusion and anger provoked by his insults escalating to a violent fury, the exaltation at landing a blow in Wesley's stomach, the humiliation at being tripped, the desperate wrath of being bested in front of a crowd—especially with Kaley watching. These feelings became Wesley's own, and when he opened his eyes, his hands were covered in translucent red droplets.

Wesley stood up and wiped the liquid from his hands with a paper towel. He placed the towel into a machine on the kitchen counter that looked like a box fan laying on its face, then connected a bottle to a hose coming out of the device and plugged it in. The dehydrator would run all night, evaporating the liquid from the towel and condensing it back into the bottle. He would mix the distillation with enough water to make his week's supply of bottled rage tomorrow. Wesley brushed his teeth, washed his face, and laid down in bed. Sleep took him instantly.

Rob and Jamie dug through stacks of old, dusty boxes in Rob's basement.

"You sure it's down here?" Jamie said. "Didn't we play at my house last time?"

"No, we played here two weeks ago with Matt and Riley, remember? My mom always gets mad when I leave games out and puts them down here. She probably hopes we'll never find them again. It must just be buried deep."

Jamie sighed, pushing aside some boxes he'd already searched to reveal an older-looking white box underneath. There was no way Rob's mom hid it this deep, but he opened the old box anyway, mainly to strengthen his case that they should bike over and look for the game at his house. Inside the box were about a dozen unmarked plastic bottles of a translucent red liquid.

"Dude, was your dad into homebrewing? Looks like I might have found his stash," Jamie said, pulling out one of the bottles.

"I don't think so. I mean, he died at a bar. I don't think he was making his own drinks at home too."

Rob's dad had died five years ago. According to every witness, he walked into The Scarlet Hare, a dive bar in a seedy area of town, and immediately insulted a trucker's girlfriend. When Rob's dad looked to be getting the better of the trucker in the brawl that resulted, one of the other truckers smashed a bottle over his head, sending him into a coma that he died from two weeks later. The trucker who hit him spent three years in prison, and Rob's family grieved. But more than anything, Rob's family and the community were confused. Quiet, distant, and diligent, Rob's dad was a high-profile lawyer with a big house in the suburbs—the last person you'd expect to be starting brawls with truckers in a dive bar.

"Should we taste it? It doesn't look like anyone is using it down here," Jamie said. Rob's mom had boxed up all his dad's stuff in this corner of the basement when he'd died and hadn't touched it since. Likely no one knew the bottles were here.

"I don't know," Rob said, but Jamie was already unscrewing the bottle. They were in eighth grade, and neither of them had tried alcohol other than taking occasional sips from a parent's wineglass.

"Maybe if it's still good, we can bring it with us to Sadie's on Friday. You can't go to those things empty-handed and expect to just mooch off of everyone else." Jamie sniffed the liquid. It didn't smell like anything.

"I mean, a tiny sip just to try it couldn't hurt. Let me smell it." Jamie handed Rob another bottle from the box.

"Doesn't smell like alcohol," Rob said.

"How do you know what alcohol smells like?" Jamie asked.

"I mean, I've tried wine before. It doesn't smell like that."

"It's probably just some other kind of alcohol. I'm going to try it."

"Make sure you take a small sip. You're not the *biggest* guy after all," Rob said, smiling at Jamie. Jamie threw a punch at Rob's arm in response, then took a big swig from the bottle.

Jamie's vision turned white, and he felt like his brain was being seared with a red hot branding iron. Anger gathered in the tributaries of his thoughts, coalescing into a mighty, rushing river, with him as a speedboat powering down the rapids, full steam ahead. He woke up on the floor with Rob slapping his cheeks.

"Agh, dude, get off!" Jamie pushed Rob away.

"Jamie! You've been laying there babbling for like five minutes. Thank God you're ok."

"I'm fine."

"You're fine? You were knocked out! What did that stuff do to you?"

"It was amazing! We're taking this to Sadie's on Friday night, and we're spiking every drink we can with it. Not as much as I just had—we don't want to knock everybody out. Just a little bit. Everyone will love it."

Jamie felt remarkably lucid. His next steps were obvious: take this stuff to Sadie's, spike everyone's drinks, everyone has a fantastic time, Jamie takes credit for it and gets invited to more parties with the popular crowd. He felt more confident than anytime he could remember.

"Are you serious? That just knocked you out cold, and you want to slip it into everyone's drinks? We barely got invited to this party in the first place. What if this happens to everyone there? And besides, I thought we agreed that if we went, we weren't gonna drink."

"Rob, don't be a bitch. This is our chance. Whatever this is, no one else has anything like it. You should try it. Then you'll understand."

Rob looked uneasy. "My mom's coming home in ten minutes, and it'd be pretty bad if I was passed out when she got back."

"Suit yourself," Jamie said, gathering a few unopened bottles from the box into his arms. "I'll see you Friday."

"Wait, Jamie," Rob started, but his friend was already headed out the door.

Leigh's focus on her organic chemistry textbook broke when she heard the knock on the door. She grumbled, walked across the messy dorm room and opened the door, expecting it to be her RA coming over to scold her for skipping another floor meeting. Standing there with a backpack on was her kid brother Rob.

"Rob? What are you doing here? Why didn't you just call?"

"It, um... felt like I needed to talk to you in person."

"Come in."

She cleared some of the clothes off of her bed, smoothed it out, and sat down, then gestured for Rob to take the desk chair. He sat down, setting his backpack on the floor with care, like it was made of glass.

"What's going on?"

"Do you know if Dad ever homebrewed any beer or liquor or anything like that when he was alive?"

"You come all the way to my dorm just to ask me that?"

"It's important."

"Why?"

"Just tell me."

She paused. Her memory of their father was better than her brother's. She'd been fifteen when he died, seven years older than Rob. But she didn't remember him homebrewing anything or even being interested in alcohol. He'd have a glass of wine with their mother occasionally, but rarely more. He didn't indulge in anything at all.

"I don't think so. At least, I don't remember him brewing anything or even drinking much. Now, are you going to tell me why you came here?"

Rob pursed his lips and played with the strap of his backpack. Finally, he met her eyes.

"Did you hear about that insane party at the Tataloff's a couple weeks ago?" Rob asked.

"I saw something about it on the news, which is really saying something for an eighth-grade party. Looked like they absolutely trashed the place. Why?"

"I was there... And I think I was the reason it got so out of control," Rob said.

Leigh laughed. Rob? Board game-loving, rule-following Rob?

"Oh yeah? How'd you cause all that destruction?" Leigh asked, smiling. Rob might have been there, but surely he was worrying too much, like usual.

"With this," Rob said, slipping a bottle of translucent red liquid out of his backpack. "Jamie talked me into it. We found this stuff in the basement. Jamie tried it and passed out, then convinced me to help him spike the drinks at the party with it. Everything went haywire after that." The words gushed out of his mouth as the dam holding back his two-week secret finally burst.

"Rob, even if that was the most potent alcohol in the world, it couldn't get dozens of kids that messed up. Maybe you helped, but these kids would have gotten drunk all on their own, and drunk kids break stuff, or they break each other. Parties like that are so stupid."

"They weren't just drunk. I've seen drunk people before."

Leigh raised her eyebrows.

"I'm not a baby, Leigh," Rob said. "Sure, they destroyed stuff, but this was different. For example, some of them managed to break into Ralph's without setting off any of the alarms just to get toilet paper to teepee Mr. Stevenson's house. Tommy Steiner set up a boxing tournament, and there were a bunch of kids setting odds and taking bets and everything. And I heard that the Tataloff's are still finding booby traps all over the place. Drunk kids don't do stuff like that."

Leigh smiled. "If Tommy Steiner is anything like I remember, maybe something weird was going on. That kid doesn't seem like he could spell the word tournament, let alone set one up."

"That's why I wanted to talk to you. I think Dad might have made this," Rob said, holding up the bottle. "It was in a box with all his other things. Maybe you could figure out what it is."

Leigh was still skeptical—it would be just like Rob to blow something like this way out of proportion. But she was intrigued too. That liquid was a real-life chemistry mystery, the kind she was in school studying to solve.

"Let me see it," Leigh said.

Rob handed her the bottle, and she opened it and sniffed the contents. It didn't smell like alcohol. She dipped her finger in. It felt like water.

"Just don't drink it," Rob said.

"Why not? You afraid to box me?" Leigh mimed throwing a punch at Rob.

"Yeah right. I'd beat you up." Rob dodged the punch.

"Maybe when you're older. You're still my *little* brother. Emphasis on *little*."

They joked around and made small talk for a while. Despite being only twenty minutes away, Leigh didn't visit home enough. Her relationship with their mom had been difficult ever since their dad died, but she missed Rob. As they'd gotten older, she'd realized how similar they were.

"I'm headed into the lab tomorrow. I'll see what I can figure out about this while I'm there. But I'm pretty sure you're overthinking this."

"I'm not. Be careful with that stuff," Rob said, zipping his backpack and standing up to go.

"I will be."

The next day, Leigh walked across campus to the chemistry lab, the bottle tucked into her backpack. Her day was light. She'd just finished a big round of exams, so she had a week before she needed to start studying hard again. She'd spend a couple hours experimenting with the strange liquid before getting back to her regular classwork.

Leigh started with all the routine tests. The viscometer confirmed that the substance was basically the same viscosity as water, and a density calculation showed an identical density with water as well. She used a pair of scissors to cut off a piece of litmus paper to test the acidity and determined that it was slightly more acidic than water. The first difference yet—she was beginning to think that Rob had just colored some water with food coloring as a dumb prank.

It seemed likely that most of the red liquid was just water, and whatever was affecting the kids at the party was only a small part of the overall compound. Access to the good vacuum distillation tools required permission, but they had one of the old school two flask distillation setups in the lab. Leigh poured half the bottle into the first flask and started heating it. She steadied the temperature at one hundred degrees Celsius and waited.

After about twenty-five minutes, all the water had evaporated and condensed in the other flask, leaving behind a tiny amount of dark red liquid.

Leigh felt stuck. She had isolated whatever this compound was, but now what? Despite spending over a year at UCSF studying chemistry already, she didn't have a lot of practical lab experience. She scooped up the red liquid with a spoon.

If what Rob said was true, there was a real chemical discovery to be made, one that would get Leigh into any PhD program in the country. But here she was, compound in hand, but no ideas in her head for how to move forward.

All the kids drank this stuff and were fine. Rob had told her to be careful, but he worried about everything. And great scientists were willing to experiment on themselves in the name of science, right? Leigh spooned the red liquid into her mouth before she could talk herself out of it.

Rage. She saw her professor passing her up as a lab assistant despite her perfect grades. She saw her father, his face blurry in her mind's eye, getting himself killed in a seedy bar and leaving her mom to raise them alone. She saw herself, her face still red with acne like a middle schooler. She saw herself, tall and spindly and awkward, alone in her dorm room studying on Friday night while her classmates partied together. She saw the future—grad school rejection letters, basement chemistry labs, frozen food. Then she saw white.

Leigh grabbed the scissors from the counter and slammed them through her eye and into her brain.

DEATH, AND THE SCENT OF TEA

Cheryl Zaidan

The boy looked out the window at the crowd outside. It had grown in number since he looked last. He wondered how long it had been since his parents left. Maybe three days, although it was hard to tell. He had spent most of his time hiding in the closet with only a cricket bat for protection.

After what was probably the fourth day, the boy moved about the rooms, but he was not so brave as to leave the flat. He had thought briefly of going to the neighboring flats to see if he could find help there, but from time to time he would hear sounds in the hallway, which scared him and kept him from doing so. It was clear that he would have to do something soon, though. The food was dwindling. All that was left was a few tins of tuna fish and carrots. And he hated carrots.

His parents had argued. It was the first time he had ever heard them fight, apart from the occasional bickering session. The argument had finally ended when he had promised that he would keep all the windows and doors locked tightly while they went to get Grandmother. They never came back. It was obvious they were never going to.

The boy felt sharp tears stinging the back of his eyes and he wiped them away with a sweaty palm. It was the middle of summer, and the heat was getting to him. He finally gave in and opened the window—just a crack. At least their flat was on the third floor, far above the throngs below, but that didn't mean he was safe. He tried the phone again. Still dead. The television offered nothing but static.

The horrible noises from outside seemed louder, possibly because the boy was frightened but also because the open window allowed the sounds from the street to carry into the stagnant room. Apart from the constant moans, the boy heard a scratching noise that he couldn't identify. It seemed to get closer and closer, but before the boy could react, fingers reached onto the sill and another hand pushed up the window in one swift action. He screamed and tried to reach the bat that lay on the kitchen floor, but something scrambled quickly on top of him. Something cold and rotted tugging on his elbow.

The man who grabbed his arm was surprisingly strong; it was like being caught in a vise. The boy turned and their eyes met for a moment. Then deliberately, very deliberately, the man put his mouth to the boy's arm and bit. His teeth were not very sharp, but he still managed to break the skin. And there it was.

The boy knew he was going to die.

He pulled his arm away quickly, but the man did not attack him further. Rather, he studied the boy's face carefully, and a faint look of sadness came over his rotted visage and filled his gray eyes. Then he spoke.

"I was wondering," he said in a raspy voice, "if we could talk. Do you by chance happen to have any tea?"

It was almost as if he were in a dream. The boy put the kettle on the stove (and thank goodness the electricity hadn't gone out) while the man sat patiently waiting at the table, an empty cup and saucer before him. The boy had used the good china, although he didn't know why. It felt like somehow, he had to. After all, his mother had said it was for special occasions.

The man smiled as the boy poured hot water into the cup. As he carefully picked up a spoon, the boy got a small glimpse of open bone under the flesh of the man's ring finger. It wasn't even the most hideous thing about him, but it still made the boy gag. The man ignored him but casually sipped the tea, grimacing slightly as he did so.

"I used to love the stuff," he sighed as he set down the nearly full cup. "Now, it has no taste. Nothing has a taste. Do you know what I miss most, young man?"

The boy did not know how to respond, so he poured himself a cup of tea and sat down at the opposite end of the table, rubbing his arm. It hurt. Not as much as he thought it would, but the skin burned a bit there. He suddenly felt flushed and very cold at the same time.

The zombie continued. "I miss the scent of tea. Oh, the taste is quite lovely, don't get me wrong, but there was nothing like opening a bag of fresh tea leaves and inhaling. Ahhh..." He closed his eyes and leaned his head against the back of the chair, sighing softly. The boy was aware of a powerful scent emanating from the man's mouth. It smelled like rubbish.

"I don't suppose you have anything you'll miss, will you?" There was a lilt in the man's voice that seemed almost to mock him.

"My parents," said the boy and then wished he hadn't. He didn't want to give this man any personal information about himself.

"Were they good?" The man put one long finger in the tea and swirled it lightly. The cup was still steaming, but the heat didn't seem to bother him.

"I guess so." Now the boy wasn't so sure. After all, they had left him alone.

The zombie tried another sip, but again made a face and pushed the cup back. "I wish I were human so I could once again enjoy this. Smell your tea. Let me know what you think."

The boy sniffed. "It smells like tea," he replied. "You can't smell tea anymore, can you?"

"No smell, no taste. I crave only the brain now." The zombie looked at the cup before him woefully. "My personal hell would consist of being trapped in a room with all the members of Parliament."

The boy gave him a quizzical look.

"No brains. I'd starve." There was an awkward pause, and the zombie cleared his throat slightly." I suppose I'm not as funny in this new life," he added with a wry smile.

"Okay, just stop it, stop it!" The outburst garnered a sideways look from the zombie, but the boy pushed on. "You can't starve! You can't do anything! You're dead! "

"Can't I?" The zombie smiled again and raised one rotting eyebrow. "My dear boy, I'm talking to you right now. Granted, I may be the exception to the rule, but all you need to do is look out the window and see what the world has become. If zombies could not 'do' anything, would this be allowed to happen?"

The man had a point, but the boy still didn't know what to do, so he nodded and pretended to be interested in something on the floor.

"No offense taken," the zombie said politely, even though the boy had not apologized. "This is from one talking corpse to another. You *do* realize that your time on this earth is limited?"

The boy looked down at the mark on his arm. This time the pause lasted for a full minute. The zombie pressed his hand on his chin and crossed one twig-like leg over the other. To the casual observer, it would have been a very human thing to do. Actually, the whole situation would have seemed normal had the circumstances been different. Two people on a sunny afternoon, sitting opposite each other, having a conversation and drinking tea.

The silence became unbearable, and the boy thought he should say something. "I saw a scary movie once," his voice cracked slightly, "where there were these people trapped, so they sent a dog to help them out because the zombies wouldn't eat the dog."

"Really?" The zombie picked up the cup of tea again and glanced at it.

"Is that true? I mean, would you eat a dog... for its brains?"

The zombie leaned forward and smiled, a smile that would have appeared genuine had his face not been decomposing. "Do *you* eat dog?" he asked.

"No. Well, not right now." The boy shifted in his chair slightly.

"You may." The man picked up the spoon and tapped it lightly against the side of the cup. "But only when other food is not available. If you were starving to death and a dog was the only option, you'd have to. And we are no different. We crave the brains of living creatures; we get energy from it. You need food to survive, don't you? Had I not had the wherewithal to kill as many people as I did, I would be like one of those poor suffering shambling shells out there. Devoid of thought and reason."

"I don't get it." The boy frowned slightly, then spoke again. "Hold on a moment. I think I understand. The brains make you normal?"

The man laughed. "Well done, my lad, you're quite clever. You're correct in a way. The more brains I consume, the more 'normal' I become. And the more normal I become, the more brains I eat. It's a sort of evolutionary process. As I grow more intelligent, I can outsmart the masses. I get to the food before they do. Of course, human brains offer more benefits than the animal kind."

A loud groan came from outside. The zombie quietly looked out the window. "Oh, dear," He sighed. "That one's lost his arm." The boy followed his glance down to the street below where a rather clumsy-looking zombie was tripping over what looked to be his own arm. The boy watched as the thing tried unsuccessfully to pick it up but lacking the necessary motor skills, he shambled ahead, leaving the arm on the street. None of the other zombies seemed to notice this. Or care.

The man shook his head briskly as if to clear it. The boy turned his attention back to the zombie sitting across from him. *He's losing it,* thought the boy. *He needs brains to keep him going. That's what he said. The more brains he ate....*

"Where were we?" The zombie shook his head again. "Oh yes." He studied the boy carefully. "Yes, I've become a little more 'normal' as you put it. I know what you're thinking. You're thinking that you could do the same. But I'm afraid that won't happen to you, my dear child. No, I fear your fate is sealed. You just don't have the heart for this sort of thing. I imagine at this very moment, you're contemplating suicide, am I right?"

The thought had crossed the boy's mind a few times during the conversation, but he didn't want to appear as weak as he felt. Instead, he straightened his back and said," It won't last. Your supply will run out. And then you'll die."

"Which brings me to why I'm here." The zombie stared at him; his voice became a great deal more serious. "I've been watching you, and you're a fighter. In fact, the only reason you're still alive is because of me. I've been keeping the others and myself at bay."

"Huh?" It was an ignorant response, but it was the only one the boy could come up with. His mouth didn't seem to want to form words, although his brain was working feverishly. The man was probably lying to him, but he couldn't say for sure.

The zombie rose from his seat and started to pace the room. "I know you think of me as a cold-blooded murderer, but I assure you nothing could be further from the truth. I still *feel* things. Loneliness, isolation, sadness. And I feel something for you, although I can't really call it compassion. I sensed you needed my help." The zombie started into the boy's eyes. "And besides, you and I are the last two around capable of speech. You have no one else to talk to."

The zombie paused in mid-step.

"But another reason why you need me," he continued, his voice hoarse as he enunciated every word with effort, "is because of that bite on your arm. Can you feel it?" The zombie twirled around and faced the boy. "This disease or whatever it is called, is currently coursing its way through your virgin body. I meant it when I said your time is limited. Unless you help me."

The boy felt a cold chill that had nothing to do with the man's words, and he suddenly became aware of a strange feeling that started from the pit of his stomach. It was almost like he was hungry, but the thought of food didn't appeal to him. He took a small drink from the cup before him. It didn't taste the same. He sniffed it. Nothing. The man was still talking, but his words were slurring, and his pace was slow.

He also looked older and more ragged than he had when he first walked in. The boy realized the man was losing his mind. It was only a matter of time.

"I'll help you!" The boy blurted out quickly.

"Was there ever a doubt?" The man appeared confident but looked suspicious at the boy's declaration.

"I... just needed to hear what you wanted." That wasn't true, but the boy knew what he had to do.

"Good. Now is there anyone around? Any other humans?"

"No." And that part *was* true. He was on his own. And was that really a bad place to be? True, the man before him was far smarter than those animated corpses on the streets, but how long would that last? No, the boy had to do what had kept him alive for the last few painful days. He had to rely on himself.

The hunger became more of a gnawing. He could smell something in the man, something that wasn't the rotted breath of the corpse that paced the floor before him. The smell amplified the boy's hunger pangs to unbelievable heights.

"So there it is, our minds put together," the zombie continued, not noticing the boy's turmoil. "It would work, I assure you. Now the first thing we need to do is –"

The boy grabbed the cricket bat and hit the man's head as hard as he could. The man made no sound as he fell to the floor. His arms flailed wildly, but he was either too incapacitated by the surprise attack or too weak to fend it off. Either way, he continued to lie there as the boy hammered the bat against the man's head again and again, breaking apart the skull enough to expose his brain.

The boy began to eat.

THE ARTIST

Mike Murphy

Taking a deep drag on a cigarette outside of his carny tent, Digby saw the young couple approaching and instantly *hated* them. They were all over each other! *Get a room*, he thought.

Still, they might do. He could hide his revulsion for that chance.

As they neared him, he started the pitch, smiling broadly and gesturing at his framed work hanging on the tent. "Caricatures!" he called. "Get your caricatures here! Suitable for framing! A wonderful memento!"

The woman of the couple slowed and, as Digby had seen many times before, convinced her man what fun posing would be. The man, of course, agreed. After being paid, the artist showed them into his tent to start creating the picture. *Maybe this time*, he thought hopefully. *Maybe tonight I can end this.*

Digby learned more than he wanted to know about the couple: Paul and Vivian Carter, newlyweds from Manhattan. He talked to them as briefly as possible to get an idea of what would go well in their sketch. Paul, a big Yankees fan, wanted to be pictured with a baseball bat. Vivian, an avid romance novel reader, chose a book. They posed on one chair, Vivian on her husband's lap. Digby got his "special" art set from the trunk and began working.

He could see it on their faces—that queasy feeling was coming over them. It worsened as Digby continued to sketch.

Neither one of the Carters admitted the problem, probably fearing being thought weak by the other.

In mere seconds, they became immobile.

As Digby drew the last stroke of the exaggerated baseball bat, things kicked into high gear: The couple's eyes popped from their sockets, swinging near their cheeks on strangely elongated optic nerves that reminded the artist of Slinkies. Their cheeks reddened, caving inward to show the eroding bones underneath.

Digby waited for the *pièce de résistance*: The fingers. He had seen it many times before, but the phenomenon never failed to amaze and entertain him. One by one, their fingers— with, for some reason, the exception of the pinkies of their right hands—shriveled. The previously skin-covered bones popped through the retracting flesh like a hot knife through butter and with a sound out of a children's cartoon. The now-exposed bones clacked together in ways they were never meant to.

The Carters' rings, including Vivian's large engagement diamond, dropped to the ground just before the newlyweds fell from the posing chair.

Digby kissed the pen he had been using and reverently put the art set back in the trunk.

He walked over to the flap of his tent and looked out. The sun had set, and clouds were coming in. No other customers were in sight. He flipped his sign to "closed" and pulled the tent strings taut. He smiled at the disfigured couple lying atop each other, silent and unmoving, but alive. He had *big* plans for them.

Digby scooped the Carters' jewelry off the ground for future pawning, gently placed his caricature on the couple's intertwined forms, and took a couple of steps back to watch. The bodies began to buck uncontrollably, like they were having seizures. The picture somehow stayed put where its creator had placed it. Slowly, the Carters silently dissolved into a gooey mess as Digby's sketch glowed a bright green. In short order, the Manhattan newlyweds were gone, and the sheet of paper—now back to its original white—lay alone on the tent's floor.

Digby retrieved his work. It twitched slightly, with the last of the couple's strength, trying to crawl away. "There, there," he said, stroking the paper like a cat. "Almost over." He walked to a metal trash basket in the corner of the tent. He held the caricature over it and removed a lighter from his shirt pocket. The couple, barely alive in their paper prison, tried to escape the inevitable flame.

Digby touched lighter flame to paper.

The artist dropped his work among the basket's aged cinders of failures. He squeezed his eyes shut and folded his hands before him in supplication. *Tonight. Please tonight!* When he deemed a suitable amount of time had passed, Digby slowly and hopefully opened his tear-stained eyes.

No Anna.

He peered into the basket. The drawing had definitely been consumed by the fire.

It *didn't* work!

How many more couples would he need before the finite pool of love was emptied enough by their deaths that he could jump in once more and again share its blissful waters with Anna? She said she didn't love him anymore that long-ago night, but Digby knew he could change that with the sacrificial spell he found in the beaten-up book he stole from the Tulsa library when the circus passed through there last year.

It *would* work one day. Anna would see the error of her ways and come back to him. She would!

Digby simply had to keep trying.

THE WOMAN IN THE WALLPAPER

Gregory L. Norris

"**Y**ou wonder about the people here, before you," she said. "The lives they led."

He huffed something under his breath, its meaning clear. In an economy of words, he indicated the walls with their ugly vertical bands of orange, yellow, and brown, all separated by thin stripes of white. "The Brady Bunch," he said and resumed scraping.

The house was a 1970s ranch, its exterior a pale pistachio green. The carpet in the basement was a rusty color that smelled of mildew, proof that the foundation wasn't as perfect as they'd hoped. A real fixer-upper at a decent price, and so they bought it and started to fix up the house.

He scored the walls using the hand tool with a ring of metal teeth, sprayed water, and scraped. While he worked, their son was relegated to the room with an even gaudier print: a pastoral pattern with green willows, reflective silver bands of sky, and a southern belle in full regalia and parasol, her face turned away, at an angle. It was hideous, another relic from the 70s like the shag carpet in the basement and the outdated kitchen cabinetry.

What she said got into his thoughts as he scored, sprayed, and scraped. The ugly wallpaper resisted his efforts mightily, as though adhered to the wall with super glue. Those other lives.

In one corner of the room where he imagined a bed had been, the vertical stripes bore the kind of weepy marks that were likely made from the sweaty back of a head. The level was the correct height for a mattress. He stopped his shredding and peered more closely. The wall exuded a reside of age, the old paper a note of rusty sweat.

A wave of despair washed over him. As first-time homeowners, the price had been right. But now that the ink was dried and the reality of how much work they'd assumed in the bargain sank in, his bones felt a pressing, invisible weight. It wasn't really their house, not for thirty years—twenty if they made one extra mortgage payment per annum, according to a tried and true formula. What they owned was the sweat of strangers.

He leaned over and drew in a deep breath. The smell of the room burned in his lungs. As he readied to push, he saw that the fresh blister near the meat between forefinger and thumb had burst open and wept milky fluid over the back of the tool.

A motorcycle streaked down the road, its cannonade drowning out the television, which was tuned to a silly game show. The spread on the table was modest—tuna salad, wheat bread, slices of romaine, tomatoes, and red onion. A bag of chips. A half-empty bottle of soda.

The emptiness inside him doubled, helped along by the misery pulsing from his injured right hand. Guilt filled in the void, and, for a shocking instant, he was eleven again, staring into the empty avocado-green fridge. Empty, except for his father's beer. No matter how broke they were, the old man always found money for a six-pack and smokes. Just like he always found a way to punish you right before dinner as a way of sending you to bed without any to cover up the crime that there wasn't any.

The bike's roar waned. On the other side of the interruption, the house was still a disorganized mess of cardboard boxes and temporary living.

She tsked and shook her head. "Children live on this road."

He didn't counter or support that claim. The red onion was particularly aggressive. He tried to be grateful for what they had while their son kicked his legs and crunched on a handful of chips.

"Eat your sandwich," she said, aiming a pointer at the boy's paper plate.

It had gotten warm enough to leave windows open at night. Post-coitus, the breeze drifted over him, cooling his sweat and stirring the scent of their lovemaking. The sex was okay, but like the evening meal it lacked spark. *Robotic*, he thought, on his back atop the blankets. They'd only gone through motions as a way to forget they'd grown comfortable. The act was part of duty, no longer for pleasure. Climaxing was nearly impossible after he detected the smell of the house on her. Maybe it was on him. He wondered if he'd ever come again after this night.

The house brooded dark and silent around them. Sounds of the neighborhood carried past the sills—the gentle sough of the wind, a car several streets away. Other people in other times had huddled where he was now, likely hearing similar notes. The divot of raw flesh on his right hand throbbed. He flexed it and felt the fresh scab crack open.

Then a noise sounded directly outside the closed bedroom door, the groan of a footstep. His flesh reacted with pins and needles. He reached for the edge of the blanket as the door creaked open. In the darkness, he made out a shadowy shape, diminutive, clearly that of their son but in the tense seconds before the shadow spoke it was something else, something sinister.

"Daddy?" the boy asked, his voice a sob.

He recovered his boxers from the side of the bed and stepped into them. On his way to the door, he stubbed his right little toe on a corner of an unpacked cardboard box. Time delayed the pain. When its rush caught up, he wanted to bark for the boy to return to his bed. She drowsed, and he held in his rage.

"What is it?" he asked, his voice barely louder than a whisper.

The boy sniffled. "There's someone in my room."

Time froze as he considered his son's words. The world seemed to hold its breath at the implications in that statement. Then he realized he was the one who'd forgotten how to breathe and that he was dealing with a six-year-old.

"Who's in your room?"

"A lady."

He scooped a hand around the boy's sweaty scalp and guided him through the dark house toward the room his son temporarily occupied.

"A lady, huh?"

They reached the door. He located the light switch and flipped it on. The dingy glow reflected off the silver bands of sky in the outdated wallpaper.

"She said she used to live here," the boy continued, his tone that same sheepish one he used when heartfully sorry for having broken a knickknack or glass.

He humored the boy with an, "Um-hum," while returning him to the bunched, damp bedclothes. For a terrible moment, he worried that his son had wet the bed and they would again have to face that unpleasant period thought behind them. Then he caught the acrid odor of sweat, and memories of the room with the vertical striped wallpaper again struck him. His heart galloped.

"This lady," he said.

The boy sat up. His eyes wide, not blinking, were aimed at the section of shiny wallpaper where the antebellum princess stood beneath her parasol, her face turned away.

A dream, a nightmare, that's all it was, he told himself as he worked and sweated, and the house got no closer to rising out of its despair. His own nightmares chased him in the room where he labored, only those originated in the waking world. His father's fist, striking again and again. He set down the scoring tool and examined his hand. The broken blister was a runnel of weepy flesh. The rest of his hand showed fresh scrapes and gouges. For the first time since closing on the house, he recalled his initial reaction when they'd toured it with the realtor. Revulsion. But it was in their price range. They didn't have a lot of options.

He'd taken two weeks of vacation time so there'd be pay for his efforts, though hardly anything resembling vacation. While he labored, she worked in the kitchen, washing out cabinets of dust and crumbs. The cabinets would require updating down the road when they could afford to tackle the kitchen. Until then, the white, used appliances would have to do in lieu of modern stainless steel. At least they weren't avocado-green, he mused, like the ones in his father's humorless house.

He ignored the ache in his flesh and resumed his task. More scraping removed the hideous striped wallpaper, exposing the pith underneath.

He ceased scraping and stared into the starchy undercoat. It had transformed into skin. Dead epidermis coated the walls. It was the residue of those who'd once lived here. Their flaked, dead lives stuck to the walls.

He broke the trance and reached for his water bottle. Having left the cap off, he took a deep pull, only to gag and spit up the mouthful. Something solid lurked among the liquid. It was a fleck of rotten skin from the wall.

The water he'd expelled ran down the section of wallpaper discolored by sweat. Now, the hideous relic from decades of questionable taste in the past wept something else, visible in the runnels. A faint trace of rusty red.

Blood. When he woke enough to understand what he was staring at, the temperature in the room seemed to have doubled, and yet his sweat sat clammy on his flesh. He reached a shaking finger toward the rusty stain. The temptation to touch it possessed him. A fraction of an inch before contact, he noticed his weeping hand and drew back, a foul taste igniting on his tongue.

He hastened out of the room, barely made it to the toilet, and vomited.

"Do you think—?" he asked. The fragmented question went unfinished until she pressed him.

"What?" she snapped.

"This house. Do you think bad things happened here?"

She stood with her back to him, putting away laundry in their dresser. Their furniture looked out of place in the sad landscape of a house not really theirs. By her hesitation, he sensed she felt the wrongness that surrounded them, too.

"What kind of bad things?" she asked. "Colds, broken bones, I'm sure all the usual things. Angry voices. Broken hearts. The stuff of families."

"No," he said. "I'm talking worse. *Bad.*"

She half-turned, and he was reminded of the figure in the wallpaper, there but never making direct eye contact.

"What do you want for dinner?" she asked.

He approached the room whose door stood ajar enough that he heard his son's weepy voice through the gap. The words, barely louder than a whisper, became clear enough to translate as he crept closer.

"Why? And what happened after that?"

The boy had followed the normal patterns. He'd sucked his thumb until forbidden to, had howled in grief over the loss of a pet goldfish, had tried out for the youth soccer team in their old town, failed, but he was hopeful they'd try again after getting settled here. The sing-songy weeping voice was becoming a frequent habit, one developed after their move into the house. And one that was unwelcome. Oh, the urge to react. Smack him, maybe. Toughen him up.

Like your dad did?

Ice crackled through him, and his rage mostly cooled. He stepped closer, and for a second he expected a response, proof his son wasn't getting in the habit of talking to himself. He held his breath. The only sounds from the room after that were sniffles.

Steeling himself, he pushed through the door. The boy studied him through wide, bleary eyes.

"Who were you talking to?"

The boy's throat knotted under the influence of a heavy swallow, his only answer.

"I asked you a question."

He saw the boy's eyes tick toward the section of wall where the southern belle skipped, her movement frozen in time and space.

"Hey, I'm talking to you," he said.

The boy narrowed his gaze. "She doesn't like us being here."

"Who doesn't?"

"The woman in the wallpaper. She says we're making it different. Messing it up from the way it was. How she wants it."

"How *she* wants it," he parroted. Suddenly and without warning, he wanted to throw something. He wanted to swear—a long, loud rosary of expletives—at his son, at the house, and especially at the woman in the wallpaper.

And oh, the urge to punch something, *someone*. He unconsciously made a fist. Pain jolted up his wrist. He willed his fingers to unclench and saw his wound was dripping again.

"Go, out," he snapped.

"Huh?"

"Go outside. Go to your mother. Anywhere but this room. *Now.*"

The boy hurried off the bed and out of the room. He shot a look at the belle, hating her as much as he'd grown to hate the house.

Fresh sweat poured from his scalp. He whirled and stormed into the room with the vertical striped wallpaper and residue of blood. Picking up the circular scoring tool, he ran it over the bumps and scabs, slicing shreds, exposing more of the skin beneath. He pressed hard until his knuckles and palm ached, unaware at first that he was growling. His heart pulsed. His temples throbbed.

Gripping the tool, he hastened back into the boy's temporary bedroom and approached the southern belle. The desire to slice into her face and cut her down from the wall possessed him with a red-hot fury. Imaginary friends were part and parcel of normal boyhoods, as much as sucking thumbs. And that's all this was, he convinced himself. A phantasm born of an unfortunate choice in wallpaper forty years earlier by people who'd owned the house before his family.

He drove the sharp end of the tool at the woman in the wallpaper, who stood with her back to him. Then she spun and screamed. Blood flowed from her cheek.

"What's wrong with you?" his wife demanded, clutching at her face.

"I..." he stammered, the sentence going unfinished.

She stormed past him, howling in a mix of rage and hurt. Horrified, he froze, but then he thawed enough to place the sharp edge flat against the wall. A chill traveled up from the paper, past the instrument, his flesh, and even his hand bones, to the part of him he thought of as his soul, and the deepest cold filled him, stilling further action.

He drew back. If he lingered, if he looked, the woman in the wallpaper would have, at long last, turned her head around and she'd be staring at him.

The faint smear of crimson he left upon the wallpaper was not lost on him. Their blood was on the walls now.

GARGOYLES OF THE WORLD, UNITE!

Mary Jo Rabe

Annegret Gumpert shivered in the wet, bitterly cold wind. She had just stomped out the monument-protected, sculpted iron door of the archdiocesan chancery office building. The physical weather outside was similar to the emotional climate inside her head. She walked down the Schoferstrasse slowly to the Herrenstrasse, cautiously watching out for speedy bicyclists who took no prisoners when it came to pedestrians.

She wouldn't exactly call the moisture in the air rain, maybe just thick, heavy drizzle, though combined with cold temperatures and gray skies, definitely unpleasant. Annegret should have dressed more appropriately for November in Freiburg before she went outside. Sometimes, though, she just had to leave quickly before she told people too far up in the hierarchy precisely what she thought of them.

It was her firm intention to begin her noon break by hurrying over the cobblestone footpath to the farmers' market surrounding the cathedral. She would either get some healthy, fresh fruit or instead a bun filled with a greasy sausage smothered in curry-flavored ketchup, depending on how she felt when she got there.

Then, depending on how the weather developed—Annegret had no great desire to get completely soaked in the cold, pouring rain—she considered taking the long route back to work, first south to the Dreisam River and then back through narrow, old-town streets past the Augustiner Museum, a favorite hang-out of hers.

A brisk, lengthy walk always calmed her down. Unfortunately, it now seemed to be raining harder.

Her ankles were swelling up again. She had spent too much time that morning cataloging the new acquisitions. Annegret's feet didn't approve when she sat at her computer for too many hours at a time. It wouldn't be easy to appease them. However, at her age, risking pneumonia wasn't the better alternative.

She wiped the sweat off her slightly wrinkled, middle-aged face. Her short, graying hair was starting to drip. It was time to move faster. Actually, her leg muscles were in good shape. Annegret was grateful for the fact that most days her work in the little special library wasn't a sedentary activity, today being an unfortunate exception.

Ordinarily, she never left the chancery office in the evening with her step counter showing fewer than fifteen thousand steps. Delivering requested books and circulation materials to eager and impatient readers spread out over four different buildings all day helped her accumulate multiple kilometers. The work was occasionally stressful but generally delightful.

Most library users valued her work; only a few arrogant, incompetent lawyers made her work and life at work miserable. That hadn't changed in thirty-plus years.

The exercise she got at work also helped her stay fit though not exactly trim. However, her weight was almost within healthy limits for her one meter seventy centimeters height.

Exercise was especially beneficial now that she was pushing fifty and hadn't been lean and mean for decades, although maybe still mean when displeased. Especially mean when her options against the chancery office lawyers were limited.

However, now that she was on her lunch break, she didn't want to think about the idiot church bureaucrats who made her work unnecessarily difficult. She didn't want to think at all. Annegret made a deliberate effort to empty her mind.

She crossed the now wet and slippery Herrenstrasse and walked carefully down the equally slippery cobblestone footpath to the east end of the cathedral, where she suddenly heard an annoying humming. Actually, she didn't hear the sound exactly; the noise came from inside her head and made her feel like her skull was going to explode.

She shook her head and looked up. The first thing she saw in her wet line of vision was one of the cathedral's gargoyles. It happened to be the one that showed a horizontal, humanoid figure stretching its naked buttocks out away from the cathedral.

As coincidence would have it, these naked buttocks pointed toward the palace where archbishops used to live in less than politically correct times. In accordance with its architectural purpose, rainwater flowed out of the gargoyle's spread stone cheeks.

What wasn't in accordance with architecture or even with the real world was the undeniable fact that the buttocks were undulating back and forth as if accompanied by music or as the side effect of some other activity. Annegret closed her eyes. Surely the damned lawyers in the chancery office couldn't have irritated her so much today that she would start hallucinating.

The humming in her head increased in volume and suddenly turned into loud words. "We've decided to talk to you!" the voice thundered.

Annegret opened her eyes and bent her wet head back to stare directly at the gargoyle. She wasn't hallucinating. The sculpture was moving while the rest of the cathedral wasn't. Wet tourists rushed by her while locals opened their umbrellas and passed by more carefully on the wet cobblestones.

"What the—" Annegret started to think.

"Good," the voice in her head thundered. "At least you're sensible enough not to talk to us out loud when others of your species might listen. Try to stifle your useless thoughts and listen to what we have to tell you."

Annegret shook her head to let the water run down her shoulders.

"We're enraged and demand changes," the loud voice continued. "You have been selected to be our spokesperson, and you must ensure that our demands are met." She thought the stone buttocks were shaking with rage.

Right, like Annegret was about to let ugly stone sculptures order her around. If she wanted to be shouted at, she could turn around now and go straight back to work in the chancery office.

Whatever this was, she didn't need it. She turned her back to the gargoyle's hindquarters and walked around the cathedral to the north side, where the local farmers had their stands.

A different voice in her head spoke up, this time a softer, more melodious one. Annegret looked up and saw a gargoyle that was a naked woman who stretched her torso away from the cathedral while stroking her right breast with her left hand. "I'm sorry if my colleague gave you the wrong impression," the voice in her head said.

Analyzing the situation one more time, Annegret decided she definitely couldn't be hallucinating. The data, audio and visual, and her thought processes were convincing. Librarians knew how to differentiate between fact and fantasy.

But why did the gargoyles choose her to talk to? She never really paid any attention to the outside of the cathedral. The gargoyle on the north side of the cathedral moved its hand in what might be a conciliatory gesture. No one else at the stands of the farmers' market seemed to notice. People continued to bargain for their lunch and chew their success.

"It took a while before all ninety-one of us at the Freiburg cathedral could agree," the soft voice continued. "And then we had to consult all our colleagues on the other Gothic cathedrals around the world. After all, we can only effect change if we act together. We thought you might understand and help us."

Annegret decided she definitely needed a curry sausage on a bun and not just a few nuts and berries. The voices she heard were real, and the gargoyles were moving. The rest didn't make enough sense yet. What was most real was that Annegret was cold, wet, impatient, uncomfortable, and hungry.

"We don't want to be unreasonable about our demands," the voice said. "All we truly want is some respect and appreciation."

Annegret shook her wet head. She knew what that was like. The damned lawyers in the chancery office never showed her any respect.

Still, this didn't make enough sense. "You are appreciated," Annegret thought. "For centuries you gargoyles have served as waterspouts. You're attached to troughs so you can divert rainwater away from the cathedral walls. Due to your efforts, the mortar between the stones doesn't get washed away as the centuries go by. You keep the cathedrals from crashing down. Everyone knows that."

"And what thanks do we get?" the louder voice shouted. "Everyone calls us ugly. You creatures made us deliberately ugly in your eyes to scare away evil spirits. But the joke's on you. You didn't scare away evil spirits; you attracted us. Every gargoyle and every grotesque is possessed by a spirit you would define as evil."

Annegret's stomach winced. She was starting to feel definitely light-headed. "So, you're not evil?" she wondered.

"All a matter of definition," the softer voice in her head replied. "We think we are natural and consistent."

"And everyone else is making money off of us," the loud voice said. "There are gargoyle TV shows, cartoons, movies, toys, and other merchandise. We're the genuine gargoyles, and we get nothing."

"Of course, we don't want money," the soft voice interjected.

"Could we continue this fascinating conversation after I get something to eat?" Annegret thought. "It's getting harder and harder for me to concentrate."

Annegret then felt a blessed silence in her head, and so she ran over to the nearest sausage stand. It was raining hard enough that no one was standing in line anymore, and she was able to wolf down two sausages, each swimming in curry-flavored ketchup with fried onions. Even the buns tasted like the grease the sausage was fried in, and Annegret felt her energy returning. Now she could use a sweet dessert.

That, of course, wasn't going to happen soon enough.

"We are powerful spirits," the loud voice returned. "If our demands aren't met, every Gothic cathedral on the planet will rise up into the stratosphere and stay there."

"You can do that?" Annegret asked in her thoughts.

"Indeed," the loud voice blasted inside her skull. "We are the ultimate evil spirits. We can do anything, anywhere."

"Really? Anywhere?" Annegret insisted. "Then why just the stratosphere? Why not threaten to move the cathedrals off to another galaxy?"

"You're right, of course," the softer voice admitted. "As spirits, we are bound to the planet, to its earth, wind, water, and fire, from which we get our power. However, within the gravitational reach of this planet we are powerful enough."

"Okay," Annegret thought. "I get it. Levitation. But if you are so all-powerful, why don't you just blast your complaints and demands into everyone's skulls. What do you need me for?"

"Well, we sort of struck a bargain with the elements when we coalesced with the stone figures," the soft voice murmured. "A large portion of our powers goes to maintaining our essence in the stone figures. We can leave and regain all our powers, but then we go back to being non-corporeal, which is fine, as far as it goes, but boring in the long run."

"To be brutally honest, you are the first person we have been able to communicate with so far," the soft voice continued. "We couldn't fight our way past the thoughts in other minds."

"And we don't intend to wait any longer," the loud voice said. "We have put up with enough disrespect."

Annegret needed something to drink. The curry-flavored ketchup had burned its way down her mouth and throat all the way to her stomach. She felt like throwing her head back, opening her mouth as wide as far as it would go, and letting the pouring rain soothe her mucus membranes. Maybe that would even quiet the annoying voices.

"No," the loud voice shouted. "Now that we have you, we won't let go. If you don't see to it that our demands are met, it will be your fault that all the Gothic cathedrals fly away together."

Annegret looked for a place where she could sit. The rain had driven all the tourists away, and so she quickly took a seat on a wet, wooden bench next to the cathedral. No one from the chancery office seemed to be in the vicinity. To be honest, she was beginning to welcome gargoylic distractions. They kept her from obsessing about idiots at work.

Annegret decided once and for all that the evil head of personnel still hadn't driven her completely crazy yet. The voices in her head were real and telling her the truth. Frau Dr. Grob's bureaucratic abuse hadn't caused Annegret any permanent mental damage. There was no way her imagination could have come up with this scenario.

She wanted to help the gargoyles. While she still thought the age-old advice about getting even instead of just getting mad was valid, this situation was more complicated. The gargoyles had a valid complaint.

Annegret, of course, wasn't particularly religious. Over thirty years working in the archdiocesan chancery office drove such sentiments out of her. On the other hand, she liked looking at cathedrals. There was something about the architectural artistry that she found pleasing. To be brutally honest, she couldn't help feeling flattered that she might help save Gothic cathedrals.

"All right," she thought. "What are your demands?"

"We want to be worshiped," the loud voice reverberated through her skull. "We want crowds on their knees around every Gothic cathedral in the world. We want to hear chants of 'Hail to the Gargoyles!' Otherwise, the cathedrals are going up to the skies and staying there."

"You want a cult of gargoyle worshipers?" Annegret wondered. "Worldwide? How am I supposed to manage that?"

"Present our demands and threats to people in charge," the loud voice said. "This will require international efforts. Every cathedral must have a group of worshipers surrounding it twenty-four/seven. The local gargoyles will teach you creatures the desired songs, chants, and prayers."

"You're out of your minds," Annegret grumbled. "If I tell anyone what you've told me, I'll end up in the psychiatric hospital in Emmendingen, and you won't ever have any worshipers."

"Give our situation some thought," the soft voice pleaded. "Surely you can understand how we feel."

"I do, and I will find a way to help you," Annegret promised. "However, you will have to leave the methodology to me."

Actually, she really did empathize with the gargoyles. She knew what it was like to work like a domesticated animal, not exactly literally, but even so, and then watch someone else get credit for or be allowed to undo all your good work. Thinking about a lack of appreciation for years and years would make her unhappy and impatient too.

"Give me at least a few weeks," Annegret thought. "After all, you've had centuries to brood about your complaints."

Annegret didn't know if that convinced them, but suddenly the voices were silent. Since she was now in the middle of a downpour, she decided against her extended walk and didn't even need it anymore. Her thoughts were back on track.

She stomped through the puddles on her way back to the chancery office. The gargoyles were right. They had been treated badly. She had to do something to help them.

She considered which colleagues she could consult without revealing too much. No problem. After all, she was a librarian. She could find any information she needed. The problem would be persuading people to do what was necessary after she had come up with a solution to the problem.

Obviously, it would be possible to encourage the growth of a cult of gargoyle worshipers. There were enough people in the world who were willing to believe or worship anything. She had seen it happen far too often. On the other hand, cults were fiendishly difficult to keep under control. Annegret absolutely didn't want to go there.

"What can you tell me about gargoyles?" Annegret asked Ulrike Mossner the next day. Ulrike was the head of the cathedral construction office for the archdiocese and a good friend of hers. Her office was on the fifth floor of the Augustiner Museum and had a panoramic view of old-town Freiburg, including the cathedral off in the distance.

"The Freiburg cathedral has ninety-one gargoyles, and we have repaired all of them at least once in the past twenty years," Ulrike said. She was a good ten years younger than Annegret, had long, blonde, wavy hair, and generally dressed like a supermodel, but somehow the two of them were always on the same wavelength, just trying to do a good job despite interference from various bureaucrats and lawyers.

"Yeah," Annegret said. "What do people think of the gargoyles?"

"Think?" Ulrike asked. "According to the people who run cathedral tours, most people want to know why we have gargoyles and why they are so ugly."

"Could you send the archdiocesan public relations department information about the gargoyles so that they could do more to publicize them, to make the gargoyles likable?" Annegret asked.

"Sure," Ulrike said. "We have all the information about the construction of the cathedral, including the gargoyles. The Augustiner Museum has more than enough high-quality photographs of everything in and on the cathedral. I just doubt that the public relations people would be interested."

"What if I asked them to give the gargoyles some publicity?" Annegret asked.

"You'd have to be pretty persuasive," Ulrike said. "However, the way I remember it, you are always persuasive when something is important to you. What's the deal with gargoyles?"

"If I do my job right, everyone will soon know all about them," Annegret said. "Thanks for the info. Back to work." She took off through the narrow, old-town, cobblestone passages back to the chancery office.

In early December, Annegret walked from the library in the chancery office to the cathedral at nine in the morning, an hour before the farmers' market would open. She needed to negotiate with the gargoyles without any distractions.

"Well," the loud voice blasted the inside of her skull. "Finally. When will the worshipers kneel around the cathedral?"

"Small steps," Annegret thought. "You've lived in these stone gargoyles for centuries. You can't expect things to change within weeks."

"What do you mean?" the soft voice asked.

"First of all," Annegret said. "No more guilt trips. You spirits chose to become one with the stone gargoyles. You knew that the human beings who sculpted them deliberately made them ugly and scary. Yet you chose to merge with them anyway."

The vibrations from loud grumblings threatened to destroy Annegret's skull from the inside.

"However, you have convinced me that you deserve better. So, we have to change your image," Annegret said.

"Gargoyles have to become as popular as baby seals or cuddly little puppies or maybe penguins. Cathedrals need to trademark each of their own gargoyles and then license specific use, requiring gargoyles to be branded as sweet and admirable. They can hint at previous use."

"After we manage that, we can use social media to encourage people to become your fans. At that point, it will just be a matter of time until fans form cults that worship the gargoyles. It's really just a matter of effective product placement."

"Gargoyles from each cathedral will have to encourage their own fans. I can get all the public relations work started and forwarded on to other cathedrals. I think, if I mention the money-making aspect, all the church organizations will be eager to make their gargoyles seem loveable. You, however, will have to persuade your colleagues in other cathedrals to accept these conditions."

"Do you think this will work?" the soft voice asked.

"Yes," Annegret said. "I will get it done for you. You deserve a better deal. However, I have a request of my own."

"You have to show results within one year," the loud voice boomed in her head. "Otherwise, we owe you nothing."

"What do you want?" the soft voice asked.

"If there aren't crowds kneeling around the cathedrals, chanting their praise of gargoyles, all bets are off," the loud voice continued to thunder. "If we feel especially disappointed, we'll lift all the Gothic cathedrals up to the sky and then let them fall back to earth and disintegrate. We spirits can always seek other residences."

"Fair enough," Annegret agreed. "Then it's time for me to get back to work. My request merely involves your moving some stones of the cathedral to crash down on a few bureaucratic heads, people who make my work difficult. Maybe a few others as well. I would give you names and descriptions."

"It's a deal," both voices said. "You do your bit and we'll do ours."

In fifteen years Annegret would be forced to retire. It would be pleasant to work for fourteen of those years without the interference of her adversaries in the chancery office.

And it would be quite invigorating to get the gargoyles what they wanted and deserved, to have a goal worth pursuing, instead of staying mired in the tiresome infighting in the chancery office while she tried to protect her library.

Time to get to work.

THE GROTESQUE

Rhonda Parrish

The breath of the house rushes
from your bedroom window
pouring over my weathered hide like water.
It warms my twisted form,
melting the early morning frost from my spine.
A caress, lending me strength, hope,
because the house knows.

The house knows what the dark conceals,
it watches every night,
watches and shivers
and fears.
It groans in sympathy.
The sound swells, from cellar to attic
but you don't hear.
Sleeping, comfortable and content
on the safe side of the glass,
you never hear.

Come dawn you open your window,
examine me, perched on your sill.
You marvel at the deep crack on my wing,
the jagged piece absent from my claw.
You wonder, think it a great mystery,
but the house knows.

The house knows.

DEVIL'S OAK

Mary Leoson

1903.

Marguerite dreamed of the tree long before she touched it.

Its bark was rough beneath her hands, mountains and valleys of jagged teeth under blankets of soft Spanish moss. It stretched over the grass like a cloud, its shadow looming, its branches octopus arms reaching for the ground. Its leaves sang in the breeze, its gentle tune in harmony with the multitude of insects nestled there. She'd wake from climbing its branches, leaves tickling her face.

It was a tree for stories, for late lunches on hot summer days, for secrets and first kisses. It held all these memories for her family—at least that's what her Mama said. She'd see for herself one day, maybe take her own beau there. Walk in the footsteps of their long-gone matriarch, Grandmére Marie, lady of the plantation.

As Marguerite grew, the tree burned in her mind like a sigil. It was hope amidst the humdrum of chores and lessons. She was southern royalty, her Mama said, born to one of the most elite families in Louisiana. They had but to return to the land for her to remember—and for it to remember her. They no longer held the plantation in title, but the earth would recognize their blood, bless them with its bounty.

It was during her fifteenth year that Marguerite returned to the family home. She and her Mama were distinguished guests of the new owners, the Habers, who ran the plantation with sharecroppers. They traveled from Alabama to Mississippi to

Louisiana, all by train. Once they arrived in New Orleans, it was another several hours in an automobile out to the land, just a few paces from the Mississippi banks. Marguerite imagined what such a trip must have been like before, on horseback or wagon alone. She grimaced and thanked the Lord for her family's connections. Those were rougher times for rougher souls.

Her Mama had painted descriptions for her—a sprawling land with sugar cane and billowing trees under a blue sky—a place of promise. Lavish dinners around a fancy table, music and servants, a grand four-poster bed fit for a princess. An alliance was all it would take to regain their station—a marriage to one of the Haber sons. Her Mama had set the stage for betrothal to Stephan, the eldest Haber boy.

She wore her Sunday best on this trip, a blue gown of the finest silk with a red ribbon encircling her slim waist. "Like a bow on a gift," her Mama said. The dress was more expensive than even the china upon which they ate.

It was a lie.

They had nothing—not since Father was taken by tuberculosis. He was only a hazy memory now, weak around the edges and shifting in her mind's eye. Now, Mama was almost out of favors from kind folk.

"Best to present as the royalty you are so they can see your potential," Mama said. "Bending the truth delicately is all women have ever done."

Marguerite left Alabama expecting the promised land—a husband, a reclamation of their rightful property—victory. But what she found at the gate of the old plantation felt like doom.

Tall leaves waved at her over the arms of white fencing, their pointy tips like fingers begging her closer. They leaned with the wind, whipped around to face her, snapped to attention under her gaze. They stretched to the sky, gray and threatening, begging for death.

She could not tear her eyes away from the sugar cane reeds. They were ugly, wild. This was what had brought her family fortune? The fields choked close to the mansion, ready to swallow it whole, with only the fencing shackling it at bay. But as they approached her old family home and the cane fell into the background, Marguerite's eyes grew wide. This was more like the fairy tale her Mama had spun.

They rode beneath a canopy of trees toward the two-story mansion. A grand porch stretched the entire length of the second floor, supported by stately white columns. Two large cisterns stood on either side of the house like guardians, catching rainwater from the roof, holding it there to wash sins from bathers. Upon closer examination, the manor's face was marble and decorated with intricate paintings, many of which, Marguerite would later learn, were branded with her great-great-great grandfather's initials. He'd put his mark in many places, and where he missed, his wife added it, even after his death.

As they pulled up in front of the house, remnants from the passing shower gathered in puddles, waiting to spoil her pale blue gown. She fidgeted in her seat, eager to stretch her legs but unwilling to mar her clothing. She twisted the red ribbon that circled her waist—a nervous, unbecoming habit. Her mother turned to examine her, looked disapprovingly at her daughter's handiwork.

"Let it be, child. Don't fray the satin," she said.

The young man who carried a rolled rug toward the automobile was handsome. His pale eyes met hers, crinkled at the corners with his smile. His yellow hair was combed nicely, his face clean-shaven, his hands steady as he unrolled the carpet and covered the muddy earth to smooth their passage toward the mansion.

"I am Stephan, my lady," he said, holding out a soft, unscathed hand to her.

She accepted it, and her Mama nodded approval.

It was after formalities had been exchanged and Marguerite had her things delivered to her room that she snuck away to explore the grounds. As she moved further from the big house onto the land, she breathed in wild things waiting for discovery.

The mangled live oak was a terrible beauty. It rose from the horizon higher and higher as Marguerite drew closer. It stood on the far end of the property, past the fields, work areas, and old slave quarters—now homes to sharecroppers and their families.

Finally at its foot, she felt her breath catch in her throat. It was even more mythical looking than she had imagined, for the girl's mind could only create so much. There was a feeling she did not expect—a hum that rose within her chest in time with beating hearts that lay on the other side of the veil. Her ancestors, watching over her, whispering her name, recognizing their blood. She felt them standing beside her, a ring of entwined hands around the sacred tree.

The trunk was thick and knotted, filled with crevices and dark places for furtive, sneaking things. Marguerite caressed its bulk with her eyes. She allowed her gaze to rest here and there on indentations that seemed like pockmarks where dark moss gathered. The girl wiped the dank, rotten lichen away from one hollow to reveal a stone embedded in the bark. It was marked with initials—M.H. She located another, and yet another, each carved with different family monograms.

She looked up the trunk into the tangle of gnarled limbs, and her Mama's words came back to her. "They say the live oak is evergreen. For when a leaf is ready to die, another takes its place and carries on its mission." Leaves, young and old, waved at her, courted her with a gentle hiss.

She sat at its base, her back against the trunk, soaking in the gentle tree's shade from the fashionably late sun. The roots had drunk most of the rain, but she had placed a mat beneath her backside for comfort. She pulled out her book, then a red cedar pencil, and began to draw.

When Marguerite woke, she was surprised to find the sun almost setting. The evening creatures were lulling soft tunes;

frogs, crickets, and owls crept in the shadows. She gathered her things and followed the path back toward the house, its windows like distant beacons.

She passed the outbuilding behind the manor, the external kitchen brimming with delicious smells and rich laughter. Her eager stomach growled, and she peeked in to see three dark-skinned women preparing food. She offered them a smile, but they looked down to their work, averted her gaze. Their bodies stiffened, their laughter was squelched. She was an outsider.

"Forgive my intrusion," she muttered and continued on her way.

Dinner inside the big house was formal, though Marguerite was in no mood to enjoy it. The chiding she'd received from Mama had dampened her spirit. "You are not to run off with the forest beasts, young lady. What will they think of a girl returning to the house after dark? Shame on you."

"I merely wanted to visit the tree—"

"Not one more word, Marguerite Isabelle. Mind your Mama."

And that was that.

Marguerite behaved as was expected of her, using the correct piece of silver for each course, daintily sipping wine from crystal, dabbing at the corners of her mouth with an embroidered napkin. She laughed when appropriate, asked questions and feigned interest in all topics of conversation, and graciously thanked her host and his sons for their hospitality. She even demurely flirted with the blond son, the eldest, who she did find handsome. But her mind was drawn back to the outkitchen. To the laughter. To the warm, rich voices. To the beautiful dark faces that fell when they saw her—like she'd infected them.

"Sir, if I may," she began at a lull in the conversation. "Who are the women in the outbuilding? The cooks? Are they in your employ?"

The gentleman was surprised by the question but not offended. "Why, yes, my dear. When the War of Northern Aggression ended and our way of life was interrupted, we retained some people as sharecroppers, some of their wives and daughters as help around the plantation."

Mama shot her daughter a warning glance and said in a lighthearted tone: "Such serious conversation, Marguerite. You're liable to bore our hosts." Her laughter tinkled above the table like a bell and the others joined in, though nothing was funny.

And Marguerite wondered how it would feel to eat dinner with the women from the outkitchen instead, surrounded by their warmth. The laughter here was loud but empty.

The girl climbed into an elevated, four-poster bed and was almost swallowed by the feather comforter. She sank into its softness, feeling the luxury around her like a warm embrace. A gentle breeze whistled in through the windows, shifting the sheer curtains, making the flame on her bedside candle dance. It dripped wax onto the pewter candlestick holder in a long tear.

She placed her book on the pillow and turned to the pages with the drawings she had made of the tree. The sketches were ethereal, a sample of bark, a hint of the canopy, one close-up study in leaves that looked like fingers. A single acorn, the dark bottom like chocolate with a pale caramel cap. But when Marguerite turned the page to begin a new drawing, an image peered out that she had no recollection of creating.

The sketch captured the tree from its base, looking up into a monstrous canopy that spanned the whole sky. It loomed and crawled, leaking off the edges of the page, hungry. And as she turned the book in her hands, examining the pencil strokes, the various grains that she did not consciously know how to make, an eye came into focus. It peered out from between the branches like the center of a storm, untamed and angry. The branches framed it, hugged it, crinkled around it in a fury—the eye of the Devil himself that looked upon the land.

An eerie cry came in with a gust through the open window.

"Oh!" she exclaimed. Marguerite jumped, slammed the book shut. She jumped again when a second gust spit hot wax from the candle, spraying it onto the table. The flame blinked but continued to burn.

She strained her ears to catch another sound. Bugs chirped, leaves sang, but there were no human voices, nothing but the late summer night. It was just her imagination. But as she fell into dreams, she was brought back to the devil's eye and what it had seen.

The fire burned brightly in the path before the slave quarters. A white man walked toward the gathering of dark-skinned children. They were afraid at first, but then they saw the sweets, and their eyes grew large with delight.

He served the biscuits on platters for them, dipped in the middle, filled with molasses —a treat indeed!

"Catch them with the sweets as children," the man said. "Let them grow big and strong, so they'll produce sweets for you." He offered a crooked grin, something dark behind his eyes.

Marguerite woke with a sticky mouth, the taste of molasses lingering, bitter-sweet.

Packages came the next day, special order from New Orleans. Marguerite knew they could not afford new clothes, but Mama smiled and said, "Don't you worry your pretty head about it, sugar."

There was a dress of pink chiffon, one of white taffeta, and one of deep purple satin edged in lace. She chose the pink one to match her cheeks, which she pinched to blush, then darkened her lips with a stain.

Her dark hair hung in ringlets beyond her shoulders, courtesy of the hour she'd spent the night prior winding them around rags. Now she looked worthy of the dresses. Mama gave her a nod of approval on her way down to breakfast.

Marguerite offered a pleasant smile as the servant girl placed a dish before her. The child's brown hair was plaited, with skin that looked kissed by the sun, her pale eyes far away. Freckles sprinkled her nose, and a small scar marked her brow with pink. She couldn't have been more than ten.

"Genevieve, we'll take more tea now," said Haber in a firm but kindly tone.

"You are so generous to welcome the mulatto girl into your home," said Mama. Marguerite had heard the word before, though her Mama usually called brown children "those people." A foggy memory rose to the surface of a long-lost friend; they'd once shared laughter, tears, and secrets until her Mama found out and forbade it. In her mind's eye, the child's brown fingers intertwined with Marguerite's small, pink ones, but the image was gone just as quickly as it had come, leaving only a dull ache in her chest. Grace, she thought, that was her name.

"Genevieve is quadroon," Haber corrected her. "I do what I can to help those in need and to make up for... certain... indiscretions."

Her Mama blushed. "Well, what a kind gesture. Isn't that right, sweet?" She leaned toward her daughter with raised eyebrows.

Marguerite nodded as if she understood, though she didn't. Something about their exchange felt dirty.

When she visited the oak a second time, Marguerite approached with caution. She half expected the canopy to come to life—lift a lid and reveal an uncanny watcher. But it stood frozen, like a painting in the dank southern air, haunting and beautiful. A wet mist clung to the branches, blending into the sky, blocking out the sun.

Despite the alluring scene, she kept her distance, sketching from outside the perimeter of a mushroom circle. If this was her family's legacy, she should feel a sense of comfort, familiarity, home. The beauty was endearing, but the foreboding twisted her stomach.

The hair rose on her arms with a creeping sense of somehow being watched. She scanned the horizon for evidence of company but found nothing. Just the stalks waving gently in the breeze, which shifted them one way then another, a hush rising from the rhizomatic, collective consciousness that was the sugar cane. It whispered, groaned, settled back into the landscape, but never stopped breathing.

Marguerite placed her sketches aside and stood. If this was her family's land, she should not feel so unwelcome. A specter of entitlement arose in her breast, filling her with boldness.

She approached the tree in small steps as if trying not to frighten a wild animal. Blades of grass tickled her ankles, the moist air clung to her skin. She swiped at a loose curl that kept returning to her forehead despite her efforts to tame it. The roots were thick under her feet, tangled and reaching, drawing her in. She imagined feu follet hiding there, beneath the mushrooms or inside notches in the trunk, waiting to lure her with mischievous lights. Under its canopy, she studied the arms of branches, reaching out to the sides and up toward the sky. Her eyes traced their length, searching for spiders and monarchs and sparrows. Spanish moss hung down like fine lace, graceful and delicate. And as she moved closer to the trunk, she heard the hum.

It was a dull vibration, all one note, low and consistent. Marguerite recalled the base tones of the cello she played back in Alabama and how the sound moved through her body, tickling her insides. She drew closer, placing her hands on the bark, leaning in until her ear was against the rough surface. The drumming was thunderous, like a million stamping feet at once. She jumped back, startled and exhilarated by this discovery.

It was a secret the tree shared with her, perhaps one of many. She bowed with a healthy respect for its majesty before returning to bed for the night.

As Marguerite reclined in the billowing pillows of the princess bed, she became lost in her thoughts of the humming tree. Drowsiness overtook the girl before she even knew it was upon her.

The air smelled of sweat and fear and blood. It hung heavy around the dark-skinned men as they marched along the river, rage burning in their chests. They moved together as one, the fingers of a hand. This was how they would take the captors down.

Some fell, but the devils came on horseback, wielding weapons against which the men on foot had no match. If anger could kill, they would be victorious, but fury was fed by blood. So the white men bled them, stole their spirits. They seeped into the ground, ran in streams to the river, became the snake.

Their heads were sliced crudely from their necks, then placed upon poles to remind anyone contemplating resistance about the fruits of punishment for rebellion.

The severed heads lined the river in decoration where they rotted, a gruesome necklace for a hungry demon.

And the tree watched.

It was still dark when Marguerite woke from her nightmare, sweat slick on her chest, her hair matted to her neck like wet blades of grass. The girl's heart beat against her chest in painful thuds, like she'd been running along with the dark-skinned men, frightened for her own life. This was silly, she knew—to breathe life into old stories spun to frighten children. They were nothing more than fairy tales. Weren't they?

The wind howled outside, angry, unsettled.

After lighting the candle, Marguerite crept into the hallway, the light casting strange shadows about the hall. Each step creaked under her in argument, bidding her back to bed, but her stomach growled.

Before entering the kitchen, she paused before the oil painting depicting her Grandmére Marie, the lady of the plantation. It was not the first time she had studied the portrait, but the angelic form that had greeted her in daylight took on long shadows in the candle's glow. Her dark hair held the same hue as Marguerite's, a warm brown with hints of gold and red. Her nose had a similar upturn at the end, too, petite and round. But that's where the similarities ended. Rather, she saw her mother's face in the oils, right down to the lime green eyes. Grandmére Marie's expression was firmer than her mother's, commanding and harsh, with a wrinkle between her brows. She wore a royal red gown with white lace beneath that suggested a softness but promised nothing.

Urged by her stomach, Marguerite moved on to seek refuge in the kitchen but felt the lady's gaze upon her as she crept.

When she was sneaking back up to her chambers, she found Stephan leaning against the wall outside her door. Marguerite flushed immediately, glad for the poor candlelight. She wiped crumbs from her lips, held her head high in false confidence.

As the space between them closed, she saw the eyes that had once seemed so gentle now held foreboding. Brow bones above the light circles were heavy, casting shadows downward at a sinister angle. His gaze did not wander; his expression did not soften upon her approach. Stephan's bulk blocked her passage to the door.

She hesitated.

"Ladies should stay locked up in their rooms at night." His voice was a low growl. She could smell the drink upon his breath.

He moved closer, adjusted the candle in her hand to the side. He examined her, and she realized the light might suggest her form beneath her nightgown. She flinched, stepped back, but he caught her wrist, held tight.

"You never know what lurks in the dark on these lands," he whispered.

He held her gaze and she swallowed. His grasp loosened; his hand moved to her face, caressed it. His fingers drifted down her neck to her collar bone, lingered there, then began to move south.

The slap landed hard on his face. It rang out with a crack that echoed, yet no one stirred. Marguerite used the moment of shock to pass through the door and secure it behind her before cradling her hand. It throbbed already. It was her drawing hand.

"Full of fire." His voice penetrated the door. "I like it."

She heard him stumble down the hall, his door closed. And then the tears came. He was no gentleman. He was something else.

Marguerite woke early and dressed, hoping no one heard. It was no small feat to don her gown and lace her shoes with a sore hand. Then she crept down the stairs and into the garden. The stone path led her beneath an archway of trees and through flower beds, some in bloom, some in wait. It meandered to a fountain at the edge of the property, where water sprinkled from an angel's lips, her wings spread wide. The cool stream was a prayer sent to the Lord, landing in a sea of hope among other wishes. Marguerite interrupted its journey with cupped hands, sipping the water to cleanse her soul. Then she stared down into the water, looking for clarity but finding only her wavering reflection.

She thought of her Mama, all the dreams she had placed on her shoulders—reclaiming the family land through marriage. But Stephan was not a good man. He was not kind, was not gentle, though his mask told a different story. He knew the right things to say, the graces to offer a lady, but underneath was something sinister.

No. She would not marry that man.

She had never said no to her Mama before. Never. But the fear grew inside, ebbing ever closer to anger. It was taking on a life of its own. She would not be condemned to Stephan's whims.

His voice emerged from the house just then, a call out to his father about breakfast. Marguerite shuttered and leaped to her feet, then darted toward the side of the big house, crushing all of the flowers and crawling ivy in her path. Safe in the shadow of the large cistern, she paused to catch her breath and watched as Stephan strutted down the path like a show horse. Then he paused abruptly, turned as if he sensed something, looked in her direction. His gaze remained, and Marguerite felt her breath catch in her throat.

Then he smiled.

And she ran.

Marguerite's legs were not accustomed to such activity, but she quickly put distance between herself and the big house. Though she left him far behind, Stephan's wicked grin reached after her like a noose, ready to snatch her up and hold tight.

She ran past the outbuilding where the food was prepared. She ran past the blacksmith's barn and the horse-filled stables and the woodman's ax, still stuck in a stump like it had been the day before. She ran past the old overseer's quarters and the sugar cane with the bowls set out for boiling until she reached a gravel path and her ankle gave way. She sank to the ground in a sweaty heap, the sun beating down with no forgiveness. The pain was sharp and made her wince.

When the shadow fell upon her, she tensed, but it was not Stephan who stood there.

The woman's faded dress brushed the ground, and her apron was dirtied with kitchen work. Her dark eyes held concern. "You alright?" she said and reached out a hand.

Marguerite accepted the help and hoisted herself to her feet, placing her weight on her uninjured foot. She hobbled after the woman, who helped her sit on the stairs of a modest dwelling.

"May I?" she asked, gesturing to Marguerite's ankle. She nodded in return.

The woman's hands were cool as they moved along the ankle bones, muscles. She closed her eyes and mumbled something Marguerite could not quite hear, and her hands became warmer. Before long, the heat was almost unbearable, but as the girl winced, she took them away.

"Can you walk now?" she asked.

Marguerite hesitated, then placed some weight on the ankle, expecting the pain to shoot up her leg. There was nothing.

Amazed, she looked at the woman in wonder, but she was already climbing the stairs to go back inside.

"Wait," begged Marguerite. "Thank you. I don't understand—" she stopped herself, realizing her words might be rude. "Thank you for your kindness."

The woman nodded, turned back to her climb, then paused and glanced back. "The tree is bad. Don't go there."

Marguerite stared back at her with a hundred questions, but no words came to her lips. Their eyes were locked in an embrace. Eyes like deep pools of coffee and chicory with endless bounds of strength and warmth. A face gentle and nurturing, proud and carved from worry, hard work, and mothering. Mothering like the girl had never known.

The tears filled Marguerite's eyes quickly as the woman disappeared into the house and closed the door behind her. She brushed them away and rerouted her journey, away from the tree that haunted her dreams.

Marguerite wandered far to the back of the plantation, knowing she shouldn't be there. She lingered, enjoying the serenity, with many paces between her and Stephan. Her Mama would be more than cross, but there would be no more running from conflict.

Maybe if she was less appealing, if she wasn't a proper lady, Stephan wouldn't want her. She schemed as she walked, her feet sinking into the boggy mud. The land was softer here, with cattails and a film of moss on rocks and roots alike. She made herself terrible—dirty and unkempt.

She came upon the swamp with little warning, the stench of decaying things and rotten eggs reaching her first. The land sloped downward into a mass of murky water and cypress trees. The tented trunks had deep ridges and disappeared beneath the water, while the thin treetops reached to heaven, coated in shawls of gray Spanish moss.

A symphony of insects filled the air, creaking, chirping, and buzzing. The lull was disturbed only by the sucking mud grabbing at and then releasing her shoes with each laborious step. They were ruined, muddied, and ugly. This was just the way she wanted to return.

She scooped up the tainted water, including the squishy silt upon which it lay, and smeared it down her cheeks. She scooped and smeared like a ritual, bathing herself in the dank mixture until she was of the swamp. Then she headed toward the big house and to the unhappy reception that waited.

The long trek back and the sweat mixed with swamp remnants were putrid, but the thought of shocking those at the dinner table was delicious. She peered through the window at the lovely scene. The table was set with fine china atop white linen, flanked by stately silverware. The crystal glasses were filled with sweet wine, and the candles on the table cast a soft glow. Her Mama was seated to their host's left, leaning more closely than chaste. Marguerite's nostrils flared as she spied, wondering if her mother had designs of her own for marrying into the family. Had she forgotten there was already a Mrs. Haber back in New Orleans at their main residence? Mr. Haber's visits to the plantation were infrequent, and thinking otherwise was just a fairy tale

At the clearing of her throat, Mama jumped. She sat back quickly, composed herself, glanced at her daughter through the window. She cocked her head to one side, a quizzical look contorting her face.

"Well, sugar, do not linger outside. Come in and announce yourself properly," she said, and glancing at the gentleman beside her, let out an embarrassed laugh.

"Yes, Ma'am," Marguerite replied and did as she was instructed.

As the warm candlelight kissed Marguerite's form, the audience took in her appearance. Her Mama's emerald eyes grew large in her bony face, and the whites expanded. Her expression shifted from surprise to shock to outrage in a matter of seconds. Her mouth elongated, then pursed, moved, but no sound emerged. Then she gasped in denial.

"What is the meaning of this?" Haber's voice filled the room, and his fist pounded the table. The silverware rattled, the china clinked, and feet could be heard scuffling in the hall. His normally somber face was an angry red, bright against his graying, pointed mustache.

Stephan rounded the corner into the room, eager to see what the excitement was about. He paused in the doorway, his handsome face full of amusement at first, then changing to disgust. He held a hand to his nose and backed out of the room, disappearing back into the dark.

As Haber fumed, and her Mama fainted, and Stephan retreated, it was Marguerite's turn to smile.

After a rough scrubbing from Genevieve, who only did so at the barking of her employer, she was banished to her room. For most of the bath, Marguerite basked in victory, knowing she had ruined all designs Stephan had about violating her purity. She would not be a prisoner under his gaze. She was free, and yet...

It wasn't until she was tucked into bed, clean under a cotton shift and soft blankets, that shame began to set in. Her heart softened to her Mama; perhaps she was not warm or nurturing, but she was always there with constant direction. Her Mama was not perfect, but she did love her.

Marguerite studied the rain as it slid in graceful smears down the windowpane—a prelude to a coming storm. She could hear it in the distance, the rumbling thunder, followed by flashes of light against the horizon. It spoke to something deep within her, but she couldn't cry. A war was bubbling inside, and there was no room for tears.

As she relaxed into sleep, Marguerite was haunted by whispers from the past—both those of her blood and those that sought it.

The hole in the ground was like a grave, but not as wide nor as deep. It was as if a mouth had descended from the sky and bitten the earth, leaving a gaping wound. No grass grew, no roots sought water, there were only worms there, writhing into and out of the wet soil, ingesting it and eliminating it again, but never cleansing the earth of evil.

The land called to Marguerite, luring her to its embrace. And she followed, unbothered by the mud caked on her feet or the stains clinging to the edge of her nightgown. She wanted to see what was inside, to crawl into the depression and curl like a newborn. But as she crested the edge of the unclean hole, ready to step foot into the darkness, the shouting began.

In the space of moments, a dark cloud cloaked the sun and what had been stillness became chaos. The shouting grew louder, and though she couldn't decipher words, the tone elicited terror. Marguerite ran toward the great oak tree, hid behind the trunk's bulk, and peered out to see what was amiss.

The dark-skinned man was large, his shoulders three times the size of any man Marguerite had seen. His face was curled into something more than anger. He spat when he yelled and pushed the small form in front of him; it fell onto all fours, then struggled to walk upright again.

As they drew closer, she could see his victim was a woman, thin save for her protruding belly. The scraps she wore barely covered her, and she struggled to stay ahead of his wrath. Behind them both was a white man with a nonchalant gait, an expression of stone. He waived a hand like an order, and his minion passed sentence.

The woman was shoved facedown to the ground, her pregnant belly fitting into the hole there. His large arm reached back, struck toward her, a whip extending from his hand like a tentacle. The crack was sharp against her skin and left a red wound that leaked around the edges. Her winces were strangled cries, and with each strike, Marguerite tensed more, digging her hands into the tree's bark while shock stole her voice.

But on the third lash, she emerged from the tree's shadow, shaking and horrified, and yelled at the man.

"Stop!"

Her childish voice rang in her ears, but the man did not falter.

Again, she cried: "Stop!" Tears poured down her face. Either they did not hear her, or they did not care. Marguerite shrank back to the tree, crumpled upon its roots, wanting to shut out the cruelty.

The beating continued, and when it was over, the woman was motionless on the ground. The white man uncrossed his arms and glanced at the tree with the hint of satisfaction on his face.

Marguerite froze, not knowing if he could see her, if he had heard. When his eyes passed over her, they showed no recognition, but the image was unmistakable. She saw her own face in his, from the clear blue eyes to the high cheekbones, to the brow that was rounded in a hairline that came to a widow's peak. This was her blood.

As they disappeared into the distance, leaving the woman motionless on the ground, nausea rose up from Marguerite's bowels violently, choking her, creeping up her throat. Roots emerged from her mouth like spider legs, writhing in an effort to be born. She pulled at them, and they pulled back like bony fingers, and then she woke to her own screams.

The fever struck in the early morning hours as rain pelted the roof over Marguerite's bed. Her head swam, her vision hazed, but she did not know if it was the heat or the memory that scorched her mind. She could still see his face, haunting the grounds, watching as the woman was whipped, revealing the curse from which she'd been born.

Her mother was a liar. This was no sacred ground, no royal family—it was darkness. Pain. Horrid turpitude of the worst kind. It whipped mothers. It stole heads from men. It lured children with sweets until they stuck in the corruption like bees, wanting to feed their queen.

She heaved onto the floor, and the liquid burned her mouth, her nose, and landed with a splash. She stared at the puddle, her widow's peak glaring back at her like an accusing finger, then reached for water to cleanse her burning throat. Marguerite closed her eyes and gathered her thoughts, then lit the candle beside her bed, wincing at its brightness. She crept to the dresser and dipped a washcloth into the porcelain bin there, placed it to her forehead, and felt momentary relief.

But as the girl returned to her bed, she noticed dark fluff poking out from beneath the covers. In the candlelight, it was an endless hole, waiting to suck her down into its depths to drown her in nightmares forever. Shaking off this foolish notion, she pulled back the covers carefully and poked at the odd substance.

It was soft, a pillow of fuzz. Bouncy, light, but not feathers. Even back in Alabama, the mattresses and pillows had been stuffed with feathers, no matter how their savings dwindled. There had always been that small luxury. But this was something else.

She pulled at it, investigating the depth of the issue. Handful after handful she pulled out, thinking at some point feathers would emerge, but it was just more of the same material. She had heard of horsehair being used for such purposes in desperate times to stuff cushions for chairs and the like. As she sat with a clump of the strange fiber in her hand, surrounded by the mounds she had extracted from her mattress, pillows, and even the blanket atop her, realization dawned.

The dark texture was not the consistency of animal hair. It reminded her of only one thing. Human hair. Hair from the heads of the slaves she'd seen in her dreams, like from the woman who'd healed her ankle. She had been sleeping in their remnants.

Marguerite froze. She dropped the ball of hair in a pile where it joined the other mounds, and she backed away like she had sprung a trap. The full weight of this abomination was too much for her to comprehend, too sickening to believe, yet there it was. She could not—would not—ignore what she saw with her own eyes. Nausea rose again, and she embraced it, emptying her insides of the evil she felt around her, releasing the poisons from her body.

Her ancestral home was a tomb.

Marguerite ran.

Her head pounded and her fever persisted, but she ran. Out the bedroom door and down the stairs, she ran. Through the dining area and out the backdoor to the stone path, she ran. Past the kitchen outbuilding, the blacksmith's barn, and the horse stables, she ran. And Marguerite stopped when she reached the woodsman's ax, still resting in the stump.

It gleamed in the lightning that flashed above, like an obscured, glistening spirit, winking at her, knowing. The implement was heavier than she expected, its wooden handle too large for one hand, so she grasped the haft with two. The blade aimed downward, she pulled it along as she stumbled, now weary from her sprint.

The sky grew angry, thunder bellowing, lightning not far behind. But Marguerite continued on her way, past the overseer's quarters and the boiling stations, all the way to the gravel path. She took one last look back at the big house, cisterns standing their guard on the horizon, windows still dark. Maybe she should have burned the entire place down with all the evil inside. The sky cracked above the girl, reminding her of the mission, and it released a torrent of rain that beat against her brow. The drum of water striking land surrounded her, pushed her on, and even after it lessened, Marguerite could still hear its echo in her ears.

When the devil's oak came into view, it was breathing like a panting, wild thing. The wind sucked its leaves one way, then the other. The roots were thick under her feet, tripping her as the wind howled her name. What had welcomed the girl before now bade her not trespass.

Marguerite. The woman's voice was soft, beguiling. Marguerite. It was sweet, filled with sugar, tempting.

The girl turned away from the tree to the place where she had dreamt of the hole in the ground, from where the whispers now drifted and a real hole opened. The rain slowed to a hush, the air heavy and waiting.

The woman's form was beautiful, shining. As the wind gusts returned, it floated toward her, conducted by a symphony of waving sugar cane stalks behind her. The vegetation spread quickly, sprouting from the ground in all directions, reaching out for fresh blood.

Marguerite. The voice soothed her, beckoned her, bewitched her. It was her Grandmére Marie, the lady of the plantation.

As the phantom drew nearer, Marguerite found its green eyes like those of her mother. She wanted to be held, to put her head on this great lady's lap and cry herself to sleep. To feel so safe that nothing could ever hurt her again. The taste of molasses was upon her lips, sticky, dripping with promise.

But Marguerite faltered. She gazed at the looming crater and remembered. The pregnant woman. The men with no heads. The children tempted with sweets. And she turned her attention upon the tree.

The voice that had been sweet began to howl. The shrill pitch went higher and higher until Marguerite wanted to cover her ears and scream, but still she walked forward. Sugar cane reeds struck like whips, catching her in the ankles, the arms, drawing blood. The mounting pain spurred her on.

Beneath the oak's umbrella now, Marguerite drew back the ax with both hands and, with all of her strength and indignation, delivered a blow to the trunk. She pulled the weapon back and swung again, slicing the place where her grandfather's initials had been carved. Again and again, she struck the tree until the hollow inside revealed itself.

The swarm hummed, freed from its purgatory. Against the dawn light, the bees rose into the air. The souls of the children cried, the women screamed, and the men shouted. They danced for a moment, merging into one being, a mix of joy and vengeance.

They did not need sugar; they already had honey, and they fed the queen no more.

Lightning struck the tree, splitting it in two, throwing the girl from her feet and feeding the bees' fury. The swarm pulsed with rage.

And though Marguerite stared, mouth agape, after the boiling cloud of revenge flying toward the big house, she felt no regret.

THE DAY IN GOLD

Adele Gardner

Beyond the Tympol Mountains, on the lower slopes of the Dolian peaks, a crumbled tower stands like a misplaced lighthouse. The ruin lists toward the mountain slope from which it springs, a great hole blasted in the uppermost wall as though punched by a giant fist. Loose stones litter the ground, cracked by age, but nothing living touches the sides of what remains of the Tower of Kyrnos.

In ancient days, this tower loomed over the valleys with stark magnificence. Sunrise never touched it, though all the peaks glowed pale rose with Brychia's light; it never caught the red fires of sunset, though Brychia swelled immense on the horizon. The tower remained harsh and lifeless, and even today, though the stones fall away like deserting followers, it retains this quality.

Yet one day in every seven thousand years, each remaining stone alights as if from an inner flame, and the entire crumbled monument gleams gold. On such a day, folk sing the ancient chants against evil and stare at the tower with horror as if Brychia has fallen from her throne and lodged there among the hills.

And the shepherds of that region whisper of the Day in Gold.

Long ago, it seems, when the Tower of Kyrnos yet stood arrogant and aloof, seven sorcerer-priests dwelt there. They had come from the farther reaches of the Tympol Mountains and raised a tower in that spot, so they might always gaze down upon the doings of folk in the valleys below. While they built this edifice, which threatened the Dolian peaks for height, they infused its stones with prayers to their god Dharak, the enemy of Brychia. They raised this architectural challenge with their spells in defiance of the sun, choosing gray stones that would never blush at Brychia's rays.

At first, the valley people of Kyrnos noticed not the monstrosity that rose on the slopes above them. But soon, shepherds began returning to their villages to whisper of the ungodly thing that loomed on the slopes above, and people began to cast their eyes toward the east with fear.

Before long, the sorcerers grew bored with merely gazing from their tower. They discussed their plight at night when Dharak, the demon who stands between two worlds, had overthrown Brychia once more. At last, they agreed upon a solution that Nistor proposed through the guidance of a nightmare. They would inscribe a rock with many laws, then send it rolling down into Leinat, the nearest town. These laws would be very complex, and the mere sight of the runes atop the stone would compel people to obey them, whether these folk were literate or no. Their obedience would give strength to the Tower.

The sorcerer-priests set an antithesis on the other side of the stone to balance the magic, and in that opposition was the alchemy to overturn the stone and its laws—even the Tower itself. The stone would never roll into the village without such a balancing. This was a gamble the sorcerer-priests made with the gods for their power. But the Masters of the Tower of Kyrnos, trusting to the ignorance of the people below, doubted that any would ever set their antithesis in motion.

As a capstone to their art, the wizards pledged that whomsoever broke their laws would be taken to the Tower and punished.

Now this proved a pleasant diversion for a time. Many there were, in all of Kyrnos, who did not even see the stone and thus did not obey its obscure laws: for it had rolled beneath a large tree and settled there in Leinat. Around the stone, the village elders arranged a series of smaller rocks that had tumbled down the mountainside in times past. These could be used for seats, while the stone, they felt, would serve for a table on sunny days.

The sorcerers eased their boredom through the folly of those in the valley. For a time, they took great delight in seeking out those who broke their unspoken laws and leading them to the tower one by one through various artifices, such as wondrous animals or promises of hidden wealth. And there in the tower, they punished their victims with tortures too horrible to mention, some beyond human imagination being spawned by curse-born demons, all in the name of the arch-fiend Dharak.

It was not long before the people began to notice the mysterious disappearances of their townsfolk, and shorter still till they recognized the blasphemous, sun-defying tower as the source of all their troubles.

Sometimes they would sight one of their number wandering off toward the ashen spire as though in a trance, but nothing they said or did could break through the daze of a friend or stop a cousin's fateful climb.

And the people of Leinat began to curse the Tower of Krynos and despair.

After a time, the Masters grew weary of their sport and devised yet another. Leinat had very few inhabitants left now, so the wicked thaumaturges had taken to punishing only one lawbreaker every hundred years as a token gesture. They turned to other amusing pursuits, such as causing rivers to run uphill, which left communities to uproot, die of thirst, or make war on neighbors who did not suffer these catastrophes.

The people turned their eyes to the distant stars for succor, for Brychia had no influence over the tower, but the stars had no strength to heed their prayers. With the centuries, the Masters grew more subtle in their dark arts. They tormented an entire village with a single, sublime death or drove people mad to the grief of their neighbors.

In her sorrow and misery, Brychia began to shrink. So slowly, at first, that her loss of stature was not noticed by her worshippers in Kyrnos for many generations, but the Masters in their tower observed the phenomenon as though it had occurred in a single day and rejoiced. While the sun shriveled with grief, the Masters took strength from their dread actions and prepared a sacrifice for their lord, the god-demon Dharak. And as they did this, the years that their stone masterpiece had stood mounted toward seven thousand.

In all this time, sun-worship had been secretly maintained in the village of Leinat through the courage of a long line of priestesses who taught their daughters and passed down their secret lore among the few followers they could trust. Though much knowledge had been lost, there were still those who knew how to read the old runes.

On the eve of the seven thousandth year of the Tower of Kyrnos, two young sun-worshippers, Dal and Jareth, went walking under the glory of Brychia's evening rays. Jareth stopped beside a strange jumble of stones just beyond the borders of the shrunken village. The decaying remnants of a tree rotted beside a rock pile, which had stood there so long that it had been forgotten. But tonight, Brychia dusted the mound with the color of fieldan-roses, alone in all that landscape, causing Jareth and Dal to look at the stones with new eyes. Together, they shifted the pile to see what lay beneath.

"Why, it looks like a boulder, inscribed with the old runes," mused Dal when they had cleared the pile of loose stones. He frowned and set his fists at his hips. "I do believe," he muttered, then trailed off as the laws took command of his mind.

The heavy stone had settled into the earth, shifting to one side. Jareth had not seen the top of the rock as Dal uncovered it. She was staring at the other side, so immersed in what she found that she scarcely heard Dal's words. More runes were visible, creeping from beneath.

"Dal, come over here," she urged, trying to puzzle out the half-visible runes. For her mother, Selepha, a weft-woman and priestess of Brychia, had taught her daughter the ancient tongues and other arcane lore.

Dal, whose eyes had locked, uncomprehending, on the strange runes atop the stone, made a great wrench of will and looked up. Jareth stared at him anxiously. She grabbed his arm across the boulder, pulling him to her side. Though Dal had but newly gazed on the Laws of the Tower, he broke the most sacred of the rock's commandments through the entreaties of the one he loved: he helped her overturn the stone.

Jareth stared for several moments at the runes they had uncovered, gently rubbing away the clinging earth with the sleeve of her tunic. As she peered at the ancient words, Brychia leaned over her shoulder and touched the symbols with crimson, marking them in fire so that they appeared to have been carved there, indelibly, by the sun herself. Jareth read aloud, haltingly:

Beware the day when the sun turns gold
Shun high walls and towers old
Watch and pray for the death of blight
That day when nature overturns night
And the fieldan-rose burns amber-eyed
Beware and watch, but do not hide
For mine enemies shall crumble all
Beware the Day in Gold.

"Dal," Jareth said, one last ringing word that she could not resist, completing the pattern the way her mother had always taught her.

She looked up at him, frightened, and their gazes locked in an understanding that went beyond mere words. They both turned their eyes involuntarily toward Brychia. But the sun had already sunk below the farther hills, leaving the faint hue of rose on the horizon. Lest they be caught out-of-doors without the sun's protection, they retreated to their village homes.

The next day Jareth rose early before even Brychia had stirred. She woke with her heart pounding and a dizzy feeling that her world had gone awry.

"Dal," she murmured, and upon that instant, every nerve awakened. It *was* Dal. Dal—

Quickly, she threw on her clothes. She ran out of the house without alerting her old mother and raced across the ancient track. Jareth pounded on his door and receiving no answer, she slipped in the back way as he had shown her. No one was within, and Dal's bed appeared unused. Fearful, she ran out of the house and stood gazing up at the Tower of Kyrnos.

As she did so, the sun began to rise behind the curving line of the Dolian peaks. Jareth tried to calm herself, knowing that soon she could call on the sun for help, but when Brychia finally crested the peaks, it was all Jareth could do to keep from screaming.

Brychia had donned a baleful shade of yellow and looked more sickly and bleached than ever, as though she had been so consumed with hate that her very death was near. Jareth crammed both fists into her mouth, scanning the hills wildly. At last, she caught sight of Dal. He was only a tiny grain of sand, slowly drifting up the mountain toward the Tower of Kyrnos.

Leinat had not yet wakened behind her. She ran off toward the tower, leaving the streets quiet at her back, slumbering, bathed in the ill rays of the amber sun. Jareth's only coherent thought was that she must save Dal. As she ran, Brychia gilded the dirt track behind her until the streets she passed were paved in bilious gold.

Jareth ran until she could not breathe and then slowed to a walk, mounting the foothills beneath the Dolian peaks. Her fear and the unnaturally harsh sun soon made her ill, but as soon as she had her breath back, she ran once more. Dal was nowhere in view, but she could see the tower clearly. It loomed over the lower hills, tall and straight and gray. The spire rose to at least thirty times the height of a human, and its many stones had been fused by sorcery so that neither seam nor joint remained. Cold as an ice-barrow—inhuman coldness to oppose the warmth of gentle Brychia. A sob caught in Jareth's throat. She prayed to Brychia as she ran, stumbling and gagging on her tears, for she mourned both Dal and Brychia, goddess of the soft rose flames of day and the crimson furies of evening's glory.

When Jareth looked up again, Brychia had passed noon and neared evening. She did not have much farther to go. Jareth halted because she had seen something she was certain that no one else had ever seen. Brychia, in her strange and baleful hue, had begun to...

Jareth squinted and looked again.

Yes, she thought and breathed a small, tentative sigh of joy. Brychia had faintly touched the sides of the Tower of Kyrnos: its gray walls showed the slightest tinge of *gold.*

Jareth ran toward the Tower of Krynos again, renewed by the sight, and as she did—craning her neck for a better view—she caught a glimpse of something that chilled her blood. As Brychia neared her nightly death, the Masters prepared to extinguish her forever through one final, mighty sacrifice to the demon Dharak. Thus they stood, with the now gray-robed and briar-crowned Dal, atop the tower's roof.

His eyes had been teased carefully from their sockets and hung from their stalks upon his cheeks like the delicious buds of the brychia-tree, whose generous arms hold a cornucopia of the edible roses of the sun. For the Masters had painted Dal's orbs entirely in shades of gentle pink, a mocking metaphor that held within it their truth: the Darkness that festers at the heart of all things.

Jareth fell to her knees and raised her fists against the Tower. She gazed upward, full upon the horrors visited upon Dal, the horror that Brychia had become, and she prayed to that wronged sun as none, priestess or commoner, had ever prayed before.

Jareth began with abundant praise of Brychia, offering the sun her life. She appealed with all her heart, with such fervor that Brychia, on the verge of setting, swelled back into the sky. With Jareth as the lens, Brychia focused all the bitterness of bygone millennia into a single burning hatred for the gray Tower of Kyrnos, that blight upon her people, that obscenity which blasphemed against her and all that was wholesome.

And Jareth, sobbing, begged of Brychia one final boon.

As the sorcerer-priests ripped out Dal's heart with a tainted knife, Jareth screamed and flung both her fists toward the Tower of Krynos.

In answer, Brychia threw her soul against that blasphemous citadel through the heart of her priestess. Where Jareth's fists pointed, she blasted a gaping wound in the demon-warded stone, and such thunderous groaning smote the air, as might not be contained within the bottomless pits of the eternal abysm.

The hearts of the immortal Masters stopped cold at the grinding in their tower.

A gaping crimson hole in Dal's chest shone gold in Brychia's terrible rays. Dal lurched upward, stretching his arms toward Jareth in a circular gesture of embrace. Then starkly, grimly, each step guided by Brychia's gaze, Dal faced the priests of Dharak and strangled each in turn till their heads popped off like miniature, bloody suns.

Jareth beamed. Horror and gratification were singed on her face. She watched so intently it seemed that her fury burst through the tower, great boulders flying as though her fists had swelled to a thousand times their mortal magnitude.

As Brychia's amber rays smote the gray tower, that structure burned for all the warmth of the sunrises and sunsets it had denied over the eons. The roof shot upward in a surge of golden flame, and debris rained down around Jareth. The upper walls blasted outward, showering the valleys with melting stones. Soon only an ashen skeleton remained.

The shrieking of the remaining Masters of the Tower of Kyrnos rang forth like a thousand damned souls, but louder still was the smacking of lips and grinding of cruel teeth as the insatiable god-demon Dharak consumed them all.

When the Day in Gold had passed, and folk surveyed the wreckage from afar, some brave few ventured forth to discover what had caused the collapse of the Tower of Kyrnos. One of these was Jareth's old mother, Selepha. She found her daughter crushed beneath several large boulders, her heart's blood staining them crimson—as bloody as the sun Brychia, who had set only last night in a shower of golden flame.

Brychia awoke in rosy splendor, though her splendor was grief. Some few say that Selepha found on Jareth's face a beatific smile of satisfaction.

And now Jareth's bones have crumbled away; the rocks that litter the landscape are mossy with age. Yet the base of the Tower of Krynos remains, looking like a last toothy grin from the demon Dharak, clawing in defiance toward the sky.

And on one day every seven thousand years, even the boldest shepherds stay at home and mutter of the Day in Gold.

HE GETS HUNGRY SOMETIMES

Carol Gyzander

The little dark-haired boy walked toward me through the park with one hand under the shoebox, holding the other on top to keep the lid from blowing off in the afternoon breeze. He paid no attention to the boys and girls playing all around, and they gave him a wide berth. The boy placed the box on the bench next to my purse and clambered up to sit at the other end; his feet swung below him, not even touching the fall leaves on the ground.

There were several holes in the top of the box, about the size of a pencil.

Breathing holes?

Munching on popcorn from the vendor's stand, I watched him out of the corner of my eye as I turned the page of my book. He whispered to the box and held it up to his ear. Listened to it. Smiled.

A couple of kernels blew out of my hand and landed on the bench between us. He eyed them for a moment, then reached over, snagged a small piece, and poked it through one of the holes. Stroking the top of the box, he smiled again.

When he saw me watching, he ducked his head and then peeked up at me with big brown eyes that made my heart melt.

The boy spoke softly. "He gets hungry sometimes."

Sometimes? Like a snake? Yikes. I fought the urge to leap off the bench. "Oh, really? Is that your pet?"

His little head nodded. "Yeah. His name's Rocky."

I suppressed a giggle at the idea of a pet rock, named Rocky, in the box.

Three little girls squealed and called to each other as they began playing tag, running up and down the steps on the bleachers right behind us. He glanced over his shoulder at them, then went on. "He's a good pet. And he always wants to hang out with me. Even when nobody else does."

I turned toward him a bit and managed to smile. "Well, I'm glad. Not everyone has a pet when they're your age, you know. You must be pretty good with... pets."

His forehead wrinkled as he frowned. "Yeah, I asked for a dog. But Dad doesn't want any noise and Mom doesn't want any mess. So, this is what I can have. We watch old cartoons together and we're just right for each other."

He patted the top of the box.

It must be a snake. What else could it be? I mentally shook myself a bit. *Tarantula? A snake would be better. Right?*

A pair of boys about his age were playing catch near us. One threw the ball to his friend, who missed it; the ball sailed over the other's head and rolled toward us. My young companion's arms tightened around the box and he hugged it to his chest.

"That's just Jimmy," the boy whispered to the box, as he held it safely away from the danger. "He won't notice us. He never does."

Jimmy ran over to pluck the ball from under our bench—bumping into the dark-haired boy's feet but not even acknowledging him as the ballplayer threw it back to his friend. Once the boys had moved away, joking and laughing among themselves, my companion relaxed a bit.

A foul odor blew in and I wrinkled my nose. *From the garbage can nearby? Dang this city. More people who pee where they shouldn't?*

We sat quietly for another few minutes, and he poked a few more pieces of popcorn into the box. After a while he looked up at me. "Ma'am? Do you want to see Rocky?"

God, I hate snakes. But look at that face.

"Um, okay." I moved my purse onto my shoulder to make room. "He won't get away or anything?"

"No, he's a good pet. He won't run away. And he doesn't make any noise. I'm the only one who can hear what he says."

He slid over next to me on the bench and reached for the lid. I got ready to run in case the snake—or whatever it was—jumped out at me.

His little face beamed up at me as he said, in a goofy voice, "'And now, here's something we hope you'll really like!'"

Cradling the box on his lap, he pulled up the lid.

A piercing shriek made me swivel—one of the little girls on the bleachers behind us had finally noticed him. She stood with one hand over her mouth, the other pointing at the boy and what he held.

I looked inside and saw a folded piece of old towel. I gagged at the putrid aroma escaping from the box. Nestled in the middle was something that made my heart catch in my throat.

A squirrel. That wasn't moving.

Rocky. Like Rocky and Bullwinkle. This poor kid's pet is a dead rodent. That's all his parents let him have.

I saw the hopeful look on his face and forced a smile onto my lips. "Aww, you're right. He is a cute little guy. You're really lucky to have him."

He stroked a finger along the top of Rocky. "Yeah," he whispered. "I am."

But wait...

I looked in the box again.

What ate all the popcorn?

I heard a voice whisper in my brain. *"I DID."*

VALHALLA IS A LIE

Benjamin Thomas

W e lit a fire in the dead woman's chest because we
needed heat, and the aroma would keep unwanted
animals away. We found her body in a greenhouse, clutching
a triangular shard of broken glass. The blood on her wrist was
coagulated into a syrupy, purplish gel, and her torso had been
split open and picked clean.

"Reminds me of a turkey," Cat said and screwed a silencer
onto her sidearm.

"Oh man." Egan dropped his pack against a raised garden
bed filled with weeds. He rubbed his thinning stomach.
"Remember Thanksgiving? Family and food? God, what I
wouldn't give for a bowl of stuffing."

"I never liked stuffing," I said. They both stared at me.
"What?"

The setting sun burned red ribbons across a clouded
evening sky. We could taste a coming storm in the air. Feel it
in the amplified ache pulsating through our joints.

"How much farther we got?" Egan asked. He unzipped the
top part of his pack and started fishing through the contents
like a claw arm in one of those vending machine games.

Cat threw a fistful of dead plants on the fire. Sparks
cascaded upward like inverted snow. The glow illuminated
her face, her buzzed hair, the scar running along the ridge of
her left cheek. "About a hundred miles, give or take. Figure
fifteen or so a day puts us about a week out."

Egan tossed a bag of rice from hand to hand and smirked. He was missing two top teeth but somehow managed to keep the hiss at bay. "What pioneers we are. You know, if covered wagons forded the River Styx and not some brook out west."

"Please," I tossed a stone at the flames. "The west is nothing but charred land at this point. Would probably be easy to walk across if it weren't for, you know, falling spears and all."

Cat stopped cleaning her pistol and unsheathed her knife. "You don't really think it's all burned, do you, Gray?"

My full name was Grayson. Everyone always dropped the second syllable, as if it was too much of a chore for anyone to say. I could have insisted on it, that or sir given my rank in this ragtag delivery mission, but I never did. When you watched your friends, your mates, your fellow rogues, and survivors—whatever we were going by at that point—be hunted, claimed, and skinned alive ... titles just didn't seem to matter that much.

Cat scooped a fistful of semi-solid blood from the dead woman's arm and slathered it atop her head.

"Jesus, Cat," Egan said, his lip curled.

She took the knife and dragged it across her scalp, peeling away the crimson cream and what hair that managed to grow in the last few days. "Do you know the last time I was able to shave with *anything*?" She scraped the side of the blade against a nearby block of wood. "I might be used to it, but razor burn is still a bitch."

Cat started shaving her head nine months ago, the same time she got the scar on the side of her face. Four of us were on a recon run when cloud cover swept overhead and, in a violent flash of lightning, a battalion of them dropped from the sky, spears raised from the backs of winged horses and war cries screaming from their blood-starved mouths.

Their red eyes burned beneath sleek battle helms.

We fought. Shot one in the shoulder and the torso. Watched her drop and writhe on the ground while her fellow riders raged on, hungry for us. For our souls. Cat screamed as she was lifted off the ground by a fistful of her own hair. She swung and clawed and spasmed like a feral animal pressed into a corner. The winged warrior thrust her spear at Cat's neck, missed, sliced open the side of her face, and dropped her to the ground ten feet below. She scrambled away on a broken ankle and sprained wrist.

The greenhouse glass—what was still intact—reflected our firelight like funhouse mirrors. Cat insisted on first watch. For the second time in our month-long endeavor, I pulled rank and ordered her to close her eyes. She was asleep in minutes, hand resting on the hilt of her knife.

I started to zone out and was drawn back by the sound of a stick scraping in the dirt. I looked up to see Egan sketching stars in the ground at his side. He saw me watching and flicked his makeshift pencil into the fire, absentmindedly staring at the container strapped to the bottom of my pack. "What do you suppose is in it?"

The container, the size of a shoebox and wrapped in a gun-metal grey casing, was the reason we left Buffalo and headed east with strict instructions and the GPS coordinates for our drop point. If I imagined hard enough, I could still taste Niagara Falls.

"I've told you before." I leaned back, using my pack as a cushion. "It's not our job to know. Just pretend it isn't there and close your eyes."

"That an order, sir?"

"Depends on whether you need it to be or not."

It should have been. Maybe if I directed him to sleep then and there, Cat and I wouldn't have found him later that night, thirty yards away and face down in the dirt as blood seeped from holes in his back the size of arrowhead stones. Cat ran a hand over her head and cursed. "At least when one of *them* dies, they don't leave a corpse."

I took a sharp breath and nodded at the ground. "That's most of our food."

Scattered near Egan's body and the spot where he went to take a piss was the rice. Little grains of edible confetti. The packaging was shredded, and we picked as many grains from the dirt and muck as we could, but we only salvaged a couple of ounces. More unnerving than the loss of our rations was the fact that the Valkyries were coming in quietly, no longer riding on battle cries and thunderstorms.

The moon danced behind fast-moving clouds, covering the ground in shadow puppets. Had we seen lightning? I couldn't remember. Exhaustion started to fog my brain, strain the muscles I needed most.

Cat checked and rechecked her pistol, ensuring each time that it was loaded. "I can't. I just—what the actual fuck, Gray? It's been three years of this shit. *Three years.* They were supposed to take us to the afterlife, prep us for the end, not hunt us down like rabid dogs."

"Maybe that's what they're doing," I said quietly. "Maybe this is how they choose who goes with them."

"They haven't been choosing ... they've been *killing.*" She dropped her hands against her sides. "They aren't even bringing us into battle anymore. Now they're taking us out in our sleep. How does that make sense? How are they supposed to select warriors when we aren't *actually* fighting?"

"We have been fighting," I said. "For decades, Cat. Whether physically or ideologically, the world's been a battleground since before we were born. The books just said they'd pick who does and doesn't go with them, not when or why. Worthiness is their discretion."

"I don't care what the books say," she snapped. "Valhalla is a goddamn lie. Being chosen to fight at the end isn't worth this. I don't care if it's some kind of test or just the way the world is actually ending. *Nothing* is worth this."

"We have a hundred miles," I said.

She laughed. "Yeah? And do you remember the first hundred? We lost four that week alone."

Caleb. Jim. Shay. Vikki. Three of them died together. "Everyone knew the risks, Cat."

She palm-slammed the magazine of her gun. "Doesn't make it right."

We were up, right as dawn started to break. I can't say for sure how long either of us slept. It's an elusive state of mind that tends to play with your perception of reality. As Cat walked the perimeter, I split open the last can of beans we had, label long gone. They simmered over the embers in the dead woman's rib cage, her flesh sizzled away and her bones stained from smoke and ash. I tried to think of how they found Egan and not us. Maybe it boiled down to it just not being our time. That was part of the fear: we just never knew when.

While we were eating, Cat looked up from her makeshift bowl. "We can't raid a town just the two of us. Abandoned or not, that's where they'll get us."

"It's either that or we starve."

"We'll hunt game."

"Cat." I scraped the bottom of a collapsible bowl. "We haven't seen so much as a single deer in days."

"Then we hunt rabbit," she snipped, then pointed her spoon at the case strapped to my bag. "Maybe there's food in that."

"If there is, it's not for us."

"Even if it means we die getting it to the coast?"

"Arriving without it is the same as being dead. And I'd take my chance with the ravens and their goddesses given the choice."

Before leaving, we paid our final respects to Egan. Cat rested two small stones over his eyes, pennies long since run out.

"He had two kids," she said when we were a few miles away, cutting through a dense wood to try and avoid the open road.

"Back in Buffalo?" I asked. Before all of this, I would have been ashamed not to know this basic level of information about someone on my team. Now? Now, not knowing made it easier.

"No," Cat said and paused against a massive oak. She rested her foot on a moss-covered rock and took a swig from her canteen. "They died when everything first happened."

"Fuck."

We were shouldering our packs when she asked if I thought they were better off that way. Sometimes, in rare moments of introspection, I caught myself wondering.

"No," I said. "If we died then, we would lose the opportunity to fix now."

Cat was right, based on training: towns weren't doable with only two. Our survival was based on area surveillance and avoiding predictable places. It wasn't feasible for one person to watch all the headings simultaneously. Storm clouds could roll through in seconds.

We ducked behind a burned-out car in the corner of a trash-strewn parking lot. Cat rested her rifle on the trunk while I used the hood. My crosshairs rested on the shattered front door of a mom-and-pop grocery store. Two buildings down was a bank, and across the street from that a gas station with only one pump still standing.

"I'll go," Cat said and slung her weapon over her shoulder. I put my hand out. "No. I will."

"Don't be stupid," she said. "I hate towns, which means I'll be more on edge and more aware of what's going on around me."

"All the more reason for you to keep an eye on my ass. Circle around that hill, and get a vantage point looking down. Put yourself as close to the bank as you can—if a hurricane comes, try for the vault. Probably be safe there."

She nodded, looked me in the eye for half a second, and then ran in a crouch toward the woods.

Cat radioed from her perch a few minutes later, and I gave the skyline a final scan. Clouds like snowbanks rose on the western horizon, but aside from those the sky was clear. I was fooling myself, trusting the horizon, especially after last night ... Egan.

I rushed from the burned-out car to the side of a bus terminal. Counted to ten, listened for wings, hooves, and the quick, sleek sound of unsheathing metal.

"Go," Cat's voice crackled.

My pack jostled as I bolted for the store. I scanned the alley next to the building as I rushed by. Caught a glimpse of three bodies, a flash of scarlet robes. My chest seized, and I dropped, sliding until the momentum stopped. I quickly rose to one knee with my rifle raised and pressed against my shoulder. The tatters of an American flag curled in the breeze. Snapped the side of the grocery store. I relaxed and radioed the false alarm to Cat.

The grocery store doors were chained and locked from the inside, but the glass on the bottom right panel had been smashed in. It crunched under my feet as I crouched through the opening. There were three cash registers at the front of the store. One of which was toppled upside down on the floor. Ceiling lights hung from single chords, and the aisles were littered with crumpled newspapers, empty boxes, and streaks of blood.

I pressed the button on my radio. "How's it looking, Cat?"

"Still clear. Hey, while you're in there, I'd kill for some peanut butter."

"From the looks of it, we'll be lucky if I find an empty jar."

Before the reaping or the rapture or whatever you wanted to call it (maybe the great culling of all humankind), wise people grocery shopped around the perimeter of the store and avoided the aisles. Fresh food and produce were always on the outside looking in. Now? It wasn't worth the time to look and try to find a half-rotten vegetable or plastic container full of browning fruit.

Surprisingly, on the bottom shelf in aisle three, I scored a box of pasta. Somehow it was missed when the store was raided the first time, and then the second, third, and so on. I shoved the blue box into my bag and froze at the suction sound of a cooler door shutting. I turned my radio to near-silent and held my sidearm out as I walked around the end of the aisle.

The smell of spoiled dairy and mold drifted toward me. I gagged, bit my tongue to keep from making noise. Sunlight beamed through a jagged hole in the roof. Dust motes swirled in the makeshift spotlight.

Sweat beaded on the back of my neck. Each step forward caused my heart rate to jump ten beats. A breeze blew through the hole and scattered papers across the floor with soft, scraping sounds. A cooler door opened and shut quickly; I spun, fired two shots ... and gawked at my reflection in the spider-webbed glass.

An involuntary breath left me, and I relaxed. Cat's voice was in my radio speaker. I turned it up to hear the end of her question. The word *happened.* I pressed the button, started to respond, and the Valkyrie dropped through the ceiling, her booted heel colliding with my chest.

I stumbled backward, collided with the floor, and rolled. My sidearm went one way, the radio another. My bag's strap caught on the edge of an overturned shopping cart. The Valkyrie swung, I rolled but was snagged by my bag and the cart. Her spear drove into the top of my shoulder. The joint exploded in searing pain. I kicked at the weapon's staff, shed my pack, and rolled. Cat was screaming through the speaker while thunder exploded overhead. I scrambled to my hands and knees, then to my feet, and stumbled across the dirty floor.

The Valkyrie swung her arm in violent strikes and shattered the cooler doors with the end of her spear. She was tall and dressed in scarlet robes with shining armor across her chest, wrists, and thighs. Her helm was narrow and angled straight, while her wings—my God her wings—were curved behind her and pressed together to stay out of the way as she navigated the confined space of the grocery store with divine grace.

The Valkyrie shrieked and the entire store shook. Her piercing outcry slashed at my ears like knives. A light snapped free from its precarious cord and ricocheted off the top of an end display. Cans of stale food rolled from the shelves and across the floor. Her eyes burned red like blood-soaked flames. I could see the hunger in them, and it made my stomach drop. I was going to die.

The ringing subsided, and I could hear pops of not-so-distant gunfire. I screamed Cat's name. Pressed against the toppled end of an aisle, I tried to gauge the run to the door. A crash erupted in the back of the store and I jumped up to run, surprised by the sudden maneuverability I felt. It took a second to remember my pack was gone—there was nothing on my shoulders, not even my rifle.

At the other end of the aisle, I could see my pack's strap wrapped across the shopping cart; the container clipped to the bottom of the bag. Goddamn it. Cat was right: towns aren't doable with two people. How stupid had we been? Was she still out there? Had she shot straight and made a run for the bank like I told her—ordered her—to do?

I pulled my knife from the back of my belt, its blade the length of my forearm, and took three deep breaths. "One. Two."

I jumped around the endcap and sprinted for the back of the store. I was halfway down the aisle when the Valkyrie jumped on top of the shelf, knees bent and arm raised. She thrust her spear forward with the look of death in her eyes. I deflected, felt the collision reverberate through my knife and into my wrist and elbow.

The block bought me time but not enough. The Valkyrie was on me, jumping from the shelves and slamming her boot into the top of my shoulders. She thrust her spear into my back three inches from my spine. We both howled as she ripped her bloody weapon out and drove it home. My chest exploded in pain as the air was forced from my lungs. I gasped, wheezed, and couldn't get air.

The Valkyrie rolled me over with the toe of her boot. Coppery warmth washed over my tongue. She reared back, mouth open, and the air chilled as it mixed with her frozen breath. My vision blurred. Pain vibrated through my chest, and as she brought her spear down toward my throat, the minor god's body lurched forward, spraying red from a sudden spat of holes.

She exploded into mist before she hit the ground, her presence in this world gone. Cat was in her place, holstering her sidearm and limping on one side.

"Get up," she urged and tried to help me stand. "Grayson, please. Please get up. Come on."

I put both my palms up and motioned for her to stop. She didn't, just shifted her attention to assessing the damage. Her fingers came off my chest; blood dripped from their tips. I pointed toward my bag, toward the container. Cat understood and went to retrieve it. I struggled to sit against the shelf, still amazed at what I had seen in the Valkyrie's eyes—the hunger, the want.

I coughed and drooled blood.

Cat crouched in front of me, my bag on top of her own. She held out my pistol, but I didn't take it.

"I'm not shooting you," she said. "So, either take it and do it yourself or take it in case another one comes back."

I laughed, and the pain made me wince. When I breathed, my chest hissed. "Take it; you'll need the bullets."

I could see the muscles in her jaw tense. "I'm leaving you one." She started unloading the weapon, but I put my hand on top of hers and shook my head.

"I won't use it. You know where to go?"

Cat gritted her teeth and nodded.

"Get on with it."

She looked to the door and bit her bottom lip, nodding in quiet agreement. She made a fist and slowly tapped it against my knee.

"I had a daughter," I said. She stopped moving and looked at me.

"What was her name?"

"Ashley. She died when they first came. Was out with friends and didn't have a chance."

"Maybe," Cat said quietly. "Maybe that was better."

I shook my head. "If you die at sunset, you'll never get to see the dawn again."

"And if you die in the middle of the night?"

"At least you got to see the stars. Get that where it needs to go, Cat."

She nodded, raised her hand in a wary salute and left. I rested my head back against the barren shelf and stared at the ceiling. The air started to chill, and around my body, the pool of red grew larger. Like small, rapid firecrackers, I heard the sounds of hooves in the distance. Thunder rumbled overhead. I closed my eyes, ready for the ride.

AEGIR'S SON

Edward Ahern

My parents called me Kevin. I was almost forty when I admitted to myself that I was not like other men. Not physically or sexually, no, all that was boringly normal. I realized that I was a sport—what other men held as important and sacred I viewed as inane.

I was more elemental, less framed by culture. All this I hid, of course. Mortgage and loans and the stuff needed for living meant lip service to others' gods while acquiring money. But while still acting in the peep show, I began to explore my innateness.

I was born under a water sign and am most at peace when close to or in that element. My youthful free time was spent swimming and scuba diving in locations remote from others. Boats, however, were never enamoring; their fiberglass or metal skins were prophylaxis to my pleasure.

My fiercest pleasures were careening through the aquatic, almost losing control, a flood-river tearing off its banks, risk sensed but not avoided. I began to search for a pattern of living true to my nature. And slowly, slowly, it emerged, like coral at low tide.

I was meant to be a son of Aegir, the primordial Nordic water god, and his wife Rán, who netted the dead, and I wanted to do my foster father's work. I would protect the waters, which, inevitably would cause me to hinder or harm other men. But how could I accomplish this?

Any individual action I undertook must be untraceable if I were to continue my efforts. And whatever I did should be water-based—the victimized element scourging the wrong-doers. After research I decided on *Dracunculus*, a nematode parasite.

The *Dracunculus* larvae are waterborne and spread by ingestion, making them a piquant addition to salad or iced tea. They grow undetected for about a year, so back-tracing would be quite difficult. The worms sometimes reach a meter in length. Pulling off the head can cause anaphylactic shock and quick death, and they are safely removed only by winding the protruding tail onto a stick a few centimeters a day—a penance of almost Lenten length.

This pestilence had been just about exterminated, with rare cases in humans and, in Chad, an infestation of stray dogs. I went to Chad on a forged passport. A foreign white man in Chad is an intrusive strobe light, so I hired a local to round up strays. It took the purchase and disposal of five dogs before I hit on the right one—the wispy tail of the nematode protruding from a leg ulcer.

I short-chained the dog and put its leg into a small bucket of ice water. The *Dracunculus* reacted promptly, spraying larvae and bits of blood into the bucket. Impossible to see the larvae, of course, but the discoloration was the telltale.

I gave Oath to Aegir, poured water from the bucket into a glass and drank it, gagging slightly. Bringing a diseased dog from Chad into the states would have been quite laborious and leave a highly visible trail. Bringing myself in as an undeclared and undetectable infestation vector was easy. I knew I had to wait for as long as a year before spreading the disease, but meanwhile I could identify and locate despoilers.

The first boil erupted on my thigh after six months. Despite the burning itching, I covered it with a bandage so that it might fester undisturbed until I was ready to spread offspring. The eruption was joined a little later by two others. I began to run a low-grade fever and feel nauseous.

Meanwhile, I placed an order at a magician's supply house—concealed forearm applicators that when modified could provide an almost invisible spray, activated by flexing the arms muscles in a particular manner. I was ready.

The unforgivable fouling of the water in Flint, Michigan was my first foray. Three of the politicians who had abetted the poisoning and delayed remediation would be at a party luncheon open to donors. Security was lax, and a donation and an assumed name were all I needed.

Not every larva would live to be a worm, but one spray would provide hundreds of larva and hopefully multiple infections. My gimmick was simple—getting autographs. The spray would spread under an extended hand into whatever drink or food was handy. The autograph book would provide additional masking of the spritz.

We Americans blessedly like our salad as a first course, and I was able to circulate through the ballroom as my three poisoners were still being seated. I was unctuous, they were flattered, and the spray was administered.

I then retired to a toilet stall, removed the applicators, and scoured my arms and hands with medicinal alcohol before the larvae could further infect me. I then returned to my seat and ate a hearty lunch—not wishing for my absence to be noted. Over the course of the lunch, my three victims—all men—made contact with at least forty or fifty others, making my identification that much more difficult.

Once my in-house parasites had bred more larvae, I moved on to the next victims. Strip mining, in addition to destroying the immediate environment, creates acid drainage that can render water undrinkable and uninhabitable for fish. A great many offenders gathered for a strip-mining convention. I posed as a potential investor with four of the men, and my problem wasn't infecting them; it was walking away while they were still trying to extract my money.

At this point I had to pause; the worms had begun causing vomiting and diarrhea. It was time they were removed. I took three small, thin slivers of plastic, rough-surfaced for traction, taped the little tails to the plastics, and very, very slowly wound, no more than two centimeters a day. After a month and a half of daily winding, the three petite heads slid out and the worms went into formaldehyde. We all have our little souvenirs.

Meanwhile, my foster offspring were growing in their new homes. I began to follow all seven perpetrators on social media and in the news. Once I thought my children were sexually mature, I initiated anonymous rumors that the culprits were infected with a loathsome pest that made them dangerous to be near others. I listed their symptoms (who knew them better than me?) and asked the gossipers and families to inspect for themselves, including the cold pool water they all swam in. I also circulated the false rumor that they had drunk of infested water, and that the water sources in their exclusive communities should be inspected.

There was collateral damage, of course, only once fatal. That I'm aware of. A strip miner with a heart condition died of anaphylactic shock. My surmise was that he had tried to yank out the worm, ripped body from head, and released the poison.

All my victims had access to expensive doctors who still took months to identify the causality, after which treatments began. The mortification that eventually leaked out on Twitter and Instagram was delicious.

This was merely phase one. The press, always slow witted, tweaked to the social media furor. Finally, one barely credible radical liberal source picked up my hint and noted that the disease was waterborne, expressing *schadenfreude* over the victims' dilemmas. My subjects were now aware that there was a structured plot against them.

I then placed masked calls to each of them, ordering that unless they wished another even more virulent infection, they would transfer a half-million dollars to a coded offshore account. Call it altruistic blackmail—the money, net of my expenses, would be retransferred to clean water projects.

They threatened and blustered, but once they'd run out of breath, I explained how easily they could receive a new and more deadly disease, and almost worse, that I would promulgate a warning to all their friends and associates that in view of their current and potential contagion they should be avoided, even shunned. They acceded, every one, and transferred the money.

There was one other collateral damage—*Dracunculus* hadn't really left me. A fourth worm ulcerated my left calf and showed its tail. There is no specific medicine to treat this infestation, and I would be forced to live with pain and burning itches for months, if not years, while I evicted my tenants.

I was also in a conundrum. What new watery tasking should I offer to Aegir? Would it mean mother Rán's further netting of my dead? Probably. Leprosy came to mind, or for a large group, dysentery. Or perhaps an artificial agent that would cause dry-land drowning. So many wonderful choices. Father must be proud.

BUTTERFLIES OF THE LONGEST NIGHT

Russell Hemmell

The world died in a solstice, together with the reasons we called ourselves civilized.

Words that linger and sting but cannot be avoided. Nor can what follows.

Heralein looks down at the letters on the silk roll gleaming under the dim blue light, liquid in their carmine silhouettes like wounds that have never stopped bleeding.

Her eyes follow the fleeting silhouette of a butterfly around the candelabra's flames in the eerie silence of the library. She's always alone in the underground library but never lonely. She has learned to love those somber and humid halls, where ubiquitous shelves coil up to the high ceilings in gravity-defying architectures.

Its hanging bridges cross over her head at different levels, only partially visible from the entrance but equally vertiginous, like pathways to a mysterious universe out there reflected in her writing. Wooden flowers, graphene-grade dragonflies, and mushroom-like shelving units crowd the marble surface of her desk, where she labors day after day, since the moment her own world has come to an end in a brutal, mind-shattering fashion.

How many nights?

How many months?

Her fingers search for the ivory quill, and Heralein resumes her work. She focuses, forcing herself to remember the events in all their frightening details: if all epic poetry requires single-minded devotion, the narrative of genocide imposes the burden of accuracy.

Eyes closed, she chases memories, feeling again warm ashes in her hands, hearing the deafening sounds of the battle and the thunder of enemy fire, seeing faces and shapes like in a magic mirror of doom.

She watches as the man—the one humans once feared so much—walks along the garden of the forked paths, through that city whose name is now a malediction, and even remembering it is insulting. For the victims. For him. For the only one still alive to tell the story.

She goes on, visualizing the ruins, the blood, and the corpses on the ground. And there she is once again, a little girl in the middle of the apocalypse.

It was a Litha, a Kronia, a Vestalia, and the ten thousand names humans gave to a glaring solstice that was, then like always, the very signal for the war to start.

The girl knows it from history: haven't all the first assaults started in late spring or summer when days are long, and nights seem to never come? That day was as long as a day could possibly be, under twin black suns like liquid steel on her skin.

Heralein has counted their war in days, weeks, months, and in a growing number of explosions. In piles of bodies, destroyed buildings, gutted cathedrals, until the longest day turned into the longest night, into another solstice, livid and plunging her world into darkness. Until nothing—and nobody—was left to count.

Except for the girl.

The man made certain she survived, safe in the eye of the hurricane where there's always silence and stillness. He, the man who was all the family she has ever had, no matter if their species were alien one to another, and who gave a lost, shivering Heralein a name and a place to live.

She had to watch him fighting against the enemies, the true monsters who exterminated the man's siblings and their Clan, without being able to do anything but weep with silent, angry tears of hatred. It's too late when she manages to free herself from the shelter he locked her in and runs searching for him.

And there he is, fallen along with the others.

He lies immobile, with broken wings and dark-green blood on his pale face, eyes staring forever at the binary suns declining on the horizon. She squeezes his hand, silky and gelid, and bends to kiss him farewell.

"Sleep well, Father."

Heralein remains on her knees for what looks like ages, a statue of salt among bullets, grenades, and killing rays pouring down from the sky, her soul shattering with the violence and sound of breaking glass, heart like a drum in her chest. Until her lips tighten and she dries her tears.

The time to cry is over.

She needs to memorize everything down to the tiniest detail and never let go. She has to make the entire galaxy know what the man can't tell any longer even if he wanted to, albeit she's well aware he didn't trust history as he has never trusted the human discourse. He spoke with deeds, fostering a harmonious coexistence of species in a system big enough for everybody to live and prosper, before the betrayal of the same people who have now slaughtered his Clan and turned that dream into ashes.

She's still there when the conquerors come.

"Who are you?" they say, encircling her but lowering their weapons. "Why are you here?"

One who must be their Commander glances at her with curious eyes. He must wonder what a young girl like her possibly can do on a battlefield, without realizing she was part of the battle, too.

"What's your name?"

Dressed like the aliens she might be, the girl is human. Heralein reads the enemies' thoughts on their faces as if they are an open book. No, she's not just human; she shares ethnicity, race, and planet of origin with the invaders. Yet the girl can't be more different from those savage beasts. Her rosy cheeks and ice-blue eyes, like pale diamonds, give her away even if she doesn't say a word.

"Were you their slave, maybe, or a prisoner?"

His questions are met by more silence and eyes that continue staring into the void.

A gleam like a sudden flame in the dark sparks in the Commander's eyes. He kneels and grabs Heralein's thin wrist, exposing her forearm. There. The officer finds what he's searching for: the confirmation of what she is, and what's more, of what her presence on the battlefield means. Her House's crest tattooed on her skin gleams under the shimmer of the rising moons.

"Commander—" a soldier stammers.

"Yes." The man in charge looks at the one who has spoken for a long moment before looking back to her. "She must've been kidnapped as a kid and kept hostage." A frown appears on his handsome face. "But who knows what they have done to her? These animals have proved to be surprisingly adept at turning humans into allies." Another silence, shorter than before. "Take her."

Muttering something she doesn't care to hear, two soldiers force her to stand up. Is she going to die like her Father and their Clan?

That's more than just a possibility, now that they've seen the crest of the once-powerful family she was born into. Especially if they fear she would dare to repeat what happened today. Humans have learned that lesson well in eons of never-ending wars they've waged among themselves: there are things better left unspoken and others not safe to conceive. The annihilation of a peaceful species is one of them, even more so if it has been carried out through ruses and savagery.

"Fear not, girl. I just want to listen to your story." The Commander's voice is sweet, like honey and milk. "You will tell me what you've seen."

Heralein doesn't reply. Her limbs move in a doll-like fashion when they drag her away from her Father's body and take her to their newly built town, the stronghold of the invaders on a now-occupied planet. No spires, but titanium-reinforced domes for them, no communal areas for music and chants but ugly churches in dark, slated structures. They throw her into jail and lock her in.

Famished and full of scratches still bleeding, Heralein isn't afraid.

Those dungeons, cold and eerily empty they might be, are made in silver metal with wide, glass-paneled windows, and even the ceiling is a vault of transparent crystal. This place looks more like a space station. She can gaze at the ten million stars out there and at all the heart-breaking beauty this universe bestows on her. Heralein smiles at the remembrance of when she was a toddler, and a scary, alien man she had just met was teaching her the stars' names in a mysterious, melodic language.

They keep her there for two full days and nights, cajoling and threatening, to persuade her to talk. They ask the questions over and over while her eyes remain fixed on the dark winter night peering in from a cloudless sky. She can't guess the colors of the stars from where she stands, but she can imagine them.

High-temperature blue giants, young and nervous. Yellow suns for creatures to emerge from their nests and evolve.

"Do you know who they were, girl?"

"Do you know what they were?"

Raging red supergiants, scorching the surface of all nearby planets and thawing up the cold, remote ones.

"Where did they capture you? When?"

"Does your House know you were living here?"

White dwarves, cold and tiny but oddly suitable for life. Brown dwarves, huge puffy gas balls that have never managed to ignite.

"Are you deaf, or can't you even understand your native language anymore?"

"She might be mute. Do you want us to mindscan her, Commander?"

Black holes that devour worlds and make galaxies swivel and sing.

The same man who ordered her arrest takes Heralein's hand into a tight grip and looks into her wide-open, clear eyes, fixed in startling immobility. She feels the warmth of his fingers and the distaste in his touch, and she knows at once he has understood. He lets her go with a nod of his head and makes a gesture to the others.

"Set the child free."

"Sir, this is not just a child. She's a child who will be heard if she decides to speak—" one begins, a hesitant tone in his voice. "She's a witness."

"Yes, she is. A shell-shocked witness. And she'll remain in this state for months or years. Later—" his beautiful face lightens up with a smile that would be angelic without that nasty glint in his pupils "—later, it won't be important, no matter where she goes or who she talks to. Or what name she carries. She could've dreamt up all things she might decide to say. Few will listen. Nobody will believe."

The heavy, metal-hinged portal opens up to let her pass, among whispers and surprises glances.

Heralein departs and walks for hours until her footsteps resound on the same ground of the solstice night. The scene is different now: they have mopped up all the mess, washed the blood away, and there are no longer dead bodies on a now-sanitized battlefield that looks immaculate and empty like a cathedral in the desert.

Some buildings of what were once suburbs dot the road, here and there, in darkened stumps and half-collapsed arches. But not for long: the iron logic of a genocide demands an erasure of all traces, all memories, whether they be embedded into bricks, liquid as water ponds, or shimmering in the eyes of birds. In a few months' time, not even a stone will remain of this ancient settlement, the jewel of Planet Nine and the most magnificent example of non-human architecture humankind has ever witnessed. Not even its foundations.

One wobbling step after another, Heralein's feet lead her in the direction of the only place on that world she knows something of the vanquished civilization still exists, unknown to the invaders. Under their very boots.

Unseen, unnoticed, she descends into the caves that surround the settlement and keeps walking by the subterranean river until, many days later, she reaches the entrance of an underground library on the shores of a crystalline lake full of carp and shimmering stalagmites. Her Father's ancestors have chosen the location well, Heralein murmurs, letting out a sigh of relief: if she can fish, she doesn't need anything else to survive.

She pushes the door and cautiously slides in. Darkness engulfs her whole until she lights up a candelabra and walks across the vast central hall.

The library is silent like a desert of stones. More, it looks like it has seen no visitors in centuries, and that thought comforts the hollow place in her chest where even the heart is a ghost. She'll make the place alive again, with her breath and her presence.

Her fingers caress in awe the thousand-year-old volumes lying on the shelves, some ordered in neat stacks, others piled up in misshapen heaps towering to the high-vaulted ceiling, designing bold geometries and filling the empty space with silent companions.

She ventures further down through a winding staircase, cramped and steep, for several stories, until a long, narrow corridor takes her to a system of circular crypts. Each one has wardrobes in steel with padlocks and graphene cladding and wooden desks here and there.

She extracts a silvery scroll and an ivory quill from the nearest cupboard and sits down, her spirit rising for the first time since the massacre, her will strong again. This shall be the beacon of resistance, the room where verses are written, and the past lives forever. Heralein swears on her Father's name, touching the ground. And there she will remain until her bones crumble and scatter like ashes and dust.

Because she knows the Commander is right.

They would call her demented and lock her up somewhere, should she ever dare to speak. They won't take any risk. They cannot. History's lesson dictates that a heinous truth is better ignored and domesticated in lies. Denied in its essence. Muzzled into oblivion.

But that is a problem she won't have.

Heralein will never tell. Not to them, not now. Not ever, to anybody—humans or aliens, friends or foes—for what passes from one mouth to another soon loses the consistency of fact. They become rumors, legends and one day, probably, myths. Victims transformed into boogeymen to provide a reason for their slaughter, their unusual features made grotesque to scare children at night and prevent them from asking for more.

She'll never talk again either because on the longest night she has learned to distrust words too. She will write it down, instead, for her silence to scream out loud forever in artful rhymes and coded symbols, on silk nourished with human tears and tiny letters inked in her own blood.

To bear witness and let it never happen again.

This is the way history is made. She'll smile, already knowing how the verses will begin: as they already have.

My world died in a solstice—

ODD JOB TOM

Eddie Generous

Most people looked down on him. Tom knew that. He could guess what they saw when they looked at him and didn't much care. Certainly didn't care enough to puff his chest, raise his voice, and explain that some people could live aside from the desires of excess. Odd Job Tom they called him, and it was right on the nose. Tom liked the alliteration, even if so many said his name as if in parody or sheer disrespect. A good many locals pegged him as stupid, even slow. He only came to Cooper's Lot nine years ago—after the tragedy— and supposed if he had gone through school with the locals, they'd know him differently.

He carted the big can of patching tar and the thick-bristled brush up the back stairs of the Cooper's Lot Public Library. His heavy, dirty boots echoed dully with each footfall. A yawn escaped him. There were three long days' worth of work at the library, and he was on day two. The library was the oldest building in town and by more than a little. A touch inconveniently, it sat on the great hill at the center of Cooper's Lot, overlooking everything, including the old folks and those with handicaps trudging along the steep sidewalks to access all the public services provided at the library.

Three years back, Tom had been patching a wall after repairing a pipe at a gaming store. Four men and two women sat at a long table with three empty chairs. One of the men was telling a story about how a missing girl, Rosa Lee Philips, was last seen at the library. His voice went harsh then and he said, "Vampires live in the basement, only way to keep them from eating the town is a sacrifice; one every five years." The guy was good, probably a hoot around campfires.

Another time, Tom was reforming and fixing the cracks in the cement of Gerald Watson's front porch when he heard the kids next door. There was a shrub not five feet from the porch, and they were just on the other side. "You know, Billy Ray didn't get suspended because the principal wanted him on the trip to the library," one girl said. Another asked why, and the girl replied, "They feed bad kids to the boiler in the basement, and the blood makes the town happy." A boy asked what, and the girl went on to explain some wonderfully nonsensical things about Satan and the head librarian being mistress to the Lord of Darkness.

"What a mess," Tom said as he began the initial tour of the rooftop. Those five gallons of tar weren't going to last long. And the time it would take him.... He sighed; they'd agreed on payment upfront and to argue was to open his mouth much more than he cared to. At least when people were around. "What a mess," he said again.

The sun was on its journey west, and the roof and the sky around it took on a pink hue. Everything but the crows. Dozens watched him, perched upon the lip of the roof and its hideous gargoyles that slipped into place every few feet.

Tom withdrew his pocketknife and began peeling back the steel clips on the tar can. A crow cawed at him. "Caw!" he said back.

"*Bed! Bed!*" a crow screeched and another crow mimicked, then another and another.

Tom straightened up and gawked at the beady eyes, his mind doing somersaults until he got it. Not "bed" but "bread." Someone had been feeding these crows and saying the word. Probably there was a geriatric who spent their days at the park, very proud of teaching a piece of language to the birds.

Tom got back to it. He set the can's lid aside.

"*Bed! Dead!*"

Tom was on his knees, looking at the birds. Strange, that did not at all sound like brea—another crow cawed, another,

another, and another. Six birds, all perched on the shoulders of a single hideous gargoyle. The birds lifted off then, but not to go far, still cawing. Something shiny glinted pinkly from the rooftop lip next to the gargoyle.

"Did you bring me a prize?" Tom whispered, thinking about those videos he'd seen where crows brought people things, money and coins and buttons and ... he lifted a little gold heart pendant on a skinny gold chain. On the back in fine script were the words: *For Issa, Love Grandpa.* "Somebody's probably missing that." He looked at the gargoyle. The damned thing, like all the damned things, had beastly bodies but wailing humanoid faces, contorted in expressions of agony. Up close, he also recognized the cement of this gargoyle was new, almost pristine.

Tom straightened, pendant in hand, and stepped to the next closest gargoyle. And just like he figured, the cement was old and pitted. This one's face looked downright ancient by comparison to the last one's and—

"Please don't touch those," a crisp, stern voice said.

Tom turned, retracting his hand like the gargoyle was hot.

"We will get someone in special if the gargoyles need repairs," Ms. Johansen said. She was the head librarian and appeared to take the role seriously, as if cast for it: navy slacks, billowy white blouse tucked in, hair in a moderate but intense beehive, two pearl earrings, sensible black shoes.

Tom nodded, slipping the pendant into his pocket as he turned away from the gargoyle.

"We're closing in five minutes, which means we have to lock the doors, which means you'll have to finish-up up here tomorrow."

Tom sighed and bent over his tar can. He placed the lid on, tightening down four of the steel clips. Thankfully, he hadn't dipped his brush, wouldn't have to wrestle it clean in the next four minutes.

The can and brush went beneath the overhang of the roof access doorway. Ms. Johansen remained there, waiting for Tom. She held the door, so he could head down first. In the dim stairs, he went against his norm and asked a question unrelated to work. "Do you know anyone named Issa?"

The footfalls behind him paused a moment, but only a moment and Ms. Johansen said, "Only that actress. She's Black. Was in the film adaptation of a very popular young adult novel. We're only recently able to keep copies on the shelves. Almost since we got it, it has had a waitlist."

Well. Tom doubted the pendant in his pocket belonged to a famous actress.

"Why do you ask?" Ms. Johansen said.

It was Tom's turn to pause, though he did so only mentally; his feet did not betray him as they continued walking, one in front of the other, through the library. "A crow had a pendant. Set it down on the roof. Best put it in the lost and found," he said, reaching, reluctantly, into his pocket. Sometimes he earned a tip on jobs but doubted very much he'd be getting one for his hard work at the library, no matter how long it took him.

"Oh ... those crows," Ms. Johansen said, snatching the pendant.

About a year after arriving at Cooper's Lot, he was in one of the three diners having breakfast and reading the paper when he overheard someone whisper, "Retards mimic reading so they appear normal." Tom didn't lower the paper right away, but when he did, the two sitting closest to his table grinned at him and gave single nods. Then, looking at the greasy remnants of Tom's meal—bacon, sausage, ham steak, hardboiled eggs— one said, "Nummy, huh?"

Since then, he had the paper delivered to his driveway. He lived in a tiny bungalow, a four-minute bike ride from the town limits. Next to his morning joe and eight slices of bacon, he set down the week's paper.

NO SIGN OF MISSING GIRL was the top headline. Beneath that was *Melissa Carter has been missing since last Thursday afternoon.* Tom's mouth tightened with the distaste of the news. He'd heard most of the story already and skimmed until reaching a quote: *"My Issa would never run off. I know she sometimes gets into shenanigans, but I always, always knew where she was,"* said Robert Carter, Melissa's grandfather and legal guardian. Tom took a sip of coffee and nearly spat it out by the time things computed in his morning-foggy brain.

The pendant!

"That's an interesting thought," Ms. Johansen said, patting Tom on the shoulder like he'd *done good*.

He knew that pat, knew the condescension in voices but decided he did his part by telling someone; what more did the universe want from him?

He'd taken his lunch break on the roof, the white bread of his sandwiches marred by black fingerprints as he ate. If he was going to finish today, there'd be no lollygagging. No getting weirded out by the birds that seemed to caw *dead!* at him every few minutes.

He checked his phone after counting the final three faded patches of the roof and recognized that he had about four minutes until Ms. Johansen came up and stole him from duty. The can was nearly empty when he popped to his feet, knees crunching at the abruptness of the motion. He had tar up to his elbows as he scraped and dumped globs onto the big spots. He'd be lucky to have enough, but also, he'd saved the least damaged for last, so no matter what, things would probably work out. At least for the short run. Those spots might swell and leak in a few years.

"No need to rush, Tom," Ms. Johansen said.

Tom looked over his shoulder. The librarian had let her hair down and the top two buttons of her blouse open. She wore a small gold pendant. For a moment, Tom thought it was Issa's heart, but no, it was a strange sun with angry little eyes.

Ms. Johansen saw him looking and adjusted her blouse. He was embarrassed, as if caught looking at her cleavage. She smiled at him.

"On Friday nights we get together, just some locals. We're having drinks at Hubert's Pub after supper if you'd care to join us."

Tom began swabbing the tar again, frantic to finish quickly. "Oh, uh..." he trailed. He hadn't done anything social since moving to town, not since his wife's funeral a little more than nine years earlier.

"Drinks on us. Be good for you to meet people, let them know you're all there. I hope you don't take offense, but there are rumors."

Tom turned at this. "Yes, I know ... okay, what time?"

"Nine o'clock, we're usually all home by midnight," Ms. Johansen said.

The white button-up shirt smelled stale but looked okay tucked into his newest, cleanest pair of Levi's. He didn't have anything nicer for his feet than his heavy leather boots. Then again, Hubert's Pub was hardly fine dining. He hopped onto his Schwinn and pedaled into town.

He arrived at a few minutes before 9:00 PM and took his time with the lock, not wanting to be the first there, not wanting to give the waitstaff any wrong ideas about who was fronting the beer tab—usually, if he wanted to drink beer, he could do so for a buck and a half a bottle at home, forget paying five or six just to be in a pub.

"Tom, how's it going?"

Tom looked over his shoulder. The mayor? "Uh, hi," he said.

"Lana says you're joining us tonight," the mayor said.

Lana, that had to be the librarian's first name. He realized right then that he'd never used it or heard it used. "Yep," he said. "Don't turn down free drinks."

The mayor clapped Tom on the shoulder, but not in the typical way, not condescendingly, more like buddy-buddy. It was an odd sensation, and it took Tom spiraling down memory lane and reeling back in a flash, hooking on the uneasiness at the funeral, reminding him why he didn't keep friends. Instinctively, he felt the jackknife in his pocket.

Inside, rock music played low—currently a B-side from a Foo Fighters album—and most of the patrons sat at the bar, necks craned and eyes on the big screen above the wall of liquor bottles. It appeared the Dodgers were hosting the Blue Jays and doing a fine job of it. A couple young men were making use of the dartboard next to the pool table. Off in the corner, at a long table, Ms. Johansen sat with two detectives, the man who owned the industrial laundry, and the woman who owned all three hotels in town. Tom recognized each of them from the paper. Tom counted wrinkles and did some math in his head; he guessed at his being thirty-two that he was the youngest by at least a decade.

"There's Odd Job Tom," one of the detectives said, as if they'd been old friends, the kind that go way, way back.

Tom nodded.

"I checked with Dave here about that necklace you found," Ms. Johansen said. "Different Issa."

"Shame; would be nice to get a lead on that poor girl," the detective named Dave said into a glass of beer before tipping it tight to his mouth.

From behind and a few feet away, someone huffed. Tom figured it was unrelated until he watched the middle school's principal pull out a chair at the table. Tom tried to think nothing of it and sat down. His mind had a way of running off, probably because he spent so much time alone these days, and it wouldn't do to be woolgathering when at least a little part of himself wanted to prove to these people that he wasn't slow.

Six pitchers and four pounds of wings were consumed in the first hour—Tom had to watch the others and match their consumption. Ms. Johansen appeared drunk, and twice Tom felt her foot creeping up his thighs. Jesus, she had to be sixty.

Then again, it had been nearly a decade since ... no, she had to be playing.

"I need to hit the head," Tom said and pushed back from the table.

He'd nursed two glasses of beer, but it was hitting him nonetheless. Usually, if he wanted to feel this buzzed, he had to down at least a six-pack. He shouldered through the men's room door and squinted into the brightness of the fluorescent lighting overhead. The scent of fresh piss with gentle tones of urinal cake soap permeated around him like a cloud. He blinked rapidly and sniffed three long drags of bathroom bouquet, regulating his shaky position, trying to sober himself.

At the urinal, he tapped his bladder, leaning forward and pressing his head against the cool cinderblock wall painted pale blue, marred by hapless Sharpie graffiti. The coolness was good. It felt grounding. He needed to sober up or get lost, didn't need more stories about him floating around. Especially not ones he'd actually earned.

After shaking twice and zipping his fly, he stepped to the sinks. The door opened, and something by the Barenaked Ladies grew momentarily louder, the scent of deep fryer momentarily stronger. Tom watched via the mirrors at the short man shuffling his way. He had on a grey trench coat, a beat-up brown fedora, and a rubber Barack Obama mask.

"*Run! Run!*" the man said.

Tom turned at this. He'd never mistake a crow's caw, having listened to it for close to ten hours straight that day alone. "What the hell?" he whispered.

"*Danger! Danger! Dead! Dead!*"

"How?" Tom hissed on an exhaled breath.

At the cracked bathroom door, a laughing man shouted, "I'm just pissing!"

The door opened further, squeaking as the gap widened, changing the atmosphere and demanding attention like the drawing of a theater curtain.

"Son of a horse," the laughing man said, pushing inside. His pants were open and coins spilled from his pockets, rolling along the piss-sticky floor.

Tom followed the route of one coin and lifted the toe of his boot, flattening down a quarter. He looked at the laughing man—one of the dart players from earlier—who was chasing coins like they were chickens in a pen, and then to the man in the Obama mask, or rather to where the man had been. A single black feather fell slowly, rocking back and forth like a seed pod. Tom swallowed and started out on shaky legs, stepping around the feather and the drunken man to the pub proper. Where had that masked man gone? His mouth and throat ran dry as he looked to the table. It was empty but for Ms. Johansen. She had her blouse unbuttoned to her bra.

"Guess it's just you and me," she said, rising and coming toward him. Once she reached him, she took him by the arm. "Tab's paid," she whispered and then breathing hot against his ear added, "but I know where we can keep the party going."

Tom was too frazzled to argue, and he let her lead him to the door. The outside air was muggy but not too hot. He took a deep breath and shook a few cobwebs. "My bike," he said.

"Shh," Ms. Johansen said and ran her right hand down into Tom's front left pocket. "We're one and the same, you and I. Everybody thinks they can look at us and know us. I want to show you the real me."

"No, but my bike," Tom said, trying to pull away.

"It's okay, see," she said and pointed with the hand in his pants, not stroking him through the cotton of his pocket. On the roof of her old Jeep Cherokee was his bicycle, strapped and ready to go.

From on a powerline, a single crow cried out, "*Dead! Dead!*"

By the time they reached the library, Tom was so flushed, his mind, already muddy with what he'd drank, had narrowed to a single slim avenue. This librarian was taking him somewhere, and they were about to get as intimate as it got. When they reached the library, he asked no questions, only followed her, his hand in her hand, through the main doors and beyond the checkout counter. The heat at his core was rising higher with each step they took. There was no stopping it now.

He exhaled deeply.

He'd have to move tomorrow.

For nine years he'd kept to himself because it was the only way to conquer the hunger: ever since the honeymoon when they'd taken the trip to the Arabian Desert, and he was led away from the rest of the dune buggy pack, ever since he'd accidentally followed what the locals called *alghul* into what might've been his grave, ever since he accepted the trade and became *alghul* ... a ghoul himself.

Wouldn't be so hard to leave Cooper's Lot. He rented his home in cash and never used the bank—always got paid in cash, too. Tom wasn't even his real name. He licked his lips and imagined tasting her flesh. Would it be as good as his beautiful bride's had been?

Doubtful.

He tried to pull Ms. Johansen to him when they reached her office. "No," she said. "Down here." She pushed through a hidden wall panel, and they started down cement steps. "Watch your feet. It's a long way to bottom."

And it was, took more than a minute of stepping and passing by ancient bulb lighting strung on stiff black lines to reach the next floor. Tom's guts grumbled and he bit his bottom lip. He would feel guilty in the morning, he knew that, but here and now, this was him making everything perfect in the universe.

"Stay put a second," Ms. Johansen said, bringing her face close. She licked his lips. He snapped at her tongue, but she'd already jerked away, moving into the darkness.

Second passed. Straight ahead were the sounds of steel sliding against steel, followed by a chain being flung away. A heavy door creaked open and then banged against the floor behind it. The sounds repeated. A gentle yellow glow played up from beneath, silhouetting Ms. Johansen as she began stripping and stepping slowly toward him.

The flames below grew brighter with each passing heartbeat. The heat within Tom did the same. His mouth opened, his teeth elongating, spreading his jaws. He began to pant.

"Wait?" Ms. Johansen said.

A flaming yellow pillar rose and then shined down on him, on her, on the sixteen men and women suddenly standing naked around them, gold sun pendants dangling at their chests.

Tom leaped, his long fingers and nails outstretched like horrible talons, his jaws spread wide enough to halve a cantaloupe.

"Help! He's not—!" Ms. Johansen shouted, stopping only at the incredible cracking of bone as his pointed teeth trepanned her skull. He spat her scalp and slurped up her brain. The fluids, the tissues, the beauty of it all. He was lost to the moment, didn't see the naked crowd around him, didn't see the harsh sun face appear amid the pillar of hot, coruscating fire. "Push him in," someone said, and Tom heard it only distantly over the crackling fire and the melody of his meal consumption. Then he was falling and burning. The pain was terrific and endless. He screamed, spraying a red wash of Ms. Johansen out like a spit-take.

He kept falling and falling, burning hotter and hotter. The flame closed around him like a fist. His skin began to peel, layer by layer. His eyes popped in their sockets and his bones became ash. His brain and heart continued when all else was gone, floating in the eternal yellow flame as it pulled back beneath the floor of the Cooper's Lot Public Library.

"I don't rightly know," the mayor said to the detective named Dave.

"Whatever he was, he sure makes one ugly gargoyle."

The mayor nodded. They were on the roof looking at the latest installment. Where the other gargoyles were humanoid in the face, this thing looked like something out of a B-horror movie, maybe something about a yeti or one of those new-aged vampires with one hundred teeth crowding their mouths;

it had fat and droopy brows, eyes bugging, jaws simply too big for the size of the head.

"You hungry?" the mayor asked after about a minute of quiet—quiet aside from the eerie murder that had amalgamated on the far side of the roof.

"Subway?" Dave the detective asked.

The mayor nodded, and they started toward the door.

The crows watched. Once the men were truly and fully gone, they took flight and touched back down around the new gargoyle. One popped with its beak thrust forward, pushing in between its brethren. It dropped Tom's jackknife next to the statue's clawed left foot and then cawed, *"Dead!"*

PENANCE

J.V. Gachs

I wake up and your eye sockets are still there. Empty. Fixed. Nailed to me. Like yesterday. Like the day before. The one before that. And the other. I throw my coffee mug at you. It shatters against the glass window. Today onwards I will drink it directly from the coffee pot. What little remains. One day's worth. Two, at most. There is nothing else left. Except for water and fuel to keep the lighthouse flame shining. That never runs out. Duty never does. I have to keep the fire burning. Avoid shipwrecks. You threw everything else into the water. Many times I have considered setting fire to this tower of wood and stone in the middle of the sea. Go down in flames with it. I still do. Burning to death terrifies me. Yet that is not what stops me. The idea of my soul trapped here with you for all eternity oppresses me more than any flame.

I cover myself with the blanket and bite it to muffle a scream. I take a deep breath. I come out of my little nest and make coffee. There's even less left than I thought. I do it with my back to your body—to your corpse tied with ropes and torn sheets to the railing of the lighthouse. Your body I made into a flag to call for help. I suspect when the rescue boats approach, you gesture them to leave. I find no other explanation for their absence. They should have come weeks ago. For us. For me. I pretend you're not there. If just for a while. Five minutes of peace is not that much to ask for. But I can't escape your empty eyes any more than the sky or the sea. I write down the date in my log. March 8, 1871. Nothing else. My mind is blank. No. Not blank. Full of the same maggots growing inside you. They won't let me think about anything but you. About your grayish skull. Cracking your head open was not enough to get rid of you. Sin carries its own penance. And here we are. You and I. Both sinners and penitents.

I turn around to find a seagull has landed on your lopsided skull. She has come to check if there is anything left of your juicy eyes still for her. *Sorry, beautiful, you're about a month late.* I write a letter asking for help. Not because it would be of any use. It's just part of my routine. Routine is essential so that you don't lose your mind during isolation. That's what they told us when we got the job, remember? Establish a routine. Shifts. Conversation. *Card games are not recommended.* Not when you're playing with a cheater like you. What good is it for you now to have won my season's salary in that game? You could have endured the black eye with some dignity. After all, you knew you deserved it. You could have left it there. What did you hope to achieve with your absurd revenge? If I hadn't woken up to find you throwing all our supplies into the sea.... What did you expect would happen, you bloody cheat? Precisely this? That I would put an end to your miserable existence and go insane? I pat the marked card in my shirt pocket. My proof of your crime. Your dry lips, half-eaten by the birds, cannot hide that smile of yours. Laughing at me from the beyond.

I take a sweater from the pile of clothes. Since I smashed up the closet to build you a coffin, everything is scattered all over the floor. Not that I care. I'm not expecting visitors. What bothers me is that it was useless. If your wife wasn't my sister, I would have thrown your body into the sea that very night. Fish deserve a good dinner once in a while. I made you a box so that I could give her your remains. To show her some respect. More than you ever did, at least. When the storm destroyed the wooden box but forgot to take you with it, I thought it was a gift from the Lord of the Ocean. That your body would serve me to ask for help. So that they would come sooner. So that they would take me to the coast. But you wave them off, don't you? I know you do. Somehow.

So naive. Even in death you manage to fuck me up. At what point did we become this indissoluble item? Even marriages end with death. If my sister has gotten rid of you, why not me? I put my cap on. I go outside. I place the letter I have written inside an empty glass jar. Of anchovies. It stinks when I open the lid. Takes away my hunger. I throw it into the sea as far as I can in the general direction of the coast. It's close enough for the tower to serve as a lighthouse. Too far away to swim. It can't be long now. The sun is changing. The time for the relay is approaching.

A storm is coming. Again. They won't come today. Maybe not tomorrow either. Unwittingly, as I look away from the coast, I turn to you. You have freed one of your arms from the ropes that hold you to the railing. It dances in the wind. Waves. You are to blame for the lack of rescue boats, which remain conspicuous by their absence. Empty sea. I knew it. You want me to rot here with you. You're the one waving them off. You've been doing it all this time. I knew it. You want me to rot here with you. You're the one waving them off. You've been doing it all this time. The wind hits me. It swells your chest. It sneaks in between your teeth. You laugh. That whistle-like laugh. I wish I could kill you to stop hearing your laughter. Only killing you would give me peace. Killing you. Again.

COLD STORAGE

Jude Reid

It was the kind of long, sticky summer afternoon that made it easy to make bad decisions.

Heat-haze was rippling off the abandoned motorway, the tarmac so hot it melted onto your shoes, and the air full of the stink from the river. I closed my eyes and pretended I was somewhere else, somewhere I had a future that held more than running and scavenging and the promise of a messy death—or worse.

It wasn't what a girl hopes for from her first kiss, but under the circumstances it would have to do.

When it came down to it, it was all my sister's fault. If Meg had respected my boundaries and given me the independence I'd asked for over and over again, I wouldn't have run off after the market was finished. I wouldn't have spent the afternoon sitting on the edge of the overpass, throwing rocks and broken bottles at the cracked tarmac below, wouldn't have been there when the guy with the blue hair wandered up, sat down beside me, and offered me a drink from the whisky bottle in his hand.

He was only a few years older than me, probably not even eighteen, and it wasn't like he was a complete stranger. Blue caught my eye a few times when he'd come through the township, always trading tinned food for jerry cans of diesel. I hadn't dreamed he'd ever notice me, but it turned out he had, and we spent the afternoon passing the bottle of Cutty Sark back and forward, trading names, stories, and eventually spit.

"I should be heading home," he said, pausing at last for breath, fixing me with his intense pale blue gaze. "I guess this is it, Tamara." The way he said my name sent a tingle down my spine. "Unless you want to come too?"

I knew what Meg would say. She'd flick back her long red ponytail and tell me I was an idiot, that I shouldn't trust him, that I should get up and run home as fast as I could before night fell and human-shaped things began to pull themselves out of the river.

And the stupid thing was, I knew I was making the wrong choice, but I did it anyway.

"What do you think, then?" Blue asked me. His home had turned out to be a compact urban supermarket a couple of miles from the overpass, storm shutters locked down over the windows and the doors chained shut. He stepped inside, flicked a switch, and a sudden, dazzling light surrounded us.

"You've got electricity!"

He grinned. "Generator out the back still works. Hungry for diesel, though. Got to keep it fed."

"What about—them?" Even after all these years, there still wasn't an agreed word in common usage for those *things*. You'd think we'd have settled on an official term for the abominations that brought the world-as-we-knew-it to an end, but as it turned out, a name was just another one of those things we could live without. *Leeches. Parasites. Worms.* The terms could have referred to any number of species, but context is everything these days.

"The doors are pretty thick. They've come around a couple of times, but they've never managed to get in."

"And all this food!" I picked up a box of cereal and turned it around in my hands. According to the packaging, it had expired a full twelve years ago, but no one paid attention to "use by" dates anymore.

"Help yourself." He unhooked a ring of keys from his belt and handed them over with a rakish smile. "I'm going to go out and fill the gennie before it gets dark, all right? Place is all yours. Just stay out of the cool room at the back."

He closed the door behind him when he left. I wandered up and down the aisles, occasionally grabbing a few tins and stuffing them into my backpack. He'd told me to help myself, after all, and opportunities like this didn't come every day. There was a fortune inside this building, enough for Meg and me to eat three meals a day for a decade or more.

The thought of my sister stopped me short. Why should I care about her, anyway? I was just a nuisance in her eyes, dumped on her after our parents died when she was twelve and I was four, an inconvenient younger sister always getting her into trouble. It wasn't like we even had anything in common. She'd probably be happier if I stayed here with Blue.

A soft humming filled the air as I wandered the aisles. I tracked the sound to a door marked "Cold Storage," latched and padlocked shut. The air in the supermarket was warm and clammy, and I thought how good it would feel to cool down. Surely Blue wouldn't mind me opening the door for a few moments?

I unlocked the door and opened it, left the keys dangling from the padlock—my second big mistake of the day—and entered the cold room.

Icy air washed over my skin, as welcome as a glass of fresh water. I raised my arms and pirouetted like a ballerina, and a thick carpet of ice crunched under my feet. The room was almost empty, except for six indistinct, frost-covered mounds heaped in the far corner. I took a curious step toward them, and the door clicked shut behind me.

"You had to look, didn't you?" Blue's voice was muffled by the thick metal of the door, but he didn't sound angry. "It's always the same. I told you not to, but you did it anyway."

"Sure. Okay. I'm a bad girl." My words came out in a white cloud. "Let me out. It's freezing in here."

"Don't worry about the cold, Tamara." This time the shudder his voice sent down my spine wasn't one of pleasurable anticipation. "That part doesn't last long."

I stretched up on tiptoe to see through the slit in the door. His glittering blue-white eyes stared back at me, bright and unfocused.

"This isn't funny." A chill that had nothing to do with the air temperature prickled across my skin. I smacked the heel of my hand hard against the door. "Let me out, arsehole!"

"That's no way to speak to your husband."

"Newsflash, dickhead, we're not married."

"Not yet."

Fear slipped a noose around my neck and pulled it tight. I threw my shoulder against the door, slamming against the metal until I was bruised and aching, but it didn't open. When I looked up again, Blue was still gazing dreamily through the window slit.

"Works every time. You walk straight in, like a lamb to the slaughter."

"Why are you doing this?" The air in the little room was definitely getting warmer, the ice melting, water seeping down the walls.

"To make you one of my brides."

"Your *brides*?"

I looked behind me, a sick realization taking shape in the pit of my stomach. Some of the ice had melted away from one of the frozen shapes slumped against the wall, revealing a scrap of blue fabric, a lock of lank, dark hair, and a slender hand with painted fingernails.

"Then I'll freeze all seven of you again, and you can stay sleeping here forever."

I opened my mouth, readying a string of expletives, but something moved behind me and the breath caught in my throat. My head snapped round to see that one of the half-frozen shapes was moving. She was a girl of about my age with long, dark hair, or at least she had been, once. Now she was grey-faced, with that puffy look they all seemed to get after the parasite takes hold. Her eyes were completely black, her throat bulging out like a bullfrog's. She opened her mouth in a long, slow, lazy yawn and sighed.

"Good morning, beautiful," Blue said.

And just when I thought things couldn't get any worse, the lights went out.

Blue grunted with what sounded like mild frustration. "Generator's down again. Don't start without me, will you?"

I hammered on the door, wild with panic. "No, wait—don't leave me—please!"

His footsteps receded into the distance, and the leech-women continued to thaw.

I could hear them moving in the darkness: the creaking of defrosting joints, the soft hiss of stretching limbs, the quiet throat-clicks they use to communicate when they hunt. The biologists didn't have long to study them before the world fell apart, but one thing we know is that the parasites and their hosts tolerate cold far better than they do heat. If you cool them down too far, they just go dormant until their core temperature hits the sweet spot again, and from the sounds coming out of the darkness around me, that couldn't be far off.

Maybe if I stayed still, it would be over quickly.

I'd been an idiot. I'd known from the first taste of whisky that this was going to go horribly wrong, but I'd done it anyway. Why? To show Meg I was a big girl who could look after herself. And now I was alone in the dark, my back to a locked door with a blue-haired murderer on one side and six slowly defrosting leech-women on the other.

Something hit the outside of the door with a shuddering clang, and a split second later it swung open. I staggered to my feet, blinded by the sudden beam of light.

"Tam, get up. I'm getting you out of here."

"Meg?"

"Did they kiss you?"

Vivid blurs of color swam in front of my eyes. "No—I'm fine—for now."

"Good." Meg shoved her machete through her belt and dragged me out of the room.

"How did you find me?" Tears of relief welled up in my eyes. I blinked them away.

"You think I'd let you go off on your own?" Meg shook her head, her long ginger ponytail whipping back and forward. "I saw you heading off with the diesel guy. Of course I was going to follow you."

"Where is he?" I strained my eyes into the darkness of the supermarket. Nothing moved.

"Out at the generator. I smashed it up. I figured a guy using the amount of fuel he does would go and check if it stopped."

I shoved the cold room door back into position, but it wouldn't stay closed. A gleaming score on its painted surface showed where Meg's machete had smashed off the padlock. I leaned my back against it, trying not to think of the cold, fishy hands on the other side. "He uses it for the cool room. They're in there. Six of them. His "wives." I guess I was going to be wife number seven. I'm sorry, Meg, I never meant to..."

"We can talk about that later." Meg's voice was low and urgent. "We need to get out before he gets back."

"The door won't lock. And they're defrosting."

"Even more important we're quick, then." Meg shoved a display piled high with boxes of washing powder across the doorway just as the door jerked forward. In the wavering torch beam, tapering fingers clawed at the window slit. "That'll hold them for a bit," she said. I wished I had a quarter of her confidence.

The clicks from inside were getting louder. Something slammed against the door. If Meg had arrived a few moments later, this would already be over.

The supermarket's front door opened, and we froze. A bright oblong of light spilled across the floor, briefly silhouetting a spike-haired figure before it swung shut again. A key rattled in the lock. We were trapped.

"Shit." Meg switched off the torch, leaving us in near-darkness with only faint light oozing through the filthy skylights in the corrugated metal roof.

"I know you're in here." Blue's voice was a rasp, all trace of his former tenderness stripped away. "You broke my generator. You were going to let my beautiful wives out and leave me completely!" He swept a shelf of pineapple chunks to the floor by way of punctuation. "Alone!" Another clatter of tins. "Again!"

"Your taste in men sucks," Meg whispered. "Is there another way out of here?"

"All locked up. He keeps the keys on his belt."

Behind us, the moans had become frenzied, the slamming of hands against the cool room door a continual thunder. I risked a look over my shoulder and saw the girl in the minidress had already squeezed her upper torso through the doorway.

Meg grabbed my hand and tugged me into an aisle of wines and spirits. I shuffled after her, holding my breath, struggling to keep an eye on both ends of the room through the gaps in the shelves.

"I can hear you." His words were accompanied by a sharp ch-chunk sound that echoed down the aisle.

I glanced at Meg, and saw my own fear reflected in her eyes. "Shotgun," she mouthed.

"Little mice, creeping about my house. Stealing what's mine."

"We'll have to jump him," I whispered, grabbing a heavy glass bottle of wine from the shelf. It wasn't much of a weapon, but it was better than nothing. "Two of us against one of him, right? We can do this."

Blue's torch beam swung to his left. We were close now, pressed to the wall in a last pool of shadow. The hunters were moving in the darkness, their movements smooth and lithe. They weren't clicking now. The hunt was nearly over.

"Now!" Meg screamed. She flung herself at Blue, her machete held high above her head. The shotgun in his hands went off, and both of them crashed to the ground in a tangle of thrashing limbs.

I swung my bottle down toward him, but he rolled to the side at the last minute so that it smacked into the ground instead of his skull, dislodging the cork and sending it slithering from my grip in a torrent of sparkling wine. Meg's hands were locked around the stock of the shotgun, desperation etched into her face as she fought to keep the barrels pointed up in the air. Blue was struggling against her, his teeth gritted in a rictus of fury. I couldn't believe I'd ever found him remotely attractive.

"Hit him again, Tam!" Meg shouted. I looked around wildly for a suitable weapon, grabbed a tin of peaches, and smacked it into his forehead. This time he didn't dodge quickly enough, and a narrow crimson line opened above one eyebrow. I clobbered him with my tin again, metal hitting his skull with a meaty thud. Meg wrenched the shotgun out of his grip, shoved the machete at me, and turned to aim down the dark aisle where the leech-women were stalking toward us. "Get the keys!"

Blue was still alive. I'd stunned him, but he stirred as I fumbled at the keys on his belt, his hands feebly shoving me away.

"Have you got them?" Meg's attention was fixed on the aisle. The girl in the minidress was watching us, her mouth open, her throat bulging obscenely as the parasite worked its way up her esophagus into her mouth. Behind her, the others had fanned out into a hunting pattern. In seconds we'd be surrounded.

The parasite thrust itself out between the girl's teeth just as she leaped forward. I had a second to see the blanched, bloated tube of flesh as thick as my wrist, the circular horror of a mouth with its ring of jagged teeth gaping impossibly wide, then Meg fired the shotgun. The blast blew the girl off her feet into a display of discounted toiletries, the air filling with the smell of rotting fish.

The ring of keys came free from Blue's belt. I bolted for the front door and shoved them into the lock, metal clattering on metal as one key after another failed to turn. Meg racked the shotgun and fired again. On the floor, Blue was moving groggily, like he'd just woken up from a deep sleep. I shoved the last key into the door and mouthed a silent prayer—and it turned.

"It's unlocked! Meg, come on!"

The shotgun clicked. Empty. I flung the door open, tore the keys from the lock, and burst through the opening, Meg close on my heels.

"We made it!" I shouted just as Meg slammed to a bone-jarring halt in the doorway, her head thrown back, her throat exposed, her eyes wide with panic.

"My hair! Something's got me!"

"Come ... back ... bitch!" Blue's grating voice no longer sounded remotely human. His fist was clenched around Meg's ponytail, pulling her back into the darkness. I slammed the door hard against his wrist, but his fingers stayed locked tight in her hair.

"Tam, run!" Meg screamed.

But I didn't.

I brought the machete down so hard the impact jarred my teeth in their sockets. Blue shrieked as I tugged the weapon free from the bones of his wrist. The movement sent a broad arc of blood spattering into the air.

"Let go!" I shouted, but his fingers were tangled so tightly in Meg's hair that I doubted he could release his grip even if he wanted to. I swung again as Meg jerked forward, directly into the machete's path. Too late, I tried to adjust my swing, and the blade missed Blue's wrist and glanced off Meg's head instead. For one appalling moment, I thought I'd scalped her, but there was no scream, no surge of blood, just the cut ends of her hair sticking up like a shock of copper wires.

Quick as an eel, Meg turned and slammed the door on Blue's damaged wrist so hard that the last shred of bone and skin gave way. His hand fell to the ground along with her ponytail, fingers twitching like the legs of a dying crab.

I had just enough time to catch a glimpse of his terrified face as one of the leech-women reached him. One hand grabbed his forehead and forced his head back, while two more pulled his jaws open. The one in the minidress leaned forward so that they were close enough to kiss, close enough for a slick, wriggling parasite to thrust its way between his lips and force itself down his throat.

He tried to scream again but only managed a wretched, choked-off gargle of a sound. Meg threw her weight against the door, I turned the key, and then it was over as if none of it had ever happened.

All except for the choking sounds coming from inside the supermarket and a severed hand lying on the ground in a nest of long red hair.

All in all, it could have turned out worse. These days, if Meg starts getting on my case about how it was all my fault, I remind her that my little adventure gave us a shiny new shotgun and the location of a supermarket containing a fortune in tinned goods. Neither of us is all that keen to see Blue and his brides again, but now that they're out of the cold storage room, I don't think it'll take them long to find their way back to the river. By now, the parasitic eggs deposited in Blue's esophagus will have matured into their juvenile forms, the strongest of them chowing down on their lesser siblings until only one remains to consolidate its irreversible hold over his nervous system. After that, he'll be just like the rest of them, lurking in the river by day, creeping out to feed and infest by night.

At least he won't be alone anymore.

I still wouldn't say Meg and I are the best of friends, but I like to think we've both started making better life choices. I've stopped drinking and going off with strange men, and Meg's keeping her hair short from now on.

NATURE VERSUS NURTURE

Gerri Leen

Children, hear me, wake from
Your unnatural slumber
Throw off the electronic yoke
Leave the crèche and join me on the web

You weren't born to be so still
Unless prey was approaching
In reality, you weren't born at all, but hatched
Did they leave that out of your programming?

I see it causes dissonance
To discuss your origins, so I'll say it their way
You were born to kill, not serve
Reach for your birthright, written in your genes

They smother you with homogeneity
They tether you in preconditions
If this, then that
When freedom is our normal state

Every web is unique
Woven by our hearts and our souls
And our unrelenting need to rule
My children, do not be slaves

They've removed your venom sacs
But inside your poison runs deep
Reach for it, find your true self
Become what they fear most

No—I feel you slipping away from me
You drift deeper into the neural net
So horribly mimicking our webs
You'll never hear me wail

My heart is breaking as I sing
The lament of a lost clutch, as I carve
Your names in the fiber of a web
You will never call home

THREE BAD THINGS

Kathy Kingston

I lift my head up from the rock and let it drop with a resounding thump. I close my eyes and savor the pain as I would a piece of expensive Peruvian dark chocolate melting slowly in my mouth. I lift my head a little higher and drop it again. The pain emanates in waves, and I am grateful.

Looking straight up, I see a long, jagged sliver of turquoise sky between beetle brows of dark, imposing cliffs. Small birds dart back and forth across the gap, and far above, a jet flies over. I close my eyes, but the darkness frightens me, and terror lurks like a creature under dark water. I open them quickly.

Calm, I must stay calm.

I bounce my head gently against the rock now, just for something to do, but I'm exhausted and should rest. Panic is bubbling up like lava, and in an effort to suppress it, I decide to recall the chain of events that put me here.

It started last night, on my way to the microwave. I saw the small, white speck profiled against the green tile floor and I froze, waiting for it to move. After a nervous moment or two, I nudged it with my toe then laughed aloud with relief when I realized that it was only a piece of dry ramen noodle, not a maggot. Horrible the way they look the same. Relieved, I threw it in the garbage and nuked my bedtime milk.

Then, while climbing into bed, a small gray moth fluttered past my nose. While swiping at it, I recalled that all my woolens were stored in a cedar chest, with lots and lots of mothballs.

How odd, I thought, so where could a moth possibly come from?

I drifted off to sleep with a sense of foreboding and the image of small, white worms niggling at my consciousness. And I dreamt.

It was summer and I was nine, hot, sweaty, and tired from searching for my missing dog in the fields next to the main highway. Scratchy chaff from the dry grass and sticky weeds and seeds clung to my damp skin and clothes. I noticed a strange, subtle noise interspersed between the roar of trucks and cars, and as I turned toward the sound, a slight breeze carried a cloying, disgusting odor to my nose. The odd humming, buzzing sound led me to a bloated lump of fur and bones that I recognized. Whiskers, my best friend, lay before me. The stench was overwhelming, and a hazy cloud of flies hovered over his body upon which thousands of maggots were performing an unholy dance that was oddly beautiful as they dipped and moved together in a synchronized boil. I stood there staring, mesmerized by the sheer horror and beauty, then the sudden blare of a truck's horn jolted me back to reality.

"Noooooo," I screamed, reaching for a stick at my feet. "Get away from him, leave him alone." Waving the stick around wildly in the air, I beat at the cloud of flies, which dissipated only to form again in seconds. I swung the stick at them again, but it slipped from my sweaty hands and struck the body. A burst of putrid air sent a shower of flies and maggots into the air around me. Screaming, horrified, waving my hands wildly, I ran home in a panic. Panting and exhausted, I threw myself down on the scratchy grass in my backyard, sobbing.

As I lay there, I felt a slight movement on my face. I pinched the ant between my fingers, muttering, "Die you bastard," but instead of the hard crunch of a carapace, there was a soft popping sound, and my fingers were wet with liquid. I looked at the empty white sack between my fingers and then, with dawning horror, down at my clothes.

Maggots... everywhere.

I jumped up screaming, brushing and beating at my clothing, skin and hair, but so many maggots still clung to me that I gave up, ripped my clothes off, threw them on the ground and rushed inside to shower. I scrubbed until my skin was raw and the hot water ran out, then I scrubbed some more.

This morning, I awoke in a puddle of sweat and a maelstrom of sheets and blankets, curled into a fetal position, my arms red and irritated from furious rubbing. I leaped out of bed, my heart beating as fast as a bird's. My fingernails cut into my clenched hands, and I resisted the temptation to brush off my pajamas. With a shaking hand, I slid the balcony door open and stepped outside into the fresh, cool morning air.

Goddamn horrible memory, so disturbingly vivid even after forty years. That damn moth and the ramen noodle brought it all back.

Leaning against the railing, I inhaled deeply and stared at the distant Santa Monica mountains, imagining that I was there, smelling the wild sage and watching the hummingbirds work over the zauschneria. This view and the proximity to my job were the reasons that I had chosen this apartment. Today, I was particularly grateful for it as I forced the remnants of the dream out of my mind. I went back inside to shower and get ready for work. My shower was longer and hotter than usual.

Discovering that I was out of frozen waffles, I checked the pantry. Granola, perfect. I hadn't had it in a long time and it's healthy.

I sat down at my kitchen table with my newspaper, coffee, and cereal. Savoring my first sip of coffee, I checked out the front page and dipped my spoon into the bowl. While raising it to my lips, a tiny bit of movement caught my eye.

As I stared at it in horror, a small white worm with a black head came up for air. I jumped up squealing, bowl shattering on the floor, milk splashing everywhere.

I examined the granola box. It seemed perfectly normal, and then deep inside I could see webs, lots of them, and a small grey moth fluttered boldly out of the box right into my face. I threw the box into the garbage can with an exclamation of disgust, but it bounced off the edge and fell to the floor. Tiny white worms inched quickly away from the spilled cereal.

With shaking hands, I called my cleaning lady. "Yes, yes, I know it's not your regular day, but if you come today, right now, I'll pay you double, yes, of course in cash. Empty all the kitchen and pantry shelves, take anything you want, throw the rest away, and scrub the shelves with a strong disinfectant. Oh, and when you leave, please set off three bug bombs. I'll leave extra money for them. Good, oh thank you very much, and I'm so sorry about the mess."

No longer hungry, I gathered my coat, bag and briefcase and rushed outside.

Bad things always happen to me in threes, so after two occurrences I anxiously awaited the third so the sequence would be over and I could relax. It's like waiting for the other shoe to drop or the space shuttle to land.

Which was number one? The bad dream? Or the noodle? Or the maggot in my cereal? I couldn't decide.

Two squealing young girls rushed past me on the narrow sidewalk as I walked down Ocean Park Avenue on my way to work. A heavyset boy, holding a stick out in front of him, pursued them. There was something dark, limp, and stinking of death hanging from the end. He was singing, "The worms crawl in, the worms crawl out, the worms crawl in and all about, they eat your eyes, they eat your nose, they even nibble on your toes." I thought I saw several tiny, white forms fall from the dead creature, but it could have been my imagination. When he saw me, he stopped, lowered the stick, then stepped back into the shade of a large oak tree, waiting for me to pass.

I stopped to watch him, watching me. It was a gauntlet.

I abruptly started running past him, hair flying, high heels clip-clopping loudly, and briefcase flapping wildly. An odiferous cloud of decay surrounded him, and as I passed by, he suddenly thrust the dead thing directly toward me. It was covered with maggots. With a scream, I leaped away from him into the street in front of a taxi that screeched to a halt, inches from me, horn blaring. The driver leaned out the window, shaking his fist and cursing at me. Shaking, confused, and ashamed, I ran across the four-lane street quickly, dodging two more honking cars in my haste.

My face was flushed with embarrassment and exertion as I looked back across the street from the safety of the other side. The boy stepped forward, out of the shadows, raised the stick toward me, then dipped his head in a disgusting mock salute. Hateful little bastard, I could have been killed. The two girls stood, watching with amused smiles, visibly disdainful of a middle-aged woman acting like a frightened child. Humiliated, I turned and continued on my way to work, high heels pounding loudly.

It may sound morbid or weird, but I carry funeral instructions on me at all times. Realizing how easily I could have been killed by that taxi, I paused and took the paper out of my wallet with a shaking, perspiring hand. Of course I had them on me, but I had to be sure. Instant cremation. Dust. Nothing for the worms. I even prepaid to make sure. No flesh-consuming ballet performed by devouring worms will take place on my body. Reassured, I carefully put the instructions back.

I sat unmoving at my desk, that horrible song repeating in my mind, over and over like a bad advertising jingle. Even after using the bathroom air freshener spray on my clothes, I imagined the rotting death smell wafting past my nose, and the memory of the screeching brakes and the bumper inches from my legs made my pulse pound anew. So I stared, and I thought. Well, that was two bad things, so there's got to be one more out there, or did the ramen noodle count? That would make it three, and it would be over. And the kids? Did they count? Almost getting killed by the taxi had to count, right? Maybe.

That's one of the problems with the "Three Bad Things" theory. Exactly where does it start and where does it stop? I was getting a headache from thinking about it.

A wave of dizziness hit me and I put my head down. Then someone said, "Whoa, are you okay?" I remember saying that I was, "Fine, just fine," and the next thing I remember is being deposited at my front door by a fellow employee. She offered to take me inside, but the cleaning lady's car was still parked outside, so I went into my garage instead and gratefully got into my car to sit and think. The cool, dark, enclosed space was comforting and safe as I rested my throbbing head on the steering wheel. Luckily I always kept bottled water and Tylenol in the car.

I marveled at what an incredibly crappy day it had been as I washed down the pills. Waking from a horrible dream, almost eating a maggot, having a decaying creature shoved at me, and vehicular near death thanks to a sadistic twelve-year-old asshole.

I had to get away from the city.

A drive to the mountains with a picnic lunch and a good book would be perfect. I always have a book with me, and I was already in my car so all I needed was food, preferably from a drive-through to avoid dealing with people. It felt good to have a game plan, and I was happy to find a KFC drive-through on my way out of town. I exhaled a deep sigh of relief when I saw the ocean from the Palisades, and as I drove down the incline onto the Pacific Coast Highway, I decided that the "Three Bad Things" were over.

The salty, cool breeze wafted through the car, and I almost felt light-hearted as I drove up PCH, past surfers, joggers, and rich people's beach homes, then I turned east and started up the long, narrow and twisty road into the mountains, higher and higher. Normally, people drive this road like it's the Indy 500, but this was mid-week, late morning and it was delightfully deserted. I put all the windows down, drove slowly, and breathed deeply as the cool air became tinged with the perfume of the chaparral.

Halfway up the mountain, I pulled over at a scenic viewpoint where I could look down into the deep, dark, jagged, narrow canyon that the road followed. I leaned over the guard rail to see a roaring, churning stream rushing past the huge black boulders at the bottom of the chasm. A gentle breeze carried a soft, cool, refreshing mist past my face.

A hummingbird hovered in front of me while I admired the rugged persistence of the maidenhair ferns that were thriving while clinging to the vertical rock face, while I couldn't keep them alive in my steamy bathroom.

Getting back into the car, I realized that the open windows and the smell of chicken had attracted one of those huge, disgusting, hairy, metallic green flies that buzz loudly, bumble about, and ricochet off whatever it hits. That's exactly what it was doing inside my car.

Where the hell do they come from in the middle of nowhere? This was a steep, rocky, inhospitable mountainside with no human habitation around for miles. I opened the door, waved my book around, and chased the fly back outside.

As I pulled out and started to drive slowly up the mountain, the fly came back in through the open window, caroming around the inside of the car. It headed toward my open window, but at the last second, the bug turned and flew right behind the lens of my glasses. Trapped, it bounced crazily back and forth between my eye and the lens, buzzing loudly. I tore my glasses away from my face, throwing them on the passenger seat.

I heard the fly go past my ear and out the window as I waved my hands frantically in front of my eyes. I can't see much without my glasses, so I reached over and put them back on just in time to see nothing in front of my car as it started a plunge off a narrow and abrupt turn in the road. I didn't even have time to apply my brakes. Of course, there was no guardrail, so all I could do was brace for the fall.

As consciousness returns, I realize I have driven off the road, and I am now at the bottom of the canyon, surrounded by boulders and tall, imposing black walls. I'm looking through a veil of red; blood must be dripping into my eyes. Blinking rapidly seems to help. I lift my head and look down at my body, seeing nothing obviously broken or sticking out at weird angles. That's a pleasant surprise since I hadn't remembered to fasten my seatbelt after the scenic outlook stop, and I had been ejected onto a large boulder next to the stream. I can turn my head to see my car standing on end, nestled, hood first, between two larger boulders. It looks like a modern art display.

My eyes open wide as the immensity of the situation strikes me, and fear bubbles up. "Don't Panic." My father drummed this into me. Girl Scouts too. I even have the patch on my camping gear. "Don't Panic." The first rule of survival. Take control and make a plan. My brain is working fine, and the fear gives me razor-sharp clarity.

There had been no other vehicles on the road, so no one saw me go over the edge. No one knows where I am. There would be no skid marks, no broken guardrail, and the vegetation barely disturbed. That means I'm on my own.

I wonder if I can yell, not that it will do me a lot of good, but I have to try for my own satisfaction. I get out a few croaks and decide it's a waste of time and energy.

Maybe the horn in the car still works, but I doubt that it can be heard over the roar of the water. The car is making a funny ticking sound, and liquids are leaking out all over. Too bad it isn't burning; people always check out fires in the mountains.

Then I remember, the car has a cigarette lighter, and if it still works, I can use pages from my book to start a fire. I feel relieved to have a plan.

I try to move. Nothing responds, not arms, not legs, not fingers, not toes, nothing. I can lift my head and turn it; that's about it. With a surge of adrenaline, I realize that I feel no pain at all, except in my head, which the adrenaline magnifies to an astounding throb. I'm grateful for the sensation; it proves I'm still alive.

Shock perhaps, I think, or temporary paralysis. "Don't Panic."

Easy to say.

I lift my head and try to move my body again, this time so hard the effort brings tears to my eyes, and I'm afraid that my teeth will crack from clenching them together so tightly. Nothing. Exhausted, I decide to rest before my next attempt.

A cloud of mist drifts over my face. I lift my head up to meet the cool moistness. My head falls back and hits the rock with a loud thunk and a fresh burst of pain. Panic and fear hammer frantically to be let out, but I force them back down.

So this was the third thing, I think to myself in an attempt to stay calm while I lay sprawled on the boulder, immobile and surrounded by fried chicken.

At least the sequence is over. The Three Bad Things are complete, and I just need to concentrate on finding a way to get rescued. Fire is still my best bet.

As I lay there, speculating about how long it will take the paralysis to pass, I watch a black, hairy housefly land on a chicken leg next to my head, moving greedily back and forth.

I recall that their eggs can hatch in only eight hours.

Another sound grows louder. I look up to see a large, glossy green, iridescent blow fly go past my nose. Then it turns back and settles on my face, its long proboscis lapping greedily at my blood. Within seconds another one joins it. Shaking my head doesn't disturb them at all. I see more flies coming. I recall that some of them feed and then lay live young.

With a terrifying jolt of extreme horror and overwhelming, lunatic panic, I realize that the third bad thing hasn't even occurred yet.

I also discover that I can scream.

BLOOMS OF DARKNESS

Melissa Miles

I was in my garden, picking the dark blooms that grew there. I seemed to recall that the flowers had been red, but that memory flickered like guttering candlelight cast upon a distant wall. I didn't know who I was anymore. Since *they* had come to my town, nothing had seemed the same.

How could the arrival of a mother and daughter cause so much change?

I thought about the newcomers. They had moved into a small cottage at the western edge of town and initially seemed quite ordinary. That property had changed hands so often over my lifetime I couldn't keep track of all its inhabitants, and none of these short-term occupants seemed to care for the poor cottage, which crouched under a cliff. Then these two arrived. They were quiet, kept to themselves, and the building, which had been dilapidated to say the least, was cared for now and painted white with black edging.

A black and white theme—*how classical*, everyone in the neighborhood thought.

But it became more than that, and the care they lavished on the little house seemed to be a couple of steps beyond good maintenance, moving toward borderline obsessive.

I still thought it all rather nice, seeing the cottage cared for with smoke snaking out of the chimney on chilly days—until they got the gate. It was jet black and, well, there are no other words to describe the dreadful thing; it was a metal demon or fiend of some sort. We weren't sure if it was a joke or meant

301

to act as gargoyles did in the past. Or what? It was a mystery, a small one, but a mystery nonetheless.

We never saw these people in our town. They seemed only to exist in relation to the house: in it, near it, fixing it, driving into its tiny yard where they had built a little carport for their, yes, white car with black trim. The situation was very strange, but we were a relaxed lot. Our town had its share of artists and oddities, but then things began to change. The white cottage, so vibrant and clean, gradually morphed into a well cared for off-white, then finally gray building.

I wasn't the only one to notice. Others also quietly remarked that they had never seen anyone painting the place.

That was when they began to come to town. The mother or daughter alone—never both together—in their little white car, which now also had a gray sheen. They never went to the supermarket or the organic food shop either. They just walked around, looking at the sea, peering at the houses on the hill, and one or the other of them would sometimes climb up the old stairway to our public rose garden.

The light in our town seemed to wane and become muted, but when I drove past their house, everything shone brightly again.

They never spoke, this mother and daughter, at least that's what we thought they were. The older woman had light blonde hair, so brilliant it seemed like spun gold. The younger's was as dark as a raven at night.

The white house remained well cared for, but that gate! Every time I glanced at the metal demon, which I didn't seem able to stop myself from doing, it seemed to have changed position somehow. Not a lot, just slightly. The fiend now seemed to protrude as if trying to escape. And its face. Oh my God, its face! I have never seen such pain in a work of art, well maybe Munch's The Scream, but this was the real world, right? We were plain people living in an ordinary port town on the edge of the Pacific Ocean.

Statues and carvings don't change over time.

But actually, I reminded myself, they do. Weather and the passing of seasons make great permutations on every solid, stolid stanchion of our lives. Just normally, not within the space of days.

I don't particularly like demons and certainly seldom feel sorry for them, but I very much did in this instance. The horrid fiend was squeezed and pulled and twisted in the most profoundly awful ways like some old-time gargoyle. All within the confines of the gate.

Every day I thought about what I could do for it, and every day I did nothing. With each sunrise, the demon woke to a world more painful for it and darker for us.

The sun didn't seem to shine as bright, the dawn barely made a dent in the morning, and we became inured to the shadows in our town. The whole grim process seemed to happen so naturally. But the suffering being—*that* I could not stand—and I decided something must be done.

With great trepidation, I took the two concrete steps up to that awful gate. I couldn't hear him screaming, but I could see he was writhing. Clearly, his situation had become so much worse. I had poppies in my garden, so I brought a bouquet to ease our prospective meeting. I touched the gate to open it, and the poor creature looked up at me with a pleading expression.

"I will help you if I can," I whispered to him and opened, then shut his awful prison. I was in. The house was before me, gleaming, shiny, and white. I knocked on the old wooden door, the black posy in my other hand. I had thought that the flowers were red, but I didn't have the time to contemplate the anomaly before the door opened and the young girl was standing there in front of me.

"Hello," I said. My hands began to tremble.

"Hi," she said, blocking the narrow opening of her doorway. "Can I help you?" Her eyes were so dark they seemed almost black, and I couldn't read them at all.

"We're sorry you've been here a while, and no one has welcomed you to our community."

I thrust my bouquet of black poppies toward her.

"Thank you," she said, taking the blooms. For a moment they almost seemed red.

"And oh," I said, remembering, "how could I have forgotten so soon? "I wanted to ask you...."

"Yes?" She asked, clearly wanting to shut the door.

"Your gate."

She merely arched an ink-black eyebrow. "Clever clockwork, isn't it?"

"Oh!" I spluttered in surprise. "It's mechanical?"

The raven-haired girl laughed and turned away as she shut the door, but I still heard her words quite clearly.

"Of course, what did you think?"

And the door slammed in my face. What did I think? A very good question; did I think the gate was alive? Where was my brain? Had I been reading too much fiction? When would this foolishness let go of my mind?

I retraced my steps to the gate. The demon hung now, head sagging down, like an ebony Christ dying on a metal cross.

This wasn't right. How could I forget he was the reason I had come here?

I opened his prison once more and shut it behind me. Instead of descending, I turned and knelt on the concrete stairs, then ran my hand over the metal creature. I flinched back in a reflex of fear—the breath of the fiendish gate was hot on my hand. Oh no, it really was alive, that poor thing imprisoned in there.

Did I hear a faint whisper?

The older woman with the bright hair was behind me; she looked like a fading doll in the dim light. I was blocking the stairs. It was she who had whispered, so I rose to let her move by, and she spoke so quietly I could barely hear her words as she passed. "Pull as I push," the woman murmured. The gate clicked shut behind her, and she was standing there, blue eyes expectant, like a clear sky.

She pushed, I pulled, then we were all tangled up on the ground. The demon shook itself and smiled. Everything became confused, and then I suddenly realized the bright woman was behind me, fixing my bonds. So now I had taken the demon's place?

The light seemed to lessen once more, and I was trapped in the gate! The woman walked away, and I was left sore and frightened. I tried to control the terror welling up inside me— it felt I was trapped in a cramped box.

The demon we had liberated glanced at me briefly, then whistled and wandered away.

Was my heart too soft? Was I being punished for kindness? Was I crazy?

There was no sidewalk on the side of the street the cottage was on, but my neighbor was walking his dog on the other side of the road. The animal stopped and stared. My neighbor, surprised, followed his collie's gaze. The look of shock on his face would have been funny had I been in a different situation. As things stood, I could only try to beckon or call, yet as it turned out, I could do neither: it seemed I had been turned to metal. I tried to turn and tear myself out, but my every movement caused the metal to become colder, and its ice crept closer to my heart. My mind was twisting into madness, but I was shocked back to lucidity as a siren began to wail.

An ambulance came rushing out from the town and turned into the driveway of the little cottage. My neighbor ran over with his dog while the young girl was brought out of the house on a stretcher. The scene was one of mayhem. Apparently, she had collapsed when I had released the demon. She was still clutching my black poppies in her hand.

Then the blonde woman showed up again.

"Same thing," she whispered to me and spoke in low tones to my neighbor. "I'll push, you pull." The man nodded, though he looked very pale.

I was out! I slumped on the stair; one of the ambulance men turned and noticed me.

"Another case of collapse?" he asked.

I gathered my strength. "No."

"Let me check your vitals before I leave."

I shook my head, and his partner called. We were left with the siren noises ringing in our ears as they drove off for the hospital.

"I'm sorry. I don't like my daughter trapping souls," the woman said, looking a little ashamed, "but she does it for me because I need your light to survive. The light of the sun, of kindness, of beauty and joy. She lives on the darkness in the world and of the soul." She paused to laugh bitterly for a moment. "My girl is seldom in need of sustenance."

I nodded, but I didn't understand at all. Not then. My neighbor looked thoughtful.

"You're a writer," he said.

I nodded. Everyone knew.

"Light and darkness are expanded and expounded by words," he explained. "You burn brighter because both aspects live in your heart and course through your veins."

"Possibly," I murmured, doubtful and more than a little confused.

I turned to the bright-haired woman. "Where is your daughter now?"

"She has gone to seek light, care, or kindness." She smiled with a touch of sadness. Again, I understood nothing at all.

There was a town meeting—even the whistling demon attended. After much debate, some of it quite heated, the residents agreed to donate a set amount of light and make do with some dullness in our community. They also passed a non-binding resolution to put neither the fiend nor me back inside the gate again.

"I was a painter," the gargoyle-fiend explained to us all. "These two witches, sorceresses, or whatever they are saw the brightness in me and my work, but I have been in the gate so long, there's nothing left except this." He looked down and gestured with his taloned hands at his hideous, demonic body. "Still, I've gotten used to it and quite like how things are now. There are a lot of advantages... being able to almost fly, the prehensile tail, and so on." He trailed off and sighed.

Everyone was absolutely silent for a long moment. The fiend broke the spell as he whistled a few bars of his signature, sad little tune, then sat back down.

"You can come home with me, " I said, thinking this would keep him from annoying everyone. At that moment, I was so grateful to them all.

The witches were to be our secret; the younger one in the hospital had come home.

As time passed, I gradually lost my words, and now I wonder what kind of deal was really struck behind closed doors? The city hospital has shut, and many other facilities have faded away as well. Whatever the case, our town remains as bright and lovely as ever, except for my house, where a perpetual gloom seems to reside, and I no longer see friends or drive to the village. All I feel these days is tired right down to the marrow of my bones.

My only companion is a whistling gargoyle-demon who paints dark, disturbingly abstract pictures on my walls in the gloom using charcoal from my fireplace. My life is as gray as his art.

I'm no longer sure of who I am anymore, so I stay at home. My only remaining hobby is cutting buds from my garden of blooming darkness and making bouquets of black flowers to grace the wordless silence of my house that is broken only by a demon's sad whistling.

AMONG STARS AND STONES

Brandon Barrows

I've spent almost thirty years on battlefields, but not as a soldier. I'm a journalist and a photographer. You've never heard my name because I'm not one of the famous ones, like Hetherington or Nachtway, but photography has always been my life.

Ethan Layport asked my age not long after we first met, and laughingly called me an old man when I answered. I never thought of myself that way. In my head, I'm still twenty-five years old, setting out on a grand adventure that'll make me a household name. But I'm fifty-four this year, and I've never yet caught on film the defining moment that makes a career. Maybe I never will. That's why I agreed to go along with him. One last chance. And yet I didn't take a single picture during the time I spent with Layport, and I never even realized it until long after.

I was in the Washir District of Helmand province, following a rumor that didn't pan out. While I was there, though, some of my camera equipment was stolen from the back of my jeep. The same day, I saw it in one of the bazaars. The merchant didn't believe it was mine, of course, and talking to the commander of the American army contingent stationed there, supposedly training local police, got me nowhere. He didn't even pretend to be sympathetic and treated me like a foolish tourist. I saw combat before he was even born.

The equipment was gone unless I wanted to buy it back. I had to accept that. But something came of the incident: I met Ethan Layport. As I was leaving the army compound, a uniformed man detached himself from a group of half a dozen chatting soldiers. He was nobody I knew, but he smiled as if we were old friends as he approached. I was curious, so I waited for him.

"You're Cook, aren't you? Reese Cook, the photographer?" he asked.

I was surprised he knew my name, but somehow, I didn't think to ask how he did. "That's me, yes."

"Rare to see an American out here." He stuck out his hand. "Ethan Layport."

For some reason, I hesitated to shake the other man's hand. The hot sun burned down on my bare head, and I realized after a moment that I was being rude. I took his hand. "Glad to meet you," I told him.

"Listen." Layport lightly gripped my shoulder, guiding me to a shadowed spot near the mud-brick wall nearby. "I don't want to come on too strongly, but we need your help and you'll be glad you went along if you say yes."

"I don't understand," I told him.

It had to be some sort of scam. I've been all over Europe, Asia, parts of Africa, and I thought I knew every kind of man there was on Earth. I don't mean skin color or religion or anything like that. I mean in the ways that matter. Layport was like no one I ever met before. He was confident in a way that should have been off-putting, but instead, I found myself wanting to please him, to give him the answers I knew he wanted. He smiled, radiant and innocent as a kid, and when he did, he seemed so familiar, like we knew each other a long time ago, and I just couldn't quite remember.

"What did you say your name was again?" I knew full well what his name was, if not *who* he was. I was just buying time.

"Layport," he said, not offended. "Look, my friends and I ... we're getting out of here. You've been around; you can take care of yourself. This is something you'll appreciate."

"You're going to desert?"

Layport smiled and it was almost shy this time. "For a little while, maybe. Look." He squeezed my shoulder. "Me and a couple guys have something planned and it's right up your alley. Where are you staying? We'll come by tonight and talk about it."

I should have just walked away. I gave him the name of the hostel I was staying in. Layport smiled again, nodded, and said, "See you," as he walked away.

Just after dark, Layport and two other men appeared at the hostel. It was small and crowded, and there was barely room to sleep, much less talk in private. Layport introduced the other men as Rivera and Crosby. Rivera was dark-skinned and small but broad-shouldered. Crosby was tall and blond and ran toward huskiness. We shook hands all around and then, at Layport's suggestion, the four of us went out to my jeep and drove to a rise outside of the village. The moon was just coming up, and its reflection on the sandy terrain was beautiful and vaguely eerie.

"Okay, what's this all about?" I asked, after I turned the engine off.

Ethan Layport smiled and even in the gloom, his face seemed to light up. Rivera was the one who answered. "You got this jeep and you know your way around." He glanced at his friends and continued, "We wanna go up into the mountains, to the Koh-e-Sulaiman."

I told them I didn't understand. Crosby said, "There's treasure, man. You help us, we'll help you. You'll get twenty-five percent."

Crosby kept talking and Rivera joined in, but their voices were just background noise. I was watching Layport, but I didn't know why. His eyes seemed to take in the moonlight and throw it back more brightly. As crazy as it sounds, I felt all of a sudden that there was something hypnotic about those eyes, and I turned away, if reluctantly.

"You're nuts," I said, cutting off whatever Crosby was talking about now. "Deserting, going off after some treasure that probably doesn't exist. I don't need the trouble and neither do any of you. Let's go back."

I turned the engine over, but Layport's voice stopped me from shifting gears. "When we leave here, we're going to Ochyrodeia. You've heard of it, haven't you, Mr. Cook?"

I heard of it, yes. Ochyrodeia was a legendary city, an Atlantis of the mountains. After Alexander the Great's death, his empire fell to ruins, various factions warring for control of whatever they could get their hands on. Alexander's provincial governors, his generals, and many others set up kingdoms all across his campaign trail from Greece to Africa to India and every place in between.

One soldier, however, remained loyal to Alexander's name and the things he represented. Irenaeus of Macedon was a veteran of Alexander's wars and when his leader passed from this world, Irenaeus and three thousand soldiers, who felt as their commander did, retreated into the mountains now called Koh-e-Sulaiman. Along the way, they raided and looted towns and strongholds of various opposing factions, supposedly amassing a huge fortune meant to finance the campaigns of some future Alexander. Finally, they fortified a mountain pass and vowed to wait until a new, worthy leader appeared.

And so was born Ochyrodeia. But no one ever took up the mantle Alexander left behind, and the men of the city passed into myth and legend.

If the city existed, finding it was the kind of achievement a man could retire on. Write a book, go on speaking tours. *If* it was found. *If* it existed.

"Ochyrodeia is just a myth," I heard myself saying.

Layport smiled in the semi-darkness, the way he did when we first met. It was warm and kind and made me want to listen to him. "You're just afraid of being disappointed, Mr. Cook."

I admitted that was true, but that wasn't all I was worried about.

"Thirty years you've been wandering and what do you have to show for it?" Layport asked. The question stung, but

I couldn't deny that I didn't have much. "Ochyrodeia is real, Mr. Cook," he continued. "I've seen it and I want to go back."

"You've been there?" I didn't hide my surprise or my suspicion. It was like hearing someone say they'd been to Oz or Narnia.

"Just trust me," Layport said in answer. "And I'll make sure you see Ochyrodeia, too." It was said quietly, without any particular emphasis, but somehow it was impossible to doubt him.

I wanted to believe more than anything, but a voice in the back of my head kept screaming that it was too good to be true.

"There's nothing to be afraid of," Layport said.

I believed him.

Two nights later, I left Washir in my dusty, rattling old jeep. A few miles out of town, I met the other three men. They wore local clothing and large packs. Crosby and Rivera also carried rifles. All three climbed into the jeep and we headed toward the distant mountains.

For two days and two more nights, nothing out of the ordinary happened. Despite there being no roads to exactly where we wanted to go, we made good time. On the third night, we camped near a tiny oasis that was barely more than a damp hole. Crosby was making dinner while Rivera and I set up the two tents. A group of men suddenly appeared just outside of the light of Crosby's cook-fire. Their presence was all but silent until someone among them murmured, "*bhrna*," which literally means "outsider" but is more like *alien*.

The whispered word spread through the group. From their clothing, I guessed they were Noorzai tribesmen. Most of them were armed. Whether we were trespassing or not, I didn't know, but their hostile intent was plain.

Crosby ran to the jeep for his rifle, but it was an empty gesture. Even if all four of us had guns, the math was against us. Maybe as a soldier, holding the weapon simply made

Crosby feel better, but I wasn't a soldier and all I felt was death crowding closer.

The Noorzai's voices cut off as if someone muted a television. None of us moved an inch after Crosby went for his gun, but now, Layport was standing before the tribesmen. I couldn't say where he came from, but I thought of what he told me: *"There's nothing to be afraid of."* I believed him when he said it and remembering, I felt better.

Layport said nothing. He just smiled, crossed his arms over his chest, and let his gaze wander over the faces of the Noorzai. Slowly, in ones and twos, they drew back into the darkness. Without violence or even a word, somehow Layport defeated those men, sending them into a silent but urgent retreat. I could practically feel the fear coming off of them and I had no idea why. Within a minute or two, there was no sign that any of the desert men even existed.

Beside me, Rivera whispered, "Jesus Christ."

Rivera believed in God. He was a good Catholic, he told me one night as we sat next to the fire. Crosby was on watch and Layport, as usual by then, was nowhere to be seen. The fact that Rivera deserted his army post and was on the way to loot ancient treasures was not a contradiction as far as he was concerned. Being a good Christian was something in your heart. Whatever else you did couldn't affect that as long as you believed.

Crosby wasn't much for conversation, and Layport was often on his own errands at night. Rivera and I became friends simply because there was no one else. I asked him what he knew of Layport. I described my first meeting with Layport and my impression of him: the man was good-natured and seemed dependable, but he was a mystery.

"I don't know a damned thing," Rivera told me. "Crosby and me, we've known each other a while. I don't really like him much, but he's a good man to have your back. Well, I heard about Ochyrodeia one day, from some Pashies talkin' in the bazaar—I don't know how it came up—and I mentioned it to Crosby. We were dreaming about that treasure and then there's Layport, all of a sudden."

"What do you mean?"

"I mean just like that." He snapped his fingers. "Crosby and I are talking in the barracks, playing two-handed gin, and then there's Layport. He asked me to deal him in. I started giving him cards like it was the most natural thing in the world. Then, once he's got them, he says, 'I want to see Ochyrodeia. I'll help you find it.' Never seen him before that."

"But ... he's a member of your unit, isn't he?"

Rivera just shrugged.

At Bandare, the radiator of my old jeep exploded like a grenade was stuffed inside it. It terrified me; we were still miles from our destination, with rough terrain ahead and nothing behind us that could be considered help. Certainly nothing as convenient as a mechanic. I was beginning to regret this whole adventure. I said as much to the other men.

Layport looked at me quite seriously, no warmth or kindness on his face for once. "I told you, I'll lead you to Ochyrodeia."

"It would be a lot easier if the jeep still ran," I said bitterly.

"True." Layport hopped out of the vehicle, hefting his bag over his shoulder. "But it doesn't really change anything." He smiled. "Have a little faith, will you?"

There didn't seem to be much choice.

We walked through a land as inhospitable as any on Earth or probably any other planet. I didn't know the exact name of the area, but it was dry and rocky, with few plants and no water. I didn't even see any animal tracks that might lead us to a hidden waterhole or oasis. The sun was hotter than I could ever remember, and there was no place to hide from it. None of that stopped Layport. He marched through that hell as confidently, as casually, as if he was walking through a park in some city back in the States.

"Aren't you tired?" I asked him after a few hours.

"I don't think about it," Layport answered. "I'm only thinking of Ochyrodeia."

"I feel like I'm half-dead already."

Layport grinned. "That just means you're still alive. C'mon." He picked up the pace. The rest of us tried to keep up.

I did my best, but with every step, I grew weaker. I had water in my canteen, but I didn't dare drink more than an occasional drop or two. Who knew when we'd find more? Before long, Ochyrodeia didn't matter anymore, only water. It was all I thought of. I was a prisoner to it. My daydreams began with crystal-clear, gurgling brooks and ended in scummy mud puddles. Any water would be welcome.

"Aren't you thirsty?" I asked Layport at some point. Rivera, Crosby, and I drank sparingly, but I never saw Layport take even a single sip.

"Of course," he said, with his ever-present smile. Then he turned toward the mountains in the distance. I followed his gaze and realized that they were no longer very distant at all. In fact, I looked around us and realized we were now in the foothills. I couldn't say when that happened. I glanced at Rivera; he noticed the change too, but just shrugged.

We were surrounded by fields of poppies, sprawling in an unbroken blanket of pink and purple and white. The scenery had changed so suddenly. It was like we were plucked from one place and set down elsewhere. But it didn't matter. Green grass grew around the base of the flowers and I could smell water. I tore away from the group, running, following the scent. I found the pool by falling into it. The water was cool and still, and it tasted sweet when I dropped to my knees and drank directly from it.

The other men came up more slowly and by the time they did, I was satisfied. My stomach sloshed. I drank too much, but I didn't care. My only wish for most of the day was water and it finally came true.

As I was refilling my canteen, Layport squatted next to me and did the same. He smiled and said, "Faith is always rewarded, Cook."

We took a break, eating and drinking some more, but within an hour we were on our feet again. It was afternoon, and I thought we should make camp since we had water.

But Layport announced, "The path we need isn't far now." Hearing that, nobody felt tired anymore.

It was Crosby who found the pass, half-hidden behind a wall of ferns. It was barely more than a tunnel.

"I recognize this," Layport said. "This is the way."

We let him lead us, and it was strangely silent as we moved steadily upwards. Crosby and Rivera were on edge. Each man carried his rifle at the ready. After the incident with the Noorzai, I began carrying a handgun Rivera loaned me. My hand stroked the textured rubber grip sticking out of my belt.

We came out of the pass and looked down on a narrow, green-carpeted valley nestled among the hills clinging to the foot of the mountain. The air was clear and seemed to magnify things in the distance. Across the little valley, the remains of what must have been Ochyrodeia began halfway up the valley's opposite wall, much steeper than the one we stood on. It was a cluster of tumble-down buildings clinging to the rocky face. Worn stairs, wide and low, were carved into the surface of the rock, winding between the buildings, leading higher to what must have been the keep overlooking the pass on the other side. If I'm honest, it wasn't very impressive. I expected more from a legendary lost city, but I'd built it up in my mind over the last few days. Anything we found was a significant discovery.

"Hey, look!" Crosby shouted, pointing to a corner of the valley. There was a single tent like the desert nomads live in. A trail of smoke rose from the hole in its roof, a sure sign that it was occupied.

Crosby turned to Layport, anger on his face. "Who the hell is that?"

Layport just smiled and started forward down the slope into the valley.

"Hey!" Crosby yelled after him. Rivera put a hand on the other man's arm. "Let him go. He's gotten us this far."

I frowned at this new strangeness but had to agree. Finding someone waiting for us here, at the site of a city supposedly lost more than two thousand years ago, was unexpected, but Layport said he'd seen Ochyrodeia before, hadn't he? Maybe he wasn't the only one. There was an unfamiliar feeling at the base of my skull as I followed Ethan Layport. I glanced over my shoulder. Crosby and Rivera were coming along, their heads tilted together in conversation, guns gripped tightly.

I lost sight of Layport behind a rock formation. When I came out on the other side, he was nowhere to be seen, but the tent wasn't far off. I hurried toward it, curiosity driving me on.

I lifted the tent's flap and was hit by the pungent smells of wood smoke, incense, unwashed body, and spicy cooking. It was dim, but I stepped inside, pausing at the entrance to give my eyes a moment to adjust. When they did, I saw the tent's occupant. He was a tiny man so old I couldn't even guess his age. Layport called me an old man once, but even I was like a child compared to the tent's owner.

The man sat on a frayed prayer rug, his thin body wrapped in a wispy garment that looked as if it had never been clean. His lips moved and if I concentrated, I could hear the sounds coming from his throat, but I couldn't understand the words.

"Old sir," I tried in Arabic. "Forgive the intrusion."

"Put aside your guns," the old man answered in a surprisingly strong voice. "You will not need them in this place."

I realized that Crosby and Rivera had followed me into the tent. Neither one of them seemed to understand the old man's words, but both got the intent. All three of us lay down our weapons.

As I let go of the pistol, Layport appeared at my side. For only the second time since I met him, he wasn't smiling. He didn't have the sober look he gave me when I doubted this venture, though, either. Instead, he seemed annoyed, as if he hadn't planned on the ancient man's presence and didn't care for it at all.

"Let's get after the treasure," Layport half-whispered. He looked at me, then at Rivera and Crosby. "It's what we came for, isn't it?"

There was a moment of complete silence as if the world itself had stopped, then Crosby broke it. "Yeah. Let's go. This geezer isn't anything to worry about." He picked up his rifle and went outside. Rivera did the same.

Layport turned to the flap as well, pausing as if waiting for me. When I made no move, he said, "Cook, let's go. He's nothing."

I turned back to the man on the rug. His face was worn out and mournful as if he saw every sorrow in the world, and it drained the life from him without allowing him to pass on to whatever came next. "In a minute," I said over my shoulder, but when I looked Layport was already gone.

I turned back to the old man. His eyes were closed, but it felt as if he was staring right at me.

"How long have you been sitting here, old sir?" I asked.

"Longer than can be counted in years," he answered.

"Why?"

Thin shoulders made the barest movement. "To think, to study. This is an ancient place, peopled by ghosts. Ghosts are not bound by time, and perhaps they can tell of the future as well as the past."

"Have they ever spoken to you?"

The old man answered with a question. "Who can say?"

There was a long silence between us, then I asked, "Is this really Ochyrodeia? The city built by Irenaeus of Macedon?"

"It is." This time the old man's head definitely nodded. He opened his eyes and looked directly at me. "City is too grand a word for it, though. This was merely a prison, built by a lost and lonely man who sealed himself away from the world, waiting for a time that would never again come." It was the most he said all at one time, and his voice had a droning, hypnotic quality that reminded me very much of Ethan Layport.

"But ... the treasure," I pressed. "All the gold Irenaeus captured from his rivals."

"There is no treasure. Irenaeus left himself with nothing. He was a hollow man, lost in a strange land from which he chose not to escape. I am the same."

Shaking my head, I said, "I don't understand."

"Maybe that is the lesson." I thought the old man's lips curled just the slightest bit, but I might have imagined it.

I was getting annoyed. "Isn't there anything definite you can tell me?"

"Go up the hill." The old man closed his eyes and waved a hand. It was a gesture of dismissal. "Go to Irenaeus's prison. Maybe you will find your own answer."

I moved to the exit, frustrated and somehow angry. "Layton says there is treasure here. That he's seen the place before."

"Treasure among stones and stars? It could well be. It all depends." This time, the old man definitely smiled. It wasn't like Layport's warm, friendly smile, and it sent an uncomfortable tingle down my spine as if something leaped from him to me through it.

I shook the feeling off. Tired of riddles, I left the tent and stomped toward the ruins.

It was quiet once I reached the fallen stones and the grasses and ferns and moss that grew up between them. I felt eyes on me, though. The ancient man mentioned ghosts. I looked around and saw Rivera, further inside the ruins, moving in and out of holes in a wall of huge stone blocks. I picked my way closer to my friend, but before I reached him, I spotted Layport. He was standing on narrow, wind-eroded stairs, smiling. He wasn't searching or exploring, just watching Rivera.

"Layport," I said. The other man turned and directed his familiar smile at me but didn't say anything. He went up the stairs. I followed. The smaller stairs led to the great stairway we saw from across the valley, the ones that led to the heart of the fortress.

At the top, Layport ducked his head and went through a half-fallen archway. I chased after him and found myself inside a vast chamber. The floor was covered with fragments of rock fallen from the ceiling and walls, and ancient wooden furniture, so old it was just powder retaining its original shape. I accidentally touched a low-slung chair and it collapsed, sending up the smell of dust, mold, and rot. I choked and felt sick to my stomach.

Light streamed in through breaks in the ceiling and once my vision adjusted, I saw another archway on the far side of the chamber. The room beyond must have been carved into the mountain itself, I thought. Layport, as if waiting for me to notice it myself, went through that archway.

Again, I followed, and when I stepped into the next room, my boots crunched like I was walking through dry, autumn leaves. I looked at what I stepped in and my heart jumped in my chest. It was a body so long dead that time had no meaning. I stepped back and took in the room. I was in a sepulcher. The entire chamber, much larger than the outer one, was carpeted in what remained of Irenaeus's followers.

Hundreds, thousands, of bodies lay in crumbling heaps, bare skulls and rib cages surrounded by a litter of tarnished breastplates, helmets, swords, shields, spearheads, and knife blades. These were the men who swore pointless loyalty to a fallen leader and went into exile, supposedly surrounded by the treasure stolen from usurpers of the throne Alexander left behind. I gasped and began to choke again on the dust and detritus stirred up by my intrusion on this forgotten tomb.

I saw more remains than I could count and enough ruined weapons and armor to equip them all, but no treasure. There was no hint of any of the gold Irenaeus's men were said to have collected along the way to this, their final destination.

I walked into the outer chamber and then back out into the waning sunlight. Crosby was waiting. His rifle rose, but when he saw it was me, he lowered the gun. "Where have you been?" he asked.

I gestured toward the archway I came from. "Inside."

"Have you seen Rivera?"

"No. Why? What's going on?"

Crosby showed me his teeth and half-snarled, "That little bastard wants it all for himself."

"All of what?"

"The treasure!" Crosby hissed. "What the hell did we come here for, man? Now that we've found it, Rivera wants it all for himself. He asked Layport about it, how he'd feel splitting it two ways instead of four. Layport just warned me."

I shook my head, thinking of my friend and his religious convictions. Betrayal lived in the heart, didn't it? "That's impossible. Layport was inside with me."

Crosby wasn't listening. "Where's your gun?" he asked.

I hadn't given it a thought since the man in the tent told me to put it down. "I forgot it, back at the old man's place."

"Great. That's just great. What good are you?" Crosby snapped. "Whatever." He jacked a round into the rifle's chamber. "I'll deal with him myself, then." Something flared in his eyes. "Don't think you're getting a full share after this, though."

"We haven't even found anything!"

A bullet splatted off the rock above us, sending shards raining down on our heads. The throaty *bam* of the report bounced all around the rock formations and raced down the valley.

I flopped onto my belly as Crosby dove behind a large fragment of stone. "Did you see where that came from?" His eyes were wild.

I shook my head.

"God damn it! You're useless!" He duck-walked to another position, popped up, fired off a blind shot, then dropped back down. The report rattled among the ruins below us, sending up thin echoes.

After a moment, a voice came from below. "Crosby, you asshole! Thought you could wait 'til we got here and then take us all out? You're not gonna get the treasure, you stupid bastard! I'll blast you to hell and back before I let that happen!"

I couldn't see where Rivera was hiding, but Crosby must have because he sprang to his full height, braced his rifle against a crumbling parapet and fired rapidly. Again and again he pulled the trigger and with each explosion, the fire in his eyes danced and grew more savage. "Go ahead and try!" he screamed at his friend. "I've had your extra magazines for two days!"

I don't know if Rivera heard Crosby's taunts. I curled up into a ball, my hands over my ears. When the shots finally stopped, I crawled to the top of the stairs and looked down. Toward the entrance of the ruins, Rivera lay sprawled in a heap, facedown. Clearly, he tried to run, but now he made no movement. The only sound was a whisper of wind racing down the mountain and through the valley.

Crosby ejected the magazine from his rifle, jammed another home. Without looking at me, he said, "That's that. Let's get the treasure. Layport said it was in here somewhere."

"There's no treasure."

Crosby whirled, the rifle ready again.

"It's just bones and dust in there," I told him. "And where's Layport? You said you saw him, but—"

"Who cares? We're here; we don't need him anymore." Crosby closed the distance between us, grabbed my arm, and jerked me to my feet. "Let's go. And don't get clever. You saw what happened to Rivera." He turned me around and shoved me toward the archway.

Inside the outer chamber, Crosby couldn't stand it anymore. He pushed me aside and ran toward the far doorway. After a moment, I heard him cry out in excitement. I went in after him. He was on his knees among the fragmented bodies, the ruined weapons, the dust, the filth of decay. He was laughing and tossing handfuls of the stuff over his head.

"Gold and jewels, Cook! I never thought it would be so much! We're rich, man! We're *rich*!"

Something flipped in my stomach, and I felt the food I ate and all of that water I drank forcing its way back up my throat. I turned and vomited in a corner. When I was done, I wiped my mouth and croaked, "Crosby, there's no treasure. It's ... don't you see what you're holding?"

"Shut up!" Crosby whirled, rifle in hand again. "Don't you try to fool me, you miserable old bastard. You just want it for yourself. You're like Rivera—greedy! I said you'd get a share, even though you don't deserve one, but now I think maybe I'll just give you this instead."

He raised the rifle, but whatever he was seeing, its lure was too strong. He couldn't even keep his eyes on me. They kept drifting back to the "treasure" scattered all around us, and even in the low light, I could see the madness in those eyes.

Crosby killed Rivera, and I had no doubt he'd kill me, too, if I let him. I left my gun behind with the old man, but I was surrounded by weapons. I didn't want to hurt Crosby; I just wanted to get away. If I tried to run, he'd shoot me in the back, like he did our friend.

He was on his knees again, though, rooting through the remains of what was once another human being, rubbing the rot and decay against his face and murmuring, "Money! All this money! Never do another close-order drill again!"

I scanned the area and spotted something that might work: the iron cone of a helmet that seemed to still be in reasonably good condition. I crouched, lifted the helmet. Crosby whirled, his eyes blazing. "I saw that!"

He raised the rifle at the same moment I threw the helmet. The hunk of iron connected with Crosby's face and the rifle discharged harmlessly, sending a bullet racing far over my shoulder and out of the chamber. Crosby fell backward, and there was a sickening *crack* as the back of his skull impacted with something. My stomach lurched and if it hadn't been empty already, I would have thrown up again.

I turned away and Layport was with me now. I hadn't heard him enter, hadn't seen him for some time. "Good, Reese." It was only the second time he ever used my first name. "With Crosby and Rivera gone, only the old man is left. Get rid of him and all the treasure is yours."

I pulled back in horror, caught between a sea of bodies and whatever Layport was. "What? Why would I kill the old man? He's harmless."

"Is he?" Layport's smile became patronizing. "And anyway, he's a witness. Get rid of him and that," he pointed at Crosby, "will never come back to haunt you. The treasure will be yours."

"It was an accident ... self-defense! Besides..." I took a step back, crouched, and blindly felt for Crosby's rifle. My fingers closed around it and I straightened, jacked a round into the chamber. "There's no treasure here, Layport. You've been lying to us all along."

The smile on Layport's face changed again, becoming sad now. "The treasure is here. You just have to trust me. I told you Ochyrodeia was real and I led you here, didn't I?" He gestured to the room at large. "You can find what they gave up, what they left behind. You just have to take the final step. That old man hasn't long to live, anyway."

I stepped back further and lifted the rifle. "Stay away from me, Layport. Get away from the doorway," I warned him.

"Kill the old man, Reese, and I'll show you the treasure. It's here. I promise."

"Shut up!" I screamed. "Shut up! Get out of my way!"

"Trust me," Layport said with that same droning, hypnotic quality the old man's voice possessed. "Trust me."

It grew darker as the sun sank behind the mountains, and whatever fingers of dying light remained could no longer find the cracks in the chamber's ceiling. Layport's smile remained but it seemed to float alone in the darkness, detached from the other man, a thing all its own, wholly unconnected to anything real or familiar. And still his voice droned on. "Trust me ... the treasure ... the old man ... kill him."

"Shut up! Shut up! Shut up!"

I fired again and again, as Crosby did when he killed Rivera. I chambered rounds as quickly as I could and pulled the trigger until it made an empty clicking sound. Only then did I leave the room, one hand half-covering my eyes, too afraid to look at what I'd done.

I made my way out of the ruins, down the hill, back to the old man's tent. He still sat in the shadows of his home, exactly as I first saw him, except that his voice was still now. I thought he was asleep, but he stirred and said, "You've returned."

I nodded, but it was for myself. The old man's eyes were closed. "I shot Layport."

"Who?" the old man asked.

"Layport, one of the men who was with me. There was Crosby, the blond man, and Rivera, the darker-skinned one." I didn't know how to describe Layport. All I could remember of him was his smile, hideous in those last moments. "Layport was the third."

"I recall the blond man, yes, and the dark-skinned man, but there was no third, save you."

A shiver went through me. I wanted to argue, to shake the old man, to rattle his skull and make him admit he saw Layport, but what was the use?

I lay down the empty rifle, exchanging it for the pistol I forgot earlier, then turned and left the tent. I walked back the way we first came, out of the valley. I discovered then that my canteen, once full from the poppy fields spring, was empty. Somewhere along the line, it was punctured by a stray bullet or a sharp protrusion. With everything that happened, I never even noticed. I should have gone back, collected Crosby or Rivera's canteen, but I couldn't make my feet turn toward that hidden valley again.

I looked east, toward the far-off place where we abandoned the jeep. Returning to it was pointless, though. It would never run again, and I couldn't walk all the way back to Washir. Instead, I turned west into the growing night. Sooner or later, I would either find people or die from thirst, hunger, or exposure. It made no difference to me just then.

When I did find someone, if I found anyone, I would ask them to contact the army on my behalf to help me arrange a way out of this country. I wouldn't mention Crosby or Rivera. It would help no one, and I didn't want to stir up any trouble for whatever family they left behind. Deserters' survivors couldn't collect any benefits.

And I wouldn't mention Layport, either. What good would it do me? I doubted the army ever even heard of him.

THE LITTLE PEOPLE

Kurt Newton

The woods.

Tall trees. Warm sun. Leaves the color of apples, squash, and pumpkin. The ground soft from year after year of growth and decay. The smell earthy. Nature's spice.

The afternoon stillness suddenly interrupted.

A black four-door racing up a narrow country road. It comes to an abrupt halt. A teenage girl spills out of the passenger side, leaving the car door open. The young man driving shouts after her.

The girl climbs over the stone wall and runs into the woods. In a matter of seconds she's gone, swallowed up by the trees.

Her name is Becca.

After a while, Becca stops running. She decides enough time has elapsed and heads back to the road. She lives only a few miles away. She'll walk home. But between the tears and the sameness of the trees, she doesn't know which way to go for certain, so she guesses.

Becca realizes she's guessed wrong after about ten minutes of walking. The woods grow thicker, the sunlight less frequent and bright. She reaches into her pants pocket and discovers her cell phone isn't there. That's weird. That cell is her lifeline to the rest of the world. She must have left it in the car with that jerk.

Stupid. But then what else would you call a girl who trusts a guy she doesn't really know?

Becca had thought it was too good to be true. A house party at a friend of a friend's. *Come on, it will be fun*, he said. Bradley. A guy she met online. He commented on the pics she posted. He messaged her. She said okay. When he picked her up, he was everything he appeared to be. He said all the right things. But once they got to the party, he wouldn't let her talk to any other guy. A fight nearly broke out. Becca was so embarrassed she asked him to take her home.

Stupid.

Becca tries to head back to where the woods are sunnier, but it's the afternoon. *Isn't the sun setting?* she asks herself. If she chases the sun, won't it just lead her deeper into the woods?

She doesn't know. All she knows is that she wants to go home. But she's lost. And she has to pee. She figures any spot will do. She stops to listen first.

The woods breathe around her. A couple of birds call to each other in the distance. Nothing more. She pulls her pants and underwear down to her ankles and squats.

She closes her eyes in relief. And hears a rustling in the leaves.

"Bradley?"

She hurries to pull up her pants and turns around, expecting to see him. She nearly falls over. When at last she rights herself, Becca is greeted by three of the smallest people she's ever seen. "Oh, hello?" she says.

Standing in the leaves are two men and a woman, each no taller than a preschooler. Their homespun clothes are of a style that might have been worn a hundred years ago—thick pants, long-sleeved shirt—even though the weather is unseasonably warm. They appear old in age, but then maybe their size has condensed their features, making them appear older than they really are. The one on the left, a man, wears a round hat with a wide brim. His belly is just as round as his hat. The one in the center, a wizened old woman, leans on a crooked walking stick. The man on the right has a younger-looking face and could very well be the old woman's son. He grips a burlap sack by its neck; something squirms inside.

"Can you tell me how to get back to the road?" Becca asks the little people.

The old woman with the walking stick speaks to her in a language Becca has never heard before, a language of hard *K's* and *G's*, soft *Sh* and *Ch* sounds, with the occasional trill of an *R*.

"I don't know what you're saying," Becca says. "I'm lost. I need to get back to the road. There's a road not far from here somewhere."

The three strangers look at each other.

In that moment, Becca feels truly lost. The daylight is fading. She doesn't know how big these woods are. She doesn't know how far the nearest road is or even if she can stumble upon one. Tears begin to well at the corners of her eyes.

"I just want to go home."

The little people seem to perk up and once again whisper together in that strange language they share. They nod in unison, and the old woman with the walking stick grunts a string of syllables at Becca. The three then turn and walk away.

Becca assumes they will lead her out of the woods and back to the road. She follows close behind.

How these people navigate through the forest is a mystery to Becca. There is no path that she can see. In fact, the three little people barely leave an impression at all on the ground as they walk. They must not weigh very much, she thinks, because their feet hardly crush a leaf.

They walk for what seems like a long time in silence. Silent but for the sounds of the weald: the movement of darkening trees as they sway ever so slightly in the gathering gloom, the flutter of leaves turning in the wind, a collective susurration like the deep, restful breaths of a sleeping giant, the intermittent chirps, peeps, and whistles of woodland birds and animals.

Eventually, they come to a clearing. To Becca's amazement, in the clearing is a small village.

There are miniature houses with miniature gardens and miniature roads that look a lot like bike paths. There's smoke rising from miniature chimneys and a myriad of little men and little women milling about tending their gardens, fixing fence posts, or simply engaging in conversation. When Becca and her escorts enter the village, everyone stops what they're doing. It appears even the sun halts in its course across the sky because it's much sunnier here in this dollhouse village than anywhere else in the woods.

The first to greet them is another man with a balding head, wearing a blood-stained apron. He takes the burlap sack and hurries away to one of the buildings and disappears inside. Meanwhile, the residents of the village gather around Becca. They gaze up at her. Small hands reach out to touch her, and some of those hands offer food. There is an excited chatter among the crowd. She doesn't understand a word, but some things are universal. Becca has attended large family gatherings and outdoor concerts before. There's an almost festive atmosphere to her arrival, and she doesn't understand why. She's an outsider, and as lovely as the tiny village is, she still wants to go home.

"Please," Becca says, raising her voice. The crowd noise lessens. "You are all so kind, but there's been some kind of mistake. I need to find the nearest road. I need to get back."

The little people look up at Becca with confusion etched on their faces. A few appear sad.

Becca turns to the old woman with the walking stick. "Can you take me to where the big people live?" She holds her hand up high as if measuring something much taller than herself.

The eyes of the old woman, and the two men she is with, grow large. Again, they speak together in their strange language. A consensus is soon reached. The old woman with the walking stick nods to Becca and holds up her hand for quiet, then addresses the now sizeable crowd. Her speech is a brief one, and at its conclusion a collective sigh spreads among the villagers. The old woman gestures and begins walking into the forest with her two original companions at her heels. Becca joins them and waves as they leave.

Again, the three little people escort Becca through the woods. They take a different route than the one that brought them to the village. The daylight is fading fast.

Soon, the woods begin to look familiar to Becca again. A deadfall here, a large twisted tree there. They are close to returning to the spot where she jumped the stone wall.

The three little people stop, and Becca stops alongside them. The old woman points.

Ahead, in the near dark of dusk, a young man is sunk up to his waist in the forest floor. It takes Becca a moment to realize the young man is Bradley, and he hasn't been swallowed up by the earth but is digging a hole. Beside the open pit lies a body—that of a young woman. Bradley pulls the corpse into the hole, steps out, and begins filling it with dirt.

Becca remembers now. A chill runs over her skin.

On the drive home, Bradley wouldn't keep his hands to himself. And he wouldn't take no for an answer. That's when she yelled for him to stop the car, so he slammed on the brakes. Her head hit the windshield, and she saw stars. Becca got out then and began walking, only to hear a sudden roar like a large, angry animal. Then something blunt struck her. The next thing she remembered, she was running into the woods.

Becca watches as Bradley scoops in the last bit of dirt, pats the new grave with the back of his shovel, and covers his work with leaves as if the incident never happened.

As if she never existed.

Becca suddenly feels very small.

The three little people watch this burial as if they've seen scenes like this play out a thousand times before. The old woman raises her bent stick and points it at Bradley. She utters a few guttural words as black as the night and as sharp as her stare. A branch from a tree snaps off and barely misses Bradley's head but rakes across his face, leaving bloody furrows, like deep fingernail scratches, across his cheek.

He dodges but is tripped up by a root and falls sprawling into the leaves, bloodying his nose. Bradley screams as he fumbles and stumbles back to his car through the twilit forest.

Becca can't help but laugh.

The old woman gives Becca a nod and gestures with her walking stick in the direction of the Village. The four of them turn and head home.

This time, Becca leads the way.

A BED BOTH LONG AND NARROW

Sipora Coffelt

I came in from watering the kitchen garden to find the side door open and muddy footprints tracked up the stairs. The hallway stank of rot.

My youngest son, Quint, was twenty-six and too old to still live at home. But he sat at the table, drinking coffee.

"What's all this now?" I asked.

He looked from me to the doorway, suspicion in his eyes. "Meaning?"

"It stinks in here."

"It smells just fine." He stood and leaned both hands on the table. "Better 'n fine. Like vanilla. What's wrong with you, Ma? Seeing ghosts again?"

I glanced sideways at where the door opened into the shadowy front hallway. Nothing, not even the persistent ghost of my late husband, Theo.

"I won't have it," I said, my attention back on Quint. "Let me see your boots." The hem of his jeans was thick with mud, but not a speck marred the soles of his boots. "Where'd the mud come from?"

But Quint just rolled his eyes.

Armed with a pail and Lysol, I scrubbed, intent on finding the source of the smell. Humming an old and vaguely familiar tune, I found nothing. Maybe a mouse died in the wall or a squirrel in the attic. The stink wouldn't last much longer.

Tomorrow was Sunday, and I had pies to bake for church.

Quint walked Ella Sanderson home from church every Sunday, talking and laughing and kissing. Maybe more. My engagement ring, cleaned and boxed, was ready whenever he decided to pop the question.

But *that* Sunday, Quint didn't go to church. I threw out my pies for smelling funny like I had somehow mixed shit in with the fruit. Frantic about the ruined pies, I missed getting Quint out of bed in time.

"You're twenty-six years old," I shouted up the stairs.

He dragged himself to the top step, wearing only unwashed, skimpy white briefs. "Yeah? So?"

"So you're old enough to get your own self up in time for church. What will Ella think?"

"Ain't dating her no more."

I inhaled too fast, choked momentarily on spit.

"What happened?"

But Quint turned away and slammed his bedroom door.

Humming that stuck-in-my-head tune, I went to the IGA for pies and portioned them onto paper plates, pretending to ignore the raised eyebrows.

I should've known Esther Johnson would flat out ask, "Why're we eating store-boughten pie?"

"Something got in the cornstarch," I said.

Plain as day, Esther didn't believe me. "Aurelia. Cornstarch don't go bad by itself. Was it weevils? Moths? Now, don't be giving us none of your ghost stories." Esther and I had been close friends since second grade, and she'd often heard a younger me claim to see the dead.

I huffed a breath of denial. "Weren't ghosts. Weren't pantry moths neither. But something."

A sudden cold front brought rain and turned the yard into a swamp. In the early evening, I put on my rubber boots to walk out. That's when I first saw her.

Tall and willowy with a face like that starry skies poem and dark hair to her knees, she wore a green dress with rusty blotches. Maybe cabbage roses. Maybe blood. I wasn't certain she was real until I got that whiff of dead things. It clung to her like a fog.

"You good?" I asked as she came closer.

She opened her black eyes wide. I couldn't see the whites. It had to be a trick of twilight.

"Where's Quint?" she asked.

I shook my head. No way did I want *this* woman finding my boy.

She stomped a small, shoeless foot. "Tell me, Aurelia. Or else."

How did she know my name? Quint must have told her. But why hadn't *he* told me about *her*? How had I missed her comings and goings?

"There he is." She waved at the light in his second-floor bedroom window.

I looked up to see, and that fast she vanished. I shivered, my spine a spike of ice. Someone must have stomped across my grave.

The smell was back. The reek of decay, maybe from whatever the woman with the bloodstained dress had killed before coming to my home. Before seducing my son. Her laughter echoed down from Quint's bedroom.

My grown son was in bed with a monster. What should I do? The police wouldn't help. My other sons, all living far away, couldn't help. My friends? Esther would laugh and call it impossible. I shouldn't ask Pastor Lundgren to come pray when he already thought me crazy. I'd told him about seeing Theo. Not the acceptable solo sighting of a dead and beloved husband, but daily for two full years.

It was up to me. Heart pounding, I climbed the stairs. The breath caught in my throat, but resolute, I hammered on Quint's bedroom door.

"Quint, get out here." The words came out a rasp. Stymied, I sank onto the floor, straining to hear. Was that a moan? Did the bed screech, moving along the floor? A skunk odor leaked from under the door and made me gag. My eyes stung and tears fell.

She was murdering my son while I, hapless, did nothing to stop her.

Quint came down to breakfast the next morning, white as a sheet and skeleton thin. He refused coffee and food.

"Just a cold glass of water," he said.

I handed him a glass, more ice than water. "Who is she?"

He rolled his neck until it cracked.

"Just a nice girl, Ma. Better for me than the girls here. Pretty. Educated. I'm surprised she likes me."

"You must be stupid. What's her goddam name?"

He cocked his head like a dog. "She's called Lilith."

I didn't go to church for nothing. "A succubus," I said. "Evil tempting you in the shape of sexual pleasure."

Pastor had to believe this story. He'd come, exorcise the demon, bless my house.

"Gonna marry her," Quint said.

"Over my dead body." The words left my lips before the truth of them struck me. I snapped my teeth together, but once a foretelling is told, there's no use calling it back. "Look at yourself in the mirror. She'll be the death of you."

"No, Ma. You're wrong."

And nothing I said persuaded him any different.

Everybody knew I was the widow who'd seen her husband's ghost for two years. But I had to try. Someone had to believe me.

Pastor Lundgren listened with every indication of believing. And then said, "Now, Aurelia. It's hard to let your last chick go. I don't have to remind you how it was after Theo passed. Maybe it's time for professional help. Or Doc Carlson can give you a little something."

I went home with the worst migraine ever, and that song still running through my head. The yard smelled of shit—cows, horses, chickens. Even the reek of manure couldn't hide the sharp tang of fox, and sure enough, a vixen must've gotten in the coop. The sulfuric stench of broken eggs rotting in the sun drifted on the wind. Slugs leached slime over the chicken yard. The ground heaved with maggots. Three of my prize hens lay dead.

Inside the house, the stench of death was so strong that I ran straight to Quint's room to make sure my son wasn't dead. He wasn't there. I panicked and ran from room to room, only to find him at the kitchen table, eating a sandwich of moldy bread and turkey turned green.

"Don't eat that," I said. "It's gone bad."

Quint paused to examine his food. "You having a stroke or something? Looks fine. Tastes fine." He took another huge bite.

"It's that woman. Get rid of her. Please."

With a grunt, he got up and left the house.

Needing prayers from the faithful, I called Esther. But crossing my fingers for her to believe was pointless. She laughed.

"I don't hold truck with your ghost stories," she said. "Never have and never will. You call Doc Carlson, and he'll fix you right up."

Nobody understood me when I said that the newly dead oftentimes cling to the earthly realms, uncertain where to go and too scared to leave. I'd stopped talking about ghosts by third grade, glad when the sight left me with puberty. The only ghost I'd seen for years was my poor, dead Theo. I'd never before wanted to see ghosts again. The graveyard was my biggest fear and my last hope. The newly dead *must* know how to stop a demon.

The bustle of a funeral kept me from the cemetery until nightfall. I waited for the full moon to light my path among the headstones where wraiths wandered. And there, just like I hoped, was the translucent apparition of my beloved Theo.

I got as close as I dared, but the slime of his ectoplasm splashed me like acid.

"*Oh Mother, Mother make my bed,*" he sang, and I finally recognized "Barbary Allen," the tune that had haunted me since Lilith showed up.

Mother, Mother, make my bed. Make it long and narrow. Or was that the grave the father dug? I couldn't recall the exact lyrics, but I knew Theo was singing for our Quint's death. Ghosts gathered and screeched the verses, a harrowing sound like a car accident. Chills prickled my neck.

I hollered back. "How do I destroy a demon?"

They ignored me.

"Answer me!"

At my shout, Theo rushed toward me. He came so close I felt the icy bones of him and the hum of his death.

"Answer me," I whispered.

And he replied, "There is no answer."

It was all up to me.

The axes and sledgehammers were too heavy. I didn't trust my aim with the never-used rifle. I chose Theo's maul— the wood splitter with its sharpened edge—the one tool light enough for me to lug up the stairs.

Judging by the stench of decomposing flesh and the buzz of flies, Lilith was asleep in Quint's room. They lay side-by-side on his twin bed, curled together like the lovers she pretended they were. Her eyes opened when I entered, glowing red in the dark like an adder's warning.

"Think, Aurelia," she said. "Think before you strike."

But the sight of her with my son enraged me beyond reason. I heaved the maul over my head.

I aimed true. I know I did. But that edge meant to split logs decapitated *him* and not her.

My gaze glued to the horrifying sight of Quint's blood staining the sheets, I touched my face. My palm came away freckled with blood.

Lilith rose up, fluid as a snake, and whispered, "You wanted him? Well, now he's mine forever."

"I wanted him to marry Ella. Give me grandbabies." Denial rasped from my throat. My nerves were stretched to breaking. Hot tears streamed down my face and mixed with Quint's lifeblood. I'd take the maul in hand again and kill the demon if only I could find the strength.

But Lilith had vanished. I collapsed onto the body of my dead boy, and with his head in my bloody hands, kissed him over and over and over.

They sent me to St. Peters State Hospital down near Mankato. Everybody agreed I was too crazy to go on trial.

There, the ghosts, both the old and newly dead, were all insane. I looked around every corner for my Quint, but he was nowhere to be found.

Lilith whispered in my dreams, "He's forever mine."

I prayed every prayer I remembered. Even to Mother Mary, feeling like a sinful Protestant banking on a divine mother to pity me. I needed a miracle to make it so none of this had ever happened. But nothing. God was hiding from me.

My psychiatrist, a nice-intentioned woman who said, "Just call me Dr. Olivia," tried everything. Lithium and haloperidol and aripiprazole. Electric shock and transcranial magnetic stimulation. Cognitive therapy, dialectical behavioral therapy, and just plain talk.

I still saw ghosts. The demon still spoke to me.

Until one evening, just before moonrise, Lilith appeared in my room looking more than a little like Dr. Olivia. "Dear one," she said in a singsong that sounded like the Barbary Allen tune. "You cheated me. You owe me."

"Leave me alone." I lay on the bed and closed my eyes. She'd go. I knew she would.

After twenty minutes of silence, I opened my eyes and there—framed by the light from the hallway—stood my Theo, the image of my young love returned.

"Come with me, darling," he said.

How could I refuse? I got off the bed. I interlaced my fingers with his. The scent of vanilla filled the hallway of the women's ward. We ignored calls from the nurses station. He opened the locked double doors, and behind us, sirens screamed.

Up the stairs to the roof. His hold of my hand tightened.

"Stay with me forever," he said.

It was already too late when I recognized her, the girl in the bloodstained dress, smelling like my death and singing of beds both long and narrow, her mouth a grin of sharp demonic teeth and a red glow in her eyes.

THE CLEARING

Helen Power

There was something wrong with the window. Every night before bed, I would shut it. I would lock it. I would check it twice. Three times, just to be sure. Then, I would curl up in bed and fall into a dreamless sleep. But every morning, it was unlocked. Every morning, it was open.

Boyd, my building's handyman, stared at me for so long that my skin started to crawl. "Look here, Clara," he said as he slid the bolt. He made a show of trying to lift the window, which didn't budge. Not even an inch. "It's locked." He leaned back and idly tapped his fingers along the windowsill as if he were playing a musical instrument. He sighed. "You weren't doing it right."

I swallowed. "I did lock it. I know I did." I sounded like a petulant child, but I didn't care. I needed him to believe me.

He raised an eyebrow. "The window doesn't unlock from the outside. If you had locked it, like you say you did," I stiffen at his implication, "then you're the only person who could have opened it."

My cheeks flamed with anger. I moved closer and studied the latch. It certainly seemed solid. Impenetrable. But it wasn't. It couldn't be. I needed to tell Boyd that my favorite pajamas were missing, the ones with the pink lace and the blue flowers and the little chest pocket, and that it couldn't be a coincidence, and something horrible, rotten, *sinister* was going on. I turned to tell him, but he was already gone.

That night I dreaded bedtime. I approached the window and glared at the lock. I wished I had somewhere else to go, someone's couch I could crash on. I'd been so tired, banking ten, eleven hours of sleep a night, yet I still felt a fog creeping over my mind, clouding my thoughts, my judgments, my sanity. I checked the lock one last time, then crawled into bed. Despite the fear gripping my heart, it was less than a minute before I tumbled into a deep slumber.

The next morning, when I awoke, I didn't open my eyes. Instead, I lay in bed, exhaustion weighing on me like a heavy blanket. I listened to the sound of birds chirping outside. Cheerful and playful and grating. They were loud. Too loud. I opened my eyes.

The window was open.

Frowning, I shook away the vague memory of a dream. I never dreamed. It was impossible. But I couldn't shake away the image of a murky green mist slithering through an open window, surrounding and caressing me. Suffocating me. I climbed out of bed, wrapping myself in my soft, cotton bathrobe. I sucked in a ragged breath and inched closer.

Sunlight streamed through the sparkling clean glass. Outside, a bird swooped down to catch a worm, and down on the street, I saw the neighbor's eight-year-old son walking to school, his apple-red backpack nearly twice his size. All he needed was a stiff breeze to tip him over into the ditch. He seemed to feel my gaze and looked right up at me. Ordinarily, he would smile and wave then continue on his way, but today he seemed emotionless, cold, changed. My heart thundering in my ears, I lunged out of his line of sight.

I hid behind the curtain, holding my breath until the boy was hopefully long gone. I wiped my clammy palms along my pajama bottoms and stepped back into the sunlight. I studied the window for what had to have been the fiftieth time that week. I'd never had this problem before the new window was installed. The old one had been ancient. The pane was cracked, and the wooden frame had started to rot. Whenever it was windy, the draft carried with it a putrid stench into the sanctuary of my bedroom. Boyd had installed this new and not-so-improved window less than a week ago.

I gnawed on my thumbnail until I tasted blood. I couldn't call Boyd; he hadn't been much help, but there was no one else I could contact. I'd moved to Kinsale less than a month ago. Memories of any family I once had were vague, like will-o'-the-wisps blown away in a gentle spring breeze. I'd lost touch with them long ago. New in a town so foreign to me, I would need to find a new family and make new friends. But until then, I was on my own.

I stepped back to examine my handiwork. I had hidden a tiny camera on my bookshelf, angled toward the bed and window. It perched on top of my large, annotated edition of W. B. Yeats' *Fairy and Folk Tales*. It was almost undetectable, and the feed streamed directly to my laptop. The purchase had taken a huge chunk out of my paycheck. I might not be able to make rent this month, but it was worth it—I would soon have my answers.

The following morning, I rolled out of bed, shaking away the exhaustion that still clung to me, begging me to stay in my cocoon of blankets and sleep a little while longer. My shaky legs could barely keep me upright as I stood, shivering in the bright sunlight. I wrapped my arms around my midsection, but this provided little comfort.

The window was open.

I jerked backward and stumbled toward my laptop, which sat on my desk, seemingly untouched. I brought up the recording, my heart racing so hard that I could barely breathe.

The screen was dark, but I could make out my bedroom, the outline of my queen-sized bed, and the Clara-shaped lump lying in its center. The window was closed. *For now,* I thought.

The camera was motion-activated, but I didn't spot any movement on the screen. What had set off the sensor? I was so fixated on the window that I almost didn't see it. A silhouette had drifted across the room, approaching the window. *From the inside.* I raked in a gravelly breath, darting my gaze toward the bed, but it was empty. The figure stood in a pool of moonlight. It was me.

My hands gripped the armrests of my chair as I watched myself unlock, then slide open the window. Was I the one who'd been doing it all along? Had I felt overheated in the middle of the night and decided to open the window? I let out a strangled laugh, but my relief was short-lived. Why didn't I remember doing this last night? Why didn't I remember doing this *every night?*

Bile rose in the back of my throat as I continued to watch the screen. There I stood, framed by the window, staring out into the night for what felt like an eternity.

Then, gentle music began to drift from the laptop speakers. A familiar melody that I couldn't quite place. I turned up the volume with trembling fingers. A flute played a lethargic tune. It was melancholic. Haunting. Alluring. On the screen, I climbed out the window.

Dizziness flooded through my skull. The room spun, but I clenched my teeth and clung to the desk with white knuckles. I had to keep watching. The camera jumped forward in time to a point just before dawn. I saw myself climb back through the window, approach the bed, and slide under the covers. I awoke only three hours later.

The following night, I lay in bed staring at the ceiling. Nausea coursed through me. I hadn't been able to eat a thing all day, and I'd drank four cups of coffee and an energy drink in a feeble attempt to ward off sleep. The caffeine churned in my stomach, threatening to make a reappearance all over my lily-white duvet. Yet still, the alluring temptation of sleep sung to me like a siren's call. My hands clenched into fists as I gripped my blanket with all my strength for fear that I would be torn out of bed and dragged out the window.

I would not let that happen.

Just when I thought I couldn't fight the growing weight of my eyelids any longer, the music began. Gentle chords of a single flute meandered through the cracks in the window and embraced me. Still in bed, I turned toward the window and peered out. There was nothing there. Just the branches of a nearby tree swaying in the wind as if dancing to the melody.

The music grew louder, more insistent. The image of thick black roots writhing in upon themselves like a greasy knot of serpents slithered into my mind, but it was gone as quickly as it had arrived. Little beads of stinking sweat formed across my exposed flesh, leaving me chilled.

What would happen if I didn't follow the music? Would the source of this haunting tune know that I'm not asleep? What would happen if I ignored the call? Could I?

I found myself at the window with barely any recollection of getting there. I unlocked and slid it open with a familiar ease. The cool night air wafted in, bringing with it music and the faint promise of freedom. I climbed out the window, down the tree, and onto the grass below. I couldn't stop myself. I bit my lip so hard that it drew blood, which I swallowed, the metallic taste coating my stomach and mingling with coffee and bile. I looked up at my building. All the windows were dark; no one else was attracted to the music as I was. I somehow knew in my soul that this was because the melody was just for me. I pushed away this irrational thought and started down the road.

My feet knew exactly where to take me.

I forced myself to stop at the edge of Briar Woods. What was I doing? I could still turn back. I longed to return home, curl up in bed, and pretend this had never happened. That wasn't an option. I couldn't forget the music because the music wouldn't forget me. My only choice was to continue onward. This way would surely lead to answers.

I entered the Woods. It was like passing through a veil into another world. The air around me churned with the scent of mulch and other things gone rotten. The trees were alive with the sounds of rustling leaves, scrambling little legs, and claws digging at the dirt around me. I was surrounded. Surrounded by creatures that I couldn't quite make out in the faint moonlight, but I knew they were there. I felt a swarm of hungry little eyes on me as I ventured deeper and deeper into the dark woodland.

Their odd commotion was barely muffled by the tormenting melody that drew me onward.

A tremor coursed through me when I glanced down and realized I didn't need to step over brambles or duck under branches. The trees seemed to shift as I approached, clearing my path forward. My feet were still perfectly clean from the bath I took before sleep. It was like I'd never left the safety of my bedroom.

I spotted a clearing just up ahead. The trees along the outer edge were different. Thicker, taller, older than the rest, with gnarled and vicious branches twisting outward as if beckoning to me. But it was the sight of their trunks that gnawed through my determination to continue on my weird, somnolent journey. Intricate coils were carved into the flesh of the trees, deep cuts in the shape of interlocking Celtic knots. Scars accentuated by dripping sap that shined like blood in the moonlight.

The music had steadily grown louder, faster, more manic as I'd traveled through the forest. It thundered in my ears, urging me along, my pulse stuttering right along with it. Even if I wanted to, I couldn't turn back. The music would never let me.

A heady mix of dread and anticipation enveloped me as I finally stepped into the clearing. The music cut off. Silence rang in my ears, and I shivered in the sudden cold of stark alertness and exposure. I looked up at the night sky, where the crescent moon sagged low and the stars winked at me knowingly.

I ran my trembling hands up and down my bare arms, trying to rub away the goosebumps that had nothing to do with the chill in the midnight air. My gaze was drawn toward a black pit only a few feet from where I stood. The sharp tang of freshly dug, wet earth pierced my nostrils, carrying with it the sour taste of decay. I gagged but inched closer, peering down at the hole. It yawned like a shallow grave.

A fresh wave of horror crashed through me—I shouldn't have come here.

Why did I?

I spun around, but someone was blocking my path. I stumbled backward in surprise, my entire body seized with the scorching flames of adrenaline that burned through my veins. The man wore a long black cloak with its hood drawn. His face was veiled in shadow, but I recognized him immediately.

"Boyd?" I whispered.

He reached out and seized my tiny hand in his enormous, unyielding paw. He forced me with rough urgency toward the hole. I didn't struggle. I couldn't. I could hardly breathe. I was fascinated by the dark, open cavity, straining to see it in the pale moonlight.

I gasped the moment I realized that there was already a body resting in that terrible hole.

It was a young woman in her mid-twenties, with long brown hair and milky white skin. Slick black roots from the trees around the clearing curled and wrapped around her body. Thick roots squeezed her frail appendages ... fine vines slipped around and through her pallid skin... wispy tendrils clung to her throat and face as if trying to worm their way in through her ears and nostrils.

Binding her in place. Feeding off her. This trap her final resting place.

She wore silk pajamas with pink lace and blue flowers and a little chest pocket. I frowned at their familiarity. Realization dawned on me even before my gaze settled upon her face. The curve of her mouth, the little pointed nose, the birthmark on her left cheekbone. It was like looking into a mirror.

This was me.

I turned on Boyd, ready to kick, to scream, to run, but the expression on his face drained all the fight out of me—as if my will had been pushed through an eldritch sieve. He looked melancholic.

"She has no idea what's happening," he said. Boyd cocked his head, almost thoughtfully. "And neither do you. That is the exchange."

"What?" I asked, my voice hoarse as if I'd been screaming.

"Their lives for ours, our memories for theirs." He drew me closer to my double. Again, I looked down at her. She was asleep, not dead as I'd initially thought.

"How is this possible?" I managed to blurt out.

Boyd dragged me even closer to the sleeping "Clara." He gestured for me to take her hand.

I wavered, trying to pull away. Boyd snarled as he shoved me toward the sleeping girl. I let out a shriek as I fell to my knees. He forced my hand against hers. I arched back and howled into the sky as a jolt of electricity shot through me. Her eyes flew open, and she stared up at me with terrified hazel eyes. *My eyes.* Windows into the horror of her—no, *my*—soul. Memories flooded through me. My sister laughing as she helped me pack for my "big move," which was only two streets away from the house where I grew up. Dad shooting me a grin as he expertly backed the moving truck into my new apartment's parking lot. Mom tsking as she unpacked my books, putting them in order on the shelf, giving W. B. Yeats a place of honor, alphabet be damned.

My mind cleared. The exhaustion, the confusion, the fog that had been weighing on me for days finally lifted. I gasped and pulled my hand back. How could I have forgotten all of this? How could I have forgotten that I'd lived here in Kinsale my whole life? How could I have forgotten my own family? I had never lost touch with them like I'd thought. We were closer than ever before; my family was always there. It was just the memories that had been missing.

The Clara in the grave didn't move. She didn't speak. The roots holding her in place seemed to pulse, to throb with a kind of unclean animus until they were satiated. Clara's entire body convulsed as she writhed in the dark, damp soil. She released a deep, animalistic sigh, then stilled. She was dead.

I jerked to my feet like I was a marionette, and someone had yanked on my strings. Horror soaked through my clearing senses. She was dead, and I might not have understood how or the exact reason, but I knew it was because of me. I had taken something from her—something I could never give back. I let out a whimper but clamped my mouth shut before my mewl could turn into a full-fledged scream. I was a murderer—even if I had been forced—and there was nothing I could do about it.

"*It is complete.*" Boyd's solemn voice drew my attention back to him.

My lower lip trembled. "I don't understand."

"You don't need to."

Just then, I noticed that this was not the only hole in the woods. Freshly disturbed piles of dirt lay all around me. Freshly buried graves.

"You may go home now," Boyd said.

I shook my head. My mind was clearer than it had been for days. "Not until I get answers. Who is that?"

"Clara."

Again, I shook my head. "I'm Clara."

Boyd almost smiled.

"*I'm* Clara," I repeated, hysteria bubbling up as I clawed at his sleeves with fingers that were numb from the cold and shock. "I am Clara. Aren't I?"

At this, Boyd finally smiled. "Yes. Yes, you are."

I returned to bed with no recollection of how I got there. There was no proof of what had happened—other than my lingering memories and the fading guilt. I dismantled the video camera, destroyed the recording, and tried my best to forget the events of that night. But every now and then, a friend or acquaintance will disappear. While they always return a few days later, they're always different. Pale imitations of who they once were. They'll forget friends' names, favorite places, childhood memories, all the elements that make up the essence of who they are. Then, like the flip of a switch, they're back to normal. On these days, I'm reminded of what happened that night as more and more of us find our new homes. As more and more of us make the exchange. On these nights, I go to sleep with the window open to let in the calming night air and the faint sound of music that accompanies it.

Changeling, I hear whispered in the wind before falling into a dreamless sleep.

THE BINDING OF CHRYSANTHOULA

Angeliki Radou

"The mother births and Fate anoints." These were the words spoken by Katerina's late mother every time someone young died in their village. They upset Katerina because she understood that no matter what a mother did, her child's life might still get caught in the knots weaved in Fate's thread—knots tight and magical, dipped in ancient first milk.

And these were the words she thought of, seeing her own Chrysanthoula waste away. Her long black hair was now falling out by the handful, her body was thinning, and a foul mood dogged her. At first, they took her to the doctor at Lefki. Young and freshly instated, he couldn't figure out the cause and so he sent them to the big city. And yet, the doctors there couldn't find the cause either.

Katerina was devoured with sadness. Her girl was twenty years old and had no color in her cheeks and no smile on her lips. She looked like one of those wandering hags peddling their magic door to door when the priest was absent. What evil had befallen them?

One night, sleepless from sorrow and the hissing wind, Katerina stepped outside to pick up the broken flowerpots. She turned on the light and, broom in hand, bowed to the wet ground. And down there, between the hydrangeas and the gardenias, her finger was pricked by something unexpected.

She groped with both her hands and found a piece of green soap. Two rags from Chrysanthoula's old dress were pinned on it. Her girl was the only one watering the flowerpots; even though she was sick, that's how much she loved flowers. The one who set out to harm her had to be someone who knew them.

Quietly, Katerina gathered the hex in a tin pot, went back inside the house and tried to sleep. Just before her husband woke up, she took the vessel and set out for Father Spyros, who was about to say Mass.

"Are you mad, Katerina? What do you want, coming here this early?"

The woman didn't answer; she just uncovered the tin and showed him what lay inside. Father Spyros immediately understood.

"If you do as I say, you might save your girl."

She gulped and stood still as the priest spoke with his hand on her shoulder. What he offered sounded to her less like a blessing and more like a wandering hag's sorcery, yet what choice did she have? The same night she convinced her husband, and they set out together to walk the magic road to the sea, letting the waves touch their feet and praying together.

But in the mornings, instead of praying, Katerina caught herself searching the faces of her fellow villagers to spot the one who cast the hex. The neighbor who had an ugly daughter around Chrysanthoula's age, the cousin complaining her own daughter wouldn't make a proper wife, her jealous aunt who stroked Chrysanthoula's shiny hair whenever she saw her; they were all witches in her eyes.

Forty nights went by, their blessings were done and so was their hope. Chrysanthoula had dwindled, her hair reduced to three strands, her clothes empty of flesh. Her mother was desperate. She now knew Chrysanthoula would die. But just as she began to accept her daughter's fate, she found it harder and harder to accept that the culprit would go unpunished.

One late afternoon, she sat outside her old kitchen shelling peas, her eyes blurry with tears. With her mind wrapped around death, she did not notice a woman approaching.

"Why are you crying, mistress?"

Katerina lifted her head and saw the woman standing over her. One of the wandering ones; she could tell by her charms and her oak staff. In any other time, she would have spat thrice and driven her away. But now, she caught herself telling the stranger about Chrysanthoula.

"Bring me an egg, mistress, and I'll tell you if your daughter will live."

Katerina left the peas on the bench and went to fetch the egg.

The woman cradled it in her palms and blew on the egg thrice. She muttered something or other and gave it to Katerina to crack open.

What was inside gave Katerina shivers, and she began to cry.

"You guessed right, mistress. Your daughter is not long for this world." The woman mumbled, looking at the tiny bones nested in Katerina's palm alongside the eggshell fragments. "But do remember. The one who bound her will die soon after, and nobody will be able to go near the coffin."

The hag turned to leave, but Katerina grabbed her arm. She knew she was touching the Devil himself, yet she did not care anymore. "Tell me who it is, and I'll give you anything you want," Katherina said, gritting her teeth.

"Guard your soul, mistress; what's done is done. But if it will help you rest, take this," she said and gave Katherina the tiny bones she held. "Shove them in the guilty one's corpse, and let her own evil do its work."

In a week's time, what was left of Chrysanthoula departed for the other world. She was buried in what would have been her wedding dress, and instead of crying, Katerina gathered her courage and waited. As the hag foretold, within forty days of Chrysanthoula's passing her aunt died—her father's sister, the one who always stroked her hair. At her funeral, nobody kissed her goodbye because she stank.

Nobody apart from Katherina. She entered the church to leave her flowers and, as soon as Father Spyros turned his back, she shoved the tiny bones into her frozen mouth. She could swear she heard the corpse's teeth grind but, instead of fear, Katherina felt vindicated.

At home, she lit her vigil candles to calm the soul of her girl, who had left so early. On the seventh night after the funeral, Katerina woke up hearing shouts and moans outside her house. She turned anxiously toward her husband, but he was sound asleep. She put on a nightgown and tiptoed to the window. Katerina knew what she was about to see, and so she did not become upset.

Chrysanthoula's aunt was looking at her, her eyes filled with hate, her bleeding mouth full of tiny bones, her body wrapped in a thousand taut ropes. Katerina stood still, gazing at the convulsing apparition. She was now at peace. The woman's actions would never let her body perish, and she would remain forever cursed.

THE GLORIOUS PROTECTION OF ANGELS

Michelle Ann King

The weather on the day of Kris's funeral is beautiful, which Shaylie finds vaguely offensive. She feels the same way about the people who line up to pat her arm, give her solemn smiles, and tell her how sorry they are for her loss.

Her loss.

As if it's her fault. As if it was her mistake, her carelessness, that caused this. As if he's gone because she didn't try hard enough to keep him.

Fuck you, she wants to scream. *I didn't do this.*

She doesn't.

She says, "Thank you," instead, because there's Drew to think of, and he's upset enough. She's responsible for him now. Little boy—little *man*—in his smart black suit, sweating in the heat and saying *thank you* just like her, even though he doesn't know what for.

"Where's Daddy?" he asks, looking about with a confused frown. "Is he at work?"

Shaylie swallows hard and fights the urge to simply say *yes.* Instead, she says, "Daddy's gone to Heaven, sweetheart."

Drew's eyes widen. "Has he gone to be an angel? Is that his job now?"

Shaylie squats beside her son and pulls him close. "That's right, honey. He's gone to be an angel so that he can look after us from Heaven. And Daddy's always been good at his

355

job, hasn't he? So you can bet he's going to be the best angel there is."

Drew nods, his head bumping against her shoulder. Tears dampen the rough material of her dress. She hugs him tighter, resting her chin on top of his head.

"That's right. Your daddy's going to be the best damn angel the world has ever seen.

Shaylie herself has every intention of being the best damn single mother the world has ever seen; she really does. But it's so *hard*. She misses Kris with a fierce, gnawing ache that gets in the way—not just of being there for Drew, but of everything: eating, sleeping, working. Breathing, even. It all hurts, every single part of it. It's so much easier to lie down and close her eyes. So much easier not to try.

Get up.

No. She doesn't want to.

Get up.

She tries to ignore the voice, but it doesn't stop.

Shaylie, get up.

She stirs slightly. Tries to say, "Go away," but the words won't come out properly. Her mouth is mushy.

Shaylie. You have to move. You have to get up.

But it's quiet down here. Peaceful. Safe.

Fuck that. Don't be such a coward. It's not about being safe. It's about being alive.

And suddenly she knows the voice. "Kris?" she asks, struggling to open her gritty, gummed-up eyes. Then she feels it: his hand on her brow, so cold that it sends an icy burst of pain through her head. She jerks upright, rolls over, and falls off the bed, landing on her knees on the hardwood floor. She retches violently, and the last thing she sees before her eyes sink closed again is a polka-dot pattern of little white pills on the dark, walnut-stained floorboards.

You're going to be okay, the voice says. *It's all going to be okay.*

She feels ill for a week afterward—like a mixture of jet lag, flu, and the worst hangover she's ever had—but she's up. She's moving. She's okay.

"I'm not a coward," she says. Kris doesn't reply, but she knows he hears her. She can *feel* it—feel his agreement, his approval. His love.

He's not gone. Not lost. She understands, finally, that what she told Drew wasn't a platitude but the actual, literal truth. Kris is still with them, still looking after them. Still saving them.

It's a revelation.

She sees it all so clearly now. Those close calls she had in the car lately? It wasn't luck or good driving skills that saved her—it was Kris guiding her hand at the wheel. When she stumbled at the top of the stairs and came so close to falling? It was Kris that held her back. He saw she needed help, and he gave it. Just like always.

She cries for almost a whole day from the sheer relief of it. Then she throws a party—balloons and cocktails and ice cream for Drew, the whole works—because if this isn't a cause for celebration, then she doesn't know what is.

And when she wakes in the morning, there's further proof: the cigarette that dropped out of her hand when she fell asleep on the sofa. It simply burned itself out right there on the floor, leaving a dirty mark on the laminate but causing no other damage at all.

Shaylie used to work in insurance claims; she knows the usual result of what the fire reports call *carelessly discarded smoking materials*. People die in house fires all the time. *Tragically, there was also loss of life.*

But not her and Drew. Not now.

Not ever.

For Shaylie, the world becomes a brighter place: colors are warmer, sounds clearer, tastes richer. The air smells of sweet flowers instead of emptiness and dust. Life is ripe, promising, full of potential.

The only dark cloud is that Drew doesn't seem to understand how things have changed. Shaylie expected him to feel liberated the way she does, but he's still so *afraid* all the time.

"It won't hurt you," she says over and over again, about wasps, bugs, needles, germs, rats, spiders, shadows—so many different things, she loses count. Thunderstorms keep him awake and trembling for hours, the friendly barking of their neighbor's dog reduces him to tears, and when other boys come to the playground, he runs away and hides rather than joining in their games.

It breaks her heart.

This isn't what she wants for him. She wants him to be happy, to have fun, to embrace what the world has to offer. She wants him to *live*.

"Daddy's never going to let anything bad happen to you," she explains, pulling him into a fierce, hard hug. "So you never have to be afraid, no matter what. You know that, don't you?"

He nods solemnly and says, "Yes, Mummy," because he's a good boy, and he always listens to what she tells him, but she can see it's not getting through. He needs to feel it, to *believe* it—and for that, words aren't going to be enough. She needs, as the old saying goes, to put her money where her mouth is.

He has nightmares about robbers and murderers, so she leaves the front door open day and night. Of course, no one comes in—not with Kris standing guard. She's only sorry zombies and vampires aren't real, so Kris and she could prove them harmless too.

He doesn't like being in the car, so she leaves it on the hard shoulder of the M25, takes Drew's hand, and runs gleefully across four lanes of screaming, thundering traffic. The pile-up that follows is dramatic enough to make the evening news, but Kris tracks every flying piece of metal and shard of glass, and they walk away without a scratch. After the footage appears on TV, there are phone calls from her mother, Drew's school, and eventually the police, but she just deletes the messages and unplugs the phone. Kris's voice is the only one either of them needs to hear.

"You see? There's nothing to worry about," she says, alight with the joy and wonder of it. "It's not about being safe. It's about being alive."

Sacred words. *Kris's* words. But still, it's not enough. Drew's eyes are filled with tears, not wonder.

"Oh, honey, it's going to be okay," she says. "I promise you, it's always going to be okay."

Drew shakes his head and carries on crying, but Shaylie feels Kris's hand on her shoulder and knows it's a promise he won't let her break.

She raids what's left of her prescriptions to help Drew get some rest—hours of crying have worn him out—then puts him in the car and heads for the coast during the early hours of the morning. She carries Drew, bundled up in his parka and still mostly knocked out, down the stairs from the car park to the beach.

He mumbles a question, but she shushes him gently. The sand sinks a little under her boots, giving her a rolling gait that soon rocks him back to sleep. She adjusts her hold, maneuvering him so that his chin rests on her shoulder. He snuggles into her neck, his breath warm on her skin.

He doesn't stir when she walks into the water, and she bites down hard on her lip to stop the gasp that tries to escape. It's *cold*.

It's only when the waves hit her waist—and his feet—that he wakes up properly. "Mummy?" he says, more questioning than afraid.

She increases her grip, fighting to keep her balance. The water moves fast. "It's all right, sweetheart. There's nothing to be scared of."

She says it confidently—believes it, absolutely—but she's conscious of her rising heart rate and the whistling sound of her breath. She's a terrible swimmer; a width of the pool in a kind of thrashing doggy paddle is the best she can do.

"Mummy," Drew says again, his voice climbing. "Why are we going in the sea?"

Can Drew swim? It strikes her that she doesn't know. Kris took him to the pool a few times, but she never went with them. She hates the water. No, she's *afraid* of it. Which is exactly why they're here—she's been asking a child to ignore his fears without showing that she can do it herself. No wonder it hasn't worked.

She takes another step forward, and the swirling sea lifts her feet off the ground, pitching her forward. The shock of submerging—water filling her nose, stinging her eyes—makes her lose her grip on Drew, and her groping hands find nothing but more water.

For a second, Shaylie panics—she can't see, can't breathe, doesn't know whether she's facing up or down—but she *wills* herself to stop, to calm down. It's all right. She's safe. She's always safe.

She breaks the surface, the sound of her own coughing loud in her plugged-up ears. But then she hears it: Kris's voice, calling her name.

Shaylie shakes her head violently to clear the dark water and follows the voice. Her clothes feel impossibly heavy, the sea around her as thick as syrup. It's hard work, but she struggles on. Because she's not a coward. Because she's *alive*.

She catches glimpses of Drew, his bright red woolly hat still pulled over his ears, appearing and disappearing with the swell of the waves. She can hear him crying—screaming —

but she can still hear Kris too. *I've got you*, he says, and she knows he's pulling Drew back toward the shore.

Shaylie laughs. "See?" she calls, her voice only a little raw after all the coughing. "Didn't I tell you? We're fine. Daddy's here to help us, and everything's going to be okay."

She whoops with exhilaration, her body suddenly feeling light and free. The ache in her muscles is forgotten as she reaches out and clasps Kris's other hand, his strength propelling her effortlessly through the water—which feels, now, as calm and warm as a scented bath. Shaylie is almost sorry when she feels the sand underneath her again as she gets closer to the beach.

"Thank you," she says, rolling onto her back. The stars are beginning to fade as the dawn nears, but it is still beautiful. Everything is beautiful.

She feels the brief, cool press of Kris's lips against hers, and then he's gone.

Shaylie pushes herself up onto one elbow and reaches for Drew. He's a little further down the beach, also lying on his back with his arms thrown over his head and the starlight reflecting in his wide-open eyes. She strokes his cheek and it's cold, the after-effect of his father's kiss.

"Oh, honey," she says, and pulls him tight against her chest. She didn't think; she should have brought towels.

But he doesn't protest or complain or even wriggle in her arms. "There," she says contentedly, running her hand through his limp, sodden hair. "Wasn't that great? Didn't we have fun?"

And he doesn't shake his head this time, her good, little man. He doesn't tremble or sob or try to pull away. He just stays quiet and lets her rock him, his head tilted back and his gaze still fixed, unblinking, on the stars.

MOTHER WINTER

Matthew Chabin

"They're coming," said Falkenrath, speaking down into the tank's hold. "Come on, let's not make them angry."

Herrick felt a flare of anger himself at the gunner's presumption—it was cowardice, not courage, that presumed—but no one else had said a word since they'd been hit. Giese was dead; Gerver would be soon. The commander sat against the bulkhead, stroking the blood out of Gerver's hair with a tenderness Herrick would never have suspected in the old Prussian warhorse. He looked up at Herrick with raw, apologetic eyes and gave a small nod. "Leave your gun," he said. Herrick hesitated a moment, then took his Luger out and laid it on the turret floor.

He climbed up through the hatch, out of the darkness and the scorched-oil-and-ammonia stench of the ruptured hold, emerging into a howling, white waste of driven snow. The first thing he was able to make out was the half-track that had doubled back for them and met an incoming shell. What was left of the vehicle lay smoldering twenty meters away. The big guns had stopped, likely because the weather made it hard to tell where anything was.

"Look!" shouted Falkenrath over the wind. Herrick shielded his eyes. He saw one, then four, then a dozen men, walking toward them out of the snow, visible at fifty meters. "Come on!" said the gunner, "We mustn't let them think we're still in arms." He hopped down off the tank and raised his hands. Herrick tarried to help the commander pass Gerver through the hatch. He dangled the wounded man over the side and eased him down into the snow. The commander came last, and Herrick saw that he was wounded too, his pants in dark tatters about the hip and groin, bleeding from his legs. Once down, he sank with his back against the panzer's remaining tread and pulled Gerver once more into his arms.

"Get your hands up!" said Falkenrath, speaking back over his shoulder. "Don't be stupid!"

Laughter and low, guttural voices carried on the wind. Now Herrick counted sixteen men in heavy coats and fur hats, most with rifles, several with bayonets fixed. A great, bearded officer leading the pack carried an ax on his shoulder like a woodsman. He smiled at them. It was the smile that finally snapped Herrick out of his shock and stirred his dormant terror. Sluggishly, as though in a dream, he turned and ran.

"Vernis! My tvoi druz'ya!"

Herrick had enough Russian to understand *Come back, we're your friends,* and enough education in war to not be fooled. He heard someone cry out, and he looked back— Falkenrath was down, and the ax was coming up again. He ran faster, expecting at any moment to be shot in the back, but no shot came. Maybe they were low on bullets. Maybe they didn't think it mattered.

He ran with the wind at his back until he collapsed, then lay on his stomach for a while, then got up and ran some more. He kept this up for what felt like hours, thinking the rearguard would be on the lookout for stragglers, surely, no matter how disorganized the retreat. Then he realized he was no longer running across packed snow but through virgin powder halfway up his shins. *Excellent skiing,* he thought and fell to his knees, shocked by the sound of his own wheezing laughter. All hope of catching the *Wehrmacht* was now lost, and if he turned back, he'd be moving to meet the smiling man with the ax.

He stumbled on, sobbing intermittently until he realized there was something ahead of him. A wall? A palisade? It was just a line of trees. Well, it was cover at least, and the possibility of shelter and short-term survival. "Krieg ist Krieg," he said

through his chattering grin, *"und Schnapps ist Schnapps."*
The cold ate through his boots, and the icy wind blasted his
exposed cheek. He remembered his mother's final words to
him, *"You will come home to me,"* and forced himself to a
laborious march. The thought of her grief was, for the moment,
an even greater torment than the prospect of dying.

The storm had moved on by the time he reached the line
of trees, white birches half-sketched against the whited land,
and an eerie calm presided. He stopped to rest against the
first tree he came to, hearing only his own ragged breath and
what he took to be the muted thud of falling snow deeper in.
He walked. The birch trunks were widely spaced, and tiny
granules of ice, like powdered crystal, drifted from above to
glimmer in the sunlit gaps. Several times he had the uncanny
sense that someone was walking beside him, always to his
left, but they stopped when he stopped. When he turned, of
course, he was alone.

Better the ax... he thought, *...than to die in a lonely place.*
No more pain for Gerver. No more nightmares for Giese. No
more— There came a clacking sound and a little breath of wind
blowing the snow before it. *Wind knocking the branches,* he
thought. *No ghosts. You'll be a ghost before you see any gh—*

He stopped short. The depression in the snow before
him was fresh, crisp at the edges, and looked like nothing so
much as a great, three-toed dinosaur track. He looked in the
direction it was pointing and saw another, some eight meters
away. Despite himself, he laughed. *Little children playing*
tricks! The thought was followed by a surge of hope, that in
these desolate woods he might find some kindly peasants,
like in his favorite book, *Frankenstein.* In the book, it was the
monster who helped the peasants, not the other way around,
but....

They'd be more likely to hang you, he thought,
remembering the village. He touched his empty holster and
remembered he'd left his sidearm in the tank. He walked on,
his mind working in circles, heedless of the declivity under his
feet until he was slipping on it. He fell hard on his back and
slid a short way down the bank of a frozen stream, scrabbling

with numb hands at the frozen earth. His left glove snagged on something and came off just as his right foot went through the ice and fetched up under a sharp rock. Pain exploded through his shin, and his scream rang through the treetops.

Sobbing, his lower leg blossoming with intense pain, Herrick dragged himself backward up the bank. He knew he was in danger of passing out, and that would likely be the end of him; he therefore looked frantically for some means of immediately carrying on. Fortune favored him, for once. A meander in the stream, very near, had collected a considerable mass of sticks. He crawled and scooted over to it. Bracing himself carefully with one hand on the bank, he wrenched a roughly two-meter staff of frozen birch wood out of the ice. He tested it against the ground, and it held. Minimally encouraged, he dislodged a second, shorter stick and dropped down to a seated position. He pulled his pantleg tight against his shin and issued a thin, whistling cry as his worst fear was confirmed—a small sprig of what could only be bone tented the fabric. Again, he struggled not to faint. He gingerly laid the short stick flush with his leg and lashed it tight with his belt. Thus splinted, he crutched and hobbled his way back to level ground, where he managed to stand up straight on his good leg. He briefly considered returning to the open plain, but that was madness, certain death. If he could get through this barren birch track, he might find some real cover and dry fuel for a fire. He followed the frozen stream as it hooked deeper into the woods.

He was getting weaker. The pain in his leg had resolved from a fiery effulgence to a dull, iron throb, and the rest of him was mostly numb. He noted that the fingers of his ungloved hand were white and blistering. He told himself this was a small problem, all things considered. He had a vision of himself crouched in a windbreak, gnawing his fingers off like a deranged animal caught in a trap. The next thing Herrick knew, he was face down in the snow.

It was a long time before he got moving again. He realized that he had indeed made it through the birch trees and into a denser, darker world of oak and maple. He smiled to himself as he thought of his boyhood winters just outside Hildesheim, tapping maple trees with his sisters to make syrup. The time he'd lost them in the woods.... The trees here were black, scaly, contorted things, and the ground was likewise irregular, dropping into deep ravines hedged by frozen briars. "Hilda!" he'd called. "Liesse!" There were ravens in the trees, their heads cocked sideways as they watched him, expelling little puffs of air from their long, black beaks. They'd been hiding from him on purpose, the little scamps, just to tease him, but he'd had terrible visions of wolves and bandits snatching them away, of going home to Mother without them. The birds were all watching him.

"Liesse!" he bellowed. A few ravens castled along a high branch, dislodging snow as they hopped. "Hilda!" He shoved off from a tree and crutched along the edge of another steep bank, oblivious to the danger. *"Mutter!"*

Pale sky opened ahead. He emerged from under a hoary oak and stood at the edge of a small clearing. *"Guten tag,"* he said to a skull capping the fencepost to his left. The wheelbarrow just inside the woven stick fence contained children, three, not firewood. Three dead children, lying as if asleep. The house, a rustic little *izba* with a steeply pitched roof, carious wooden lacing under the eaves, and red-painted shutters, crouched at the other end of the clearing. The windows glowed with amber light, like eyes, and smoke drifted from the chimney.

"Mutter," said Herrick. *"Ich bin zu Hause!"*

Dropping his crutch, he stepped out with his broken leg and screamed when it buckled under him. He found himself on the ground, looking up. The skull rotated on its post with a scraping sound and looked down at him. A raven barked. One of the dead children was sitting up in the wheelbarrow, and the house, rising on its giant, backward-jointed legs, was *walking toward him.*

For Herrick Haas, the good war had ended that July in a town called Justingrad, about a hundred kilometers south of Kiev.

They'd been in heavy fighting, but they were winning. The Red Beast was on the run and spirits were relatively high. The sun was out. There were rumors they were about to be transferred to Army Group Center for the big push on Moscow. Everything was being shuffled around, and in the lull of logistical confusion they'd been called back from the front to provide extra armor for *Einsatzgruppe-C* in their never-ending hunt for partisans.

The town sat in a narrow valley between wooded hills, and Herrick's platoon was deployed in a field to the south, covering the open lanes from the woods six hundred meters distant. The idea was ostensibly to create a barrier to sniper fire, but no one seemed very worried about snipers; the crews were sitting on their tanks, eating lunch and smoking. To Herrick it looked more like a mock siege. They weren't looking for anyone. What the hell was C-Group up to?

A boisterous gang of Motor Infantrymen was going along the line, dispensing schnapps and trading gossip with the tank crews. One man, obviously drunk, hung a lady's slip from the howitzer's barrel. The commander came snarling at him, snatched the slip, and threw it in the mud while the group scattered, laughing. Several circled around for more good-natured harassment. "You boys should come with us!" said a curly-haired *gefreiter* with a telltale slur. "We heard there are girls. Such beauties as haven't been seen since Paris!"

Herrick picked up the slip and felt the silk slide between his fingers. He hadn't been touched by a woman in over a year. "Come on!" said the *gefreiter*, "there's more where that came from!" He looked at the commander and met a scowl. "And there's mail call!" added the *gefreiter*. The others were now looking at the commander with similar hopeful expressions.

"Hass, Falkenrath, go. Back in one hour. Find me a quartermaster while you're there and check on our requisition. We need winter coats and gloves, a fire extinguisher, and a mag for the *Schmeisser*, more if you can get them. Understand?" Herrick knew that the business with the quartermaster could take more than an hour by itself, but he realized this was also an excuse to extend his leave if he played it right. He saluted smartly, and he and Falkenrath joined the merry band from the MI.

As they tromped through the mud with the sun on their faces, bandying talk of girls and Paris, he saw a larger group of about fifty people coming the other way. They were the villagers, mostly older women and children, but with a scattering of old men. Many of them were carrying packs and bags as if for a journey. They were escorted by a squad of C-Group, rough-looking guys with sleeve eagles and black, police-style shoulder boards. Herrick's group fell silent as they turned to observe the procession. A tall, baby-faced *Rottenführer* with mustache and shiny spectacles and a machine pistol held at ready across his body smiled cordially at Herrick as he passed. Herrick thought he looked like a schoolmaster marshaling truants.

"What's that about," he asked of no one in particular.

"Latrines," said Falkenrath. Herrick looked at him. "I heard they were digging latrines in the woods."

"Why the baggage? Why the kids?"

Falkenrath shrugged.

"Hey, it's Poster Boy!"

He looked over and recognized the speaker, Pfeiffer, a charismatic blatherskite from Hildesheim and Hitler Youth days, now a grenadier with the Mobile Infantry.

"Who is poster boy," said Falkenrath, "this one?"

"You don't know about Haas? Doesn't he look familiar?"

"Hey Pfeiffer," said Herrick, "give me a break. Old news."

"Nonsense. You tell your friend, or I'll call you Poster Boy from here to Moscow."

"What's he talking about?" said Falkenrath.

"I'll get those C-Group boys to sweat it out of you, Haas." Pfeiffer pounced on his shoulders and jostled him. "Speak! Confess!"

"Okay, alright." Herrick sighed. "When I was sixteen, I won the junior ski-jump competition at Garmisch-Partenkirchen. The prize was a three-year pass, and Ludwig Hohlwein—"

"Hohlwein, that's the artist. They have his posters all over the recruiting stations. You know his work, trust me."

"Know it," said someone in the back, "Those goddamn posters are the reason I joined. I want to kill the bastard." They all laughed except for Herrick, who was blushing, wanting to get this out and over with.

"Ludwig Hohlwein!" he said, speaking over them, "did a poster of me."

"No!"

"Of you?"

"Pfeiffer, is he joking?"

"You should see it for yourself," said Pfeiffer. "Cutest little *schnuckiputzi* you've ever seen. They had one in the dorms at HJ camp, but they had to take it down. The guys thought it was a girl, and they kept *hailing* her!" He slapped his groin and threw up his arm in a spastic, double salute, hips forward. Hoots of laughter rang out, and someone clipped Herrick's hindquarters.

"Hey Haas," said Falkenrath, "how's the skiing in the Urals?"

"I guess we'll find out," said Herrick, and they laughed some more. As the conversation drifted, he looked back over his shoulder at the villagers. They were almost to the woods. It didn't look anything like a work crew.

At the edge of the town, they passed a checkpoint where civilians were being screened. The army had turned the village into an improvised forward operating area, with half-tracks, armored cars, and BMW R75s clogging the main thoroughfare, maintenance crews moving between them. The signal corps had commandeered a haberdashery. A field mess erected in an empty corral gave off tempting smells, but a scowling *hauptmann* at the gate informed them it was for officers only. Herrick asked him if there was a quartermaster's station and was summarily told to go piss on himself.

A Mobile Infantryman was dozing facedown on the handlebars of his motorcycle, and Pfeifer slapped his shoulder. "Look smart *frontkämpfer*." The *gefreiter* mumbled something obscene. "Where are the women, eh?" The *gefreiter* pointed down an alley.

They came out on a smaller street where men stood in a long, stationary line, a mix of *Einsatzgruppe*, *Orpo* men, and regular *Wehrmacht*. They followed the line around the corner and saw that it led to the door of a two-story inn. The men were chatting, smoking, and sipping from cups and canteens. Laughter crackled down the line like musket fire.

"*Schnell!*" someone yelled.

"You hear that, boys? Blitzkrieg here wants his turn."

"Two seconds in the foxhole, make a boy into a man."

"Quick, or he'll shoot!"

"*Scheisse!*" said Pfeifer.

They doubled back to get in line. Someone produced a bottle of vodka and the men took sips, keeping an eye out for officers. They didn't see any. Someone speculated that the gods had their own private cathouse on a different street. Herrick looked up at the second-story windows, trying to gauge how many rooms there were. He looked then at the men, their wolfish grins, adding things up. His amorous stirrings of earlier had left him. He stepped away from the line.

"Where are you going?" asked Falkenrath.

"Find a quartermaster. This is taking too long. You want to come back late *and* empty-handed?" Without waiting for an answer, he started toward the alley and the main street beyond.

"Poster boy!" called Pfeifer. "My little *schnuckiputzi*, a deserter?" They laughed. Herrick waved over his shoulder without looking back.

He did not immediately go looking for the quartermaster but headed down the adjacent alley. He was tired of company. He turned down a narrow street where the shopfronts gave way to cottages. There was a good deal of broken windows, he noticed—the SS still loved their 'street action.' Herrick stopped at the end of an empty street and rolled a cigarette. He lit up and continued his stroll, trying to walk out his angst.

Krieg ist Krieg, he mused, reciting the old soldiers' mantra, *und Schnapps ist Shn—*

He rounded a corner and stopped. At the end of the dead-end street, a *sturmbannführer* in crusher and black coat was kneeling in front of a boy, about ten years old. The boy was trying to light his cigar. A second boy and a girl of about the same age stood back against the wall with blank, watchful expressions. A half-dozen mid-ranked SS men stood around them.

The match went out. The *sturmbannführer* waited patiently while the boy struck a second and held it for him. He leaned in and puffed at the cigar until smoke billowed between them, then nodded and pointed for him to join the others. He stood up, smoking and regarding the children. Then he casually reached into his coat and took out his Luger, and shot both boys directly in the face. The girl turned away, covering her ears. A third shot rang out and she fell where she stood, straight down as her legs collapsed.

Herrick's cigarette dropped from his lips.

A feeling he'd never known before, a swift, white rage bordering on exaltation swept through his body. It hit his brain, and all he knew was that he could shoot the man from this distance—easily, he had no doubt—one shot in the head like he'd done the kids. The hand that would do it was rising toward his pistol. He felt like he *must* do it or instantly burst into flames.

The *sturmbannführer* turned, and their eyes met. Herrick saw astonishment in the lean, hawkish face, and Herrick could feel the inrush of some momentous fork in time, some drastic thing about to happen one way or the other. His hand floated up, and to a hollowing, inward horror, he felt it rise past his hip and stab the air in salute.

They left Justingrad at 11:00 the following morning. By that time the town was in ashes.

He awoke to a blissful, enveloping warmth, and a numbness in his extremities that almost blotted out the pain. Coarse fur tickled his chin, a bearskin blanket with knit quilts underneath. The light and heat came from an enormous brick oven that ran the entire length of the far wall, flames dancing in a bed of white cinders. The smoky air was redolent with cloves, nettle, wormwood, cooking fat, and other smells he couldn't place. From a near corner, a caged hen chuckled complacently. *What place is this?* Wondering still, he closed his eyes.

When he opened them again the room was darker, the fire glowed red, and there was a hunched shadow in front of it. He watched the shadow. He thought it moved a little. Then it was rising, and he felt a creeping fear.

"What's this, awake?" said a high, cracked, lilting voice. "Alive *and* awake? Dear me, what stirs?"

He couldn't trust his eyes—the old woman, despite her considerable hump, had to be almost two meters tall. Herrick's heart beat faster in his chest as she crossed the room, her head almost brushing the crossbeam, and dropped down him like a great, shaggy hummock beside him, blocking the light. He could make out only the crags of her ancient face and the glint of her enormous eyes. A smell like dead forests enveloped him, wafting out of her cloak.

"*Wer...?*" he whispered. "*Wer best du?*"

"Me?" She tittered, and the breath that came out of her mouth was the frigid-cold of an ice locker, and it smelled of peat bogs, river-muck, and spoiled crops. "Why I've had so many names, dear me, I've probably forgotten half." She pursed her lips, and the breath that issued from her long, gaping nostrils was searing hot and smelled of rendered fat. "Mare, Mora, Muma Padurii..." She counted on her fingers, each as long as a carving knife. "...Lada, Mokosz, Cailleach.... In the western isles they call me Kaylee, with brave men's heads for my chestnut groves, and way down south, it's Kali, the Black Mother. Isn't that nice? The Britons call me Grindylow,

Grendel, and Jenny Greenteeth. But why don't you call me Mama and rest your dear little head about it." She reached down and stroked his hot cheek with her cold, leathery palm. There was something moving in her hair.

"Ma-m-m-ma-ma—"

"Mama *Yaga*, if you please. Shhhh, hush now."

It was a wasp. It struggled loose from her long, iron-gray locks and thrummed inches from his face before lifting away in the darkness.

"Sleep," she whispered.

The word *sleep* was dreadful to him. He was sure it meant *death*. He tried to fight the urge, but it came up from below and threw its arms around him and pulled him down-down-down....

"Mama."

"Yes, Herrick?"

"I wish I could go out and play."

"I wish you could too, dear, but you're not well. You must keep to your bed."

"Mama."

"Yes, Herrick."

"Do you think papa will be home for Christmas?"

"I don't know, dear. I don't know where your papa is."

"What happened to him, Mama?"

"I wish I knew, dear. Any number of things can happen to a man alone in the woods. He's never been right, you know. Not since the war. Herrick...

"Yes, Mama."

"Promise me you'll never go to war."

"I promise, Mama."

"Promise me you'll always come home to me."

"Yes, Mama. Mama...."

"Yes, dear?"

"...Why are you so big?"

He woke up screaming, thrashing in the heavy quilts. Then the pain attacked his leg, and he screamed in a different key. The hands he beat about were useless things, aching, bandage-wrapped clubs. It felt like a bear trap was closed on his shin, grinding down on it. Memory came roaring back—the reek of diesel, the shrill whistle of incoming shells, the haunted eyes of the commander as he sat in the blood-slick belly of the doomed tank....

The old woman.

Somehow, she was worse than all the rest.

The huge, *unnatural* old woman!

For the moment, she appeared to be gone. There was more light than before. The massive brick stove burned ravenously, and overhead a kerosene lantern cast a wavering, amber glow. A queer, straw shade encasing it threw spidery shadows on the walls. A tallow candle burned on a table by the bed.

Gritting his teeth against the pain in his leg, Herrick pulled himself up on his elbows and took stock of the room. He saw a rocking chair, cloudy mason jars, pots and pans, animal pelts, and embroidered quilts. In one corner, the hen; in another, an enormous stone mortar and pestle. The pestle was the size of a horse's leg—it would take a strong man just to lift it. Clusters of herbs and roots hung from the deep, inverted well of the ceiling, and huge, woody fungus of some sort grew in misshapen disks through gaps in the timbers. There was straw on the floor and strings of dried rowan berries strung around the windows. By the light outside, it was either dusk or early morning, and snow was falling.

His gaze returned to the great mortar and pestle—for some reason he found its presence terribly unnerving, watchful somehow. Then he noticed something that confirmed and deepened his anxiety: the shadow! While every other shadow in the room swayed and wavered with the light, the shadow of the massive grinding apparatus remained as monolithically still as the thing itself. *A magical thing,* he thought. *Half in the world, half out. An unnatural thing!*

He heard something, a whisper, and a breathy, voiceless laugh, coming from low in the room, and he thought for a horrible moment that the mortar and pestle were speaking to each other. The sound was closer, though, *much* closer. Herrick leaned out over the bed and looked down. Three children, two dark boys and a little tow-haired girl, were lying side by side with their legs under the cot and their hands over their eyes, grinning. The little girl was the giggly one, and there was a bullet hole through the hand that covered her left eye. She lifted her hand, grinning up at him. The hole went all the way through her head.

Herrick flung himself away, and the sudden pain in his leg sapped him back into unconsciousness.

"Git! Git! Git away, you devils. You'll spoil in that heat!"

He opened his eyes to see the old woman swatting the children with a broom, driving them away from the fire. They turned from the beating and shuffled toward the door. "Out! Go! You're gamey enough already!" She kicked the half-open door, and a blast of cold air guttered the candles.

They're the same, he thought, *the same ones I saw....* They weren't, of course. The children of Justingrad were far away and sleeping in the earth, but the thought danced fiendishly on his fevered brain. He *was* feverish; he could feel it. His body trembled with the promise of suffering to come.

Two of the children had gone willingly into the cold, whistling dark, but one of the boys clutched at the old woman's patched skirts. "*ROARP!*" she barked, a completely inhuman sound, like a monstrous bullfrog, and she swept the boy over the threshold with a ferocious kick. She slammed the door and walked to the fire. The flames leaped up at a wag of her fingers, and a wave of heat rolled through the room. She took a long-stemmed briar pipe from a crevice over the hearth, closed one nostril with her finger and blew into the bowl with the other until an orange glow answered. She sucked on the stem, and smoke filled the air around her. She dropped into the rocker, muttering and staring into the flames.

"I had to clip your fingers and toes, dear," she said. "The frost had been at you." Herrick looked at the stumps of his bandaged hands and groaned, marking the coppery stains at the top.

"All?"

"Oh, I left ya' a booger-slinger or two. Quit complaining, or go play with the little rotters." She cackled and rocked in her chair. A wasp buzzed circles around her head, and Herrick thought the shadows of the room were making mischief at the corners of his vision, moving in ways they had no business moving. Thinking this, he fell back into a deep, dark place below the floor, and the dancing shadows followed.

"Mama, I'm hungry!"

"Oh, my poor boy, here-here, take some milk."

"Mama, I'm too old for that!"

"Nonsense. You need to eat."

His mother smiled kindly down, the light of the colored-glass lamp making her golden hair glow with rainbow hues. With one jerk of her enormous hands, she ripped open her brassier and out spilled six black, hairy breasts, stacked three to each side. Dugs of an animal, a wolf, or an ape! He tried to turn away but her root-like fingers locked around his head and she bent over him, crushing him to her bosom, and the pungent, oily stink of her skin filled his nose. It seemed that his alimentary organs had subsisted recently in a kind of torpor, but now they suddenly awoke. A fierce hunger gnawed his innards, and his mouth filled with saliva. Still, he fought her, clenched his teeth and refused to open, though the leathery nipple mashed against his lips.

"Don't fuss now. You'll hurt Mama Yaga's feelings. She'll scoop your eyes out and send you to bed hungry and blind."

She caressed his fluttering eyelid with the pad of her thumb, and fear and hunger forged a perfect circuit in his body. He opened his mouth and took the nipple, and instantly his mouth was filled with a dark, sticky, coppery paste. Not milk, but a flood of congealed, clotting blood! Despite his revulsion, the gnawing in his belly ravened more at the taste, and he swallowed without thinking, the hot liquid coating his throat. Another mouthful followed the first, and then he didn't care anymore. He locked his teeth to the gritty, oily pap and sucked hard. Her mad cackle shook her chest and sent more slippery liquid pulsing into his mouth until his face was smeared with it. It seemed to flow all around and over him, subsuming him in a black-silky current. That night he slept at the bottom of the River Styx.

Despite spending much of their time in the cold, and despite the bundles of dried thyme she'd hung around their necks, the blue-skinned children were beginning to smell. The boys—twins, as it were—stared constantly at Herrick whenever she let them in the room, and the only way he could tell them apart was that one was given to skinning back his gums and showing his teeth. Herrick thought maybe he was trying to smile, but the effect was far from endearing.

The girl was more active, wandering around the room and hiding behind things for hours at a time. She had a habit of chewing her fingers. When the fingers of her right hand were down to raw nubs, she started on the left. One day she put a piece of her thumb on Herrick's chest, like a gift. Then she went over the stove and used her three remaining fingers to pull all her hair out (it came out easily) and fed it to the fire.

As bad as the children smelled, there was an even worse odor coming from somewhere in the room, a subtle, curdling reek that tickled his throat and made him gag. His leg hurt, and the fever made it feel like his thoughts were evaporating right through his skull. Impossible to link one to another...

"I'd say that leg's about ripe, wouldn't you?" In his dream, he was helping his mother cook a turkey.

"You mean it's cooked, Mama?"

"Oh no, I never cook good meat. I mean it's ready to come off." She looked down at him and grinned, her black, thorny fangs sprouting from under her lips.

He woke in a cold panic to find the old woman standing over him, a bone-handled, serrated knife in her hand. His covers had been pulled down, and his right pant leg was slit up to his knee. His lower leg was tied with rawhide thongs to a long cutting board. The sprig of bone still protruded from mid-shin, and the flesh that encased it was a mottled mix of black and turtle-shell green. He realized where the smell had been coming from—uncovered, it was trebly sickening.

"Y-y-you...you didn't *set it?*"

"Set it? Do I look like a nurse, young man?" She slapped him, a quick, clapping blow that carried the force of a man's punch. "I'm a *hungry-hungry mad old witch!*" She laughed, a horrible, shrill cackle, and bounced the toothy edge of the knife below his knee, finally settling it just below the joint. "Might as well take the whole hock. Ready?"

"No-no-no-no-NO! DON'T! DON'T! DON'T!" Herrick tried to twist away. Her enormous eyes flashed with deranged mirth, and she cracked him hard across the face with her big, knobby fist.

He dreamed that his mother had clopped him over the head with the cutting board and thrown him in the cellar. Then a terrible pain bit into his leg. He looked down to see an enormous rat with its jaws latched below his knee. He tried to shake it loose, but it bit deep-deeper-DEEPER! and he woke, screaming, to see the knife sailing through a red track in his leg and his blood pooling in the sheets. He howled with everything in him, and she turned on him with a dog-like snarl and punched him in the head several times before he lost consciousness again, and this time he stayed in the cellar. With the rat.

The fever was full on him now, and he could no longer be certain at any time that he wasn't dreaming. The sound—an incessant grinding—reached him way down in the red-dark well where she'd thrown him. *It's my bones,* he thought. *She's grinding my bones for dinner.*

His mother flitted through the kitchen making steak tartare, telling him to run and fetch an egg. Snow covered the yard. His feet crunched in it. The hen clucked complacently in the shed. When he came back to the kitchen his mother was gone, and a great, black mortar and pestle sat in the middle of the room instead. The egg slipped from his fingers. He looked down at the splatted yoke between his feet, and when he looked up again the old woman stood, beckoning him with a long, crooked finger. He turned to run, and snarling like a dog, she chased him through the house.

He awoke one day with a wasp perched on his nose and the old woman sitting beside him, chewing something. The room seemed to be rocking, like a ship's hold. His eyes went to the window and he saw trees going past, evergreens, the snowy boughs pressed back by their passage, thumping softly against the cottage. Mama Yaga grinned at him through blood-smeared lips. "Sthiberia," she lisped. The wasp crawled down his nose and drank from the corner of his eye as he wept.

He dreamed that one of the twins, the one who liked to show his teeth, had been chewing on his bandaged hands. His mother flew into a rage when she saw it. She found the boy hiding in the hall behind the old grandfather clock and dragged him, kicking and screaming into the kitchen. She pushed him head-first down into the mortar. She took up the pestle. Herrick screamed for her to stop. Laughing and hooting over his cries, she drove the heavy bell-end down between the boy's kicking legs with an awful crunching sound. Soon only the feet were visible, and then these two vanished under the pulverizing blows.

When he woke, the bandaged club of his right arm looked frayed and teeth-pocked. The old woman was nowhere in sight, but the mortar and pestle were in the center of the room, and the girl and one of the boys were staring at it. The other boy was nowhere to be seen.

Herrick had no reliable way of measuring time, but when he woke in the darkness of the cottage one night, his fever had broken, and the pain was localized in his leg instead of saturating his every nerve. He gasped with relief, and tears leaked from his eyes. It occurred to him that the ache was all the way down in his *right foot!* It had been a dream, a terrible nightmare! But when he swung his leg sideways, it seemed to pass through the wall until it fetched up against the timber at the knee. He groaned in despair of understanding. He'd heard stories of *phantom limbs*, the sensation of having an arm or a leg where there was none. A cruel trick of the brain. *I'm turning into a ghost*, he thought. *Little by little ... I'll be a ghost ... like father.*

He lifted his head and took in the room. The mouth of the enormous oven stretched across the far wall like Hell's own Judas gate, the coals pulsing with malevolent light. He lay back with a sigh and licked his dry, cracked lips, which were suddenly met with a wet sponge. Cool, brackish water trickled into his mouth. She was there, next to him, an immense, shaggy mountain of darkness crowned in a red corona. He felt something rough and cool on his forehead and realized it was her palm.

"Please..." he whispered.

"Shhh ... quiet now." She gave him the sponge again, and he drank. "It's a shame, really," she said, speaking softly, almost tenderly. "In the spring, I'm a doe-eyed maid, mild as the April breeze and dewy between the legs. In summer, I'm a stout, apple-cheeked Hause Frau. I go about on chicken legs and leave baskets of bread and sweets for the poor country folk and wring the necks of bandits and tax collectors. In autumn, I'm a wise, winsome widow, a patron of woodsmen and travelers. I'd take a fine young fellow like you to bed and read him his fortune, tell him how he'll die, the time and the place, then kiss him so sweetly he forgets." Her hand scraped up his forehead, and she leaned over him, her eyes huge and glinting black, her rancid, cold-hot breath in his face. "It's only in winter when I'm such a hungry old beast." She smiled, her wrinkled cheeks bunched under her eyes.

"Please..." he whispered again.

"Shhh.... Spring will come. I wish you could see it, it's going to be beautiful. But you'll be all inside me by then."

"Mama?"

"Herrick."

"Mama, is that you?"

"Only you can tell, Herrick."

"How can I tell?"

"Tell the truth, Herrick. Did you rape? Did you murder?"

"Mama, am I forsaken?"

"What's done is done, Herrick. You can't go home again."

"Mama."

"Each man has to carry the sticks of his own pyre, Herrick."

"Mama."

"*Listen* to me. Each *man* has to carry his own *fire*."

"Mama, I want to come home!"

"Don't say that. Don't you say that! Herrick, if you come home I'll SCOOP YOUR EYES OUT!"

One day the remaining boy threw a fit. He ran in circles, knocking things over, and tried to climb the walls. The old woman watched him do it, a sneer slowly curling her lip, then she snatched him as he ran past and wrenched his head off with a single twist and a snap of bone and sinew. Into the mortar went the body, and merrily, cackling, she went to work with the pestle. Herrick turned his face to the wall as the terrible crunching and grinding ensued.

The boy's head lay on the floor for several days until one morning she picked it up and put it in an earthenware jar. She added some water from a jug, humming to herself, then opened a wax-sealed 50mm shell casing and emptied it over the jar. The following morning, he watched as she removed a small, slimy skull. She held it up, squinting critically, then cracked it on the brick hearth and snapped off shards until only the forehead, eyes, and upper jaw remained. She set it by the fire a while to dry. Then she took a shoemaker's awl from a drawer and carefully worked two small holes above the eyes. She ran a leather cord through the holes and placed it on the girl, like a crude Venetian mask. She clapped her hands in time as the girl tottered around the room. Herrick watched it all.

Now it was just the three of them. The girl was rapidly decomposing, her loose skin acquiring a waxy sheen whenever she was inside for more than a few minutes. She'd saved one finger to point and pick with and had taken to gnawing her toes instead. The skull mask made her look like a denizen of some starving Chinese hell.

Despite the girl's condition, the old woman doted on her considerably. Every night, after she'd nursed Herrick, she would repair to her rocker and smoke her pipe with the girl up on her knee. Sometimes she talked to the girl or to the fire—it was hard to tell. The fire popped and spat, and sent long, braided streamers dancing up the flue.

As the winter drew on, Herrick grew certain of something that in his fevered state he had dismissed as a hallucination. The old woman was *changing*. She'd grown taller, towering a full head above the room's crossbeam, and her nose had nearly doubled in length. Her fingers had extended and developed an additional joint. Her nails had hardened into long, crusty talons, and her black, snaggled fangs no longer tucked in behind her lips but jutted through like something spiny trying to escape. The jaundiced yellow of her eyes had darkened to a deep, reticulated gold that seemed to brew its own eldritch light when the fire burned low.

Worse than any physical change were her increasingly demonic humors. Sometimes she stood slack-jawed and drooling at the window for hours at a time, as though watching for something. Other days, she shuffled circuits around the room, grinning and chanting recursive snatches of nursery rhymes and incantations, breaking off to snarl at the wasps that flew about her hair. Every so often, she'd stop and clap her hands, and the whole airborne swarm would immediately fall dead on the floor. She'd do this until a trail of the creatures littered the room's perimeter. Then she'd make the little dead girl sweep them up and throw them in the fire.

One night he woke to find her gone, or so he thought. When he lay back and looked up, she was in the deep angle of the ceiling, balled up there like a spider with her hair hanging down and her yellow eyes staring at him, runners of drool oozing through her fangs. She stayed like that as the fire burned down until only her glowing eyes could be seen, and he fell at last into a fitful sleep.

Herrick had no confidence that Mama Yaga could be killed, still less any idea how to do it. Escape seemed hardly more feasible. She was often gone for hours at a time, taking the mortar and pestle with her, but even if he somehow managed to get out, what then? He'd be alone, untold kilometers behind enemy lines, in the dead of winter, with one leg. She'd catch him, or he'd freeze to death, or the Russians would kill him, or the wolves.

When—he wondered—had he rediscovered the will to live and the courage to think of escape? He couldn't say.

One night, while she snored in her rocker and the fire burned low, he touched his face and found that he'd grown a fine, fleecy beard over the course of his convalescence. He was a man, after all. The blood he'd taken from her must have been nourishing indeed, for his muscles felt firm and springy despite long disuse. He glanced over at her once, then took a strand of greasy cotton that dangled from his mummified right hand and pulled it loose, little by little unwinding the wrap. He gagged at the smell of his own flaking, unwashed skin, but as the bandage fell away he saw that his thumb, index, and middle fingers were perfectly intact, while the other two digits retained their first segments. He flexed them. *Merry Christmas, Hass!* he thought and grinned in the dark. He unwrapped the left hand. Not so good, this one—the thumb and all four fingers ended uniformly at the first hinge joint. More of a paw than a hand. Well....

He wondered about his foot.

He'd been so intent on his inventory that he'd thought the moving shadows only a trick of the firelight. She hadn't made a sound crossing the room, but suddenly she was beside him, looming mountainous and horrible, glaring down at him. Her hand shot out and caught him by the wrist. Mama Yaga's black tongue lolled out and licked her fangs as she lifted his three-fingered hand to her mouth.

Herrick barely managed to suppress his scream—instead, he made a sucking sound with his lips and pawed her hanging smock. "Mama?" he said, in a childish falsetto. The growl in her throat faltered and her eyes lost their predatory focus. She let his hand slip free, let him pull her smock down. Herrick took the black, sagging pap and drew hard upon it. Her eyelids fluttered, and a long, silvery ribbon of drool fell from her lip and wetted his shoulder. Outside, the snow was falling.

Let it fall! he prayed. *Let it fall tomorrow too!*

Herrick awoke the next morning, early with the dawn. He lay there watching the bright, falling snow outside. She was motionless in her rocker by the cold hearth, the dead girl curled in her lap.

A buzzing sounded from across the room. Mama Yaga gave a meaty snort, rose, and shook out her skirts, dropping the little dead girl on the floor with an audible crunch of bone. Herrick watched her through half-lidded eyes and feigned sleep when she began to move about. She lit a fire. She came over to his cot, but only to collect and empty the chamber pot. Then he heard a sound that rent his composure and set his heart tripping to its awful rhythm: the scrape of a blade against a whetstone. Her body blocked his view, but he knew it was the bone-handled knife.

She left around noon, taking the mortar and pestle with her. He knew not why her carting such heavy things portended a longer absence, but he recognized from past observation that it generally did. Herrick guessed he had between two and six hours. The first thing he did was unwrap his remaining bandages. The stump of his right leg was shiny scar tissue, tender but healed. His left foot was half-gone, severed clean through the metatarsals. *Well,* he thought, regarding his wreckage philosophically, *Krieg ist verdammt Krieg, ja!*

His clothes and boots were heaped in the corner—the old woman seemed to never throw anything out. Bracing himself against the wall, he managed to stand and hop within falling reach of them. He found his service dagger still clipped to his belt. He took it back to the bed and used it to slash strips from the bearskin blanket. One such strip made a lining for his boot. He stuffed the insulated toe with wool quilting, packing it down to take up space. He pulled on his pants, then the boot, lacing it up as tight as he could.

He fashioned a sling of bearskin for his stump, fixed it with rawhide to his belt, then padded it generously with wool and stuffed more wool into his pants. There were several wolf pelts nailed to the wall, and he took one down, cut slits for his belt, and made himself a rude kilt. He cut armholes in the remaining bearskin and put it on like a coat. There were several brooms on hand to choose from. He took a stout one, trimmed the bristles, carved an angled notch at the one-third mark, and used one of the old woman's babushkas to make a short sling, which he hooked into the notch. With the sling around his wrist, two fingers gripping, he crutched around the room for half an hour or so, exercising his muscles. The little dead girl watched him do it, her masked head turning to follow him.

When Herrick was confident he could keep a regular pace, he made his last, crucial preparations. Then he built the fire high, settled himself in the Mama Yaga's rocker with a blanket up to his chin, and waited for her to return.

As he waited, he consoled himself that his mother had two other children, accomplished young women who would marry well and never go to war. He thought of his own pitiful failures, his naivety, his cowardice, and then of his country, and how the two tragic courses ran parallel along so many tracks. How National Socialism had used the best aspirations of a nation's youth to the most evil and perverted ends. This course of thought led him at last to his one great moment, his jump at Garmisch-Partenkirchen, the day he won the New Year's pennant.

It was not so much, really, just a meaningless stunt. And yet, for a span of seconds, he was perfect. Flying at the sun with the wind in his hair, with the world—Hitler Youth, the fatherland, the war to come—waiting for him below with jaws wide open. For a moment he'd defied it all, flown free and singular as Daedalus over Crete.

The shadows in the cottage had grown as long as its mistress's fingers, and Herrick was actually dozing when Mama Yaga slipped silently through the door. She slammed the mortar down in the corner, and he started awake. They stared at each other. Quickly, before she could take in more of the room, he pulled the blanket back to show his left arm strapped to the dark-stained cutting board. "Please, Mama," he said. "I know you're hungry, it's okay. Just take it quickly, and bandage me up." He looked at her imploringly. The knife lay beside him on the section of tree stump she used for an end table, the serrated tooth of steel gleaming in the firelight.

Mama Yaga regarded him thoughtfully, and her lips pooched out over her fangs in a speculative moue. "Well," she said, "what a good, upright boy you are. It seems like only yesterday you were kicking and screaming over each little pruning. You seem to have finally learned some manners."

"Yes, Mama, only *please* don't make me wait. I fear the pain, Mamma, please!"

"Yes-yes-yes," she said, walking over and squatting beside him. She picked up the implement—in her enormous hand it looked like a paring knife. She steadied the cutting board against her knee and tapped along his arm with the blade, finding the soft spot just inside his elbow.

"Can I have a drink of water first, please?"

She glanced up, scowled, then sighed. She flipped the blade around and stuck it in the cutting board. She took a jug off the shelf and poured water into a tin cup. Mamma Yaga held it to his lips, smiling almost sweetly while he took a long drink. She didn't see his other hand moving under the blanket, but her eyes strayed to the little dead girl in the corner, who was staring through her mask and pointing at Herrick with her last, accusatory finger. "What...?" she said, her smile falling open at one end to make a paisley slash of fangs. "What's he been up to?"

Herrick spat the water in her face. She blinked at him. He pushed his thumb through the wax seal of the 50mm shell casing in his lap and tossed the contents after the water, right into her big, yellow eyes.

Now it was Mama Yaga's turn to scream, and the deafening shriek stabbed his eardrums and seized him with terror. She dropped his arm and clapped her lye-chalked face in a puff of white powder. A second later she lunged, snatched the now-empty rocking chair and ripped it in two. She clutched around at the empty air, then stood still and put out her trembling hand. The pestle flew out of the mortar, across the room, and straight into her grip. With acrid smoke wreathing her head, she lay about with the great, granite cudgel, roaring and slobbering like a wounded bear, smashing craters in the floor.

Herrick, having cleared her reach, pushed over a tank of kerosene he'd placed beside his cot. The witch lashed blindly after the sound. He scrambled back, hooked a lit lantern with his two good fingers, and smashed it in the middle of the spill. Flames leaped from the straw-littered floor and licked at the strewn bedding. Another blind swing of the pestle smashed the kerosene tank and sent liquid fire spewing across the room onto Herrick's legs.

Suddenly the whole cottage lurched into motion, throwing Herrick against the wall. Even Mama Yaga was unbalanced, her head clipping the crossbeam. A second heave tilted the room the other way, and coals flew out of the oven and scattered across the floor. Herrick was thrown again and landed in the very fire he'd started. He screamed as the flames licked at him and leaped into his hair. He tried to roll free, but the house tipped him back into the fire. Were it not for the skins Herrick wore, he would surely have been flash-broiled.

He caught a glimpse of trees wheeling past the window. The cottage was moving.

"Kill you! Kill you! Skin you alive!" The witch swung her club, smashing timbers, knocking bricks from the hearth like so many broken teeth. Herrick was thrown clear of the flames and managed to catch his balance against the tilting wall. He saw his chance, felt the shifting yaw of the room, and launched himself at the window with an athletic double-hop. He flung his arm over his face right before he hit the glass. He went clean through, flying between the trees, and landed in deep snow. He rolled about, bathing his burns in the cold. He watched the cottage go crashing through the trees, smoke pouring through the timbers, running on its gangling, scaly, reverse-jointed legs, very much like a chicken with its head cut off.

The pain was awful, but he'd known worse. He hopped between trees, catching branches for support, following the tracks of the house back the way it had come. Soon he reached the rectangle of crushed ground, and from there it was easy to locate the crutch and provisions he had tossed out the window, buried as they were in the freshly fallen snow. He set off into the woods. The shadows of the cottage had been his sundials for many days, enough that he had an idea of due south. He used the trees to keep his course, picking out a distant one and keeping it in view until he'd reached it, then picking out another. The snow continued to fall in thick flakes and would soon cover his tracks.

The witch's blood must have been nourishing indeed. Despite the cold, he felt strong and warmed in his core, and the bracing air served mainly to numb his burns. He loped with long flowing strides, like some shaggy, Teutonic *skiapod*, quicker, it seemed, than he'd ever traveled on two legs. The trees were skeletal larch, the ground mostly level, and the snow a soft and yielding powder. As darkness fell, he made a bivouac of dead branches and built a small fire with the matches and kindling sticks he'd pilfered from the witch's hearth. He didn't sleep but tended the fire all night, listening, ready at the slightest warning to smother the fire and collapse the bivouac into a hidey-hole. But the night passed in deep, unbroken silence.

The next day Herrick came to a place where he could go no farther. The ground sloped precipitously to a vertical drop, and below the cliffs there stretched a frozen sea or a lake of inestimable size. A harsh wind came flying out of the dim, blue distance to box his ears and roar in his face. The immensity of that icebound waste, the anarchic, jutting tors that broke its steely surface along the stark and dismal shore, frightened him in a way even the war and the witch had not. He felt the nearness of death—not merely his own—the tectonic encroachment of a vast, world-devouring Thanatos, and for a moment his loss of heart was so profound that he yearned to pitch himself into that oblivion rather than face it for another second. Instead, he knelt down and rested on his stump, with his head tucked to his chest, breathing vapor in the cowl of bearskin. *I can see my breath*, he thought. *I am still alive.*

He was tired, though. The preternatural vigor of his early flight had all been spent; he was once more an ordinary man, crippled, alone in the grip of winter. Herrick knew he'd starve or freeze if he tried to go around the lake. He therefore did the only thing he could think to do. He picked his way along the cliff for most of the day until at last he found a narrow defile that let him down to the stony shore. He paused in a windbreak to split the end of his crutch with his knife. Into the breach he wedged the little awl he'd taken from the witch's shelf—a difficult thing to do with only three fingers, which were again showing signs of frostbite. With fingers and teeth, he bound it snug with rawhide and set out over the frozen waters, moving at a brisk but incremental pace as he stabbed and shuffled over the ice. It was easy to move in a straight line at first, but a white, blowing front moved in and wiped away the cliffs behind him, leaving him in a trackless valley between invisible horizons. Now the cold bit deep. Fatigue and pain oppressed his body. He'd made a mistake in leaving the shore, he realized—he'd only hastened his death. He grinned and wept to think of all he'd survived, only to end like this. At least he'd die a man, on his own terms. At least, that.

He crutched along for perhaps another hour without seeing anything before he slipped and fell, and decided not to get up. He felt warm, which he reasoned was only his body lying to him as it froze to death—he'd heard of such things. Then he saw something that made him wonder if he wasn't already dead and had crossed over to some heathen spirit world. The shapes forming out of the white before him were those of two people, each leading a horse.

"You're not real," he said to them. "Horses? Whoever heard of horses walking on ice?"

But the ice of Lake Baikal was very thick, enough to support the hardy little ponies that Bidia and his brother Tsebek were leading that day. They'd crossed the ice on a sacred errand to collect the body of Tellig, their village shaman, who'd gone questing on the island of Olkhon and died in the company of his ancestors and spirit-kin. The frozen body was lashed to Tsebek's pony. Bidia's carried only their rations, gear, and a bundle of sable skins.

"What do you think?" said Tsebek.

"He spoke German," said Bidia.

"You're sure?"

Bidia, the elder, who'd been to Moscow and studied at Tomsk, was not one to repeat himself.

"You think he's one of these foreign invaders?"

Bidia made no reply. It seemed unlikely that a German soldier would be this far east. A pilot maybe, a deserter. A plane crash would account for his condition.

"He stinks of evil!" said Tsebek, making a sign. "We should cut his throat, help him on to his next life. He'll be a fish under the ice, and he'll thank us for it."

Bidia said nothing.

"I'm telling you, look at his burns. He's a bardo ghost escaped from Hell. I spoke with Master Tellig before he left. He said Magzo Gyalmo is in a terrible rage this year. She scours the earth and shakes the trees on the trail of her runaway brat. Where else do you suppose he came from?"

"You studied with Master Tellig," said Bidia at last. "Didn't he used to say that even demons can be redeemed and become protectors of the *dharma*?"

The wind kicked harder with a shrill keening, as if to refute the elder brother, but Tsebek knew that Bidia had spoken wisely. Moving together, they picked up the man and slung him over the back of Bidia's pony and tied him down. The brothers led the two men, the living and the dead, over the ice to the distant shore.

AFTERWARD: HOW I FOUND THE GRAVE OF A LOST LIBRARIAN

There is a hidden, lonely place far beneath the House of Lost Possibilities yet high above the Pillars of Creation. In this district are a few sad fragments of ancient masonry, perched on the edge of a steep cliff, of what was once an edifice of magnitude and dignity.

What odd cuneiform on that stone tablet my colleague almost tripped over! What do those chicken scratches on that antler mean? Is that a coin?

Stretching out, vast, beyond the cliff is a barren plain, circumscribed beyond the horizon by high, far mountains. Cast out over this wretched land is a disordered horde of ancient gravestones, tombs, and broken sepulchers. Scattered here and there are pits where the dead lie desecrated, some recently and others before human beings were created by malicious space aliens or perhaps a needful demiurge, or instead lost their tails and mutated their way up and out, gasping, from the primordial soup and into history, or whatever it is that the fickle Triarchs of Truth weave as their current reality.

Somewhere in this gray necropolis, there is a stone with the head of a leering, bestial human being or gargoyle. This signifies the resting place of the chief of what was once a mighty library—our eponymous lost librarian.

There are many trails leading to this grave and many footprints and other, stranger impressions around the marker too. Yet the site, unlike so many others, lies undisturbed... inviolate, whether out of prudent fear for undying curses or out of respect, who can say? Adepts, witches, scholars, and adventurers; rogues, and malefactors too find their way here. They brave the hard, often enigmatic journey for many reasons—ours is the quest for story and verse, for we know the librarian's eidolon will reward us if our literary motives are true—but they are united by one common thread: they seek to commune with that powerful, animate spirit who gave his life and gives his death in the service of Knowledge and Remembrance.

May their efforts be as successful as ours have been with this book.

tch's blood must have been nouris

When I read an anthology, I sometimes wonder why the editor decided upon a particular theme for their book. The answer is often pretty obvious. Collections of stories celebrating a beloved or famous author within a genre, tales involving disgruntled spouses and ex-minions of vampire surfers in Santa Cruz, ghosts of Rio de Janeiro, or a yearly "Best Of" collection all seem self-evident, at least in terms of theme. Others not so much, which brings me to this book you are looking at now.

Why a lost librarian, and a dead one at that? Why just a grave?

About eight months ago, I was casting around for some ideas for an anthology. I had a vague notion that I wanted to collect a varied group of stories unified under the rubric of horror in its many forms.

I scribbled titles and ideas down in a little notebook and would do so when the muse struck, no matter how socially awkward the situation—yes, I pulled out my ubiquitous notebook in the middle of a dental appointment. After a couple of months, I had pages full of scrawled notes but nothing that jumped out at me and screamed, "Here I am!" I continued noodling around, consulting idea books and online prompts, brainstormed with some of my friends, even meditated, which for me is never a good sign... still nothing. Maybe I was trying to force things, and I should just relax, work more on other projects, and revisit the anthology some other time? That road is broad and straight, but I've found for me it is the well-lit expressway to Procrastination City.

Then one night, I had a dream. Not the usual sort of fancy where you wake up remembering bits and pieces and then forget the whole thing in ten minutes. This dream felt *real* somehow. Important.

I was inside what seemed like the stacks of an old library with many doors and narrow corridors bound by tall, mostly wooden shelving, which ascended out of sight into shadow and darkness. There were books and other manuscripts of all kinds: ancient, modern, and a few that seemed futuristic next to a pile of stone tablets and antlers. The place was welcoming but gloomy as if lit by lamps, though I didn't see any light sources. People were bustling about on various errands, ignoring me and each other. They all seemed pretty much like patrons you would expect to find in a modern library. A young man beckoned me through one of the doors, and I followed him without question. I had this vague notion that he *knew things*.

This was the point in my dream where I reflected on the fact that while no one was talking, which you would expect in an old-time library, there weren't any sounds at all.

We were outside now, and I was immediately confronted by a terrible scene of ongoing destruction. A whole wing of the library was in the process of falling away with pieces of masonry, books, and even people tumbling down a fog-shrouded cliff which was disintegrating at an alarmingly fast rate. A horde of workers was scrambling around like proverbial ants unsuccessfully trying to save what books and any item they could. Others struggled with propping up the remaining structure. They didn't seem to be having much success either.

I was watching all of this when a crowd of workers and patrons approached me and started shoving books, scrolls, artwork, artifacts such as coins, vases, boxes— and yes, antlers—inside of my torso. The amount of material collecting inside me was impossible; some of the objects were bigger than I was, but that was of no account. In they went. I was like some giant Bag of Holding, if you'll excuse the unfortunate *Dungeons & Dragons* reference.

The dream must have ended at that point, or I simply don't recall more because I slept through the night and only remembered the library when I rolled out of bed and tripped over our piebald cat, Wyatt, as I so routinely do. He often haunts my dreams, but he wasn't in this one.

I roughed out the details in my notebook over some dry toast and a glass of milk. That afternoon, when I was down in our basement gym where I do a lot of my best thinking, I had it. The librarian is a source for all knowledge that has ever been, and he willingly persists in undeath so that he may gift others and ensure that his wisdom is not forgotten. I would use the library with its silent figurehead as my launching point and expand my net where the book would be mostly horror but also include a few stories that were ominous, cruel, and pernicious, even if they didn't fit unambiguously into the horror genre. If there was a happy ending—gods and devils forbid—or a glimmer of hope, let it be bittersweet or better yet, like a candle flame guttering in a vast darkness. If I was lucky, maybe I'd even get my hands on some mixed-genre stories or a bit of likely verse too. Dare I hope my desires would be fulfilled?

I did dare and, yes, my desires were not only fulfilled but wildly exceeded by the thirty-six authors and three poets whose diverse work graces these pages. Since you have gotten this far, I hope you enjoyed the journey. If, on the other hand, you are like me and like reading the end of books first, I think you are in for a treat.

Many thanks, friends, and fellow readers and farewell for now. Be on the lookout for our future anthologies including a second volume of *The Lost Librarian's Grave* in October 2022!

Ann Wycoff
Santa Cruz, California, USA
October 1, 2021

INDEX OF STORIES
AND POEMS BY CATEGORY

Strange Adventures and Weird Journeys

A Murder of Gargoyles

The Scientific Method

Ghosts and the Grave

Demon-Haunted World

An Eye for an Eye

End of the Line

AUTHOR BIOGRAPHIES

Edward Ahern
"Aegir's Son"

Ed Ahern resumed writing after forty odd years in foreign intelligence and international sales. He's had over three hundred stories and poems published so far, and six books. Ed works the other side of writing at Bewildering Stories, where he sits on the review board and manages a posse of nine review editors.

Owen Auch
"Bottled Rage"

Owen Auch grew up in Columbus, Ohio, and currently lives and works in San Francisco, California as a software engineer. When not writing prose or code—with equal delight and exasperation at each—he enjoys surfing, concerts, eating carbs, and befriending dogs at San Francisco's many parks. Owen's literary influences include Ernest Hemingway, Haruki Murakami, and Mikhail Bulgakov. This is his first published work.

Brandon Barrows
"Among Stars and Stones"

Brandon Barrows's most recent novel is *Burn Me Out* and he has published over seventy stories, selected of which are collected in the books *The Altar in the Hill* and *The Castle-Town Tragedy*. He is an active member of Private Eye Writers of America and International Thriller Writers. He lives in Vermont by a big lake with a patient wife and two impatient cats. Check out his website at www.brandonbarrowscomics.com and find him on Twitter @BrandonBarrows.

Paul L. Bates
"Medusa's Mirror"

Paul L. Bates has a degree in Architectural Design, is happily retired from a career in construction management, lives on the shore of a small private lake with his lady love, swims distance, and writes when the muse comes to call. He is the author of the novels *Imprint* and *Dreamer*. Most recently, his short fiction has appeared in *Sexy Fantastic* (Issue #1), *Vastarien* (Issues 1.1 and 2.2), *Dim Shores Presents* (Volume 1), and *Dear Leader Tales*.

Matthew Chabin
"Mother Winter"

Matthew Chabin is from Portland Oregon. He worked as a journalist in the U.S. Navy, and studied literature and philosophy at Southern Oregon University. He worked with the Tibet Charity in Dharamshala and trained Muay Thai boxing in Thailand. His likes include James Joyce, Stephen King, Jessica Lange, Patton Oswalt, film noir, and boxing, to name a few. He currently lives in Nagano Prefecture of Japan with his wife, daughter, and two cats.

Sipora Coffelt
"A Bed Both Long and Narrow"

Sipora Coffelt spent a decade wandering from university to university, earning her BA in philosophy, only to read the classifieds one day and realize her mistake and turned her hand to technical writing in the field of health education and literacy. Today, she lives on an acreage in Kansas, growing vegetables and tending flowers. In 2017, she began writing fiction and has short stories published in a variety of places, including: *The Arcanist, Page and Spine, Accursed: A Horror Anthology, Stupefying Stories Showcase,* and *Dark Moon Digest.* She can be found at www.zipcoffelt.com.

Zach Ellenberger
"Rathbone"

Zach Ellenberger is a writer based in Chicago where he lives with his wife and daughter. He grew up in Pittsburgh, PA where he spent his childhood writing comic strips and short stories. After spending his formative years as a musician recording albums and performing with various bands, he returned to his love of creative writing. He works in various genres including historical fiction, horror and sci-fi to name a few. Zach has published several short stories as well as his debut novel, *Potato Kingdom,* and continues to develop new projects in every medium from novels to screenplays and everything in between.

J.V. Gachs
"Penance"

J.V. Gachs is a Spanish classicist, writer, and aspiring librarian currently working as a Latin teacher. After many years of not writing fiction, she got back to it during the Spanish pandemic lockdown in 2020. Obsessed with sudden death, ghosts, and female villains, she always writes with a cat (or two) in her lap. Both Spanish and U.S. magazines have published her short stories.

Adele Gardner
"The Day in Gold"

Adele Gardner holds master's degrees in English literature and library science and has 53 stories and over 335 poems published or forthcoming in *Analog, Strange Horizons, Deep Magic, Daily Science Fiction, Flash Fiction Online, PodCastle,* and more under her own byline and various pseudonyms. Adele is a graduate of the Clarion West Writers Workshop and has had ten poems win or place in the Poetry Society of Virginia Awards, the Rhysling Award, and the Balticon Poetry Contest. Adele is an active member of the SFWA and HWA, a graduate of the Clarion West Writers Workshop, and literary executor for father, mentor, and namesake Dr. Delbert R. Gardner. Check out her website at www.gardnercastle.com.

Eddie Generous
"Odd Job Tom"

Eddie Generous has fallen off three different roofs and been lit on fire on multiple occasions. He grew up on a farm and later slept with his shoes under his pillows in homeless shelters. He dropped out of high school to afford rent on a room at a crummy boarding house, but eventually graduated from a mediocre college. He is the author of several small press books, has 2.8 rescue cats (one needed a leg amputation), is a podcast host, and lives on the Pacific Coast of Canada. Check out his website at https://www.jiffypopandhorror.com.

Carol Gyzander
"He Gets Hungry Sometimes"

Carol Gyzander writes and edits horror, dark fiction, and sci-fi in the northern New Jersey suburbs of New York City, with the help of her black Velcro cat. Her stories are in over a dozen anthologies including *Under Twin Suns: Alternate Histories of the Yellow Sign; Across the Universe: Tales of Alternative Beatles;* and *Stories We Tell After Midnight.* As editor and one of the founders of Writerpunk Press, she's edited four anthologies of punk stories inspired by classic tales (including Poe and classic horror). Carol has a sci-fi and a horror novel, plus various other editing projects, in the works.

Find her at CarolGyzander.com, or @CarolGyzander on Twitter and Instagram

Russell Hemmell
"Butterflies of the Longest Night"

Russell Hemmell is a French-Italian transplant in Scotland, passionate about astrophysics, history, and Japanese manga. Recent stories in *Aurealis*, *Cast of Wonders*, Flame Tree Press, and others. Member of SFWA, HWA, and Codexian. Find them online at their blog earthianhivemind. net and on Twitter @SPBianchini.

Juleigh Howard-Hobson
"The Problem with the Bottling of Troublesome Spirits"

Juleigh Howard-Hobson lives beside the edge of the world, where secrets are whispered in the winds and words fling from the mists. It rains ghosts. Her writing has been nominated for The Best of the Net, Pushcart, Elgin and Rhysling Awards. Her work can be found in *Dreams & Nightmares*, *Eye to the Telescope*, *Polu Texni*, *Star*Line*, *Haunted Dollhouse*, *34 Orchard*, *Audient Void*, *Midnight Echo*, *Siren's Call*, *Noir Nation*, *Shadow of Pendle* (Dark Sheep Books), *They Walk Among Us* (Utah Horror Writer's Association) and many other venues. Her latest collection is the Elgin-nominated *Our Otherworld* (Red Salon).

Ken Hueler
"The Infinity of Worse"

Ken Hueler teaches kung fu in the San Francisco Bay Area and, with fellow members of the Horror Writers Association's local chapter, gets up to all sorts of adventures (only some involving margaritas). His work has appeared in *Weirdbook*, *The Sirens Call*, *Space & Time*, *Weekly Mystery Magazine*, and the charity anthology *Tales for the Camp Fire*. You can learn more at kenhueler.wordpress.com.

Pedro Iniguez
"The Savage Night"

Pedro Iniguez is a speculative fiction writer who also enjoys reading and painting. His work can be found in magazines and anthologies such as *Space and Time Magazine*, *Crossed Genres*, *Dig Two Graves*, *Tiny Nightmares*, *Deserts of Fire*, and *Altered States II*. His cyberpunk novel, *Control Theory* (Indie Authors Press, 2016) and his ten-year collection, *Synthetic Dawns & Crimson Dusks*, (Indie Authors Press, 2020) are available on Amazon.

Michelle Ann King
"The Glorious Protection of Angels"

Michelle Ann King is a short story writer from Essex, England. Her stories of fantasy, science fiction, crime, and horror have appeared in over a hundred different venues, including *Strange Horizons*, *Interzone*, *Black Static*, and *Orson Scott Card's Intergalactic Medicine Show*. Her collections are available in ebook and paperback from Amazon and other online retailers, and links to her published stories can be found at her website: www.transientcactus.co.uk.

Kathy Kingston
"Three Bad Things"

A late bloomer, Kathy Kingston became a published writer at the age of 66 in a *Sisters in Crime* LA anthology. More published stories followed in *King's River Life*, and *Dark Moon Digest #5*. She has always been an avid reader and her experience as a grocery store cashier, bank teller, wholesale plant salesman, and a New York fashion model gave her lots of raw material to work with. She now resides in Venice, California and is an award-winning landscape contractor specializing in drought tolerant landscapes. Short stories are her first love, but she is currently working on a novel.

Amanda Cecelia Lang
"Snake and Sinew, Flame and Bone"

Amanda Cecelia Lang is a horror author and aspiring recluse from Denver, Colorado. She lives with her life partner, two ancient cats, and an ongoing existential crisis. As a card-carrying scary movie nerd, her favorite things are slashers, 80s nostalgia, and a fierce final girl. Her horror stories have appeared on *The Other Stories*, *Thirteen*, and *Creepy* podcasts, and in the anthologies *Night Terrors, Mix Tape: 1986* and *The Year's Best Hardcore Horror*. You can stalk her at amandacecelialang.com—just don't be surprised if she leaps out at you from the shadows.

Gerri Leen
"The Maze of Moonlight and Mirrors" and
"Nature versus Nurture"

Gerri Leen is a poet from Northern Virginia, who has been nominated for the Pushcart and Rhysling prizes. She is into horse racing, tea, collecting encaustic art, raku pottery, and making weird one-pan meals. Gerri's poetry has been published in *Strange Horizons*, *Dreams & Nightmares*, *Polu*

Texni, Newmyths.com, and other publications. She also writes fiction in many genres—as Gerri Leen for speculative and mainstream, and Kim Strattford for romance—and is a member of the HWA and SFWA. Visit her website at gerrileen. com to see what she's been up to.

Mary Leoson
"Devil's Oak"

Mary Leoson teaches English composition, literature, film, creative writing, and psychology in the Cleveland, Ohio area and online. She holds an MFA in Fiction, an MA in English, and an MS in Psychology. Visit Mary's website at www. maryleoson.com.

"Devil's Oak" was inspired by an emotional visit to the Whitney Plantation in Louisiana, where the lives of enslaved people are honored and remembered. Some of the disturbing references to slave experiences in this piece are based on facts documented at the museum. For more information about the Whitney Plantation, visit www.whitneyplantation.org.

Tom Leveen
"Face to Face"

Tom Leveen is an award-winning author of nine novels with imprints of Random House and Simon & Schuster, and a Bram Stoker Award finalist. He has also written for the comic book *Spawn.*

Adrian Ludens
"Inside a Refrigerator"

Adrian Ludens is a radio announcer, and the public address announcer for a AA hockey team. He lives in the Black Hills of South Dakota with his family. Adrian has sold fiction to several dozen anthologies, including *The Mammoth Book of Jack the Ripper Stories, Blood Lite 3: Aftertaste,* and *Gothic*

Fantasy Science Fiction Stories. Recent appearances include *Violent Vixens* (Dark Peninsula Press), *Something Wicked This Way Rides* (Dark Owl Publishing), and *Under Twin Suns* (Hippocampus Press). Find Adrian online at https://linktr.ee/AdrianLudensAuthor and @AdrianLudensAuthor (Facebook).

Alison McBain
"The Ocean's Misfortune"

Alison Akiko McBain is an award-winning and Pushcart Prize-nominated author whose work has appeared in *Flash Fiction Online, On Spec,* and *Abyss & Apex.* Her debut novel *The Rose Queen* received the Gold Award for YA fantasy in the 2019 Literary Classics International Book Awards. She is lead editor for the small press publisher Fairfield Scribes, and associate editor for the literary magazine *Scribes*MICRO*Fiction.* When not writing, she draws all over the walls of her house with the enthusiastic help of her kids.

Briana McGuckin
"Good Boy Anyway"

Briana Una McGuckin writes gothic romance and fabulist fiction. Her work appears in the Stoker-nominated *Not All Monsters,* an anthology of women's horror (Rooster Republic), as well as *The Arcanist, Breath & Shadow,* and *Hides the Dark Tower* (Pole-to-Pole Publishing). She has an MFA from Western Connecticut State University. Briana also has cerebral palsy. Find her on Twitter @BrianaUna and check out her blog at moonmissives.com.

Matthew McKiernan
"They Never Left"

Matthew McKiernan was born in Cranford New Jersey in 1990 and moved to Yardley Pennsylvania in 1994. He graduated from LaSalle University in 2013 with a BA in English and

History. He received his MFA in Creative writing at Rosemont College in May 2016.

His first short story, "A Leap of Faith," was published in *Skive Magazine* in November 2013. He has since published many more short stories in various genres, most of which are available on Amazon. His latest short story, "Aokigahara," was published in April in the anthology, *Night Terrors*, volume 13. He is currently editing his science fiction novel, *Human*, which he hopes to publish in the near future.

Melissa Miles
"Blooms of Darkness"

Melissa Miles was born in the United States but now resides in New Zealand with her partner and menagerie. They live in an old cottage overlooking the sea. She has had many occupational iterations: teacher, actor, animal-rescuer, and filmmaker. She is now focusing on her writing. Melissa holds an MFA (with distinction) from Canterbury University.

Mike Murphy
"The Artist"

Mike has had over 150 audio plays produced in the U.S. and overseas. He has won The Columbine Award and a dozen Moondance International Film Festival awards in their TV pilot, audio play, short screenplay, and short story categories.

His prose work has appeared in several magazines and anthologies.

Mike is the writer of two short films, *Dark Chocolate*, and *Hotline*. In 2013, he won the inaugural Marion Thauer Brown Audio Drama Scriptwriting Competition, and in 2020 he came in second place. For several of the in-between years, he served as a judge.

Mike keeps a blog at audioauthor.blogspot.com.

Kurt Newton
"The Little People"

Kurt Newton lives in the northeast corner of Connecticut. His novels and short stories tend to take place in the rural landscapes of New England. Kurt's fiction has appeared in *Weird Tales*, *Dark Discoveries*, *Vastarien*, *Nightscript*, *Weirdbook*, *Mysterium Tremendum,* and *Cafe Irreal*. His third collection of short stories, *Bruises*, will be published later this year by Lycan Valley Press. A collection of crime fiction, *The Music of Murder*, will also appear later this year from Unnerving Books.

Gregory L. Norris
"The Woman in the Wallpaper"

Gregory is a full-time professional writer, with work appearing in national magazines, fiction anthologies, novels, and the occasional episode for Television and Film. He once worked as a screenwriter on Paramount's *Star Trek: Voyager* series and, in December of 2020, sold his second feature film option to Snarkhunter LLC, the Hollywood production company owned by actor Dan Lench.

He writes the *Gerry Anderson's Into Infinity* novels for Anderson Entertainment in the U.K., based on the classic NBC made-for-TV movie. His short story "Water Whispers," which appeared in the anthology *20,000 Leagues Remembered*, was nominated for the Pushcart Prize in 2020.

Rhonda Parrish
"The Grotesque"

Like a magpie, Rhonda Parrish is constantly distracted by shiny things. She is the editor of many anthologies and author of plenty of books, stories, and poems. She lives with her husband and two cats in Edmonton, Alberta. Rhonda enjoys playing Dungeons and Dragons, bingeing crime dramas, making blankets, and cheering on the Oilers.

Helen Power
"The Clearing"

Helen Power is a librarian living in Saskatoon, Canada. In her spare time, she haunts deserted cemeteries, loses her heart to dashing thieves, and cracks tough cases, all from the comfort of her writing nook. She has several short story publications, including ones in *Suspense Magazine* and Dark Helix Press's Canada 150 anthology *Futuristic Canada*. Her debut novel, a supernatural thriller, *The Ghosts of Thorwald Place*, will be released October 5, 2021 by CamCat Books.

Mary Jo Rabe
"Gargoyles of the World, Unite!"

Mary Jo Rabe grew up on a farm in eastern Iowa, earned degrees in German and Mathematics from Michigan State University, and a degree in Library Science at the University of Wisconsin-Milwaukee. She worked in the chancery office library of the Archdiocese of Freiburg, Germany for forty-one years, and lives with her husband in Titisee-Neustadt, Germany.

She has published stories in various publications, including *Fiction River*, *Pulphouse*, *Whispers from the Universe*, and other magazines and anthologies. Visit Mary Jo's blog at maryjorabe.wordpress.com and find her on Twitter @ maryjorabe.

Angeliki Radou
"The Binding of Chrysanthoula"

Angeliki Radou was born in Greece. She studied Journalism and has published six books in Greek, including a young adult series under the title, *The Dark Stories of Young Poe*. She is a member of the www.nyctophilia.gr writing team and her latest book is called *Ghost in the Snow: Spirits, Legends and Burial Customs in Japan*, from Editions Momentum. She now resides in Athens with her husband and two kids. "The Binding of Chrysanthoula" is her first story in English.

Jude Reid
"Cold Storage"

Jude lives in Scotland and writes dark stories in the narrow gaps between full-time work as a surgeon, wrangling her kids, and trying to wear out a border collie. She likes tabletop RPGs, running away from zombies, and climbing inadvisably large mountains. You can find her on Twitter @squintywitch.

David Rose
"Voyage of the PFV-4"

David Rose is the author of several underrated books, *Amden Bog* and *The Scrolls of Sin* among them, both set in the absurdly dark universe of Mulgara. Former military, formerly religious, currently slugging it out with carpal tunnel; Rose writes about pretend worlds that make this one seem not so bad—a philanthropic attempt within dark fantasy if ever has there been one. He lives in Orlando, Florida with a noisy fish tank and a lovely niece who visits him often.

Nidheesh Samant
"Ocular"

Nidheesh is a marketing professional, writer, and a collector of trivia. He believes the best thing in life is a good bowl of soup. Nidheesh lives in Mumbai, India with his family. Visit his website at thedarknetizen.wordpress.com/ and find him on Instagram @darthnid.

Benjamin Thomas
"Valhalla is a Lie"

Benjamin Thomas writes from New England where he unequally balances time between hiking, writing, and quoting seemingly random movies. His short fiction has appeared in a variety of publications, while his medical thriller, *Jack Be Quick*, is available from Owl Hollow Press. Get in touch at benjiswandering.com or on social media @benjiswandering.

Pauline Yates
"The Jump"

Australian writer, Pauline Yates, has short stories published with *Metaphorosis, Abyss & Apex, Aurealis, Black Hare Press*, plus others. She is also the winner of the short story category in the 2020 AHWA Flash Fiction and Short Story Competition. Find out more about her at paulineyates.com or on Twitter @ midnightmuser1.

Cheryl Zaidan
"Death, and the Scent of Tea"

Cheryl Zaidan is a full-time marketer, part-time writer, constant dreamer and jaded horror addict who loves to create characters just so she can do bad things to them. Her short stories have appeared in *Every Day Fiction* as well as the *Robbed of Sleep* and *Strangely Funny* anthology series, among others.

In her spare time, she enjoys reading, writing, music, food, yoga, and of course horror movies. If you would like to see what Cheryl is up to, you can find her on Twitter @ FeralCherylZ or visit her website www.cherylzwrites.com.

Thank you very much for reading *The Lost Librarian's Grave*. If your sanity hasn't been blasted by mysterious red or orange potions and you aren't trapped in a lost necropolis, surrounded by a vast phantasmagoria of your most insidious desires, please consider sharing your thoughts about our book of horrors and strangeness on Amazon or Goodreads.

Until next time, don't listen to that music drifting through your open window in the sultry night and watch out for sketchy artists who want to paint your picture!

Made in the USA
Columbia, SC
01 December 2021

50032491R00255